BLEAK HISTORY

A Novel

JOHN SHIRLEY

POCKET BOOKS
NEW YORK LONDON TORONTO SYDNEY

Pocket Books
A Division of Simon & Schuster, Inc.
1230 Avenue of the Americas
New York, NY 10020

First Pocket Books trade paperback edition August 2009

POCKET and colophon are registered trademarks of Simon & Schuster, Inc.

For information about special discounts for bulk purchases, please
contact Simon & Schuster Special Sales at 1-800-456-6798 or
business@simonandschuster.com

The Simon & Schuster Speakers Bureau can bring authors
to your live event. For more information or to book an event
contact the Simon & Schuster Speakers Bureau at
1-866-248-3049 or visit our website at www.simonspeakers.com.

Designed by Jamie Kerner

Manufactured in the United States of America

10 9 8 7 6 5 4 3 2 1

Library of Congress Cataloging-in-Publication Data is available.

ISBN 978-1-4165-8412-4
ISBN 978-1-4165-8426-1 (ebook)

For Micky with a million billion

The author wishes to thank
Michelina Shirley, Paula Guran, and Ed Schlesinger
for vital editorial input.

A little ways into the future . . . just far enough.

But the darkness pulls in everything—
shapes and fires, animals and myself,
how easily it gathers them!
Powers and people—

and it is possible a great presence is moving near me.

I have faith in nights.

—Rainer Maria Rilke

From: Dr. Helman
To: General Forsythe
Re Subject: Gabriel Bleak

As per your request, here are a few highlights from our case file on Gabriel Bleak. Some of these notations stem from our observation of the subject in childhood, while others relate to his service (US Army Rangers, see his Service File attached) in Afghanistan. He is now a civilian working intermittently as a tracer of bail jumpers.

He was one of the first among the young subjects in our prototype study to show a clear-cut response to the new release of AS energies ("AS" is a new term: *apparent supernatural*) as a result of the diminution of the [words excised from file for security purposes]. Bleak remains one of the most impressive. We suspect that there are entity-based forces who may have moved him into place for a key role in their agenda. He seems unaware of this possibility and, as a civilian, uses his paranormal capabilities largely for personal gain.

Bleak seems to have the ability to manipulate certain of the planet's inherent energy fields, and to use same to communicate with UBEs, e.g., so-called "ghosts" and certain other entities inhabiting the Hidden, though this does not appear to be a consistent capability. The inconsistency may be explained by the fluctuation of the intensity of his power. While he is not precisely telepathic he does seem to have an extraordinary level of "psychic feel" sensitivity, and, according to one unconfirmed report, may well be able to psychically sense an observer any time he is being observed, even if it is done through a concealed camera. If Bleak is being observed, he can see himself through the eyes of the observer, and sense certain general facts about the observer; e.g., their gender, their level of hostility. We suspect he has other AS skills, including extraordinary offensive capabilities, but these have not been confirmed.

He may indeed be one of those people chosen to unite with a symmetrical Astral Other, a union which could produce an especially powerful PES (psychic-energy-symmetry) pulse, that might be useful, or dangerous to our interests, depending [redaction].

As our failure to usefully connect with him while he was with the Rangers demonstrates, Bleak is a problematic subject. His psychological profile suggests he is prone to dogged independence, sudden changes of direction in life, and, when provoked, proactive aggression. Caution is urged. . . .

CCA Auto-Insert Terminology Footnote:
    A consciousness-inflected energy field connecting all life on Earth, the Hidden is, according to a supposed ShadowComm website (shut down by CCA), "the medium that provides a living environment for a spiritual ecology; for the disembodied: ghosts not yet gone on to reincarnation or the higher planes, elementals, predatory spirits, the evolved spirits that served the Light. If you have the gift to contact it, the Hidden provides a medium for summoning; for psychically affecting matter."

PROLOGUE

"Don't you just feel . . . *different* today?" Gulcher said to Jock.

"I dunno," Jock rumbled. "Bottled up in here, I dunno how I feel."

Troy Gulcher looked up at the clock in the aluminum mesh on the wall of the lockup. *They even try to cage time*, he liked to say.

The guards for Securimax Cell Block 5, a New Jersey high-security penal institution, were most of the time behind the glass of the bulletproof booths looking down on the cellblock from the second-floor tier. Gulcher could see their silhouettes up there, but you couldn't see their faces most of the time, what with the light being behind them. Like being watched by ghosts.

Jock, a tall, blond man with a heavy jaw and Aryan Army tattoos—real name Rudolph Simpson—and Gulcher, a stocky, dark man with a short black beard, heavy black brows. Both convicts were in coveralls, prison yellows, standing by the Ping-Pong table. Just toying with the paddles. Jock bounced the ball under the paddle, but didn't try to serve it.

It was almost lights out. Pretty soon the guards would tell them through the public address to "put paddle on table" and go back to their cells; it being Monday, three guards would come to each cell, unlock them one at a time, doing a quick check to see if anyone had managed to make some pruno or tucked away some other contraband.

Same old same old, for almost a year now. No movement on getting Gulcher transferred to State Medium Security, where it was so much easier, roomier, a man could hustle some drugs. "You shouldn't have busted up that security guard's shins," his court-appointed lady lawyer had told him. Snooty bitch. Like to get her alone, once he was out. Have her out of that pants suit lickety-split.

Restless. Nervous. "How about serving that fucking ball, there, Jock?"

Jock shrugged and served and they batted it listlessly back and forth till it bounced from the table and Jock went to chase it down. Gulcher waiting tensely.

Gulcher was feeling more than his usual restlessness. Something in the air about to bust open like a lightning storm. Ought to try to explain to Jock again. But it was hard to explain the hunches he got.

Gulcher and Jock had become allies, since the Jersey guys came into the cellblock; Chellini and Doloro, trying to throw their weight around. "When you get out, this t'ing's going to get you, you don't gimme what I want in here," Chellini said. "Cigarettes, whatever." *This t'ing?* Gulcher doubted that fat bastard Chellini was really a made man. If he was, he would probably have had a better lawyer. Doing any time to speak of just for stealing a car, with the jails so crowded, meant you had a bad lawyer.

It was strange Chellini had ended up in high security for stealing cars. Maybe it was his record. Maybe he'd pissed off the cops. Or maybe he was a plant, made a deal with the warden to catch the others with contraband.

"You really don't feel something, like, in the air?" Gulcher asked softly, as Jock came back with the Ping-Pong ball.

"I dunno, Troy, hey, could be I do feel funny." Jock paused, bounced the ball on the table. "Could be they put something in the dinner, one of them experiments they do on prisoners."

Jock was prone to paranoia. Craziness in your block boys was one of the things you put up with. Gulcher sighed and glanced up at the clock again.

"Don't wait," a voice whispered. *"Don't waste what . . ."* The voice faded before it quite finished.

"What'd you say?" Gulcher asked, looking sharply at Jock.

"Didn't say nothing," Jock said, returning the look, eyes narrowed.

"Thought I heard a . . ."

"Long ago, you called my name. The wave has risen. Now you can hear my reply. Reach out . . . use the red vitality . . . don't wait . . ."

There it was again. A whispering. Something about calling a name? A wave "risen"? Red vitality?

Someone whispering—not Jock. But no one else was standing close enough. Just the two of them standing at the Ping-Pong table. Whose voice was that? Sounded like it was coming from right behind him.

Gulcher looked—nobody there.

Whispering . . . but what was the voice saying? Couldn't quite make it out. "You didn't hear somebody whispering?" Gulcher asked.

Jock frowned at him. "You fucking with me? 'Cause I don't like that."

"The wave rises . . . let it guide you . . ."

Was that what it was saying? The wave rises, let it guide you? And there was a feeling with it. . . .

The whispering went with a rise in that strange, restless feeling. Like years ago. He'd never forgotten it. Started with that Aleister Crowley book he'd got, as a teen, from that crazy-stoned old friend of his Pop. Old dude with the long white hair, used to run with Charlie Manson. That strange feeling Gulcher got when he'd read the book. Not understanding all of it. . . . But when he'd drawn the diagrams, called the "Names of Power" listed in *Magick in Theory and Practice* . . .

Nothing definite had happened that night, years before; just that feeling of something unusual in the air. A tingling that seemed to want to talk to you. But—nothing that you could actually see. Next morning, 5 a.m., his father had got himself paralyzed. Slid his Harley under a truck. Which was a good thing for his son, a "blessing"—as that old drunk Father Lawrence liked to say—because it meant no more beatings from the old man and because it meant that eventually Gulcher could get his pop alone, with the old son of a bitch stuck in his bed. Could take his time ending the old prick's life. Smothering him good and slow. Which Gulcher did within six months of the accident.

Now, in Securimax Cell Block 5, the feeling grew and grew in his chest, as the whispering got louder and louder. A *good* feeling. Strong! Like when he did Dexedrine to get through a night of jacking trucks, getting them over the Penn border. You got a rise, a sensation of power inside, like no one could sneak up on you, no one could bust you, no one could stand in your way.

Another voice from nowhere—but this was the guards, talking through the PA. *"Okay, guests of the State, back to your cells for inspection, chop-chop."*

Gulcher tossed the Ping-Pong paddle onto the table and they walked back to their cells, each just a little bigger than a motel bathroom. Usually you had to share, but here in Securimax, Jock and Gulcher each had a cell, side by side. The cell doors were open but they'd be automatically closed in a few minutes, once the cons were inside.

The whispering again. *"The wave rises, no longer is it held back. Open and be guided . . ."* And something else lost in the echoes of Chellini and the other ginney shouting at one another from their cells. "Shut up so I can hear," Gulcher muttered.

What exactly was the whispering telling him to do? And why was the light going purple in here? Was he having a stroke, or what? Maybe he should ask to go to the infirmary. Fat chance. Not something they granted without his being practically dead already.

He stepped into his cell, found the plastic comb. The guards worked hard on not giving you anything you could use as a weapon on someone else, or yourself. Toothbrushes were short and soft, there were no springs on the bed, no toilet seats, and on and on. But he'd been working on the end spine of this comb, scraping it against a rough spot on the metal frame of the door, and he had it pretty sharp. Wasn't much of a weapon. He hadn't been sure what he was going to do with it. Till now.

"Don't waste any time," the whispering said. Gulcher could hear it more clearly now. *"The wave is rising. It won't continue forever. Do it."*

He sat on the bunk and took the spiky plastic end spine of the comb and bent it a little outward from the other spines, gritted his teeth—and jammed it into his wrist. It took a moment to punch through. Had to press hard. Then—he sucked air through his teeth as pain jolted through his wrist and blood squirted out, a red so dark it was almost inky. He hadn't hit anything major, just a bunch of smaller vessels, but it was more than enough blood for his purpose. He yanked out the plastic spine, then climbed in close to the wall over his cot, dipped the index finger of his other hand into the blood on his wrist and started drawing. Just letting the feeling guide him, like the whispering said. It felt good to do that. And he always did what felt good.

First he drew a rough circle, in blood, on the wall over his cot—a circle about two feet in diameter—then words within the circle, following it around its curve, inside. "The writing on the wall," he muttered. "Read the writin' on the wall!" An expression he'd heard from that Juvenile Hall judge, old Judge Kramer. Gulcher chuckled, as he wrote, remembering that.

He didn't know what he was writing till it was there on the wall. He just let it be guided. But Gulcher remembered some of the names—Names of Power, they were called—from the books he'd read as a young man. He figured they'd been stored away in his head, somewhere. *MOLOCH* was one of them. He found he was writing them inside the circle.

Gulcher heard the door of his cell clang shut behind him, the lockdown triggered by the guards, but he ignored that. He knew it wouldn't matter.

"Hey, Gulcher!" Jock shouted from the next cell. "You're right, I feel weird! I'm, like, hearing shit too! Voices!"

"Listen to them, Jock!" he shouted back, as he dripped blood on his right hand, from the wound, covering the whole palm, the fingers.

"Now, *apply the mark of your hand to the interior of the circle, to complete the connection,*" said the whisperer.

He pressed his bloody handprint into the circle. The words, the lines, the print, all dripped, but you could make it out anyway. It was an intact image.

"*Gaze on this symbol,*" said the whisperer, "*reach out with the power you feel now, connect, take power from us. . . . Use it as you see fit.*"

Gulcher stared . . .

And felt the power descend on him. He felt overcharged with

it, like he might explode if he didn't release it. He backed away from the bed, turned to the door, put his hand on it. Seemed to see the mechanisms that held it shut, inside the wall. Saw snake-like figures in there, ethereal snakes with faces, writhing, waiting for his command. Told them to push here, and here . . .

The door slid open. Followed by all the doors of all the cells in Securimax 5. An alarm started hooting, earsplittingly loud.

Gulcher stepped out and looked around—wondered why the air was so cloudy. It was like they were in a steam bath. But it wasn't steam, it was something else. Like it was the vapor of life itself. *Like it's the stuff ghosts are made of,* he thought. Like that, but spread out, choking the air. And he saw faces form in it; faces forming and falling apart . . . and forming again.

The siren howling . . . and the men howling as they writhed on the floor.

And one vaporous face seemed to dominate the others—a bigger face that kept stock-still in the air as the others rotated around it with a slippery, nauseating motion. Like one of those faces you see carved on the squatting statues stuck on the roofs of old churches. What did they call that? A gargoyle. But big, this face. Big as a basketball backboard. Big. Looking at him, its horny lips moving. *"The air serpents are yours. Formless familiars. Take territory. I will guide you to the place where I can take strength; where I can grow . . . and in time I will send more of myself, to your side."*

"Who are you?" Gulcher demanded.

"Your god, who blesses you," said the face, then it broke up, melted away. But Gulcher felt it still watching him; still just as much there, even if it was invisible. *"Call me Moloch as some did once, whose children burned in my grasp."*

"Gulcher!" Jock was yelling. "What the fuck's happening!"

The guards were running in, their faces tight with fear.

The man-faced serpents were writhing in the living steam—

were made of it, and something else—and Gulcher shouted, "Kill them!" and the man-faced serpents darted at the guards and entered into them. And the guards clawed at themselves and began firing their weapons at one another.

And they fell convulsing, yowling with pain and psychosis, as Gulcher led Jock up the stairs to the now open metal door.

ONE

A humid New York summer day. And someone was following him.

Gabriel Bleak always knew when he was being followed. This time, he could feel the tracker about half a block back. He sensed it was a woman, blinking her eyes in the hot light searing off the windows of the high Manhattan buildings. She was hurrying through the crowd to keep him in sight. He couldn't read her mind—but, as long as her attention was fixed on him for more than a few seconds, he could see what *she* saw. Attention itself had a psychic energy, a power he could feel, could connect to.

It was hot and humid, it was July in the city, and the corner of Broadway and Thirty-third was thronged with people, all hurrying along. Bleak sometimes felt as if the people were giving off the heat on a day like this. As if the summer heat rose from the body heat of the shifting, elbowing, insistent crowd; the humidity was a by-product of their sweat, their countless exhalations, their sticky, thronging thoughts.

Bleak figured that illusion troubled him because he could *feel* their lives around him.

He didn't feel any hostility from the woman following him, and none of that telltale psychic pulse that would indicate she was part of the Shadow Community. So he would take his time evading her.

Bleak stopped to wait for a double-decker tourist bus to pass in front of him. Japanese, French, German, Iowan faces looked down at him from the roofless top deck of the bus; the Statue of Liberty's face, painted hugely on the side, slid ponderously past, and it was as if she were looking at him too.

The bus passed, and Bleak pressed on through its cloud of exhaust, holding his breath. Dodging a taxi, he made it to the farther corner. Yankee Hank's Bar was up ahead. He'd slip in there, see what move she'd make when he cut the trail short.

The fingers of his right hand balled into a half-fist as he conjured a bullet of the Hidden's force; drawn from the energy field coating the world itself, the power pulsed down through his arm as raw energy flow, coalescing into a glimmering bullet shape within the forge of his fingers. He cupped the bullet in his right hand, close against his hip, so no one could see it. Bleak could see it though, if he looked. He felt it pulsing there, hot and volatile, a mindless compaction of life itself—in this form, potentially destructive. He would throw it only if he had to. If he didn't use it against his enemy, he couldn't reabsorb it, he'd have to release it into the background field—which would draw attention to him. It was bright outside, no one would see it in his hand, but in a dark room, the energy bullet would show up, as if he had a little ball of fireflies trapped in his fingers.

Bleak was aware, suddenly, that the woman following him had an apparatus of some kind in her right hand—an electronic device. She would glance at it, then hide it in her palm, cupped against her side—echoing the way he was hiding the energy bullet. He got a glimpse of the gadget from his flickering share of her point of view. Looked like some kind of handheld EM detection meter . . . only, it wasn't. What was it? A weapon?

He turned, used his left hand to open the bar's door—his right still cupping the energy bullet—and went into the suddenly cool air-conditioned room, a dark space shot through with the light of beer signs and a couple of red-shaded dangling overhead lamps the color of banked embers. Baseball souvenirs on the walls. ESPN baseball was a rectangle of bright greens and whites on the flat screen over the bar. The bartender, a man with short, curly red hair, long sideburns, was one Seamus Flaherty, who nodded at Bleak when he came in. Bleak was a familiar face here. He sometimes drank himself into a safe numbness in Yankee Hank's, when his sensitivity to the Hidden became too much to bear. He spent a good deal of mental energy separating out the material world and the Hidden; trying to stay focused, not get lost.

Bleak had learned to compartmentalize. *This is me, in the world that ordinary people share; this is me taking part in the Hidden.* That didn't always work. Then he turned to beer—and a few shots to go with it.

Seamus didn't know about any of that—couldn't see the bullet of energy glowing in Bleak's hand; it was below the level of the bar as Bleak walked by the three men on the middle stools. They were arguing about a game.

To Seamus, rinsing a beer glass, Bleak was just a medium-height, lanky, relatively young man with sandy hair who always seemed two weeks overdue for a haircut; brittle blue eyes; a man not quite thirty, in an old Army Rangers jacket, jeans, big black boots. Pretty much the same outfit most anytime, though Bleak changed the tees under the jacket. Bleak had a collection of fading rock-band T-shirts. Today he wore the Dictators.

The drinkers in the bar didn't take much notice. Yankee

Hank's was decorated with New York Yankees paraphernalia—dusty jerseys, fading autographed balls, curling baseball cards—and if you were a Yankees fan, these days, you pretty much stayed drunk, either because they were doing great or doing badly, depending on what week it was. The drinkers were slurring drunk, not sodden drunk, but they didn't notice much except the little drama on the sports channel.

As Bleak walked by, Seamus called out, "Thinking of starting up our softball team, this summer, Gabe, you in?"

"Sure, man, if I can pitch!"

Seamus gave him an affirming wink and Bleak strode on to the back room, empty except for Yankees posters and neon beer signs, two large red-felt pool tables, and restroom entrances in the farther wall. He toyed with the idea of going into the men's restroom, waiting his tracker out. But if she was really hunting him, she wouldn't let the men's room sign stop her.

He walked over to the other side of a pool table, turned toward the door, hesitated there, trying to think it through. If she wasn't Shadow Community, who was she? She could be a fed. Maybe Central Containment.

Bleak decided he wanted to know whom she was working for. And what the instrument in her hand was.

He couldn't see her, now, because she'd lost sight of him. He only had sight of her, psychically, when she had him in sight. He waited.

The energy bullet had lost some of its power through the attrition of time, but it was still hot in his hand. Holding it there for that long, he might get a slight burn on his skin. Still, he pulsed a little more power into it, building it up to full strength.

Over the noise from a television ad for a men's perfume *absolutely guaranteed* to attract women, he heard Seamus ask someone what he could get for them. It was her. Bleak thought she said a glass of chardonnay, but he couldn't hear it clearly, then she asked a muffled question, and Seamus said, "The *ladies'* is back there, miss."

She was still tracking him. But whoever she was, she was staying undercover about it.

His grip tightened around the energy bullet, compressing its charge a little more. But he kept it out of sight below the edge of a pool table.

She walked in, then, a pale woman with bobbed raven hair; she wore a conservative dove-gray dress with a matching jacket, red pumps, matching red-leather purse over her left shoulder, nails the same color. An expression you'd expect on a prosecuting attorney added hardness to an otherwise appealing, heart-shaped face; pursed full lips. Her paleness wasn't unhealthy, it was like something he'd seen in Renaissance paintings. She was a head shorter than Bleak—but there was no sense that she was intimidated. She stopped just inside the billiard room, standing there with her feet well apart. He noticed she had her purse open. He could just make out the top of a gun butt in there. In her right hand was what looked like one of those devices carpenters use to find metal studs hidden in the walls. Only it was more complicated looking, sleeker. And as she came closer, she held it low enough so that he could see its little LCD screen. Where a tiny red arrow was pointing right at Bleak.

The gun butt convinced Bleak there was no use in playing it cute. "It'd be better if you left that gun in your purse, miss," he warned, keeping his voice gentle but raising his hand, opening his fingers enough so she could see the energy bullet shifting through orange, red, purple, violet, incandescent blue, yellow; back to orange, red, purple. "And that other thing you have pointed at me—mind telling me what it is? I mean, it's only fair." He smiled. Hoped it was a disarming smile. "If I had a creepy little device pointed at you, I'd tell you why."

She stared at the energy bullet cupped in his hand, fascinated, her eyes widening fractionally. Her voice surprisingly husky, she said, "Okay. You're the real thing. Gabriel Bleak, you are required to come with me—and right now. The federal government requires your presence."

He looked closely at her. When she'd said, *The federal government requires your presence*, he'd sensed ambivalence. She was a strong woman, and she could make an arrest. But she didn't quite believe in the job. She wasn't completely one of *them*. She'd do her job. But he could hear the doubt in her voice; see it in her eyes. Too bad he had no time to persuade her to let him go. Other agents would be not far away. And they'd be here soon.

Bleak shook his head. "Like to help you out. But last time the government 'required' me, things kinda . . . didn't work out."

He tossed the energy bullet from his right hand to his left, as if one hand were playing catch with the other. The flaring, hissing passage of it startled her—she took half a step back. He grinned.

"Easy with that thing," she snapped. "Just—get rid of it. Trust us and it'll be all right. I can't guarantee your safety if you don't surrender."

"Mind telling me, for starts, what happens if I go with you?"

"I was just told to get a . . . a confirmation on you. Then I bring you in. I don't know any more than that."

She delivered the disclaimer believably. But Bleak could feel dishonesty the way someone else might feel a sudden cold breeze. She'd been honest right up to *I don't know any more than that*. He looked into her eyes—and felt himself held there. An indefinable familiarity hummed between their interlocked gazes, in that long moment. As if he knew . . . not her face—but something inside her.

She glanced over her shoulder, showing a flicker of irritation—and not irritation with him.

He tossed the energy bullet back to his other hand. It made a sizzling sound passing through the air. "Expecting someone?"

She looked at the glow of power nestled in his hand. "Put that thing *out* and just . . . come along. We'll talk, Mr. Bleak. All right?"

"Love to have a drink with you, if you had a different profession, miss. I might even have gone with 'just come along.' But . . . just 'come along' with a government agent?" He shook his head. "I've got work to do, for one thing."

"You're a skip tracer, from what I've heard. You can do that anytime. We don't need to be in any kind of . . . of confrontation, here."

"Sure, okay, but—come to think of it . . ." He tossed the energy bullet up so it hissed and spiraled, caught it in his right hand. "You haven't even shown me ID. They make up badges for your department yet?" He smiled. There was something about her . . .

She grimaced, glanced over her shoulder again.

"Someone slow to back you up?" Bleak added thoughtfully, "You're not NYPD or FBI. I'd have had their badges stuck in my face till I was blind . . . so that leaves CCA, right?"

She looked at him flatly, then tilted her purse so he could see the badge clipped to the inside flap: HOMELAND SECURITY, CENTRAL CONTAINMENT AUTHORITY. "CCA agent Loraine Sarikosca. So you know about CCA. Not many are aware it exists. Lot of you people know?"

"I think I read about it on the Internet somewhere." Truth was, all the ShadowComm knew. A few had escaped and told their stories. And the Hidden disclosed a good many secrets.

She gave a small shake of her head. "The Internet. I don't think so."

"Way it is now, anybody can be detained. So I guess I won't ask what *authority* you have. But"—he tossed the energy bullet from his right hand to his left—"what *excuse* do you have?"

"What?" She seemed startled. As if she'd been wondering herself.

"What rationale? What excuse? To just take people away."

Her eyes followed the energy bullet as it went back to his right hand. "There is a . . . a national security directive . . . having to do with extraordinary paranormal capabilities. The risk to the public . . . the possibility you could be of . . ." She broke off, licking her lips.

"What were you going to say—about the possibility? That I could be useful?"

"We'll talk about it in the car."

"Will we?"

Bleak saw the uncertainty in her eyes—and saw it locked away, a moment later. Her eyes going cold.

"Yes," she said, her voice flat. "Now . . . I'm going to ask you to make that little fireball of yours go away. Here—I'll turn off the detector. Even steven." She clicked the device off with a flick of her thumb, put it in the purse as casually as a woman putting away a cell phone—but her hand came out of the purse with the gun.

Bleak knew the gun was coming and was already releasing the bullet with a snapping motion—like a man snapping a whip. The energy bullet sped from his hand like a spinning meteor, straight at her rising gun-hand, whistling faintly as it went. She shouted in surprise and pain as the packet of energy struck her snub-nosed .38 square in the cylinder, sent it flying from her singed fingers—its metal glowing red-hot, trailing smoke.

"Get down!" he yelled, rushing around the pool table to tackle her, the two of them going heavily to the tiled floor. The gun clattered against the wall—and exploded, as every bullet in the gun went off, detonated by the energy charge, bullets cracking into the ceiling and the floor, the room acrid with gun smoke. She tried to pull away . . . he thought he felt her heartbeat, for a moment . . . hoped she knew he was trying to save her life.

"What the fuck!" yelled Seamus from the next room.

Bleak had an impulse to see if Agent Sarikosca was okay—he liked her nerviness, and he knew she was just doing her job—but he made himself get up and dodge into the men's room instead.

"Come back here, dammit!" she yelled, behind him. So good. She was okay.

"Call nine-whuh-one!" one of the barflies yelled, in the background, as Bleak turned, slammed the door shut, then shot a burst of energy from his hand to melt the metal of the lock. Not enough to hold it forever, but it'd slow her down. A moment later the door creaked as someone on the other side slammed it with a shoulder. "Call nine-whuh-one!" shrieked the barfly again, muffled now.

Two booths on the right, urinals left, sink and window straight ahead. He shook his head, looking at the glazed-glass window over the sink. Painted shut, and anyway too small for him.

But he heard her out there, talking on a cell. "Yeah, just get in here—he's blocked the door somehow—" Then an aside to Seamus: "I'm sorry, sir, this is federal business, you're going to have to stay out of here. . . . No, sir, there's no fire, just a small explosion. . . . No, sir, I'm not hurt, now you're going to have to . . ."

Bleak walked over to the sink, examined the wall. Touched it with the palm of his hand. Maybe.

Thump! as someone slammed into the door. Grunted in pain. Slammed it again.

And there were more agents coming.

Bleak sighed. It seemed he'd used up this bar. Seamus wasn't going to be happy with him.

Nothing to lose. He put his hands on the wall above the sink, closed his eyes. Drew energy from the background field, channeled it through his arms . . .

He stopped, aware of a spiritual scrutiny. Deep contact with the background field exposed any disembodied entities handy; it revealed the Hidden. And someone was there.

Bleak opened his eyes and found he was staring at himself in slightly reflective window glass over the sink—and saw that something . . . someone . . . was behind him, looking over his shoulder. A set of disembodied eyes. A face was filling in, around them.

Looked like a teenage boy, maybe eighteen. Just old enough to get into a bar in New York. He could even make out the acne, because that was how the ghost thought of itself.

A drug OD, Bleak suspected. The ghost might have been here for years.

"You ought to let go, kid," Bleak said. "You're stuck here. You're dead, see."

The kid shook his head, at first like someone shaking their head "no," then faster and faster, till his face was a blur, as he receded, his denial becoming a retreat through space itself—and Bleak closed his eyes again, focused the power he'd drawn, directed it into the wall above the sink, felt the plaster crack and shudder and give way. Something clanged noisily to the floor.

Bleak opened his eyes to see a rough oblong hole, a gap three feet high in the wall, the sink broken down on the tiles, water gushing from a pipe, wetting his boots.

He heard the door breaking down behind him—

He reached out, caught the still-hot edges of the wall, wincing at the contact, put his right foot on the pipe, and levered himself up and through, out partway into the alley behind the building. Running footsteps behind him; someone grabbed his left ankle but he twisted free, got to his feet in the alley. A car was just pulling in twenty-five yards to his left, one of the dark blue, compact natural-gas hybrids favored by the CCA. Bleak thought about invoking help from the disembodied, but he didn't want to incur debts if he didn't have to. He started to the right, looking for a way out—but it was a dead end. Trash cans against a brick wall.

He turned back toward the car rolling slowly, inexorably toward him. Someone was hurrying up behind the car—a blond man in a suit, an agent in wraparound mirror sunglasses, raising a pistol. Someone behind him yelled, "Keep your head down, Arnie!"

"You!" shouted "Arnie" from behind the car. "Hands up!

You've assaulted a federal agent! I've got every right to take you down! Hands up, do it now!" He was aiming his pistol over the top of the car.

Bleak backed up, coalescing another energy bullet in his right hand.

Agent Sarikosca appeared at the alley's mouth, behind Arnie, her mouth open. She'd been running. She glared past the blond agent.

"Bleak! Put your hands on the wall, give it up! I promise you won't be harmed!"

"Don't make promises you can't keep," Bleak said, looking up toward a fire escape. No, out of reach.

The car was bearing down on him . . . and stopped, rocking on its shocks, about thirty feet away.

He thought he might be able to hit the sedan with a compacted energy bullet to make the engine explode, but if he did that, he'd probably kill the guys inside. And he didn't want to kill anyone if he didn't have to.

He knew what surrendering to the CCA could mean. Maybe the stories about its prisoners were just rumors, but he thought it wiser to believe them.

"I'm counting two and I'm opening fire!" Arnie yelled.

That made up Bleak's mind for him.

Heart thudding so loudly he seemed to hear it echo in the alley, Bleak snapped the energy bullet toward the agent—aiming it so it'd whip close to the man's left ear. Scare him into screwing up his aim. The agent yelled, ducked aside from the meteoric energy bullet, fired his weapon as he stumbled. A bullet cracked past Bleak. He'd heard that sound often enough in his life to know what it was.

Still recoiling from Bleak's energy bullet, Arnie stumbled back—

Bleak ran straight for the car coming at him. As he went, he reached out to the planetary field, felt it concentrated between the narrow walls of the alley. A pretty strong water source must run under the pavement. That helped.

He stretched out his arms wide as he ran, caught the energy in his opened hands, compressed it with the extension of his senses, molding it into a shape formed by his mind.

The car's driver and passenger were opening their doors, getting out with guns in hand—but Bleak was running up an invisible ramp in the air. Right over their car.

"Son of a *bitch*!" the driver shouted—he was another set of sunglasses in a suit—as Bleak ran through the air above the car, creating more of the invisible ramp ahead of him as he went. He waved the ramp away just as he passed the trunk of the car on the far side, and the support vanished from under him. He dropped down to a crouch behind the agents as one of them, the driver, got out of the car and turned, fired at him, the bullet cutting the air near his shoulder.

Then Arnie was there, right in front of him on the sidewalk, raising the gun. Bleak used more standard combat skills, Ranger hand-to-hand. He set himself and kicked out, connecting with Arnie's wrist. Arnie yelped in pain, grimacing, as the gun spun away. Agent Sarikosca came from behind her partner, tried to barricade Bleak, but he dodged past her, like a quarterback with the football, and kept going, leaving her and Arnie behind.

Running, Bleak sensed someone he knew on the sidewalk ahead. Wondered if it was coincidence. It was Pigeon Lady: an elderly woman no more than five feet tall, who seemed to live in a perpetual flurry of pigeons; a droppings-white watch cap pulled over her spray of gray hair; she wore layers of bird-speckled wool, whatever the weather, stuck with fallen pinfeathers. And she wore pigeons like more clothing, something like thirty of them whirring and cooing about her, sitting on her head, her shoulders, her arms, whether she was feeding them or not. Her seamed face turned toward him; her watery eyes took him in, running past. Nodded distantly to him, turning to see men with suits, sunglasses, and guns five strides behind him. Feds, aiming at Bleak's back.

The pigeons erupted from her in a volcanic cloud of flapping blue and gray, making whickering sounds in their flurrying, to fill the air just behind Bleak. They flew at the faces of the CCA men; flapping wildly, blocking all sight of the agents' quarry, for several long, precious moments.

Carried on the psychic wind of their wings, Bleak heard thoughts, other people's thoughts he could never ordinarily have heard. He was not usually telepathic—not like that. Mostly he could only hear the minds of the dead.

Run, cross the street, Bleak, the Pigeon Lady thought. *We'll keep them back.*

Someone else thinking, *What the hell's up with these birds? It's like that Hitchcock movie . . . the damn things're too close to my eyes . . . the smell, the feathers—*

Where's he gone?

There—I've got a shot at him!

"No, Drake, hold your fire, you'll hit civilians!" Sarikosca shouted, as Bleak sprinted up Thirty-fifth toward Broadway, running full out, suddenly aware of the humid heat. As if he were running upstream through hot water. He drew his power from the living environment around him, but the process took something from him too—had taken a great deal for that last little gag, running on the air—and he was feeling it. And thinking, *"Drake" she said? Drake Zweig from military intelligence?* It would be a natural jump, from Army Intelligence to CCA. Maybe Zweig had ID'd him. He hoped it wasn't that particular prick.

Bleak saw the female agent at the corner, with Arnie just behind her. Trying to block him off. He took in a deep breath and cut to the right, dodging around a wheezing fat woman with runny eye makeup and a bearded man in a turban; ducked behind a disused mailbox, then cut between two parked taxis and ran into traffic, right in front of a bus. He sprinted past the front of a big city bus a whisker ahead of being run down, the bus blaring its horn—then he turned to follow it through the intersection, running along beside it. Traffic was heavy and the bus was moving only as fast as he could run.

Bleak used the bus's bulk to hide behind as he crossed Broadway, aware that a round-mouthed little girl was ogling him from a window just beside his head, her pudgy fingers pressed to the glass. He waved at her and she waved back, then, wheezing, he angled off into the thick crowd on the sidewalk, cut into a department store . . . and lost them. For now.

"WE LOST HIM," SAID Drake Zweig, coming back to the car in the alley. "*Dammit.*" Zweig was a short, middle-aged man in a gray suit tight over his barrel chest. He wore his gray hair in a kind of oily pompadour, to give him height; wide face, eyes set slightly too far apart, his mouth almost lipless. He had large hands—there was a story he'd used those big thumbs on the eyes of detainees, back in Iraq, years ago, when he'd worked for the CIA at Abu Ghraib.

"What about the detector?" Arnie asked, ruefully rubbing his bruised wrist.

"Out of range—he must've slipped off to a subway. Caught a lucky train."

Loraine Sarikosca was standing by the car, spraying her burn with analgesic, then winding a bandage around her hand. She wanted to tell Zweig he should have taken her advice, brought in four more cars for this guy. She just wondered why it'd taken so long for her backup to show, in the bar. Had General Forsythe told them to hold off—see how she handled it alone? It was quite possible.

"I can confirm the ID, all right," Zweig went on. "Gabriel Bleak."

Arnie tilted his dark glasses back on the top of his blond head, revealing pale blue eyes. "Hot as hell out here. So, Drake—how you know this Bleak?"

"Let's take it to the car," Loraine said. She knew Zweig didn't like her talking as if she had rank on him—only, she did have rank on him, so he could stuff it. She didn't want them airing this on the street.

They all got in, Loraine in the back behind Zweig, Arnie beside her. Zweig's partner, riding shotgun, was Dorrick Johnson, an African-American agent who rarely contributed more than a cynical shake of his head to any conversation. But Dorrick had good judgment. Such as the good judgment to put on the air-conditioning as soon as Zweig got the car fired up.

"How's your hand, Loraine?" Arnie asked.

"It's okay, just a little red." It hurt like a bastard but she didn't want to be taken off the job. "Your wrist?"

"Throbs. Doesn't seem broken. If I run into that guy again . . ."

"Keep a professional attitude, Arnie, okay? Forsythe wants them intact."

Zweig just then got around to answering Arnie's question, so it sounded like a non sequitur. "Bleak fucked with me on intel, of course, in Afghanistan." Zweig snorted. "He was Army Rangers. Supposed to be a tough bunch. But he was such an old lady about the civilians."

"Some 'old lady.'" Arnie said ruefully. "Almost blew off Loraine's hand. And he made us look like dicks."

"Used magic," Zweig snorted. "Didn't have the stones to use a gun. I don't really see the advantage of this weird-ass trick of his. Making a gun blow up."

"Think about it," Loraine said, gingerly touching the bandaged hand. She winced. "He shoots me, that's a real clear crime. He makes the gun explode with a power the court doesn't recognize as even existing, he just says, 'What, so your gun went blooey, why is that my fault?' No weapon, nothing the police can hold him on, really. No forensic evidence. He doesn't have to reload the thing—seems to pull it right out of the air. It's always there, even when he seems disarmed. And then there's the psychological effect—I was pretty startled, I got to admit."

"We're feds. New rules, we can take him in, don't need 'evidence,'" Dorrick pointed out. Dorrick was new to CCA—which was itself fairly new. Dorrick was a transfer from FBI. Not his choice.

Loraine nodded abstractedly. "We don't need evidence if we can get him without the police being involved—not always possible, from what I hear." Her mind mostly on wondering if the agency had brought the other detectors into the area, as she'd requested. They were testers—only a few prototypes existed. Bleak might still be close by.

She'd been standing so close to him—why didn't she just tackle him? Would he really have used that energy bullet on her, directly? She wasn't sure. She suspected he probably wouldn't have. But she wasn't sure why she felt that way.

I won't ask what authority you have . . . but what excuse do you have?

The words haunted her. She'd asked herself the same thing, more than once, since signing on with CCA. And somehow he knew that.

There was an official rationale, of course. ShadowComm types were breaking a law that almost no one knew existed. Something you were told about once you were detained: a law against using paranormal abilities—the real thing, ShadowComm abilities, not the usual fake psychics and pseudowitches. Specifically, it was forbidden to use ShadowComm powers except in a contained and controlled government context. Otherwise, the government claimed, you were doing the equivalent of experimenting with plutonium in your garage. Thought to be that dangerous. Especially since the phenomenon started popping up all over, during the last thirty years. And who knew what political orientation any ShadowComm had? Suppose they were anarchists—or Jihadists? Too big a risk.

But still, the question bothered her. Could the "containment" be justified? They were officially at war—always, always at war, with the Pan Jihad—and detaining ShadowComm, till they could be retrained, was a bit like the internment of Japanese-Americans in World War II. But even so . . .

Her cell phone buzzed. She reached for it, and its vibrating corresponded unnervingly with the throbbing in her burned hand. "Sarikosca."

"Loraine, the police are at the bar." It was Dr. Helman, at CCA's Washington, D.C., office. His low voice almost like a man parodying an affectless monotone. He seemed to consider it a classy detachment. She pictured him, a chunky little man, perhaps forty-five, with slicked-back, dark black hair and black eyes and old-fashioned, professorial suits, probably polishing his wire-rim glasses on his tie—usually a broad silk tie with hand-painted lilies and mums on it—as he spoke into a rather old-fashioned Bluetooth earpiece. She found him odious but he was her boss, and as expert as anyone in their most peculiar area of expertise. "We're sending people in to cover it for you, you won't have to go back in there."

"That's good." How would she have explained it to the cops? "We screwed up. I guess I screwed up. He got away. But . . . I got a good look at him."

"Oh, we have confirmed the ID. We know all about Mr. Gabriel Bleak. I was hoping you'd meet face-to-face. Did you . . . well. We'll discuss it later. I want a full report on your encounter with him. Everything—every last thing."

We know all about Mr. Gabriel Bleak. She opened her mouth to ask if she was being sent on assignments without a full briefing. Then she closed it again. You never got full briefings, at CCA.

Which was typical of intelligence services—sometimes it had been like that when she'd worked at the DIA. But CCA struck her as particularly "Chinese boxes" oriented: every shut box always contained another. The agency's primary mission seemed to have another one tucked away inside it. Theoretically the CCA existed to prevent supernatural destabilization of the country—and to use specially talented individuals to deflect threats to the USA. Terrorists with WMDs were hard to detect—but with the supernatural on your side, you might catch them.

Only, sometimes she thought there was another mission she hadn't been told about.

"How's the hand?" Helman asked.

"It's just a minor burn." Close enough to true.

"Good. Because you're going to be busy. Today, see if you can find Bleak, pick up his trail. This is straight from General Forsythe—Bleak's a priority."

"Why Bleak especially? There are a lot of other possibles out there."

"The general was adamant. We find him or we find another place to work."

CHAPTER

TWO

rooklyn, the same day.

At the worn end of the day, they sat on the wooden steps of the old man's back porch, behind his frame house on Avenue J, drinking a homemade ale.

"You are not going to pick up the dog?" Cronin asked, in his faint German-Yiddish accent.

"No, Cronin, you'll have to keep him a while longer, if you can," Bleak said, holding his glass of beer up to the failing light.

"Was not good, keeping a dog on a cabin-cruiser boat."

"He stayed with Donner part of the time. But I can't leave him over there—I have to move the boat. Or maybe abandon it."

"Abandon? That is your home, that boat!" He shook his head. "*Ach.* Gabriel, you are like a grasshopper with the jumping, your way of doing."

The beer had a strong, thoughtful aftertaste. Cronin had brewed it himself—Bleak sometimes called him Der Brewmeister, to which Cronin would only reply, "Your German, as ever, is atrocious."

"Just watch the dog for me, please, Cronin, I'll be back at some point. I don't think the feds know about you, but if they come, tell them anything they want to know, don't try to protect me." The bowed planks of the porch steps overlooking the overgrown backyard creaked whenever they shifted their weight. They could hear kids shouting, throwing a baseball on the street; jays made raucous sounds in the maple tree at the back fence, as if they were replying to the creaking boards.

"Too much jumping, Gabe. You talk like they're the Nazis, these people. This is not like that . . . you cannot know how bad that was."

"I know it's not that bad. Not yet. But . . . we did suspend a good many basic rights after the last attack."

The old man shrugged. "Not as bad. You must trust me when I say, not as bad."

"I do trust you. You're the only one I trust. That's why I'm leaving Muddy with you."

Muddy Waters was Bleak's middle-size, mottled mutt, his legs stubby, his body long; no one quite sure of the mixture. Maybe some dachshund, some Jack Russell terrier. Bleak could hear the dog snuffling around the side of the house.

Cronin seemed thinner these days, to Bleak. He knew the old man would never admit being seriously ill. Old Cronin sat there in his T-shirt and oil-stained dun-colored trousers, a mason jar of ale between his two hands, gazing out over a maze of fenced-off backyards—he'd been trying to fix the lawn mower, in his leaning shed of a garage, when Bleak arrived.

Bleak whistled and the dog came bounding around the corner, almost disappearing in the long grass of the yard, his snout visible as he poised to look quiveringly up at Bleak, whom he loved unreservedly. "Hey, dog—you stay with Cronin, he's gonna feed you more than I do."

"Probably that is so." Cronin chuckled, scratching an age-spotted wrist. The same wrist that had the blue numbers on it from the concentration camp, tattooed on him when he was a small child.

Cronin was the widower father of Lieutenant Isaac Preiss, who'd died on patrol with Bleak, in Afghanistan. Cronin was almost Gabriel's father too; and old enough to be his grandfather. They'd fallen into the roles, each a substitute for the other, quite easily, when Bleak had come to see him after his discharge. Come, ostensibly, to bring Cronin stories of his son's time in the Army Rangers.

Bleak had thought about telling Cronin that he had seen Isaac Preiss—that he had seen him since Isaac's death. But there was too little comfort there because Isaac's spirit, dimly seen, as if it were calling from a long ways away, had been trying to tell him something. To warn him. But Bleak wasn't sure what the message was. Isaac had been conscious enough to move on to the next world—had gone beyond "the veil," unlike the confused, muttering ghosts that haunted this world. Most spirits beyond the veil could rarely speak from their side to ours. Not easily. So-called mediums were such liars.

And Cronin knew only a little about what Bleak could do. What he had been able to do since that day when the dead had initiated him, one October, many years ago, back in Oregon, at the age of thirteen.

"I wish it was last summer again," Bleak said impulsively. He'd had a girlfriend, Wendy, last summer; he'd played softball with the bar team, and Wendy, and Cronin, had come to the games. Playing softball, bowling, playing pool—those things anchored him in the mortal world; kept him from drifting, mentally, into the Hidden. Helped him maintain that vital compartmentalization. And it felt good to be out in a park on a warm day, feeling all the parts of his body working together; the satisfaction of throwing a pretty good pitch. Once, though, in a rushed moment trying to stop someone from stealing a base, he'd thrown a ball to a ghost playing shortstop. Hadn't realized it was the ghost of a softball player; the ghost had a glove and everything. Embarrassing. Of course the ball had gone right through the glove. To the living players, who couldn't see the ghost, Bleak had just thrown the ball wildly wrong. But still . . . it made him wince, thinking of it.

"No good to think of the past, and wish for it, this an old man learns," Cronin said. "But that was good, you playing in Central Park. You were happy. You don't see that girl anymore? Nice girl."

Bleak shook his head. "No." And he didn't want to talk about her. "I'd better go."

"But where do you go, now? You will call?"

"Sure. I gave you that cell phone. Just keep it charged. No one but me has the number. I'll call that. Not the landline."

"Sometimes I think you're hallucinating, boy," Cronin muttered, shaking his head. "You have to hide, all the time. And for what?"

"You want me to show you again?"

"No. No! I don't want to see that again. Not . . . no. When my time comes, God will show me, you are not to show me. That is the commandment, the mitzvah, to wait for God to show Himself, His way. More beer? This is a masterpiece for me, this beer."

"Still got half a glass. I'm trying to drink less."

"Moderation in all things, this is smart."

"To hell with moderation." Bleak drained his beer and stood up. "I'll put this in the sink. I've gotta go."

"But where?"

"Honest, it's best you don't know. And I'm not a hundred percent sure."

"You think you can run from them, who run the whole country?" Cronin stood, his back audibly creaking. He only came up to Bleak's collarbone.

"Only for a while. I'll make some kind of deal with them, maybe. When I come back, I'll cut your grass for you."

Cronin smiled sadly and Bleak saw the old man had lost another tooth. The corners of his small brown eyes crinkled. "Sure. I fix the machine, you will cut. And we will drink beer."

A FEW HOURS LATER. The sun was just down; the buildings of Manhattan, across the river, were wearing the last glimmers of sunset like Day-Glo caps on their rooftops. Bleak stood in the screen of trees, in Hoboken, and tried to make up his mind.

There was a marina in Hoboken, New Jersey, near where Riverview Drive meets Harbor Drive. It's across the river from the Westside Highway, and Greenwich Village, Lower Manhattan. Most of the time, Bleak lived in the marina, in a tired, old thirty-five-foot Chris-Craft fiberglass cabin cruiser. Unregistered, so he couldn't be traced to it. Technically you weren't supposed to live in the marina either, but he had a friend, Donner, an old stoner who ran the place from his combo office and studio apartment overlooking the docks, and Donner pretended he didn't know Bleak lived there. He valued Bleak's chess game — Bleak could usually be counted on to lose, in the end, even though Donner was smoking pot while he played. But then, Bleak didn't try very hard to win.

Looking at the marina, now, from the screen of trees in the park across Harbor Boulevard, Bleak didn't see anything out of the ordinary. Didn't see any police cars, didn't see any obvious CCA agents over there. But they knew who he was. They'd been tracking him. So they might know where he lived, registered or not. They could be waiting in his cabin cruiser. Or watching from the small yacht tied up in the next berth. They could be a lot of places.

And he felt something. A faint sense that someone close by was thinking about him — and not Donner.

He was cautious enough to keep a small metal boat tied up, little more than a skiff with a one-cylinder, barely functional outboard motor, about a quarter mile downstream on the Hudson. There was enough gas in that little vessel to get up to the cabin cruiser, check it out from the water where they might not see him coming. He'd feel them for sure, if they were in there, once he got close enough.

He looked around, before leaving the park, though he knew they hadn't spotted him. If anyone was looking at him in any fixed and purposeful way, he'd have felt it.

It was about eight o'clock when Bleak got the boat out from under the crumbling pier downstream, started it upriver, hugging the Jersey shore. It seemed to take a long time to push against the current up to the marina. He stayed inshore, in the long shadows of the buildings with the sunset behind them.

The boat rocked in the wash from a barge. He was tired and didn't want to end up rowing. Now and then the boat's puttputting engine missed a putt, like an old man's failing heart. And he wondered how long Cronin would be around for him.

The river oozed past. The field of the Hidden whispered.

Usually he kept his consciousness of the Hidden bottled up. But being out on the river, in the slow, contemplative living stream, his senses tended to flow out of him, to widen, to reach out . . .

Until finally—a face looked up at him, from just under the dark surface of the river.

He was used to seeing them out here. Lots of guys had been dropped into the river, disposed of, weighted but alive when the water closed over their head. Funny to see the clean-shaven man in his suit, complete with a wide, checked tie; his hair smoothed back, his features quite intact, his prominent nose not nibbled by fish. His eyes looking at Bleak from under a thin sheet of dirty water. But he wasn't a corpse; only a confused ghost.

"Pal," Bleak said, "that tie is way out of fashion. You've been under there too long. You gotta get to a mall."

The man's mouth moved. No bubbles came out of it, no sound.

"Can't hear you, bro," Bleak said. "Just let go and drift with the stream. Your body's long gone. Just drift, and once you get far enough from the spot where you died, someone'll tell you where to go next."

The man sank away, emanating disappointment. Bleak remembered another river ghost, a couple years back, when he'd been out in his cabin cruiser. The perfectly preserved body of a chunky, bald man in a jogging suit, maybe from the 1990s, talking to him. Unheard. He had decided to see what this one had to say, and he'd tuned in to its mind—to its mindless muttering, really. An uncomfortable, tiring, risky process. And he'd heard, *"Tell Buddy I'm going to pay him off, he don't have to do nothing. I'm gonna get all the shit for him. My wife took it and sold it in L.A., it's gone, but I'm gonna get some more, I'm gonna replace all seven ounces, he don't have to do nothing. Tell Buddy I'm going to pay him. Tell Buddy . . ."*

"Buddy already did you," Bleak had tried to tell him. "Or somebody sent by Buddy. You're already dead. Hey, if you're gonna be a ghost, try to remember yourself slimmer and, like, in a better outfit." Bleak sometimes tried to kid the ghosts out of their self-centeredness. But they clung to it—though their fixations kept them ghosts.

"Tell Buddy I'm going to pay him off, he don't have to nothing. I'm gonna get all the shit for him. My wife . . ."

Feeling headachy and sick to his stomach, Bleak had cut the connection, like hanging up on a phone call.

Remembering the jogging-suit ghost, Bleak shook himself,

...ng around to reboot his mind. He was really good at keeping ...ad memories at bay. It was a skill a combat vet learned.

Bleak looked up from the river, saw that he was about to reach the marina. His cruiser, the *HMS Crackbrain*, was a wedge of darkness against the backlights of the marina, rocking gently on its mooring. He saw no one on it. Felt no one watching him, not from anywhere.

He cut the engine, put the oars in the oarlocks, and rowed the rest of the way. He was sweating despite the evening cool on the river. He could see lights on at Donner's place, overlooking the dock, ashore. More than one light on. But if Bleak went up to Donner's place, asked him what he'd seen, he might involve him. If he was under surveillance, they might take Donner in as some kind of accessory, or even a suspected Shadow Community rogue.

Bleak shipped the oars and let the boat drift up to the dock, near the prow of the cabin cruiser. He sat quietly in the inky darkness of its shadow, both hands holding the rope that held the cruiser to the dock, and closed his eyes. He extended his senses into the Hidden, enlarged the field of his awareness to take in the *Crackbrain*—and immediately sensed someone in the boat. No one should be there. He'd locked it, and no one else but Donner had a key.

Whoever this was, it wasn't Donner. But a faint fibrillation of familiarity tingled from the person in the cabin cruiser. And something else. Whoever it was . . .

Was wide-awake. Tensely aware. And waiting for him.

Instinct told him to get away from the dock—from any CCA backup that might be waiting nearby. And do it quietly.

But Bleak tied the metal rowboat to the line dangling from the aft of the cabin cruiser and clambered up the built-in ladder, into the larger boat. He paused on the slightly rocking deck, near the cowl for the inboard engine, listening. Nothing but the sound of a distant siren from the city, the lapping of small waves on the fiberglass hull.

He moved down the steps to the door of the cruiser's cabin—and saw that the door was slightly open. He stepped back, curled his right hand, built up power—the river helped, immediately, as running water always did—and readied himself to create an energy bullet.

The door suddenly popped open. A willowy figure came sinuously through, her eyes glowing with power.

He stared. "Shoella!"

A tall, slender black woman, her hair bristly with dreadlocks. She glared at him for a long moment—then gold teeth gleamed amidst a broad white smile.

"Bleak. Where yat? Pigeon Lady told me what happened today. If they're onto y'alls, maybe they onto us." She was a mix of Creole and other New Orleans strains; had a soft Cajun accent, though she'd been living in the North for almost ten years.

He released the energy bullet and shrugged. "If they're onto all of us, maybe they're following *you*, Shoella. Maybe they followed you here."

She shook her head. "We both know when we being followed. But *cher* darlin'? I made up my mind. You got to meet with our people . . . and decide whose side you're on."

She came a step closer, into the light from the marina. Shoella was a little older and taller than Bleak; she was almost storklike, six foot one, bony, with ropy dreads past her collarbone, a green-and-red silk Chinese mandarin jacket, a wraparound skirt of red silk, high-top, dark green sneakers, jangling copper bracelets. A sardonic expression on a faunlike, cocoa-colored face of indeterminate age. Bleak didn't know her well, though a flirtation had existed between them—at times it had seemed to break through flirtation to something more. He figured her for somewhere past thirty-five. Except for her tallness, she was not the exotic woman some expected to meet. If she was summoning ancestral spirits, or using the strange birdlike familiar that followed her, though, she took on a different aspect. She seemed to grow in bulk and density, and gravitas.

...ist now she was strolling up to the railing, to gaze out at the oozing-slow water, her bracelets jangling, singing softly to herself. Watching a barge pushing by way out on the river. Its wake slowly, inexorably worked its way over to them and lapped on the pylons.

"What I want to know," she said, "were they just after you, or they after all of us? What do you figure?"

"Right now, I'm trying to figure out how those high-top sneakers go with all that silk. Does, though. The feds are after all of us, Shoella. You were right about that."

"Then it's time to call a meeting." She made an odd twitchy gesture at the air, and in response a strange cry, and a flapping sound, came from above.

Bleak glanced up, saw a darkness shaped like a large bird—a very large bird—descending toward them. Something dark, big as a large seagull, settled on her shoulder. The Bird That No One Knew, some in the ShadowComm called it. Shoella called it Yorena. Referred to the familiar as a she though it was doubtful the creature had real gender.

The bird was dark crimson. Very dark. She was flecked with jet and a lugubrious yellow, sprayed across her belly; her beak was like a falcon's. An ornithologist had seen Shoella with the familiar and had begged to examine the creature, but when he'd stepped closer, Yorena viciously attacked him, bloodied his cheeks, and drove him away.

She wasn't exactly a real bird; she didn't eat or leave droppings. Sometimes she shed small feathers, but if you put one in your pocket, the molt was gone, soon after, like a piece of ice.

"Time to call a meeting," Shoella repeated, to herself now.

She whispered something to Yorena and the familiar took to the air, in a dark flurry of purpose. Shoella muttering, "And *laissez les bons temps rouler.*"

CHAPTER

THREE

That night. The Hudson River.

The place smelled like beer—and like the river.

River Rat's Bar and Grill was built on a dock, on the Jersey side, a little more than a quarter mile upriver from the marina where Bleak had docked his boat. The place was lit by lamps hanging from the ceiling over the bar, and not much else. It was still a bar, but had given up the grill. River Rat's was just a large shack, to Bleak's mind: warped-wooden, saw-dusted floor, wooden walls decorated with paper money brought from foreign places, lots of Italian lire; poker chips from foreign casinos, nailed up; a few cobwebby fishing nets, with dusty glass floats, hung from the ceiling. A gaunt, white-haired old man in a stained white shirt, sleeves rolled up, worked behind the dented oak bar. He had an expression on his face that wasn't far from looks Bleak had seen on refugees, walking mile after mile, in Afghanistan: a lonely look of determined endurance.

A few sailors, from the big freighter tied up down the shore, drank at one end of the bar; two other men, their backs to Bleak, sat talking at a shadowy table in the far corner.

"How'd you come to choose this place?" Bleak asked. He had never been entirely certain of Shoella's motives—in anything.

"It wasn't that far from where your boat was tied up and . . . I thought it'd be interesting."

Uh-oh, Bleak thought.

They ordered a couple of beers—the old man served up the drafts with surprising dexterity and speed—and they took them to a circular wooden table under an overhead lamp; a fishnet draped from the ceiling was spread close under the lamp, making a mesh of shadows over the table.

Bleak sat where he could keep an eye on the door and the rest of the bar. Thinking, *Is this a date? Almost feels like one.*

"You said it wasn't just you they were after." Shoella was speaking low, so he had to lean closer to hear her. "What makes you think so?"

"The agent had some kind of detector that kept her right up on me . . . but I managed to get outside its range."

"Or you're not outside its range. And they're about to bust in on us here."

"Maybe. Thing is—you think they developed that device just for me? Uh-uh. Had to be for all of us. And you know they want to find all of us." He shrugged. "Maybe I overreacted. She talked like it was just recruitment."

Shoella sniffed. "They always talk that way. But their recruitment—mo' like enslavement. What this detector now?"

"Something new. But I don't think I'm mistaken about it. The Hidden has its own energy signature."

She nodded. "When we open the gates, it's like canal locks—something has to spill through, into that space, level the energy flow. Power clings to us—and this thing smells it." She toyed with her glass, tossed her head, making her dreads bob. "That all you know, what's going on? This run-in with one agent?"

"Pretty much. It's CCA. An agent named Loraine Sarikosca all over me like white on rice. And the detector. Kind of disturbing. They can use that thing to ferret us out, make life hell."

"So maybe you want to come over to La'hood, join up close. Quit being a Rambler. La'hood watch your back."

La'hood. That's what she called the New York–Jersey branch of the Shadow Community.

"I come over when I need to."

"That's more selfishness than solidarity, Bleak," she said, leaning toward him, eyes glittering. Her accent always thickened when she was feeling emotional.

"I've had bad luck with 'solidarity.'"

"See, little white boy cheats us out of important resources when he don't come round." Shoella sipped her beer and put the glass down with a clunk. The table wobbled. "We each got our talents. We got some overlap for sure. But we might need your *especiality.*" Another Shoella term, *especiality.* "More especialities we have, more we —"

"More power Shoella has?" he interrupted, his tone casual, but knowing it would make her mad.

Shoella tensed — but after a moment he could feel her letting it go. It was something he could feel, when she let it go, as if someone had invisibly grabbed him by the shirtfront . . . then suddenly loosened grip.

"No," she said softly. "That's not it, *cher* darlin'. It's not about my power." There was a peculiar longing in her voice. Her gaze settled on his, for a moment, and he felt her longing psychically, as palpably as Spanish moss whipped by the wind to trail across his face. "Could be that you and I . . . with all our differences . . . are still . . ." She broke off, looking away. Left it unsaid.

"Our differences, anyway, aren't that important," Bleak said.

Not sure if the two of them were talking about the same thing anymore. "The Hidden is a field, and *mind* makes shapes in it . . . in the *apeiron* field." He shrugged. Made a sweeping motion in his hand as he tried to articulate it. "And *mind* enters the shapes, and sometimes the shapes survive and call themselves spirits . . . and it's everywhere." As Bleak spoke, he was aware of someone across the room looking at him fixedly—he could see himself, talking to Shoella, from the man's point of view—one of those men at the table in the other corner. That attention was hostile. He tried to ignore it. "But it's all one thing, in the big field of the Hidden, Shoella. So the *especialities* don't matter."

She looked at him with her head tilted, her dreadlocks bouncing with the motion. "And listen to y'all—hidden depths. So t'speak. Oh, here the man comes."

A figure loomed up at the table, and Bleak groaned inwardly, recognizing him. Donald Bursinsky. A refrigerator-size man in a gray hoodie, with a slack mouth and a faux-hawk and tiny, dirty-blue eyes and an ink-pen swastika tattoo on his neck.

"Yuh the bounty-hunter azzole ahright," Bursinsky said. "Yuh put me in Rikers jail."

"No," Bleak said, sighing. "No, man, you went to Rikers because you skipped out on bail. You should've shown up in court. All I did was take you back to the system—they decided where you went from there. Just doing what I get paid for." He saw a second, taller, less substantial man coming up behind Bursinsky, looking over Bursinsky's shoulder; second guy was gangly, with his hand in his pocket.

Gun in there, Bleak thought.

"Yuh know I go ahead 'n' kill uh bounty hunter, it ain't like I kill uh cop," Bursinsky said.

"Yeah, nobody gonna get that worked up about it," the other guy said.

Bleak was sorry he didn't have a gun. He didn't want to use an energy bullet here in front of these people.

He realized that Shoella was watching him, seeming bemused. "I get to watch your *especiality* now?" she asked.

"Nope," he told her, sizing Bursinsky up. The damned fool was standing much too close. "Not the technique you're thinking of, Sho'. I work with a team, when I'm bringing a man in. I've got people I call."

"Yeah, this bounty hunter was a little bitch," said the gangly guy. "Had to use a buncha guysta help him."

"If being professional about a job is being a little bitch . . . ," Bleak said, shrugging. Bursinsky was so close Bleak could smell the big lug's sweat and the corn dog he'd been eating. "You want to go back to jail, Bursinsky?" Bleak asked, levering his feet hard against the floor and leaning forward. "You've gotta be on probation."

"Now yuh threatening me wit' jail again? Gleaman . . . ?" Bursinsky turned to the skinnier guy. "Give me the—"

The moment Bursinsky looked away, Bleak launched himself out of the chair, slamming his right shoulder into the big man's solar plexus; feeling Bursinsky fold up, wheezing over him. Bleak gave another shove, with his whole body, and Bursinsky fell heavily back onto the wooden floor, making it boom hollowly; making the glasses on the bar rattle. Gleaman gaped, confused.

Hearing Shoella mutter something to her loas, Bleak straightened up and in the same motion brought his right fist up hard into Gleaman's chin; felt Gleaman's jaws clack shut, teeth crunching under the blow. Gleaman spinning, falling.

"Sorry about this," Bleak told the bartender. "Come on, Shoella," he muttered to her, turning toward the door. He got three steps—and normally he'd have "seen" Gleaman aiming at his back. But too many people were staring at him.

A gunshot, and the bullet sliced past Bleak's right ear.

Bleak spun and saw Gleaman sitting on the floor, pistol in hand. Bursinsky was getting to his hands and knees next to him—

as Gleaman squintingly aimed the Glock nine-millimeter at Bleak through a blue cloud of gun smoke.

"Not gonna fucking miss this time," Gleaman said.

Bleak began conjuring an energy bullet—but he figured it'd be too late.

Shoella was hissing to herself in Cajun French, and suddenly a translucent creature with a giant vulture's head and a man's body was hunched over Gleaman. A baka loa, one of the dark, "bitter" entities formed in the Hidden by voodoo beliefs. The apparition wore a lion's-hide skirt, and anklets of yellow grass hung over his bare black feet. The vulture's head was proportional with the body, beak opening wide . . .

And the baka loa dipped its beak to feed within Gleaman's skull. Its beak penetrated his skull without breaking the bone.

No one here could see this but Shoella and Bleak. All the others saw was Gleaman reacting in paralytic agony, flopping on his arched back, foaming at the mouth, whites of his eyes showing, the gun firing once. A glass fishing float shattered.

Bleak stepped in and expertly twisted the gun from Gleaman's hands. He looked at Bursinsky and said, "You want that to happen to you—what's happening to your friend?"

Bursinsky, getting to his feet now, was looking at Gleaman—who was spasming, chattering, and peeing his pants. Babbling: "Nuh take it out nuh take it out nuh take it out nuh take it out oh please God take it outta my head . . ."

"No," Bursinsky said in a low voice. He took a step back. "I don't."

"Then back off."

Bursinsky looked at Shoella, sensing it was her doing somehow. He looked narrowly at Bleak. "How yuh find me anyway, last time? Just tell me that, Bleak. Ain't nobody shoulda been able to find me."

Bleak shook his head. "I don't have to tell you anything except go see your fucking parole officer. You can tell your friend, if he gets his mind working, that his gun went in the drink. And don't think I can't find you again if you piss me off. No matter where you go."

Gleaman was still spasming, though the vulture-headed baka loa had vanished.

Bleak turned and walked out the door, wanting to get gone before the bartender called the cops. Normally he was okay with the police; today he was as reluctant to see the cops as Bursinsky would be. The CCA might have the cops looking for him. And he wanted to get away from the sound of Gleaman burbling.

Outside, a little breeze from the river lifted sweat from his forehead; the breeze smelled of oil and river reek. Shoella came to him on the edge of the dock, watched as he tossed the gun into the river. *Plunk,* and the pistol sank away. "You don't use your especiality at all, when you bounty huntin', *cher* darlin'?"

"Sure I do—to find them. Not to *catch* them. I want as few as possible to know."

She nodded. "Good sense, I 'spect."

"You knew that loser was in there, Shoella? That why you picked it?"

Her smile gleamed, gold amid ivory. "My Yorena told me someone with hate for you was nearby, I wanted to see what you do. Only one time I see you summon *les invisibles,* see you work." She toyed with her dreadlocks. "But I did see something in there—your manhood, that you summon and work. You summon *something* that way. From inside. Interesting to see." She glanced at him; glanced away.

"That man going to recover?"

"Oh, no, I don' think," she said disinterestedly.

He shook his head. He could feel she was attracted to him; he felt drawn to her, especially sexually. But at moments like this, it was easy for him to keep his distance.

She looked up into the inky sky, and he heard wings in the darkness. Her lips moved soundlessly. Then she turned to him, nodding. "They waiting for us. I will go to them first, you meet us. You know the dock La'hood use, sometimes, to meet?"

"Sure."

"It'll take me some time. We'll meet just before dawn. When our strength is high."

He watched her walk into the darkness; then he went back to his cabin cruiser, tied up at the end of the pier.

He had mixed feelings about meeting with ShadowComm. They made him feel less alone. But they were embarrassingly unpredictable—and maybe because he held himself aloof, most of them were vaguely hostile to him.

As he cast off, he heard ghosts, under the pier, whisper warnings to him. But then they were always warning him of something.

Everyone was always in danger, after all. From cancer, from car crashes and plane crashes, from criminals. Most people managed denial; managed to pretend they were safe.

Gabriel Bleak never had that luxury.

THE WEE HOURS OF the next morning. Atlantic City.

The noise inside the casino was like a million children's toys, the slots with their bells and tweets and buzzes, endlessly clanging and tweeting, chiming crappy little tunes. It merged together into one warbling. People at the slots banging at the buttons—not just tapping them, but really smacking them hard. All desperation. Funny to see.

"Casinos got rugs in them like my aunt Louella's house," Jock said, as he and Gulcher walked in past the smiling casino greeter. The carpet in Lucky Lou's Atlantic City Casino looked like paisley had gotten a disease. "My sister always said Louella had the ugliest damn rugs inna world."

"That greeter looked like he should be selling vacuum cleaners or some shit," Gulcher said, laughing.

They were both on a sort of high, saying things they wouldn't ordinarily say and saying them loud. Gulcher, who always knew when cop types were watching him, was aware, as they walked the aisle between rows of slot machines, that he'd already attracted the notice of a couple of thick-bodied, greasy-headed guys in casual suits. They were casino security bulls with headsets, hearing-aid-like pieces plugged into their ears. They had little blue-and-white plastic tags on Croakies bands around their necks, with their names and LUCKY LOU'S ATLANTIC CITY CASINO printed on them.

"But you know, this ain't the best casino on the street, man," Jock said. "This ain't like Trump's or one of those classier places got the spas and fountains and they look more modern and shit."

"It's just as big, and anyway it's the one I was guided to." Gulcher looked around at all the clamorous action. "Here it is, like four in the fucking morning," Gulcher added, talking loud so Jock could hear him over the endless insane chatter of the slot machines, "and we're like five steps in the door, and we got these nice new civilian clothes, and still they already doggin' security on us here."

"Hey, Troy, these places run hard twenty-four-seven, suckin' up people's hard-earned cash."

"Yeah, we been in the wrong business, Jock."

"I hear that. Where we going to start in here?"

"I'll know in a minute, I figure."

Neither of them had any doubts about what their objective was—they just didn't know, yet, how it would happen. Jock had tacitly acknowledged Gulcher as the leader, and the one with the real connection to the whisperer. Jock waited on Gulcher, and Gulcher waited on the whisperer.

Gulcher was a little surprised that Jock had deferred to him this much, Jock being so paranoid. But then, he'd seen people who were all hostile to you get friendly—temporarily, anyhow—after a few tequilas, or a line of cocaine. The whisperer gave you that stony glow without the booze, without the drugs.

Besides, following Gulcher's lead had gotten them out of high security. It was working out so far.

Sure, it had occurred to Gulcher that he was taking a big risk, hooking up with the whisperer, allying with something he didn't really understand. He was becoming *part of* something, and somehow he knew there was no going back. He was committed now. And committed also meant stuck.

So what! He was out, free, armed, with money in his pocket, and in civilian clothes. Sure he was making a deal with something like . . . the devil. But hadn't he already done that, years ago, in a way? Hadn't he crossed the line anyway, when he killed that dealer and took his weight, back on the block? What difference did it make if he got in deeper?

And it felt *good* when he hooked into that power. Good watching those pigs die, walking out those doors.

They'd found a cab waiting in the parking lot of an all-night restaurant on the interstate, a quarter mile from the prison. They'd walked right up to the cab, and the driver, one of those Paki types with a turban, he'd seen their prison clothes and tried to drive away, but murky faces swirled around the hood of his yellow cab . . . and it just stopped running. Engine just froze up. Somehow seemed like the most natural thing in the world, to Gulcher, when that happened.

The guy had jumped out and run like a scared rabbit. They'd got in the cab, ignoring the sounds of sirens whooping from the direction of the prison. People starting to figure out there'd been a jailbreak and a lot of correctional officers gone crazy, back there. And dead people . . . quite a few dead.

Jock had taken the wheel and they'd driven in the cab to a little curtained, frame house a few miles from the prison, where there were a couple of guys who'd snitched on Gulcher.

The two dudes and their girlfriends had been up tweaking on their glass pipes when Gulcher and Jock walked in, Jock grinning, with the service .45 taken from the prison in his hand, firing one two three four five shots, only one extra needed when that black chick tried to crawl away.

They'd searched the place, taking some money and finding clothes they could wear. Hawaiian shirts, jeans, Gulcher picking up a nice pair of wraparound shades. "Wonder where they stole these shades," he'd said. "Look at that, says 'Dior' on the side."

"Might be counterfeit."

"See there, you fucking rain on my parade, Jock."

Gulcher put the shades on now because the glaring overhead lights of the casino, meant to keep people awake and gambling, were irritating his eyes.

He was feeling some tiredness—normally in stir he'd be snoring about now—but he was still high, still feeling stony good.

He hadn't been tempted by any of the dope in that frame house. That was new, not being tempted by drugs. Anytime before, since he'd first got high at thirteen, he'd have jumped right into that shit.

But it seemed paltry now, compared to this.

"The suffering here is part of your power," came the whisperer, then, as they paused by the roulette table. *"Look around you, and know it."*

Gulcher had never had an interest in whether people suffered, unless he hated them—then he was *real* interested. People he didn't know—who cared? But if the whisperer said it was important . . .

There, a row of people at the slot machines. Three stumpy, little old ladies with fat ankles and cigarette-yellowed hands and droopy-sad faces: a white lady, a Filipina, a Cuban lady. Then a chunky black woman in a nurse's uniform; then a middle-aged, maybe Italian guy with buck teeth, receding hair, fake-looking gold chain. Then a big black guy in a New York Jets jersey; then a white guy so fat he was in a wheelchair from it, barely fitting in there between rows of slots; then a tall, skinny white woman in a pale pink pants suit with a crotch stain that made him wonder if she'd peed her pants because she wouldn't leave her slot machine; then a scared-looking pimply young guy, maybe nineteen; then . . .

And they were all pumping the slots, one way or another pumping at them, though the new machines, most of them, didn't have the metal arms you pulled; these weren't the old one-armed bandits, these were touch-screen and push-button, and they were all shiny with colors and panels glowing with pop icons, and they had themes, some of them, pictures of characters from TV shows on them—a *CSI: Denver* slot machine, a *Magic Girl* one, a *Disney Planet* one—and they had little lights on top that revolved when they paid, and they all went *yippety-yippety-yippety-tweet-tweet-tootle* all the fucking time.

As he watched them, a kind of ripple was in the air around each slot player, a membrane of heightened perception provided by the whisperer—and it revealed *a second face* on each person. As if each slot player had two faces at once, the second one floating behind and a little above the one you normally see. The second face was blue-white, almost like a mask, but you could see through it—a ghostly visage, with a different expression from the face the slot player showed the world, and it was looking around.

"That is the face of their souls," said the whisperer.

These soul faces were frightened and angry. They had the look of trapped people, Gulcher decided. Like they were really stuck somewhere and not sure how or why they got stuck there and they just wanted to get *out*. Like bugs in a Roach Motel.

The faces of their souls . . .

"You see it too?" Jock asked, sounding scared and sick himself.

"Yeah," Gulcher said. Wondering what the expression on the

face of his own soul looked like. These people looked like they were suffering, all right. That was funny, because the regular faces on their bodies looked like they were kind of bored, or just vaguely interested, or slightly excited. But these soul faces were like something you'd see in a mental ward. Gulcher himself had once been in a mental ward, playing crazy to stay out of prison, and he had fessed up pretty quick. Because that place was too damned depressing. He figured people's body faces in mental wards looked like their soul faces, no different.

"Those you see before you have folded their minds into the games of chance," said the whisperer. *"Their minds are trapped in the game, round and round. They have surrendered themselves; they have left an opening to anything that wishes to enter and take them. They are like puppets waiting for a hand.* Your *hands. Stretch out your hands. Two hands will do for many."*

"Two hands for many," Gulcher repeated. Not knowing why.

"What'd you say, Troy?" Jock asked.

"Shut up, I gotta concentrate and shit," Gulcher told him curtly. Jock had some ability to hear the whisperer, to glimpse the hidden things, but he didn't have anything like Gulcher's gift.

"Now reach out," said the whisperer. *"Speak the names you were taught and reach out—feel your hands beyond your hands."*

He remembered. The whisperer had guided him, as he'd destroyed the guards, opened the doors at the prison.

"It is something you were born to do," it told him. *"It is a gift."*

Gulcher closed his eyes, said the names, and had a sensation that was alien to him and natural both, when he used the gift. A feeling in his hands. As if they were rubbery, extending impossibly from within. His astral hands, reaching out beyond his physical boundaries, stretching out toward the people at the slots. And swirling around them were the steam-shapes, the man-faced serpents, going where he directed them. Unseen by anyone but him.

"Hey, you two," said the security bull, walking up to them.

Gulcher opened his eyes a moment, glanced at the guy. Short, almost freakishly broad-shouldered, froggishly wide-mouthed. He closed his eyes again as the guy went on, "What's this, standing around waving your arms at people with your eyes closed? All this grinning and laughing? We don't want drugged-up people in here, this ain't no place to be tripping on meth."

"Ha, he thinks we're on drugs there, uh, bro," Jock said. A criminal's instinct keeping him from saying Gulcher's name out loud. "Tripping, he says!"

Gulcher was stretching his unseen astral hands out to the nearest ten people, reaching into a head, through a head; stretching on to the next head, into the head, through the head; on to the next one, his reach stretching through three heads, and on to the fourth, opening them up, to stream astral familiars, the man-faced serpents into them.

Someone put their hand on Gulcher's arm—and Gulcher ignored it.

"Hey, keep away from him!" Jock warned the security bull.

"Okay, we got one with a gun here—!"

Bang of a gunshot, and the touch on his arm went away. Gulcher didn't open his eyes. He felt a body hit the floor. He knew it was the stocky, broad-shouldered one, falling, a bullet in his head. Didn't need to see it to know.

"More enemies are coming . . . reach out to more puppets."

Running feet, another gunshot, but he was ready. He opened his eyes and looked around, saw one clumsily sprawled dead man, another man crawling away, blood spreading across that funky paisley carpeting.

Men were running toward him, two of them with guns in their hands. Jock beside him saying, "Hey, man—you going to—"

Then it came together—and came rushing out. All those people, his puppets, rushing from between the slot machines at the men in the suits, the security bulls going down under a scrimmage of gamblers before they could fire a shot; a tumble of bodies, many of them old and fat and infirm, but young ones too, so many of them the casino guards were overwhelmed. And what they did then . . .

It wasn't Gulcher who made them do those things to the security bulls. He never told them to pluck out their eyes and squeeze their necks till the blood came out their mouths.

"You have tapped into their anger," came the whisper. *"Their hidden anger flows free and drives them."* Its voice oozed primal satisfaction.

Gulcher felt sick and had to look away. He didn't really care what happened to private pigs—but watching people get their faces pulled apart like that, naturally it's going to make you sick.

"What we do now?" Jock asked.

"We lock this place down, for a while, and get this mess taken care of."

"Sure to be people calling nine-one-one. Some is just watchin'. Not everyone's part of it."

"That's okay. You'll see. It's in the whole building, now. I can feel it." Gulcher turned to Jock, grinning. "This casino is *ours*."

BLEAK HAD ANCHORED THE cabin cruiser upriver; had come down here in the smaller boat. More prudent.

It was almost dawn. But here, in the shadow of a civilization, it was still dark. The sky was dark blue, showing aluminum gray of predawn; darkness draped the buildings.

As Bleak approached the rotting dock pilings, he smelled treated sewage, dead fish, decaying wood, tar, mildew. The reflection of a thin scythe of setting moon rippled with his passage, green-yellow on black. He looked back, once, to take in the baleful glower of the Manhattan skyline on the other side of the river.

His aluminum prow kissed the old, guano-frosted wooden ladder and he shipped the oars, clambered carefully forward, swearing when he nearly pitched into the drink. He grabbed the ladder, steadied himself, then tied up the boat with the painter. He could hear Shoella's ShadowComm contingent, fourteen of them up there, whispering on what remained of the old dock. He hoped no one would insist on using a familiar to probe his mind. He hated the feeling of a probe.

Bleak climbed the ladder, feeling them more clearly, up there, with every rung, their presences altering the ambient field of mind like fourteen iron spikes driven into the ground near an electromagnet. Only it wasn't a magnetic field; it was the *apeiron* field, as the Greek philosopher Anaximander had called it: the field of boundless essence that subtly took part in the other energy fields and gave birth to them; the pattern of undifferentiated consciousness from which all consciousness sprang. The apeiron was subtle yet endlessly powerful. It was the Hidden, the field traversed by planetary ghosts and other spirit beings; the energy which natural conjurers such as Bleak and the other members of the ShadowComm used as their medium of expression, each practitioner expressing himself in some personal, unique way.

Bleak climbed up onto the crumbling dock, put his hands in his coat pockets, facing New Jersey and the fourteen members of Shoella's La'hood. He was glad to be up here, where the breeze seemed fresher, pleasantly briny, coming in from the Verrazano Narrows way off to his left. But nervous, facing off with Shoella's bunch. He wasn't much liked by them.

Yorena flew at Bleak, first, just to make sure of him; to see if anyone was coming up the ladder behind him. The familiar flapped ponderously around him, leaving an acrid smell behind, and dropping a few pinfeathers; then flew back to Shoella. The creature settled on a craggy, tar-spackled post beside her: Yorena looked in profile like a big gull, except for the falconlike beak.

The pattern of speckles on her chest seemed to change configuration as he looked at them.

"Was it really necessary that we all come?" asked Oliver, stepping forward. Like most of them, Giant and Pigeon Lady aside, Oliver was quite ordinary looking. A young man with heavy-lidded eyes, he wore a Mets baseball jacket and hat; someone you'd see on the subway and not give a second thought. Even the ferret on his shoulder, a familiar of sorts, didn't seem so very exotic. "I hate coming to this part of New Jersey."

"Shoella thought it was necessary," Bleak said, shrugging. "I'm not arguing with her. The CCA is making its move on us. They tried to get me today. They've got a new way to find us. Meaning we have to keep this meeting short."

Oliver scowled. "Meaning we shouldn't have had it at all, you ask me. If they're after you, and you're here . . ." His right hand curled up as if gripping an unseen weapon—and it might just do that, since Oliver could throw energy bullets too. Only, he threw them in the manner of a hardball pitcher.

"Sounds like a risky meeting to me," someone else in the group muttered. Giant, the little person.

The others, standing in a semicircle behind Shoella, were mostly a harmless-looking mix of men and women, only one over sixty—the Pigeon Lady. A bland appearance was camouflage, but not everyone bothered: young, pale Glory was dramatically Goth in her style, while Giant, a Hispanic near-dwarf, went out of his way to bristle with piercings, and studs in black leather. To Bleak he looked like an anthropomorphic hedgehog. He'd annoyed Giant, once, by calling him Sonic. But Giant's conspicuousness could end in the blink of an eye—he had the gift of calling up camouflage sprites and could vanish against the background if he chose.

"Maybe," Bleak said, "this wasn't such a good idea. But the idea was to warn you—tell you about the detector, and maybe work together, figure some way to fly under this new radar of theirs . . ." He broke off, glanced at the sky, became aware that someone was looking at him from behind—from some distance away, up high. Pigeon Lady waddled up, grinning at him toothlessly, and he nodded to her, smiled, acknowledging the help she'd given him on the street. One of her pigeons fluttered from her shoulders, and in its wing wind he heard, *That's okay, I gots to help if I can.*

How did she get over here to Jersey, he wondered, with all those pigeons? They wouldn't let her on a subway with those things. Did they hide in her clothing?

"Shoella," Bleak went on, talking to the group, "wanted you to hear it from me." He turned and saw a light approaching in the air, still a ways off, over the river. It was almost lost in the lights of the Manhattan skyline—as if one of those lights had detached from its skyscraper and come hunting.

Giant stepped forward. "You could be working with the feds." A piping voice.

"You know that's bullshit, Giant. We don't have time for a mind probe. You see that light coming over the river?" Bleak pointed.

They all turned to look. A spotlight beam was probing down from the oncoming light; you could just make out the outline of a helicopter. Coming right at them, about two hundred yards away, sixty above.

"It's them and . . . they have a detector," Glory said. The tense little woman, her head draped in black silk, trembling as she closed her kohled eyes—peering with her mind. "I can *see* it. I see the device in someone's hand! A little arrow!"

"There's something we can do," Shoella said, looking coldly at Bleak. "If Gabriel really didn't bring them here on purpose . . . he'll help us deal with them."

"Let's do it," Bleak said, nodding.

"Everyone!" Shoella called, gesturing. They crowded around

him—put Bleak right at the center. Shoella murmured to Yorena, who pulsed the plan to their minds.

Bleak felt the someone in the chopper looking right at him. Some familiarity around the edges: it might be Drake Zweig.

"They're CCA," Glory muttered. "I've got that much."

So the feds had found him already, Bleak realized, shaking his head. That agent Sarikosca, maybe. Zweig. Coming after him again . . . and they'd be calling in backup. Which meant the others, La'hood, could go down too. They might all get swept up, trucked away to some nameless detention center for their kind.

"So they did follow you here," Oliver said disgustedly. "They're after you—and they'll get all of us!"

"I don't think they followed him," Shoella put in. "They're just flying around the area using their little detector—and picked us up."

"Let me shoot them down, Sho'," Giant said. "I've got a clear shot—they're almost in range." He raised his arms, to call the lightning down.

"No," said Bleak, shoving Giant's hands down. "The peeps in that chopper have been briefed all wrong about us. They're not to blame."

"Don't fucking touch me, Bleak."

"Focus, dammit! If Glory can make an illusion . . ."

"I can try," she said, gazing raptly at the CCA chopper, beginning to murmur to the Hidden. "But it won't hold for long."

The chopper neared; the crowd of ShadowComm muttered to one another, looking around for somewhere to run to. But running would draw too much attention to them.

"Listen up!" Bleak said sharply. He'd sometimes commanded a platoon in Afghanistan, and the tone of authority came easily to him when he needed it. "Count to three, then everyone back away from me, leave me in the center! They've got the detector focused right on me."

"No one show any power," Shoella hissed. "Blank out till they move on!"

One, two, three—and they all drew back from Bleak. He drew power, massively and suddenly, so that he'd surge with energy. That should draw the CCA detector to fixate on him, over the others—and Bleak bolted. He ducked quickly away from the fourteen La'hood ShadowComms, becoming a human decoy.

Glory projected an illusion to the observers in the helicopter—the illusion lapped out like ripples in water, undulated through Bleak's mind: the La'hood group as a crowd of the homeless, partying drunkenly at dawn around a fire in an old oil barrel, waving bottles, all blurred with a sudden flurrying of pigeons. Easy to ignore them and focus on Bleak.

Already fixed on him, the detector tracked him as he pounded across the dock—he could sense someone looking at him from above, the detector arrow sometimes entering their line of sight.

Bleak was pounding away from the ShadowComm group, through darkness, up the pier to the street, hoping to lure the chopper away from La'hood—and hoping he didn't step through a hole in the rotting wooden deck, maybe break an ankle.

The helicopter's spotlight fixed him, stayed wobblingly with him. The chopper veered to follow as, sticking to the shadow of a building, he ran up the street, then cut left along the avenue paralleling the Hudson.

Not in great shape anymore, he thought, breathing hard as he got to the sidewalk. *Second time I had to run from these bastards today. Not fit. Dial back my drinking.*

"STAY WHERE YOU ARE," boomed an amplified voice from overhead. "WE'RE SENDING A PATROL CAR. I REPEAT, STAY WHERE YOU ARE."

A patrol car. Bleak heard the siren approaching off to his right. He wondered what lie CCA had told the police, to get them to detain him.

Puffing, he turned right, down a side street, saw what he was looking for, a PATH train entrance. If he could catch a train, he'd take it a couple stops, get out, and, if he was clear of them, maybe get a cab through the tunnel. Then—where? Get a subway to Brooklyn?

No, he shouldn't go see Cronin now. Not until he'd done a better job of losing these bloodhounds. Wasn't safe for Cronin.

He could hear the helicopter's engine, feel its wind stirring the hair on the back of his head, as he jumped down the stairwell, taking the first flight all at once, wincing as he struck, pounding down the next steps.

They hadn't planned this, he decided, slowing to stride into the station. Shoella was right, they must've been trying likely areas with the detector and just happened to catch the meeting's signal.

But Bleak knew that by the time the chopper got back, the fourteen La'hood ShadowComms would have gone in fourteen directions, slipping away, anonymously, into the city, with the skill of a lifetime's practice.

Except for Giant—who didn't need to scurry off. He could literally vanish.

They were probably safe for now. And chances were he could get out of a PATH station, down the line, before CCA called someone to cover its exits. Going underground ought to throw off their detector. With any luck, he'd lost them for the night.

Bleak paid, went past the kiosk into the train station just as an early-morning train was rushing up. He got aboard a train car with no one on it but a sleepy security guard heading for a job and settled back into a seat at the other end, catching his breath. Hoping he was right to figure the others had got away.

So where did he go now? He was tired. Needed rest. But where? He didn't feel safe going to his cabin cruiser. Nowhere to lay his head.

What was that line from the Bible? *The foxes have holes, and the birds of the air have nests; but the Son of Man has nowhere to lay his head.*

Me, he thought—*only I'm not the Son of Man, I'm not the son of anyone. Going to have to be the sunless man. Hide in the dark for a while. Keep to the shadows.*

That's what he was stuck with. Another quote came into his head—from a very different source, an old hippie rock band. What was that band's name? *Knocked down, it gets to wearin' thin. They just won't let you be.*

That's what it was like for Bleak. The feds wouldn't let him be. Their Remote Viewing division—early CCA, maybe—had come sniffing around in Afghanistan, hinting about Special Recruitment. He'd wondered how they knew about him—about his talents. Suspected that they'd set him up to leave the Rangers early. As if they had other uses for him and didn't want him on the firing line.

But he'd refused to play along, after the Rangers. He'd ducked out on them. Made a life for himself in New York City, where it was easy to vanish in the crowd. A sort of life, anyway.

It was hard for Gabriel Bleak to live like a normal human being. Couldn't keep a relationship long. Had to be secretive—which women hated. But if he wasn't secretive it was good-bye, Esme; good-bye, Laura; good-bye . . . Wendy.

The train hummed through the tunnel, windows flashing with passing lights, and Bleak realized he was clenching his fists, his knuckles white. He tried to relax, but he was seething with anger. Seething at having to run from that chopper; at being tracked by a spotlight from above. Forced to run like a panicked dog with its tail on fire.

He sang the tune to himself, "'Knocked down, it gets to wearin' thin. They just won't let you be. . . .'" Muttered, "What band was that . . ."

"That was the Grateful Dead," said a voice near his ear. From some invisible entity.

"Go away!" Bleak said angrily. And felt it depart.

He was still burning inside. And he wasn't even sure whom he was angry at. Not at CCA—not particularly. Not at Shoella and her people, with their pointless suspicion of him. Not at the army, especially. Not at his parents . . . not exactly.

It was more like he was mad at all of them, and at himself, for the outsider life he had to live. It didn't make sense to be mad at yourself, he figured, for being what nature made you. But that's how you ended up feeling.

He was quietly but perpetually pissed off at who he was, and what he was, and how everyone around him dealt with it—or failed to.

It had been that way almost from the first night. The night he'd realized. The night he'd first looked deep into the Hidden. Years ago . . .

FOUR

abriel Bleak, two weeks after his thirteenth birthday.

He was living with his parents, in eastern Oregon. His parents had caught him at it out in the barn, that night. Could be they had expected to catch him masturbating over a girlie magazine, or smoking marijuana cadged from his young Native friends on the Rez, or feeling up some drunken local girl.

But this . . .

He had been a kid living alone with his folks on a ranch, just trying to keep up with homework and Future Farmers of America meetings—he'd always found being around animals soothing—and getting into rock 'n' roll, and starting to look at girls a lot more: his eyes drawn to their hair floating in the wind, their thighs on the desk chairs at school, the pale, glossy curve of their shoulders when they wore sleeveless blouses, the sudden parabolas of their new breasts; noticing the color of that girl's eyes for the first time, noticing that she'd started painting her nails.

He'd been a kid reading Marvel comics and Conan and Horatio Hornblower novels; just a kid watching war movies on late-night television. Always drawn to the military.

Why? What was it about the military?

But he knew, on some level. Later, grown-up, he'd work out the why of it: if you were a good soldier, you were part of something bigger, locked into a kind of family. A tough, ritualized, formalized masculine family. They had to accept you, if you did your job. Even if they sensed something was strange about you.

He never felt really fully connected to his parents. Not after his brother vanished. And after that day, two days past his turning thirteen, he hadn't felt accepted by them at all.

He went to church with his parents—there were devout Lutherans—but never felt a connection there, either. Not the kind other people felt. Feeding a new calf with a bottle, that gave him a feeling of connection. And there was that other connection, to the unseen, that was on the edge of his awareness . . . tingling there. Not coming into focus. Not till that night.

That night in October, Gabriel Bleak, a boy of thirteen, lay atop his bedclothes, still dressed except for his shoes, trying to read Spenser, *The Faerie Queene*, for extra credit at school—Miss Williver, his English teacher, had talked him into it. He was surprised that he liked it. He was just lying there reading the part that went

> *And forth he cald out of deep darknes dredd*
> *Legions of Sprights, the which, like little flyes*
> *Fluttering about his ever-damned hedd*
> *Awaite whereto their service he applyes,*
> *To aide his friendes or fray his enemies . . .*

And it gave him a peculiar feeling, reading those lines. *Out of deep darknes dredd legions of Sprights.* Not a feeling of dread, himself, but a sense of recognition both thrilling and unnerving.

He wished he had someone he could talk to about that. Other kids worried about talking about sexual feelings. The Bleaks bred animals, and there wasn't much mystery there. These other sensations troubled him. That tingling around the edges. *Something's there, unseen. Waiting.*

He found himself drifting into a familiar fantasy of talking to his brother. Who was gone, dead ten years now. But now and then, he liked to pretend his brother was there to talk to. He imagined saying, "Hey, Sean, I wish you could read this book, it gives me this feeling like the stuff that's so . . . that I can feel but I don't know what it is. Gives me those moments where I feel like if I'm somebody else than what people think, like that might still be okay. Like it's part of this world. Faerie, he calls it. He makes it seem like it's its own world and part of this one too. Not that I'm a fairy, dude, but . . . there's something there, it's like he knew . . ."

He caught himself. *Stop doing that! Dumb to pretend. Man, you're just a dweeb with an imaginary friend.* He wished he had a real, living brother or sister. He had a few faint memories of that other boy, his fraternal twin. Fainter every year since Sean had been killed, so his dad had told him, when they were not yet three. Some accident Gabriel hadn't witnessed. His folks were vague about it. A tractor. The boy playing unseen under the wheels.

Anyway he was gone, and Gabriel was used to that. But there was an absence in his life, an absence he could feel physically, at times. If Sean had lived, Gabriel would have had a sibling with, perhaps, the same feeling of being undefinedly different. Someone who could relate to feeling as if you had only one foot in this world. But death had taken Sean before his brother had quite understood Sean was really there as an individual. Gabriel had accepted him as part of the world like the furniture, the sky, the ground underneath, his own left hand. And then he was gone.

Sure, Gabriel had some friends—a couple of others who seemed a little "off" were drawn to him. Chester and Anna Lynn.

Drawn to him, maybe, because he accepted them; maybe too because he sometimes protected them. And there were a couple of Indian brothers, off the Rez. Joel and Angelo, he'd see them at the rodeo, at the county fair, or on the street when Gabriel rode his bike into town. They hung out and talked, sometimes.

But he never felt there was anybody he could really open up to. How would he explain? "See, there's something in me waiting to come out, it visits me in dreams, and it's always there, kinda invisible, looking over my shoulder, and I keep thinking someone is going to realize I'm not really part of this world. I have to work hard to feel part of it. It's like I'm supposed to be somewhere else wherever I go. But it's really hard to explain."

People would think he was bipolar. Which is something he'd read up on, when he started to be afraid he might be crazy, himself. One time he started talking to a guy in town, a nineteen-year-old, Connor, outside the drugstore. Connor was a notorious local eccentric.

"Hey, Gabriel, what you doing, you gotta Hershey bar, huh? Can I have a bite? . . . Thanks. What's up? Hey, can you feel the vibes right now?"

Gabriel had looked at him with interest. "Feel . . . which exactly?"

"That feeling like the ray coming at you, that you can feel in your bones and . . ."

"Well. Sometimes." Could this guy really feel what Gabriel felt? "Something kinda like that. Not exactly, it's more all over the place. I mean —"

"And it's from the agents, they're beaming them at us from orbit, it's in those satellites, and they put voices in your head that tell you to do things?"

"Uh . . ." From orbit? Voices?

"The beams come right through those faces in the clouds. The faces are from the rays."

Gabriel had winced at that. "Um . . . no. I meant something else. You can keep that Hershey bar." He left quickly, realizing that Connor was just plain mentally ill, really was bipolar, or paranoid schizophrenic. Gabriel Bleak never imagined conspiracies against him, never seemed to get "special messages" from television, the way mentally ill people did—like Connor. The only message he got from TV was that he should buy something.

When he'd turned thirteen, Gabriel had written in his diary:

> I must have some particular mental problem, that somebody could diagnose, not like Connor but something else. Something that lets me use my mind pretty reasonably, but the disease part is like I just have this feeling of knowing there's some kind of invisible world and being part of it and it's really a form of mental illness that I'll probably find in the books some day. That really sucks. Big-time.
>
> I think my mom and dad know there's something wrong with me. Mom acts like she loves me but it's like she's scared of me too. My dad goes quiet when I'm around. He used to tell me things about the world and ranching, but a couple of years ago he just stopped talking to me unless I ask him a question, and then when he answers he only says what he has to.
>
> Maybe I'm imagining all this stuff. But if I am, why? What does that mean?

GABRIEL TRIED TO READ a little more Edmund Spenser. But he was soon seized with a restlessness, laid the book down on the quilt, and stared up at the slanted, white ceiling of his room— he was in an attic room, converted to a bedroom. He had a larger bedroom downstairs but he liked the view out the window from up here. His father had seemed relieved to agree, had even painted the walls for him. Only later had it occurred to Gabriel that the move to the attic room put him farther away from his parents.

Once, when he'd got up to go to the bathroom, he'd heard them talking late at night, downstairs in the kitchen. He'd stood in the darkness at the top of the stairs, listening for a minute. Hearing his mom say, "I just think he's lonely."

"You know what could happen. They could take him. And why? What's happening . . . happening right now, to . . ."

"We agreed not to talk about that—that boy is gone, sweetheart, and we . . . don't talk about that."

"Maybe they did something to him. . . . Maybe right now."

"Please. Don't. Just . . . talk to Gabe."

"I try. But I feel like he's looking right through me . . . I want to talk to Reverend Rowell about it, but I don't see how I can."

"Quiet, I think he's up."

Had they really been talking about him? Had he heard them right? The next morning he'd awakened, remembering the overheard conversation, and wondered if he'd dreamed it.

Now, as he lay there looking at the ceiling, the wind pushed at the house, sighing, shivering the window glass. Something about its sighing reminded him of when Johnny Redbear had come over from the Rez, had called up softly to his window, late at night. Wanting him to come out and drink some liquor he'd stolen from his old man. Gabriel had refused, afraid of getting caught, but he'd been tempted. Not so much by the liquor. By the adventure. By a voice calling from outside his window. *Come on out, Gabe, come out.* He liked that. Someone out there wanting him to come out and push out the limits.

The room was warm, tonight; the wind whining at the house wasn't cold. Sometimes there was an electricity in the air before a storm, a charge that seemed to come with a warm wind. Kind of felt that way tonight. On a night like that sometimes you could see a white fire dancing along the lightning rod over the barn, a pulse of energy in the darkness. Maybe if he went to look, he would see it now.

The house faced west, and so did his bedroom window, under the highest peak of the roof. The barn was north and east. He could see the lightning rod if he climbed onto the lower roof under his window.

"*North. North and east. Look to the north.*" A voice, like a whisper. Barely audible, in the sigh of the wind.

He shook his head. Imagining stuff. From reading that book.

Maybe he shouldn't go look. Maybe he shouldn't go outside at all tonight.

"*The way is opening.*"

"Shut up," he said aloud. Maybe he was turning into whatever Connor was, after all. Losing it.

But when the wind rose again, he thought he heard a distant singing, voices singing something he couldn't make out, the sound rising and fading . . . like if you heard people singing a hymn in a church a ways off. Only this wasn't a hymn.

He snorted at himself, but he got up, went to the wood-framed window, opened it quietly as he could. A warm, searching, alfalfa-fragrant wind came in, rattling his posters: Green Day and Nirvana and the U.S. army recruiting poster. The alfalfa had been harvested but the scent lingered over the fields; and now, the window open, the perfume of reaped stalks of grain filled his room. Alfalfa and dust. *Don't fear the Reaper.*

He started to climb out the window—then thought better of it and went to get shoes. He put on his Converse sneakers, went back to the window, climbed out onto the porch roof, feeling as if he were climbing right up among all those stars crowded overhead. He steadied himself with a hand on the eaves against the wind and looked toward the barn. Was that a ghostly glow on the barn's lightning rod? He could hear the Guernseys mooing in there. And a distant *thunk* as one of the two horses kicked at its stall. They were restless too.

The door to the barn was partly open. It seemed extra dark in there, as if the darkness had thickness and weight. But was that a pulse of light in the middle of the black? And then—the deep darkness again. Bits of hay swirled at the entrance in a little whirlwind.

He could just go downstairs, tell his dad he was going out to check on the stock. But he didn't want to see his parents right now. He felt that they'd find something out about him, see it in his face, if he went. Like he was ashamed.

What did he have to be ashamed of? Nothing. Still . . .

Chorused voices—unintelligible, all singing the same song but in a hundred different languages . . . discordant and concordant, disharmony and harmony.

What *was* that?

He went to the corner of the porch roof, careful, aware of the pushing wind; he knelt and climbed down, hanging on to the gutter by his fingers so it bent a little. Letting go, dropping to the ground. Dropping far enough so it stung when he landed on his feet, tipping over at the impact.

But he was up immediately, dusting off his rump, trotting toward the barn. It seemed to him as if he were standing still and the barn was coming toward him, almost rushing at him.

He crossed to stand just outside the barn door, peering inside. Smelled hay and grain and manure; the animals shuffling their feet, lowing.

What was he here for, again? The lightning rod? Or was there something else?

He took a couple steps back, looked up at the vertical rod on the roof, a dull silver streak aimed at the stars above the open hayloft. Maybe there was a glimmer along it. Maybe not.

"Enter and turn to the north. . . . No one can hear us, but you."

Maybe someone on the highway was playing a car radio. Only, the highway was almost a quarter mile away.

He should go back to bed. But he was drawn to step into the barn.

No, it wasn't that he was drawn, like, against his will; it was like he was *finding his will* for the first time. It felt like he was finally moving into the real world. Like one of those big jungle cats raised in a zoo—escaping into the woods for the first time.

Beyond the stalls, the barn had a smaller back door that led into a corral. A light shone from beyond that door. It wasn't a color he'd ever seen before—when he thought it was red, it was blue; when he thought it was blue, it was green. But it was none of those. It was more of a prism effect, like when he tried to see inside a little diamond his mom had on a necklace.

The cows were nervously mooing, stamping in their stalls; the horses were whinnying, goats bleating.

He walked toward the back door—and stopped, looked out on the corral. Stared in amazement.

A tsunami of sullenly glowing liquid, looking like molten wax, was coming at him.

It was coming from the north, swallowing up the horizon.

Fear spiked in his heart, but another feeling, of relieved belonging, of exotic enticement, was stronger. And that delicious sensation kept him rooted to the spot, listening to that multitudinous singing, louder and louder, roaring more dissonantly as the slow-motion tsunami approached.

The silvery molten sea was languidly pouring through a breach in a giant transparent wall, beyond the corral and the graveled private road; coming through the spillway in a see-through dam, thundering as it came. The wall went up high, its top hidden in mist. The wave coming through the breach was the expression of a living sea of force, in which figures took shape and collapsed, the way waves and currents surge up a

The figures were people—and were

them seemed angelic and some diabo

without category. He was seeing the F

Gabriel knew that he was seein

what was really coming was beyond

mind had formulated this breached-

closer to comprehending it. A way to visualize the

worldwide sea of living energy.

He watched in horror and fascination as the slow-motion wave of mind-energy rushed toward him. Had just time to think, *I should run. I should hide from this!*

But he wasn't going to run. On some deep level, he knew he belonged in it. He was like a fish in an aquarium, rejoicing as it sees a flood pour into the house, the flood that will set it free.

And the onrushing tidal wave of the Hidden reared over him, a glassy wall of liquid energy . . . and crashed down all about him.

He expected it to knock him about, sweep him off his feet . . . but he felt something in his nerves, his spirit, his mind, not so much with his outer body . . . except for that crackling that lifted his hair to wave about his head like electrified seaweed; that raised goose bumps on his skin.

The currents of energy surged around him and he waited to die from its intensity, but instead he felt energized, finally *completed* by this new, living medium. The singing he'd heard was the sound its collective surging made; it was its equivalent of the sound of breakers. The singing was shaking the world, all around him, a surging cacophony of half-formed thoughts, ideas, possibilities. It was always there, usually unheard.

He felt the presence of countless other beings, in this new medium—and something else, the *potential* for beings who weren't quite there yet. He saw spirits loom up, like ethereal otters in an etheric sea, felt them looking him over. He knew, somehow, that

...re kept back from him by an emanation generated
...body—generated without his having to try. His just
...e and conscious here was enough to keep them back.
...ese beings, anyway. Certain others, more powerful and
...sh, might overwhelm that protective emanation, if they came
...pon him. Might engulf him, devour him.

But one being in particular spoke to him; an entity emanating
no threat.

"*Reach out,*" said the voice. A voice with sheer *trustworthiness*
innate in its timbre.

He remembered Connor. "I'm hearing things," Gabriel said.
"This is hallucination stuff. Hearing voices."

"*Some hear voices generated from their own faulty thinking
matter,*" said the voice from the charged air about him. "*Most who
suppose they hear the unseen only hear themselves. But you are not
like the others. You've always known that. You can feel that I am
trustworthy. You have the taste for things that are true. So listen to
me. Reach out with your other hands . . . your inner hands.*"

It came to Gabriel naturally, like a baby's first attempt to pick
things up with its fingers—clumsily at first. Still, he reached into
the luminous surging of the Hidden and felt it respond, something
like clay in his fingers, but more malleable, less definable; he extended the energy field he was giving off, used it to manipulate the
field, to extend himself telekinetically, enfolding the object nearest
to hand: a pitchfork, leaning on the cobwebby wall beside him.

And made the pitchfork lift up into the air. It hung there quivering, its tines thrumming like a tuning fork . . . then dropped
with a clang.

"*The energy of the Hidden is condensable,*" said the voice.
"*Make a ladder, like Jacob, and rise up!*"

He compressed the energy field in front of him—and stepped
up onto the energy compression.

To find that he was standing in the air, hovering two feet over the ground.

He was dumbfounded and yet, on some level, not surprised. This was what he'd always unconsciously known was there; this was the missing part of himself. This was the real world, to him.

"It is always there, but your connection to it has been locked away, muted. The device that has hidden it from humanity is weakening, and those with the gift can feel the living radiance rise."

"Who's talking to me?" Gabriel demanded, as he hovered there. "Who are you!"

As if in reply, the shape of a man formed before him, naked but sexless; the body, Gabriel knew instinctively, was a formality. It could have taken the shape of an octopus or a giant rabbit named Harvey or a Coca-Cola bottle. But just now it was solidifying, shaping to resemble a medium-size man, the body molded of the shining medium that swirled around him. The entity's "head" seemed detached, floating over the neck. There was no definite face, just an impression of eyes, gazing back at him. *"It's long since I've been here,"* said the spirit. That familiar, gentle voice. Gabriel thought of it as the Talking Light. *"There are others who want to speak to you, where the spirits of the dead linger. The Hidden is their world."*

The dead wanted to speak to him? Gabriel's mouth went dry at the thought. Who? His grandmother? His brother? "I don't think . . . I'm ready to talk to them. Just tell me—do you have a name? Who are you? Are you one of the dead?"

"I have never been subject to death. As for a name, some in your world have called me Mîkha'el."

Mîkha'el? "I'll call you . . . Mike. Light Mike."

"All right. You cannot sustain this contact long. . . . It is too new to you. If you remain, your mind will melt into it, and you will lose all shape. So quickly: ask me what you want."

His mind would melt? He would lose shape? He felt like running then. But this bright thing knew secrets. This was a chance to ask . . .

"What . . . what actually happened to my brother?" Gabriel blurted. "Sean was really little when he died but—is he there?"

"You will hear from him, in time. Someone else stands behind him, and he stands in that shadow. The wall of force is cracked and may fall completely, and when that day comes, we will see who is stronger. An enemy hides itself from you. . . . And now someone approaches, in dark ignorance, behind you. We are not alone here."

"Oh, God—oh, what is he—what have they done to him!" A choked exclamation from behind.

And for the first time in his life, Gabriel Bleak saw himself from behind. He saw himself through someone else's eyes: his father's eyes, dad at the door to the barn, seeing him framed by the doorway to the corral, surrounded by luminous fog . . . and floating in the air several feet over the floor, talking to something that wasn't there. And Gabriel saw that in his father's eyes, at that moment, his son was unnatural.

Gabriel shuddered, felt sick at the emotional repugnance he felt in his father's regard. The emotion broke his contact with the Hidden—and Light Mike vanished; the Hidden became hidden once more. The energy field disintegrated below him, and he dropped to the ground.

His father's point of view on him receded, and all Gabriel could see, then, was the barn around him, the ordinary world. He turned around to look at his dad, who'd put his boots on, sockless and unlaced, to protect his feet so he could go and look for his son; his father, in overalls and T-shirt, a big man who never showed fear, backing away from his own child . . . backing away from his son and muttering the Lord's Prayer. His mother, he saw then, standing a few steps behind him, in her long, peach-colored nightgown.

She'd seen him too, talking to something invisible, and floating in the air.

They backed away and turned their backs, his father circling an arm around his mother, drawing her protectively with him; his mother softly protesting, the two of them hurrying back to the house. Away from their son.

Gabriel heard crickets, and the horses snorting. He turned to look out across the corral again. He saw bits of mown alfalfa blowing across the dirt of the corral, and star-lit clouds parading overhead, and no other motion, nothing else. Mike the Talking Light was gone; the slow-motion sea of energy—the field of the Hidden—was gone.

No. The Hidden itself was still there. When he did as he'd been taught, stretched out his sensations, he sensed the Hidden . . . but now it was muffled. Seen through several pairs of sunglasses. Felt through a damp, sweaty sheet. A few degrees separated.

Never again would he see it quite so nakedly. And rarely would he sense the presence of Mike Light.

But he knew . . . the light that spoke was still there, removed to some metaphysical distance, but not gone forever. And it was possible to disclose the Hidden, to delve into it and manipulate it . . . and someday he would do it again.

What else was left to him?

YEARS AGO, THAT WAS, Bleak thought, as the train ground to a halt at the station he wanted. But it felt like seconds ago. It ached that much. Glorious and painful, both.

Now, just a few hours after seeing a demon chew through someone's brains at a bar on the Hudson, Bleak was rushing out of the PATH train, hurrying across the platform toward the street-exit stairs, gazing at subway ad posters but not seeing them. Seeing only his father's horrified face, that night long ago.

He never quite got over the look on his father's face. Or what happened soon after. His father, refusing to discuss what he'd seen—muttering about diabolic influences, warnings from the Reverend Rowell at the Lutheran church—making the arrangements to send him away to military school. Telling Mom, "The boy's always been into the military, let him get a good close look at it and see if it's for him."

And Gabriel hadn't been entirely sorry to go, though he hadn't been ready to leave home so soon. He'd known why his dad had sent him there, really. Because his father was afraid of his own son.

Something had seemed to block his attempts at contact with Light Mike, after that night. He was not able to ask the question, to get the answer that had been snatched away from him when his father had interrupted his first real exploration of the Hidden.

What did you say about my brother, Sean? I don't understand. Tell me about my brother!

Coming out of the PATH train station, Bleak winced at the morning light, looking for a cab. Hard to find at this hour. Glancing at the sky, half expecting the feds' chopper to be up there. But the CCA helicopter was gone.

He wondered if he'd meet her again. Agent Sarikosca. Something about her . . .

THEY WERE ALL TIRED, dead tired, gathered around the car, Loraine and Zweig and Arnie and the other agents, on the helicopter pad, outside CCA headquarters in Long Island.

It was about seven thirty the same morning. They hadn't slept—always feeling close to their quarry. Never quite catching up till that moment, hovering over the broken-down old dock. Then they'd lost him again.

The chopper was cooling off behind them, its rotors lazily

turning. Loraine Sarikosca and Dorrick in the chopper had found Bleak again—and others, it appeared—then lost him almost as quickly.

"I'm not sure what we can do legally, once we've got them," Dorrick was saying.

"Theoretically we don't need evidence for an arrest," she said, "long as we've got the Homeland Security stripe." There were things Dorrick didn't get, yet. "But even CCA likes to know they've got the right guy. I saw what I saw, but—in our line of work sometimes people start to imagine things so administration's never sure till there's film and a lot of witnesses. And it's not like we can get the police to do a Code Three on him. We'd have to explain why we want him."

"We could tell them he's a terrorist," Zweig said, thumping the hood of the car with the flat of his hand.

"We're trying not to use that one," Arnie pointed out. "Confuses the antiterrorist guys. Crosses 'em up and they get mad."

"Pretty impressive, that thing he did at the end," Dorrick muttered. "Back there in the alley. Walking on air. Can't do that with any ordnance we get issued. I kept looking for a wire." He shook his head.

"There wasn't any wire." Loraine remembered that mother and child out in Nevada . . . going straight up, in that blinding plume. Witnessing that was part of her CCA training, and she'd thought, then, *I'm in over my head.* But the paranormal had always fascinated her. She couldn't walk away.

"You could've been killed, taking him on alone, Loraine," Arnie said, with more feeling than he probably intended to show. He was leaning against the car near her; took off his sunglasses, tapped them on his knee. She stood awkwardly by the car's open door.

Loraine was aware that Arnie was sweet on her. Nice-looking guy with one of those close-cut beards, sculpted four-o'clock shadow, big shoulders, big hands, quick smile. But she didn't have time for his crush—CCA was still defining itself, and she was still finding her footing in it.

"If you're sure of the ID, what do we have on him, Dorrick?" she asked. "God, I need some coffee. Let's get in the damn car." She got in the backseat.

She'd been notified about Bleak only an hour before she'd met him. She'd been told that a CCA study subject had been located—they'd lost track of him in recent years—and she was to use one of the new detectors to track him, try to bring him in. Not much time to study his file.

"Most of what we got is right here." Dorrick, getting in the driver's seat of the car, tapped the little computer display on the dashboard. Zweig climbed in beside him.

Loraine leaned forward, looking between the two men at the small screen tilted out from the display under the dashboard. The screen was scrolling military data. Lots of it. She saw *recommended for a MoH, Silver Star. . . .* She made an impatient gesture. "I want to see early history. We know he was a war hero."

"The hell he was," Zweig said. "He was using this damn power, gave him an edge."

"Doesn't protect you from bullets," Loraine observed.

Dorrick scrolled to early history. "Says he grew up on a ranch in eastern Oregon. Horses . . . goats."

"Goats?" Arnie laughed, rubbing his eyes. "A goat ranch?"

"They raised alfalfa, had a small dairy, and he bred some kind of fancy goats, along with horses. The boy liked rock music and animals. He was in the goddamn FFA, can you believe that? Teenager, they sent him to a military boarding school. Two years of college, dropped out to enlist, Army Rangers. Made sarge. Left that and now he's a bounty hunter."

"Hmph," Loraine said, yawning. Stretching as well as she could in the confines of the car. She just wanted to get back to her condo in Brooklyn Heights, check on her cats, get some rest. "No documentation of his power early on, but apparently someone was monitoring the power and . . . expecting it. He could be going back home if he's tight with his parents . . . friends back there."

"Says Bleak is mostly a loner," Dorrick said, reading ahead. "Makes 'friends' with bartenders. Had girlfriends, only one that was long-term, she split. Played rhythm guitar with some rock band a while back, not an expert musician. Some kind of bad incident at a minor concert, exploding equipment, a fire, no one hurt but there was a small-claims lawsuit from the club—and the band split up. Bleak had a brother . . . who vanished when he was a kid. When he was a toddler, according to this."

"Vanished?"

"What it says. There's nothing more about that . . . says material was redacted from the file."

"Really." What had they censored? Loraine wondered about some of the prototype-CCA programs—she'd heard some stories about their blackest black ops.

"He knows about the device," Zweig pointed out.

Loraine shrugged. "They'd have found out soon enough anyway. The thing to do is to make more of them—we only have one that really works—and increase the range so that we can find them wherever they are. Dr. Helman says it can be done. We just need the budget."

"Who decides CCA's budget these days?" Dorrick asked. "I asked when I came on, but everybody shrugged me off."

Loraine rubbed at her tired eyes. "Couple of generals at the Pentagon got the purse strings—Erlich and Swanson. They're kind of dubious about the whole thing. We need better detectors."

She wondered if "find them wherever they are" was what she really wanted to do about ShadowComm types. After that fatal containment incident in Arkansas, her loyalty to CCA started to waver.

Loraine suspected the agency knew she wasn't completely committed to the job. General Forsythe, who ran the CCA, knew her record at the DIA—knew why she'd quit. Knew she wasn't always knee-jerk about being a team player.

She wasn't sure why she'd let them talk her into coming into the CCA. She'd always had a fascination with the occult. But was that enough? She wondered why they'd given her an assignment, authority over a crew, with so little relevant background.

Forsythe had put her to work in the field—even when he didn't seem to trust her. And for reasons she didn't fully understand, she didn't trust General Forsythe.

"That's it for me today," she said, rubbing her eyes. "Am I getting a ride or do I take a cab all the damn way to Brooklyn Heights?"

FIVE

ulcher was getting tired. But there were the cops to deal with before he could rest. Jock was already sacked out in a dressing room, in the tunnels under the casinos; snoring on a cot down the hall from the place they'd stacked the bodies. Six bodies, the ones who'd died in the melee.

Gulcher had always heard there were tunnels under big casinos, used for all kinds of behind-the-scenes business and preparation, but he'd never seen them before. In the case of Lucky Lou's Atlantic City Casino, they were tacky but clean, well-lit underground corridors, the linoleum peeling in some places. The tunnels connected dressing rooms to stages, counting rooms to cashier booths, administration to security.

Gulcher had found an administrator down here, a middle-aged guy with a nice suit. Guy who was now dead. And the suit fit Gulcher pretty good. He wore the sunglasses—they never looked out of place in a casino—and a big smile as he met the cops talking to his security people. There was a plainclothes detective and a uniformed police lieutenant with the three Atlantic City PD cops. One of the cops had a take-out coffee in his hand; the lady cop was chewing gum. The third one kept touching a pack of cigarettes in his shirt pocket, like he couldn't wait to get out and have a smoke. Somehow these casual details were reassuring to Gulcher as he shook hands with the lieutenant. The guy introduced himself. Made sure Gulcher heard the rank. Gulcher told him his own name was Presley. It was a name he'd always liked.

"Hey, thanks for coming over, Lieutenant," Gulcher said. Saying it loud to be heard over the whistle and yammer and clatter of the slot machines. People were playing again as if there hadn't been a pile of bodies here just about forty minutes ago. And the players he'd taken control of, short those who'd died, were back at it too. Not remembering anything.

"Yeah, we had a rough time with some tweakers," said Stedley, the casino's head of security. Bulky but slick guy in a tailored suit, immaculate grooming, whitened teeth. He flashed a sharklike smile. "But we took care of 'em long time before your people come. One of our guys got a gash in his scalp—you can see the blood from it."

Gulcher looked at Stedley in muted wonder. Stedley was so thoroughly Gulcher's man now. Never remembered any other arrangement. To Stedley it was as if he'd always worked for Gulcher. The whisperer, what it could do! It was just fucking mind-blowing. It was mind-*taking*, really.

The lieutenant, a middle-aged black man with salt-and-pepper hair and a little mustache, was staring at Gulcher, chewing his lower lip. Maybe starting to recognize him from the APB out on him. But the suit, the situation, and the sunglasses made him unsure. And Gulcher knew he could make him forget about it in a heartbeat.

"We'd have come sooner," the lady cop said, "but, uh . . ." She looked maybe Puerto Rican to Gulcher; small and plump but not bad looking for a cop. "But there was an explosion, a gas main went up, a quarter mile to the west—maybe you saw it on the news already. Lot of panic over there."

Gulcher figured that explosion was the whisperer's doing too.

Or maybe he should say it was Moloch's doing. Wasn't it *all* Moloch? Somehow, Gulcher didn't like to think about Moloch Baal. Who and what that was.

"Sure, I understand," Gulcher said. "You guys hadda deal with the explosion, but we had everything here under control. Yeah, it was just some tweakers on crack, or maybe meth. They jumped a couple of my guys. There was a shot fired too, but nobody hurt, and that guy got away. Just ran out. We'll send over some surveillance tape for ya. I sent the guys home, who got jumped. They're bruised up some—didn't need any hospital help. The crackheads, we taught 'em a little lesson, sent 'em on their way. I don't think they'll be back."

The cops chuckled. Except for the lieutenant, him being a real straight arrow. Opening his mouth maybe to ask Gulcher to take off those sunglasses.

Gulcher was already muttering a couple of names. And there was a squirming in the air around the lieutenant's face.

The lieutenant's eyes glazed over. He yawned. Seemed to frown, as if he was trying to remember something. Then he shrugged. His voice real dull, he said, "Yeah, okay, fellas, well, next time we'll want to talk to your witnesses. But I guess it's copacetic as is right now. You send over that video, okay?"

"Sure, Lieutenant, no problem."

The cops were already filing out. Gulcher watched them go, thinking, *I took over his mind and made him all sleepy and he just let it go.*

This was almost too good to be true. Just a little *too good.*

■ ■ ■

THIRTY-SIX HOURS LATER: 7 p.m. in New York City, the Lower East Side.

Still light out. Still hot and muggy.

Gabriel Bleak was sitting at a table in a plywood booth covered with off-white acoustic fabric, using a computer with a dicey Internet connection, having paid the shop on East Fourteenth for an hour's time. The acoustic fabric was frayed at the corners, exposing the plywood. The guy sitting in the little booth next to him was playing an online first-person shooter, and he kept muttering to himself, cursing his adversaries under his breath. "Die . . . die. . . . Come on and . . . oh, man, that's bullshit. That's . . . I'll find your ass when I re-spawn . . . change ordnance . . . change to rocket launcher, you want to play like that. . . . Noobie, using your noob-tube on me, suck this! Suck rockets! Yeah!"

Which made it a little hard for Bleak to concentrate on his e-mail. Mostly just spam. A thank-you note from Lost Boys Bail Bonds. And another client, Get Right Out Bail Bonds, had put him on its e-mail list. It appeared, according to their list spam, that now they also cashed checks. Probably give you a check for catching a skip, then offer to cash it for you in the office and use the check-cashing fees to take back part of what they'd paid you.

Bleak wiped sweat from his forehead. Why couldn't this place get air-conditioning?

He wished he'd persuaded Cronin to use e-mail. They'd talked about it but Cronin said the Internet was "bad for a man who wants to think long thoughts." He missed Cronin, and he missed Muddy. He worried that the dog was pining for him. There—an e-mail inquiry from Second Chance Bail Bonds. *Got a skip for you. Please come to office ASAP. Vince.*

Wait. He'd never worked with Second Chance. Who was Vince and how'd he get his e-mail? From the other bail outfits? Surprising, they didn't usually share skip tracers. And the guy acted as if Bleak were supposed to know who he was.

He'd check it out anyway. Not good to get paranoid and he needed the work.

It occurred to Bleak, suddenly, that the CCA could be monitoring his e-mail. So maybe it was good he wasn't communicating with Cronin that way. Time he got out of this place.

He did a disk clean, a few other quick moves to blot out his browsing history, and shut the computer down, suddenly feeling as if he might be arrested, here, at any moment.

Bleak got up, hurried out, blinking in the light spearing from the sun low between the buildings. He shaded his eyes, looked around. Didn't see that agent—rolling her name luxuriantly through his mind: *Loraine Sarikosca*. Was surprised to feel a twinge of disappointment that she wasn't there. Which made no sense at all.

He hurried down East Fourteenth to Avenue A, then downtown, looking for a certain bar where he could get a beer in a cool room and think. A bar with a back way out, where he knew he wouldn't have to bust a hole in a wall if he had to escape.

Maybe we're all going about this wrong. The ShadowComm—and me too. Maybe we should get lawyers. Challenge CCA right out in the courts. Come out of the closet more.

But he decided that thinking was left over from the days before the terrorist attack on Miami—before President Breslin had invoked National Security Presidential Directive 51, giving his administration special powers in the event of "catastrophic emergency"; powers that verged on martial law. The president controlled the courts, now. More than ever. There was still resistance in Congress and on the state level to arrests of just anyone the government designated dangerous . . . and that resistance, for as long as it lasted, was probably all that kept CCA from pushing law enforcement to put out a general APB on Gabriel Bleak.

It was almost dark when he got to Telly's Tell 'Em Anything. Cool and pleasantly gloomy inside. Only one drinker there, an old man arguing with Telly about politics. Tending bar himself, Telly was a stout Greek with muttonchops and curly gray hair and a red nose; a double shot of ouzo always in one hand, even when he was using the other to pour for a customer. He nodded to Bleak and nodded questioningly at the only draft-beer pull; Bleak gave a thumbs-up and went into the back for a quick pee. The old-fashioned men's room had a metal trough to piss in.

He was just stepping out of the men's room when a dry rustling sound and a creaky call drew his attention to the half-open door to the air shaft. It was where people went to smoke, with a bucket filled with sand and cigarette butts. And poised on the bucket was Yorena, cocking her head, shaking her feathers out.

"What?" Bleak asked.

The bird made a come-with-me motion with its head. A very human motion.

Bleak shook his head. "I just got here. You want to wait, then maybe."

He went back in the main room, found his beer waiting for him, and quickly drank half of it.

So Shoella wanted to see him. Sending Yorena was safer than e-mail. He was trying not to think about the CCA threat; didn't want it to consume his life. Figured he could dodge them till they got interested in someone else. But that was probably what this call by Shoella was about: CCA.

Bleak paid, left a tip, and headed out the front door. Long shadows slanted across from the west side of the street. A group of young tourists, in shorts, walked along talking excitedly in German. They seemed to be taking pictures of some of the elaborate neopsychedelic graffiti on the walls of the old buildings.

Bleak started to step into a doorway—and was driven back by the strong reek of urine. He went a little farther down, found a cleaner doorway, and went to stand just inside, waiting.

He only had to wait about a minute. A flapping, a shadow over the dirty sidewalk, and he knew that Yorena was there.

"Okay," Bleak muttered, "take me to her." The shadow wheeled and darted to the downtown direction. He followed, glancing up to see the familiar flickering in and out of view about two stories up. Pigeons and crows scattered to get out of its way; one pigeon was two slow; the familiar veered, struck, and the bird fell, spiraling and trailing feathers, to smack bloodily onto the sidewalk. Pigeon Lady would not be pleased.

He stepped over the dead bird and followed the shadow downtown.

IT WAS DARK WHEN Bleak got to the Battery area, at the lower tip of the island of Manhattan, and he was getting footsore. He was aware of Yorena flying overhead, but couldn't see the familiar. He wasn't surprised at meeting Shoella here; he knew she liked to stay close to running water; close to rivers and the sea. She felt powerful there. He drew power from running water too, but he suspected Shoella needed it more.

That's where he found her, on the walk overlooking the water, just beyond a small park at Battery Place. She was standing in a cone of darkness where there should have been light—a line of lampposts paced down the walkway, following the railing, the lamps all lit up, except the one she stood under, the only one that wasn't working. He looked up at the light fixture and saw that the lamp glass was blocked off; it was covered with black butterflies and moths, a living swarm of the creatures summoned by Shoella that kept most of its light muffled.

She was a thin dark figure in the oasis of shadow. Yorena flew to Shoella's shoulder, the creature nestling her head in the wildness of Shoella's black hair as Bleak walked up and leaned against the other side of the post. Behind them, lights twinkled from high metal-and-glass buildings; before them, the river surged and hissed.

"Well?" he asked, enjoying the cooling breeze off the water.

"Lots of things, *cher* darlin'," Shoella said, her voice grave. "There's a spiritual blackout, you feel?"

"Something of the sort. Last night. As I was going to sleep, I usually get a hit of the Hidden—like the big picture, out a certain distance, a few hundred miles."

She nodded. Knowing what he meant. "And?"

"And there were a lot of blank spots."

"Hey, where you staying anyway—not that boat?"

"No, in the city." He became aware that Yorena, sitting wings-folded on Shoella's shoulder, was watching him narrowly; seemed to be listening closely. He found it annoying. "There's a hotel I know, where they don't ask me for a credit card, and there they don't have tweakers making noise in the hall, and there's no bedbugs and I even have my own bathroom. Clean linen. Lot of old-time junkies there, but they're pretty quiet, they're on the methadone."

She turned to her feathered familiar. "'Blank spots,' he says, Yorena!" Shoella looked back at him, her head cocked like the bird's. "There's great holes in the Hidden, in the Northeast, holes you could drive a truck through, Gabriel. The Hidden is there—always, everywhere!—but there are places you can't see into it, now. Big places. This is new. And it is *très* persistent over to Atlantic City way."

"Yeah. But then Jersey's always a spiritual blackout."

"Hey! Not funny! Everyone got to bash Jersey. They take good care of me, many good people in New Jersey. Now—this blackout . . . there is something else there. While some places are black, other places are shining with a *volcano light*. Yorena, you are hurting my shoulder again." She shrugged Yorena away; the bird flew to the railing overlooking the river and hunched sullenly to watch them.

When Bleak looked at the creature, she snapped her beak at him.

"Your bird, if that's what it is, is getting on my nerves, Shoella." He added, in a mild, speculative tone, "I wonder if she would taste good roasted."

Yorena fluttered her wings and made an outraged squawking. "Ignore him, Yorena," Shoella said. "He's just tryin' to get a rise out y'alls."

Bleak contemplated Shoella a moment. "What did you say— some places shining with . . . volcano light? What do you mean?"

"So I call it. A nasty hot-red light. Like the light from hell! It only comes through sometimes. Comes and goes. Mostly those places, all under a blackout."

"You're under a blackout yourself." He looked up at the blotted-out streetlamp—glanced at the shadow around them.

"It was that helicopter, that come looking for us." She looked pensively at the city, her eyes searching the sky over the buildings. "That why I put up the umbrella here. Helicopters looking for me make me nervous, *cher* darlin'. Don't like to be seen easy from up above now." She looked at him, leaned a little closer. "You know that there is a 'wall,' in the north, as some calls it—that thing that keeps the Hidden . . . hidden? What keeps it quiet?"

"I've had that feeling." Bleak thought of the "wall" impression he'd had that day soon after his thirteenth birthday, on the ranch. There was ShadowComm lore about "the wall in the north." Without the unknown force from the north, which kept the Hidden muted—a force all Shadow Community felt—they would be swamped by the energies of the Hidden, would constantly see its inhabitants all around them as easily as seeing trees and cars; could see the demon known as the Lord of the Flies as easily as houseflies. And that way lay madness.

"Now the wall in the north begins to break open," Shoella muttered, frowning at the water beyond the rail. "Much more is coming to us. Maybe we can adapt. But other things come through. Things from the Big Outside. From *the Wilderness*! And there are some bad people who might be powered up. . . . And you and me, we have to sort through all this. We are stronger together, Gabriel Bleak."

She broke off, but looked at him, her lips parted . . . as if she was considering opening up. He suspected he knew what was on her mind. The tenderness in her eyes cued him. He'd felt it through the Hidden, more than once—her feelings for him. And she felt his for her. Only, hers were rooted in emotion. With him, it was just desire. And he was instinctively sure it wouldn't work out, in the end, because of that disparity. Besides—the one other time he'd had some kind of intimacy with a ShadowComm girl, Corinne Mendez, long vanished from sight, she'd fled to the West Coast over the affair. It'd been dangerous, what he'd had with Corinne. A bad kind of explosiveness. Shoella felt even more volatile.

So when Shoella seemed about to make that suggestion—he changed the subject. "You ever wonder what makes this 'wall in the north,' in the first place?" Bleak asked quickly, looking up at the dark fluttering on the streetlight. The black butterflies and dark moths muted the light the way the wall in the north muted the Hidden.

Shoella looked at him. Licked her lips. Shrugged away the unspoken.

"Yes, I've wondered. But I don't know who made it, *cher* darlin'. Who knows? Pigeon Lady is wise and she don't know. 'It comes from the north,' she says, 'like the northern lights, it comes from the north.' Scribbler—perhaps he knows. But he scribbles riddles."

"If the wall is weakening more, then there shouldn't be a spiritual blackout . . . we should see more than we do."

"That blackout comes from a thing *that came through the wall in the north*. It creates a darkness in the Hidden to conceal itself—like octopus ink, ya feel?"

"Maybe. Why you telling me this? You think I know something about it?"

"Maybe it is connected to this CCA raid. The wall begins to weaken. The power grows. Things come through—and CCA comes after you. Maybe a connection, *cher* darlin'. Maybe you learned something about that. You keep your distance from us—don't always talk to us."

He shrugged. "I don't know what it means. The agent didn't tell me much. I'm just keeping my head down."

She hesitated. "There was something else to tell you. Another reason I called you here tonight." She sighed. "The *bon Dieu* knows if it's something I should speak of. But I feel . . ."

Bleak glanced at her; saw her lick her lips nervously. He had the sense that she was about to cross a line, of some sort; to cross a bridge and burn it behind her.

"Go on," he said.

"You grew up in Oregon—the east of Oregon, yes?"

"Until I was about thirteen."

"Your brother. You had a brother, yes?"

He felt an icy shock go through him. After a moment he realized she was waiting for him to say it. "Yeah. Gone. Dead. As a toddler."

"How did he die?"

"An accident. With a tractor. Or something."

"His name was Sean?"

"Yeah." He looked at her. He had mentioned Oregon to her—but he hadn't told anyone about Sean. No one except Cronin.

"You get a familiar to tell you that? Something probe my mind when I was asleep, maybe?"

"No, Gabriel. No." Her voice was low and earnest—more personal than usual. She put a hand on the lamppost between them as if using it to make a connection with him. "I have been trying to find out what makes the wall over the Hidden—and what is changing it. I found a man who worked for a military agency. MK Omega, the agency was called. Small, elite, this thing. He is not so elite now: a lush, this man, always drinking. He talks, sure, about some things, if you buy him drinks. I met with him this morning. Something he said—I had to tell you. He say something bothered him, about this Omega group. He was part of a team that took a child, kidnapped it away. They took a boy, *Sean* his name was."

The name *Sean* sent an electric chill through Bleak.

"Out in eastern Oregon," Shoella went on, her voice softly sympathetic. "They didn't take his brother, Gabriel—they wanted Gabriel to be . . . what did this man say . . . 'a control'! That's what he called it. 'Experiment control.' Monitoring him sometimes, he say. See how he develops out in the world. This Gabriel could see the Hidden."

Bleak swallowed hard. He didn't argue.

She nodded to herself. "They lost track of this Gabriel for a time—but the boy they took, he's still with them somehow. *He's alive—and he's with them.*"

"That's not . . ." Bleak's mouth was dry. "That's not necessarily him . . . not necessarily *us*, that he's talking about."

"He remembered the family's last name. A strange name, he said. *Bleak.*"

And hearing his own name, Bleak felt disoriented, almost sick. He should be happy, shouldn't he, to hear that, if this man was not lying, Sean might be alive?

But he felt like a child who'd found a secret room in the back of his closet, with something ugly hanging back there . . . something dangling by a noose, turning slowly in the shadows . . . *something still alive.*

Why did he feel that way about it? He should be ashamed of himself for feeling that way—shouldn't he?

"So—you want to meet him?"

He looked at her, startled. "Who?"

"The man—Coster, his name is. This Coster says he knows what happened to your brother. You want to meet the man?"

Did he? After the run-in with the CCA—did he want to meet someone connected with them? Didn't seem wise.

And—there was that sick feeling. Maybe there was a reason for it.

No. That was just some leftover childhood feeling of horror—his brother vanished, and he reacted. Buried feelings, that kind of thing.

He looked skeptically at Shoella. "How'd you find out about this Coster, exactly?"

"I went to Scribbler, to ask questions about the wall in the north. He could not see much. Because the wall blocks it. But Scribbler, he *saw* this Coster—scribbled his name, the name of a city shelter. And I found him . . . Yorena found him . . . at a shelter, up by Times Square—he's homeless, this man."

Bleak nodded. *Scribbler.* A ShadowComm seer who scribbled on paper for hours, mostly nonsense. And then suddenly there it would be, a secret amidst the nonsense.

"What did Coster know about the wall in the north?"

"He wouldn't tell me much about that—said he wanted to talk to you. Said he wanted to say he was sorry he was any part of that . . . of taking of your brother."

"So he's talkative when he's drunk . . . but then he's not?"

She looked at him curiously. "What are you saying?"

"I don't know. Just—makes me wonder. A talkative drunk . . . and yet a careful one. Kind of contradictory."

She shrugged. "He talked for a while. But then . . . that one question, it scared him." She scratched in her dreads, looked out over the river. "And so? Do you want to meet this Coster?"

"I don't know." Bleak went to the railing, felt its cold metal under his hands. Watched the reflected lights dancing on the dark water.

No. He didn't want to meet Coster, not really. He knew instinctively it was dangerous. Yet he'd always wondered about Sean.

Maybe he'd always known that Sean was out there somewhere. Maybe he'd always felt it on some level.

But it was a level he stayed away from. It was someplace painful. And he suspected that behind it lay one more betrayal by his parents.

If Sean is alive, he told himself, *you've got to know it. He's your brother.*

And never knowing the truth would gnaw at his insides. Always. He'd always know he'd blown off a chance at the truth.

So he made himself say, "Yeah. Yeah, I want to meet Coster."

SIX

A concrete room in a nearly windowless concrete building, somewhere in Long Island. In the concrete room a man was strapped into an unpadded concrete chair. The chair was of one piece with the floor. The chair's restraints were made of woven plastic.

Loraine watched the man in the chair from another room entirely. A small room lined with surveillance screens.

Loraine was trying not to show how disturbing she found the scene. She was uncomfortable in the small, closed-off security surveillance station with Helman, crowded so close to him she could smell his hair pomade. Who wore hair pomade anymore? She suspected he dyed his jet-black hair too.

She was new to this wing of the CCA Rendition Building, and she had almost no experience with the Shadow Community Containment Program. But Loraine did know the name of the man strapped in the chair: Orrin Howard Krasnoff. She had read his file. Now she watched him sit there tapping his feet and hands, looking around mournfully, at the almost featureless room. Clearly afraid of what might happen to him next. Sometimes it was as if he were trying to look right through the barren gray walls.

Krasnoff was an odd-looking man, Loraine thought. The ShadowComm "containee" had a jutting jaw, dark with stubble, and his skull, stubbly itself, seemed slightly bisected into two lobes. He had a long nose, itself oddly bisected: a dimple at its tip. His sad brown eyes drooped at the corners; his eyebrows were almost not there. His wide mouth quivered, like a child about to cry, and he muttered to himself. He was a man with a paunch, but thin arms and legs—perhaps both effects from spending so much time locked up in CCA custody. He wore a T-shirt, and jeans without a belt, and plastic sandals. Bristly black hair on his pallid, bony arms.

He was not a physically appealing man, but, looking at him, Loraine's heart melted with pity.

She remembered what Bleak had said. She almost heard his voice again, speaking right out loud.

I won't ask what authority you have . . . but what excuse do you have?

Still, Loraine had accepted her place in all this. Despite her misgivings, she was drawn to this work—and she really did think it was the most important job she could do for her country. But did it have to be done like this? She kept her face impassive, her voice calm, as she said, "We ought to be able to win these people over so this kind of thing isn't necessary. They'll do better work for us if we give them a chance."

"You forget what our containees are capable of," said Helman, chuckling disdainfully and taking off his wire-rim glasses. He began to polish the lenses on his flower-painted tie. His oily black hair gleamed in the harsh light of the surveillance room; his black eyes reflected miniatures of the rows of television monitors. "Why do you think we have everything made of concrete and plastic, around this man? Because if we let him contact wood or leather or certain kinds of metal, he can use any of those things to summon certain Unconventionally Bodied Entities. We don't yet entirely understand why those substances put him in touch with those particular entities."

Unconventionally Bodied Entities: what Helman called any subtle-bodied entity that inhabited the realm of the Hidden. UBEs for short—some CCA technicians called them Ubes, pronounced "yubes." The terms annoyed Loraine. She would have preferred to call them ghosts, sprites, angels, spirits, elementals, loas—names with some life and poetry to them. But life and poetry, she had discovered, were an uncomfortable fit in CCA's Rendition Building. Here it was all about containment and control.

"You have the suppressor," Loraine pointed out. "Shouldn't that be enough to stop him from contacting any . . . thing?"

The suppressor was difficult to see on the monitor, from this angle; it looked like a short column of metal disks, behind the chair Krasnoff sat in. It was said to partly suppress the powers of the CCA subjects.

"Yes." Helman nodded—he nodded too much, almost like a bobblehead doll, as if he didn't have a lot of practice in casual communication with people. He always seemed hard at work trying to seem sincere. And always came off the opposite. "Yes, under normal conditions the suppressor would be enough. But it can only deal with so much . . . and the background energy these people draw upon is fluctuating. Sometimes rising quite alarmingly." He suddenly stopped nodding and put his glasses back on to peer at a second monitor that showed Krasnoff's vital signs. "There is a breakdown of . . . ahhh, of a *force* that kept their ability to contact that background energy in check. And certain UBEs"— he pronounced each letter—"have been taking advantage of that.

As Mr. Krasnoff might too. You see, the suppressor . . . I know it sounds contradictory . . . is an amplifier, really. It amplifies one thing so it can suppress another. It amplifies the . . . the *signal*, so to say, of the Source in the North. Which signal suppresses people like Krasnoff. Keeps them at low power. If there's no signal, or an erratic signal, the suppressor has nothing to amplify, don't you know."

"I see." Though she didn't, entirely. Where was the real source of this "signal"? She had heard of the Source in the North vaguely, but had never been intensively briefed on it. "Anyway—the suppressor's only reliable . . . sometimes?"

Helman bobbled his head. "Essentially, yes—only reliable sometimes." He returned his attention to the observation monitor. "If the suppressor cannot be counted on, we must give him as few opportunities as possible to implement mischief against us. And Mr. Krasnoff is quite capable of mischief. Oh yes. When we first had him in custody, he caused a flight of UBEs to attack the transport plane. I don't know how he thought he would survive a plane crash. Fortunately we were able to land the transport safely, after a rather tense interval, despite some minor damage."

"Um—what sort of UBEs were those?"

"I believe they took the form of what mythology called Harpies. Probably because that's what Krasnoff visualized. But we're not entirely certain. He can seem to be cooperating with us and then we discover that he's barefacedly lying."

"But . . ." Loraine was boiling with questions. "But—you do encourage him to use his . . . his abilities sometimes. Don't you? I mean, isn't that part of the point of this whole . . . containment?"

"The point?" Helman turned toward her—she saw him glance at her bosom, then look quickly away. "Yes, CCA has plans for these people. For me, the point is scientific study—to a particular purpose. An ancient one, really. The commander in chief himself has asked us to make sure that the Source in the

North . . ." He let his voice trail off and tapped his whitened teeth with a thumbnail as he considered her. "Very soon, you'll be taking a trip to the north," he said suddenly, in a confidential tone. "I know I have been tantalizing you with it for a while." He gave a smile that struck her as almost a leer. "One enjoys tantalizing such a . . ." He stopped himself, and his cheeks reddened. "I prefer to brief you when we get there. As for our containees—don't get emotionally identified, Agent Sarikosca. These people have been using their powers criminally, many of them, all along. In casinos, sometimes in robberies, to duck the police, oh, in all kinds of little scams. And Mr. Krasnoff is especially . . . well, he's one of our problem cases. One of the most recalcitrant. But also one of the most gifted. We do have a few trained former Shadow Community personnel—but *their* gifts are very limited. It's almost as if the intensity of a ShadowComm's power is in proportion to how unruly they are! As if the more problem they are for us—the better their contact with the . . . Ah—now. You see there? Mr. Krasnoff is talking to himself. He's not incapable of wetting his pants, if he gets restless, and the janitor is quite unhappy with me afterwards. Come along—and do bring that briefcase for me, if you please."

She picked up the briefcase, and Helman led the way out of the surveillance room, down the hallway—like the bland gray-and-blue corridors of the Pentagon, with flat fluorescent lights, where she'd worked before CCA—to the next-door entrance of Containee Investigation Room 77.

Helman tapped a combination on a wall keyboard, and the door opened. They went in, hearing the hum of the suppressor, smelling urine and sweat almost immediately. Helman sighed.

"Mr. Krasnoff," he said.

"Doctor, how's it hangin'?" Krasnoff said. An accent from the West. Loraine remembered from his file that he was from Pahrump, Nevada. His mother had worked as a blackjack dealer. No father around. "I'd shake hands," Krasnoff added, "but them big punkin' rollers of yours got 'em locked down."

"Well, Mr. Krasnoff," Helman said, taking the briefcase from Loraine, "formal greetings won't be necessary. This is Agent Sarikosca, by the way—Mr. Orrin Krasnoff."

She nodded to Krasnoff, but avoided meeting his eyes.

Helman knelt, opened the briefcase on the floor behind Krasnoff, who tried to turn in his chair, watch over his shoulder. "What's in that little suitcase you folks brought in?" Krasnoff asked. "You ain't gonna use that electric thing on me today, are you?" There was more resignation than fear in his voice. "Not with this pretty lady here?" His sad, droopy eyes rolled at Loraine. "Nice to look at a lady, in this place, anyhow. Something besides that stupid little room they got me in. Won't even let me watch TV, you know that?"

She started to answer but Helman interrupted, "You know you can summon things, unauthorized things, with a television, Mr. Krasnoff." Helman stood up, bringing two objects over to the front of the concrete chair. "And we don't want you to summon something troublesome."

Krasnoff looked at the objects in Helman's hands, winced, and looked away, his mouth moving soundlessly.

Helman carried a small, specialized Taser, and a rod about sixteen inches long that looked almost like a scepter, made of copper, with sections of two kinds of wood, one very dark, and a knob of white, glossy material that might have been ivory at one end.

"This chair sure is uncomfortable," Krasnoff said suddenly, to Loraine. "You ever sit in a concrete chair, missy?"

"No, no, I haven't." *Don't get emotionally involved.*

"My skinny little butt hurts on an ordinary chair, after a while. With this here thing I'm achin' near to breakin'. You know . . . say, listen, I could work on the streets with you folks, I could go out in the cars and see the world. I could do things with you folks out there and be a real help. What you got to keep me on a concrete chair for? With no TV, and no—"

"Could you really work with us, in the field?" Loraine asked. "Maybe—"

Then she was aware that Helman had turned, was glaring coldly at her. He didn't want her talking to Krasnoff, it seemed. Why was she here if she couldn't even speak to the containee? Helman had said she was to "familiarize" herself "with certain processes." Observation, then. To what end?

"Pretty lady, he's got that buzzer there," Krasnoff was saying, looking at the instruments in Helman's hands. "Like I'm a dog in some ol' Russian laboratory. He's gonna make me drool like a dog. I don't want to do this . . . I could work on the streets, I could go out in cars. . . . Sure would like to have a steak in a nice, regular steak house. There's a steak house in Carson City—"

"Mr. Krasnoff," Helman interrupted, talking, Loraine thought, as much to her as to him, as he put the little taser in his coat pocket and sprinkled a fragrant oil from a vial on the scepterlike rod, "you know that when we have tried to work with you in the field, you summon UBEs, nasty entities indeed, and two of our people had their faces badly mutilated. One man lost an arm."

"The angel tells me," Krasnoff muttered, tapping his feet and hands animatedly. "Shiny Fella gives the 'which way to go.' He says, 'You play their game 'n' you'll become game. You'll be game hunted in the Wilderness, in the After. Your spirit will run crying through the Hidden.' And, Doctor, I don't want to be in the Wilderness, when I'm in the After. I don't care that much what happens to me in this life. Shiny Fella says this life is just prep, it's just . . ." He fell silent.

Helman turned back to Loraine and spoke with clinical detachment. "You'll find that they often allude to an indifference to what happens to them in this world. Do not mistake it for depression, or passive aggression, as it might be in a subject of interest for mere psychological reasons. They feel that way because they know life-after-death intimately. The soul, we have discovered, is real—though naturally it will be found to have a scientific basis. What happens in 'the After,' as they call it, is more important to them than to most people—that is, they believe in it more. They know for a fact it exists. They have all gazed into it. They identify as much with the world of the Hidden as this one. It makes threats of execution a bit . . . weaker than normal."

Loraine turned to him, startled. "Execution?"

Acting as if he hadn't heard her, Dr. Helman turned to Krasnoff, putting the scepter in the bound containee's hand.

"Here you go, I've put the myrrh on it. Focus on it, Mr. Krasnoff."

The containee shook his head mutely.

Helman reached into his pocket and took out the small Taser. "Do not mistake the compactness of this device for feebleness. The 'jolter' uses a new kind of battery. It packs quite a punch. And it concentrates it rather uniquely, like a bee sting. Or perhaps more like a manta ray. Or indeed—the shock of the electric eel? Shall we discover together what the best analogy would be?"

Krasnoff hunched his shoulders, cringed back, shaking his head, making a low moaning sound.

Loraine wondered if Helman was testing her, by showing her this. Maybe he wanted to know if she could deal with it.

They knew she was having doubts about CCA. Had been having doubts for a while. She was sure of one thing: whatever the Hidden was, it had to be used for the benefit of the country or prevented from being used at all. But how far should she go?

She'd worked for the Defense Intelligence Agency, analyzing satellite data; later recruiting unhappy Muslim women in Syria, working out of a safe house in the old district of Damascus. Had recruited her own string of veiled wives secretly angry at the traditional oppression of their gender; women willing to quietly gather intelligence for her. When her string had been abandoned by the agency the moment the Syrian Secret Police started suspecting them, Loraine had angrily asked for a transfer away from the DIA. She'd found herself in the CCA—and was beginning to wonder if she should have stayed in Syria.

She'd heard an expression, working at the Pentagon: "Don't like it? Suck it up or move on down the road."

You were always reminded to try to see the big picture. And the big picture seemed to indicate that ShadowComm, uncontrolled, was dangerous. A freewheeling cult of loose cannons.

The Hidden probably was a natural phenomenon of some kind—ghosts and all. What did they call it? *The spiritual ecology.* But to the CCA, ShadowComm was like the arrival of assault weapons in street gangs. Chaos—a change in the balance of power. A threat to ordinary people, and to the stability of the country.

Her limits weren't CCA's limits. She remembered the debate on Guantánamo, years ago. Torture? Mild stuff, compared to the leeway President Breslin gave the intelligence agencies now, of course—he had the power to do it. Far worse was done to prisoners accused of sedition than what was happening here. And if she objected too strenuously, Loraine could find herself strapped into a chair in some barren room, somewhere.

But still. There *were* limits. Weren't there?

Krasnoff yelped, jerking her attention back to the man in the concrete chair. She smelled burnt hair and ozone. A red swelling stood out on his right forearm. She hadn't even seen Helman use the little taser.

"You can spend some time out of this building, once we get real help from you, Mr. Krasnoff," Helman said, in a gentle voice.

Panting, Krasnoff rolled his eyes at Helman. "I . . . can? Doctor?"

"Yes. We'll have to keep a suppressor near you except at certain controlled moments. But it can be arranged."

Can it really? Loraine wondered. If Krasnoff's furlough to the outside world was dependent upon the suppressors, she doubted it would happen anytime soon. They cost several million apiece, and so far as she knew, they never let them out of the building. She didn't entirely understand how the suppressors worked, but she knew there were only three of them. Delicate and expensive mechanisms. And they were not the key to containment here. Drugging and isolation were the primary methods of containment at this facility. And the suppressors were said to be less effective the farther south you went.

"I can't stand being cooped up no more. But I'm afraid . . . like if . . . if I do the wrong thing here, I'll end up in the Wilderness."

Helman had tucked the scepter under one arm and was making a minute adjustment on the little jolter. "Let's see what a stronger jolt has to say to you. You might find it quite revelatory. Possibly we might apply it to the back of your head—it might induce you to lose control of your bowels. Embarrassing, in front of the lady. But, if it's necessary . . ."

"No!" Krasnoff said, sitting up straight, struggling with his restraints. "Open it up. Turn the thing off. I'll show you what you want, if I can!" He slumped back, breathing hard, almost weeping. "But you got to promise an outing. You got to promise no more of the jolter."

"You may consider it . . . promised," Helman said silkily.

Loraine was thinking about Helman's using her to taunt Krasnoff. As a tool of torture, essentially. The thought made her stomach squirm. She wanted to grab the jolter and apply it to Helman's smug face.

But telling herself, *Stay frosty, stay professional,* she just stood there. Keeping her expression impassive. And waited.

Helman put the jolter into his pocket and handed Krasnoff the scepter. "One moment. I'll open the shaft and turn off the suppressor." He went behind the chair, turned a switch on the back of the chair. A section of ceiling slid slowly back. He threw a switch on the suppressor—and the device stopped thrumming.

Loraine looked up, had to shade her eyes against light coming through a small square hole in the ceiling, like a skylight, but it extended about three yards up to an opening in the roof where another panel had slid away. She could make out blue sky up there.

"But," Helman went on, "there are guard personnel, right down the hall, Orrin. I'll summon them to stand close by, outside the door."

Odd, Loraine thought, that he'd suddenly taken to calling Krasnoff by his first name. The psychology of interrogation?

Helman pressed a button on a beeper clipped to his belt, summoning the guard. "So just remember, Orrin, if you play false with us this time, they'll come and use that regrettable excessive force that seems to come so naturally . . . and the lady will see you at your worst. You must not disappoint me, Orrin. Not me and not the lady."

Krasnoff nodded. "I understand, boss."

CHINESE BOXES, ONE INSIDE another.

The camera that had watched Krasnoff strapped down alone in the concrete room now took in Dr. Helman and Loraine Sarikosca, with Krasnoff, and its image was being transmitted to two men sitting in quite another sort of room, a cluttered office in the Pentagon. The watchers sat at a computer terminal. Both wore the uniforms of U.S. Air Force. Both had stars on their shoulders. Generals Swanson and Erlich, officers in their sixties. The budgetary buck for CCA stopped with them.

Erlich was stocky, with thin white hair, a jowly, wide face, stubby nose. Sat in a chair to one side of the desk—this was Swanson's office.

Swanson was taller, with stooped shoulders—a bit of osteoporosis—and a thinly carven face, heavy black brows, shaven head. Swanson had been a captain, and a major in Iraq. Had seen every military tragedy, every snafu. And he was usually unflappable.

But the scene on the computer surveillance window had him grinding his teeth. "Erlich—I don't like where this is going. First of all, it was supposed to be about fighting terrorism. But we hear precious little from these people about that. CCA's not staying on task. This other stuff's not its mandate. Like this experiment now—for Christ's sake—putting pressure like this on . . . on freakish people of this kind. You don't know *what* the hell you'll get. They're connected to . . . to *things*, my friend. Things we don't want a relationship with.

"But it's the same old problem. If we don't do something with these ShadowComm types, we have no control over them," Swanson added, taking a cigar from his desk. "Same goes, Forsythe says, for the . . . things, the spirits they deal with." He smelled the cigar wistfully. He wasn't allowed to smoke in here, but he chewed on the cigar's end, without lighting it.

"The human race got by without . . . recruiting from that pool for centuries," Erlich pointed out. "They used to burn these guys at the stake."

"What I heard, they were always burning the wrong people. And things have changed. The signal that suppresses their contact is getting weaker. More of these guys are showing up. Some pretty bad ones. Guy just broke out of jail, probably using those capabilities. Forsythe's looking into that. We might be able to fix the thing in the north but . . . I'm not sure the president wants to. He wants the edge. He supports this program. Forsythe's got him in his vest pocket."

"Exaggeration. Breslin's no surer than we are. I think we ought to explore the possibility of shutting down this program."

"Forsythe's a fanatic about it, obsessed. I'm not sure what he might pull."

"Meaning what?"

"Meaning . . . I'm not sure he's in his right mind." Swanson craned his head at the surveillance window on the computer, squinting. He put on a pair of half-glasses. "What's going on in there now? Looks like they're prepping Krasnoff for a projection."

LORAINE WAS STARING UP at the skylight shaft when a brisk knock came at the door of the concrete cell. "Just wait out there!" Helman called. "Just stand ready if I need you! The door is un-locked!"

"Yes, sir!" came the muffled response from the hall.

"Go ahead, Orrin," Helman said. "Your access to the sky is open. The suppressor is off."

Krasnoff looked up at the shaft of light, clutched the scepter-like rod tighter, and closed his eyes. "Shiny Fella . . ." Loraine had the distinct impression he was speaking to someone not in the room. "I'm sorry, Shiny Fella, but I am scared to go crazy. That's worse than dying to me." Krasnoff seemed to be talking to the light coming down the little shaft in the ceiling. "If I go into a crazy place, I'll be in the Wilderness before I'm dead."

The Wilderness again. Loraine had seen a briefing paper on this ShadowComm notion. Spirits in the afterlife were protected if they were aligned with "spirits of light." If they weren't protected, they were propelled into "the Wilderness"—something like hell, a place where predatory spirits roamed free.

"And"—Krasnoff paused to swallow hard, before going on— "and tell my ma I'm sorry too, if she's gone on. They won't tell me if she died yet, with the bone cancer, and I can't get word, with the way they keep me shut down, so . . . sorry."

Having said an apologetic prayer to the Shiny Fella, whoever that was, Krasnoff opened his eyes, took a deep breath. Clutch-ing the scepter, he looked like an inbred king on a stony throne, at that moment, as he gazed up at the sky, his face awash in the beam of sunlight coming down.

"What is it you want to see, Doctor?" he asked softly. Looking longingly up at the sky.

Loraine watched as Helman hunkered by the briefcase and took out two more items. A piece of paper and a vial of—was that blood? He brought them to Krasnoff. "There's a man named Gabriel Bleak. We have a document he signed, for a bail bonds agency. He touched it and signed it. We want you to show us where he is. And here is blood, taken for a DNA sample from a man named Gulcher, when he was in custody. This man has gone missing too, and we need to know where he is and what he's doing. Both men are Shadow Community, but Gulcher didn't know it until recently. We think he has come into very great power. Can you make the connection for us?"

"Might could do it, one thing at a time. Put the paper in my left hand."

Krasnoff kept staring up at that patch of blue sky, his mouth slightly open, as Helman put the folded piece of paper in his left hand. In his right he clasped the rod of wood and copper, and he ran his fingers up and down it, over and over, rubbing each part of it with his thumb.

Helman glanced toward the camera lenses set flush with the concrete walls, one per wall near the ceiling, and Loraine, noticing an iris flicker inside the lenses, realized all this was being recorded—and perhaps witnessed by someone else.

"Shiny Fella," Krasnoff muttered. "And you who call yourselves . . ." He spoke a series of names. Loraine would try to remember the names later, discovering that not a single one remained in her memory. And she had a near photographic memory.

She felt a weight in the room then, as if the air pressure had doubled. It made her eyes hurt, her head throb. Then a red and green-blue swarm of tiny lights spiraled down the small shaft over

Krasnoff. They moved like a swarm of insects, but she could see they had no wings, no bodies, they were just minute lights swirling around Krasnoff's head. So many they almost hid his features.

He jerked his head back down so he was staring straight ahead . . . his mouth open wide, slightly drooling.

And the glittering swarm entered his ears and eyes and mouth, vanishing into him.

Strong beams of colored light suddenly projected from his mouth and eyes. Red light from his left eye, green-blue from his right, yellow from his mouth. The lights seemed to converge on the wall in front of him, as if his head were a movie projector. A circle of the tiny lights churned on the wall, then began to converge. Loraine's mouth dropped open, in awe; she could hear her heart thumping in her ears as an image, almost three-dimensional, formed in the wall: a man walking down the street. The man pausing to glance around. Walking on.

"Gabriel Bleak!" she blurted.

"Yes, I believe that is our Mr. Bleak," Helman said, nodding, pleased.

The circle of light on the wall, its edges restless with glimmering specks, showed Gabriel Bleak wearing a white business shirt, unbuttoned and untucked to hang over the back pockets of his jeans. Loraine suspected he had a gun back there, under the shirt. Under the open shirt he wore a new-looking tee that said BLACK REBEL MOTORCYCLE CLUB across it. He looked focused, in a hurry, intense.

Loraine suddenly became aware that Dr. Helman was watching her. She turned, saw him looking at her—then looking at Bleak, on the wall. Then back at her. The light from the overheads seemed to collect in the lenses of Helman's glasses, washing them out, masking his eyes.

"Was there something, Doctor, that . . . ?" she asked, not sure herself what she was asking.

Dr. Helman shook his head. He pursed his lips, as if suppressing a chuckle, and took a small cell phone from his inside coat pocket, fingered it, and spoke into it as he looked back at the projected vision of Gabriel Bleak. "Andrew? The moment you see identifying indicators, get a drone over it—I believe that's a street sign behind him, and I believe that street is in New Jersey. Collate with satellite imagery."

But suddenly, on the wall, Gabriel Bleak stopped walking—and looked pensively around.

"He senses Krasnoff, even at this remove," Helman said, with the cell phone still pressed against his ear. "Very impressive!"

A small voice muttered from the air. After a moment Loraine realized it wasn't a supernatural voice. It was from Helman's cell phone.

"Ah," Helman said. "Good. He may not sense the drone too."

Loraine, watching Bleak, who looked both powerful and vulnerable at once, had an impulse to shout out a warning to him.

She shook her head wonderingly. Whose side was she on? She had better get a grip and soon. Or she'd be in deep shit.

"Now, let the contact with Bleak go, Orrin," Helman said, taking the folded paper from Krasnoff's hand. "And take this blood . . . and show us what *this* man is doing."

The light ceased to beam from Krasnoff's mouth and eyes, as if a plug had been pulled. Clasping the vial, Krasnoff panted for a moment, blinking—then looked dazedly at Loraine. "Doctor—does she know about her and Bleak? I seen it and I think somebody should know, if . . . if they're—"

"That will be enough digression, Orrin," Helman said quickly. "Now focus on the blood. Where is the source of that blood?"

Krasnoff looked again up the shaft at the sky. Again he spoke, and summoned.

Again the sparkles spiraled down. He looked at the wall—and once more light shot from his eyes and mouth. The image formed on the wall. A point of view looking down a street in . . .

The street looked familiar to Loraine. Was it Atlantic City? She'd only been there once. Was that a casino, a few blocks down?

Then a black spot appeared in the midst of the image—and grew. It was like petroleum gushing from a hole in the bottom of the sea, spreading out in a blackening cloud. The black cloud widened, boiled, bubbled . . . and blotted the entire image.

The colored light still beamed from Krasnoff's eyes, his mouth—but the blackness seemed to boil up from the wall, into the projected beams, as if working its way toward him.

"You . . ." Krasnoff sounded distant, and almost drunk. "You got to untie my left arm here, maybe I can get a picture past this blackout mess."

Helman hesitated—then turned toward Loraine, nodded toward the restraints.

Why me? Loraine wondered. But she circled behind Krasnoff, undid the buckle of the strap that was holding his left arm.

He lifted up the vial, so that it caught the light . . . the blackness receded for a moment, then resurged. And suddenly, as if in angry response, something was on the wall besides murky cloud. *Faces—angry faces.* Some of them appeared to be multiple images of the same face as if seen in a kaleidoscope, the face mirroring itself and folding and unfolding within the bubbling blackness . . . and then a face that seemed to sum up the others, a face with a sharply drawn, three-dimensional, leathery exposition of mute fury, formed in the center of the cloud and burst out toward them—coming right at them, its gaping jaws stretching impossibly, opening too wide.

Krasnoff screamed and shut his mouth and eyes, stopping the image—though a little colored light leaked from his lids and lips—and he threw the vial of blood from him so that it smashed on the wall, its contents dripping down, dripping red. Small shards of glass from the vial clung to the wall, pasted by blood, and slowly slipped down, the bits of glass forming into the rough shape of a face.

The face from the boiling black cloud.

NOT LONG AFTER THE session with Krasnoff, Loraine found herself the only one in the cafeteria. She sat alone at a stainless-steel table, in the center of the low-ceilinged room.

The coffee had gone cold in the carafes, but Loraine had poured some into a plastic cup anyway, and now she held it clasped between her hands. She sat listening to the hum of the fluorescent lights overhead and the ticking of a big brushed-steel refrigerator in the kitchen behind the tray counter. The windowless walls held paintings of autumn woods, with a great deal of brown and dull gold in them; to her eye they looked like paintings of paintings, bereft of feeling.

"Doctor—does she know about her and Bleak? I seen it and I think somebody should know, if . . ."

From the way he'd been looking at her, Krasnoff had meant Loraine. Not some other *her*. What had he meant by that? And why had Helman cut him off so hastily?

Looking at a painting of a stream running through a boulderstrewn wood, it seemed to her that the shadows under the trees and rocks grew darker, thickened, and stretched out to meet one another; to form a deeper, interconnected blackness that blotted the painting like a big spill of ink, and in the dark spill was a face—

"Loraine?"

She jumped in her seat, sloshing coffee on her blouse. "Dammit!"

"Seems you've startled Agent Sarikosca, Doctor," said General Forsythe, chuckling. "We should have made more noise, coming up."

It was Helman and Forsythe; the general—the chief of the CCA—was wearing his USAF uniform.

She put the cup down. Helman picked up her napkin—and started to dab at her blouse. She could feel his fingers press her breasts, and she stepped back, deftly took the napkin from his hand, muttered, "Thanks," and finished on her own.

"Sorry about the coffee, young lady," said Forsythe, in his Florida accent, "but, Lord, you startle easily."

"No apology necessary, sir. I'm a bit shaken, I guess." She glanced at General Forsythe. "We had our session broken up by an unexpected UBE."

Forsythe was short, with broad shoulders, a tanned face shaped—it seemed to Loraine—like a shovel. He had once been almost movie-star handsome, but his face was sagging now, in middle age, as if the wax on a Madame Tussauds sculpture of some golden-era actor had just begun to melt. His gray eyes looked almost painted on; the lines under his fixed smile were like the incisions on a puppet's mouth.

She looked away, shuddering internally.

Maybe, she thought, *he looks so unpleasant to me because of what I've seen today; what I've been through. Everything looks kind of off to me. Even cheap decorator paintings.*

"You seemed a bit upset," Helman said, looking with solemn concern at the stain on her blouse. "When we left the containment chamber, I mean—you seemed shaken. Mr. Krasnoff can be an upsetting character."

"But from what I saw on the recordin', we made progress," Forsythe said, clasping his hands together with a clapping sound. "We got him contained and at the same time we got him working for us, all at once. Got our cake and chowing down on it too. Haven't been able to get that with many of them." He pursed his lips and looked at Loraine with a touch of amusement, adding patronizingly, "I understand you think we're going about it all wrong, Agent Sarikosca."

"Oh, well—I just thought you might catch more flies with

honey, sir." She balled up the wet napkin and tossed it into her coffee cup. "And it seems to me"—she felt a bit reckless, now, and thought she ought not to say these things, but she had to, somehow—"it seems to me that we are trying to contain things that can't be contained. Not for long. Like trying to catch moonlight with your hands. What happened in there today . . ." She thought of the face forming in the boiling blackness on the wall. "It wasn't contained. It wasn't controlled. . . . To think you can control the supernatural . . ." She shook her head. "I don't think you can. In ancient times, people made deals with it. Maybe that's what we need to do—but after today, I'm not sure we should."

Dr. Helman was making *tsk* sounds. "Now you make me wonder if you're suited for this job, Loraine. The whole point of this facility—well, shall we say a fundamental, *preliminary* point—is to demonstrate that so-called magic is not spiritual, not supernatural, it's just another form of natural energy; an unknown branch of physics. You know, radio waves are invisible to people. They can seem mysterious. Primitive people hearing a radio for the first time assumed there were spirits in the box. It's the same principle. And if it's a product of nature, it can certainly be mastered by human beings."

Forsythe was watching her closely. She didn't think she'd gain anything by just buckling under to Helman, here. For a woman in an agency dominated by men, it was better to show strength. "Yes, Doctor—I'd guess the Hidden must be something 'natural' in a way. But some kinds of natural are just past our understanding. We can't control them with machines. We can't hem them in."

Dr. Helman and General Forsythe exchanged looks of amusement. "Oh, girl—" Forsythe shook his head. "Wait—am I being politically incorrect, saying *girl*?"

"I believe you are, General," Helman said.

"Then I'll say, *Agent Sarikosca*, you'd be surprised what can hem in the supernatural. And how long it's been goin' on. I think you're just too valuable to us, with that inquirin' mind you've got, to stay out in the 'waiting room' of the CCA, any longer. Doctor— I think you should take our young agent here up north."

Helman nodded. "I was a bit dubious. But I'll honor your instincts, General."

"Well—she's got that special connection. And Sean . . . you know how Sean feels."

She looked back and forth between them now. What were they talking about? Special connection? Sean?

"I was a bit dismayed by the break in connection," Helman said. "That black-cloud effect. Curious. I've never heard of anything quite like it. As if a particular geographical area was being curtained off from us."

"Yes . . ." Forsythe's eyes had gone even blanker. "You know— it might be best if you focused on the other one, for now. On Bleak. This whole Gulcher business—just a distraction. Let it go. I'll deal with it my own way."

Helman opened his mouth as if about to object—then shut it. He looked puzzled—and annoyed, it seemed to Loraine.

"Hokay, ladies and gents, I'm off," Forsythe said, looking at his watch. "I've got a meetin'." He ducked his head in a fractional bow to Loraine. "Ma'am." And hurried off.

Dr. Helman watched him go. Then muttered, "That's truly odd. He was quite hot on finding Gulcher a few days ago. And Troy Gulcher escaped from a prison using ShadowComm abilities which are beyond any we've known, in terms of sheer aggression, judging from the stories of the few survivors. Quite dangerous. And if that was a UBE we saw, in the session with Krasnoff . . . I'm not conceding it was, but . . ." His voice trailed off.

"If it wasn't an, uh, yube—what was it?" Loraine asked.

"Hm? Perhaps—something fabricated by our Mr. Krasnoff to scare us. It's difficult to understand them, you know. They're a volatile lot, these ShadowComm types. Innately rebellious. Troublesome. Not to be trusted operating on their own."

She picked up her plastic cup. Then put it down again. "I knew, when I came aboard the CCA, that there was graduated briefing here, and a lot of need-to-know levels. But . . . if it concerns me personally . . ." She looked Dr. Helman in the eyes, to let him know how seriously she felt about it. "If it concerns me personally, I think I should know exactly what's involved. Krasnoff said something about 'her and Bleak.' He seemed to mean me. And the general mentioned something of the kind. And who is Sean?—"

Helman raised a hand, his eyes brittle with warning. "All in good time. What Krasnoff was referring to . . . I'm not convinced it's the case, what he thinks, but you've been picked to work on the Gabriel Bleak matter for a good reason. Let's just leave it at that. We find him to be surprisingly elusive. We believe you may be particularly useful. . . . Well. The details will have to wait."

"Isn't he just one more ShadowComm subject? Why focus on him?"

"No, he's not just another. General Forsythe has some particular use for him. Now . . . if your nerves are mended, we'll return to the lab and review the recording we made today. And we should be able to see some live drone surveillance of our Mr. Bleak. The UAV has been in the air for some time, and I believe they have him on camera. . . . So—if you think you can deal with what, after all, is your assignment . . . ?"

He looked at her with raised eyebrows.

She hesitated. Thinking maybe now was the time. Now was the moment to say, *I am not cut out for this. For containment. Seeing what happens to people like Krasnoff. I just don't like the way it's being done. It seems wrong to me.*

But things were different, now. Four thousand people had been killed in the terrorist attack on Miami a couple of years back, and even more basic rights had been suspended—it just wasn't safe, anymore, when you worked this close to the heart of Spook Central, to say, *I just don't like the way it's being done. It seems wrong to me.*

You didn't tell them that something seemed wrong to you, not when you knew as much as she did; when you were privy to as many secrets as she was.

Suck it up or move on down the road.

She took a deep breath. And she nodded. "I'm ready."

CHAPTER

SEVEN

That same day. New Jersey.

Walking down a Jersey City sidewalk that threw heat back in his face, past store windows that glaringly reflected the sun, Gabriel Bleak knew he was again being followed—and watched. The watching seemed to have come in two phases. First, he'd sensed someone was watching him through the Hidden—the name *Krasnoff* had come into his mind. Orry Krasnoff? Orrin? Wait—didn't he remember hearing about a ShadowComm named Orrin Krasnoff, out West somewhere? Once in touch with Shoella . . . then vanished?

Krasnoff's psychic surveillance of Bleak had suddenly ended, minutes ago. Now it was another kind of surveillance. The twenty-first-century sort. Through a machine, somewhere up above.

Where was Yorena? The familiar should have turned up by now, to guide him to Shoella and Coster. But he hadn't seen her yet. Maybe the creature was lying low because he was being watched.

This other watcher was observing him from up in the air, some elevated place—he caught a glimpse now and then. It was harder when they were using cameras—a step removed—but Bleak was able to connect with the observer's viewpoint, from time to time.

When he did, he saw himself from above. Like watching someone from the roof of a building. But the point of view seemed roughly centered above the street.

It wasn't Yorena's POV he was seeing. It was a woman, a human woman, watching him through a flying camera, he decided. Some kind of UAV flying overhead, somewhere. Hard to see in the glare. The Rangers had used devices like them in Afghanistan for recon. He knew how to duck them—knew how the Taliban did it. He would choose his moment. But it had to be soon. The UAV was just the beginning.

He thought he sensed who this woman was. *Agent Sarikosca.* But someone else was watching too, maybe more than one person. The multiplicity of viewpoint broke the connection for him, much of the time. But he knew the UAV was up there, electronically staring.

It was a small, oval flying machine, not much larger than a garbage-can lid, with rotors on its undersides, and cameras. Maybe armed. Drones could be equipped to explode.

Probably this wasn't an assassination drone. Why would they want to kill him? But then—why did they want him so much they were going to this kind of trouble?

There were other ShadowComms. So why was the CCA dogging him? Because they'd come upon him, so they were following up the nearest lead?

But maybe not. Maybe there were other reasons, considering what Shoella had told him about Sean.

Whatever their motivation, it was making him seriously angry.

And his military instinct had always been to take the fight to the enemy.

He was passing a thrift store, on his left. Several stories high. That'd work.

He ducked into the doors, nodded to the elderly, blue-haired lady sitting behind the glass counter with all the old junk jewelry in it; smelled the mild funk of old furniture and clothing as he found the stairs, in the center of the big room, that rose to the second floor.

"There's an elevator, if you prefer," the elderly lady said, as he started up the stairs.

"This'll be fine," Bleak said, and in a moment he was on the second floor, which seemed to be mostly chipped old dinette sets. Another flight, the third floor: floor lamps, rusty chandeliers, and, for some reason, used computers. He found a back stairway leading to the roof, loitered near it as a bent, old black man in janitor's coveralls went by whistling a tune. When the old janitor was gone, Bleak climbed the stairs—and found the door to the roof chained.

He put his right hand on the chain, reaching with the field of sensation around his body, reaching out to the field of the Hidden around him . . . and his attention to the Hidden revealed the ghost of an old woman, slowly wandering the stairwell, trailing her translucent fingers on the wall, softly moaning that her adult children had given her best furniture to this thrift store. And something else about being sick with cancer on her fifty-fifth birthday and no one coming except the youngest kid. Some ghosts stayed where they died; some wandered. This one had followed her furniture to a thrift store.

Why are so many of them completely useless to anyone, even themselves? he wondered.

Bleak ignored the apparition and drew energy from the field of the Hidden, pulling it down through the top of his head, directing it into his shoulders, down his right arm. He used it to form a small "grenade" of sheer kinetic volatility, which he cupped in the palm of his hand, slapping it on the chain, feeling the chain through it, though he wasn't quite touching the links. He drew his other hand quickly back, to cover his eyes.

The chain burst apart with a crinkling *pop*. Bits of steel clattered on the floor. He heard the ghost hissing in irritation at his breach of the door.

"Woman, you are dead, it's ridiculous to follow your furniture around, and it's time to move on from this place," he told her, and went through the door to the roof, as behind him the ghost muttered indignantly about "busybodies, stickin' their nose in."

It was hot up on the roof—the naked sunlight, reflected from tin sheathing, jabbing at his eyes. An aluminum ventilator exhaled the musty smell of old thrift goods.

Bleak shaded his eyes, scanned the sky—and saw the unmanned aerial vehicle almost immediately. It was glinting in the sunlight about a hundred feet above the roof, and out over the street; hovering, turning, looking for him. Seeing the drone like this, it was easy to understand how they caused so many UFO reports.

He formed an energy bullet, took several steps, winding up like a softball pitcher, and threw it underhand straight up, as hard as he could. Saw the energy bullet zip up, and up, like a small, gravity-defying meteor.

And saw it pass the UAV and fade out.

"Fuck, I missed," he muttered.

The gleaming drone turned to look at the source of the energy bullet streaking past. And Bleak saw himself, then, in someone's point of view, staring up angrily from a rooftop. Looking small down there.

Focusing on his own point of view, Bleak decided to take a chance on the noise of a gunshot. And maybe it was taking a chance of a bullet exploding in the chamber too.

He drew his gun, popped the clip out, rubbed a finger over the top bullet in the clip, extending energy from the Hidden into it. He knew how much he could infuse it with before it exploded in his hand. At least he hoped he knew. He'd only infused the Hidden's energy into a bullet a couple times before.

He quickly jammed the clip back in the gun, chambered the round, held the gun with both hands, and, squinting against the light, took careful aim up at the UAV as it started to back away from him—and he fired.

A streak of violet, and the bullet struck its target just behind the camera in its prow. The extra energy he'd infused in the bullet smashed through its armored underside and it rocked in the air, like a boat in high seas, then began to spiral down . . . and crashed into the rooftop, skidding and sparking.

Ought to get out of here, Bleak thought. The UAV would have been tracking him to set up another attempt by a CCA containment team. And maybe people downstairs would have heard the noise. He didn't want to have to explain himself to a security guard, or the cops.

A clear lubricant was leaking from the crumpled metal carapace of the beetlelike UAV.

Ought to just leave.

He couldn't resist. Chance to find out something—and maybe discourage this kind of surveillance.

He walked over to the UAV, knelt by it, held a hand close to its hot metal hull. Closed his eyes. Reached out invisibly, incorporating the field of the Hidden in his probe of the UAV; tracing back to its source.

He saw people in a room, a marine guard, a man wearing glasses covertly glancing at the woman . . .

The woman. She drew his attention. He couldn't focus on the others. But he saw her—and projected an image to her, through the Hidden. It would look like an apparition of Gabriel Bleak, to her, appearing in front of the little TV monitor they'd used for the UAV. He saw her gasp, a hand to her mouth.

He said, *Agent Sarikosca . . . Loraine . . . Why lend your eyes to a vulture? Loraine . . .*

Strange, wanting to call her by her first name. Loraine. He seemed to see her disembodied, then, a soul rising up before him, a woman-shape becoming a star . . . flaring . . . unable to stop herself from reaching out.

Bleak felt a delicious sense of contact flood his lower being— he had an immediate and uncomfortable hardness at the contact. He felt the woman's shock at the unexpected intimacy and couldn't conceal his own.

He snapped back into himself, cutting the connection. Had to adjust his pants a little before hurrying to the fire escape that led down to a side street.

He hadn't expected so electric a response—not from a woman with no power in the Hidden. He had learned that, if he chose, he could use the Hidden to enhance his ability to seduce and excite a woman—but he'd also learned that it frightened them. They felt debauched, frightened of him, so he'd stopped doing it, except, once, with a ShadowComm girl—someone too erratic to continue seeing. But this contact with Loraine—something extraordinary. He'd never felt anything like it.

The shadow of a bird rippled over him as he climbed down the fire escape, the ladder's metal warm under his hands.

Yorena.

He glanced up, saw Shoella's familiar dart over, and down, when the creature was sure she had his attention. Free to engage him now that the drone was gone.

The choppers would be here soon, Bleak guessed. Yorena knew that and wanted him away from here before CCA arrived.

He continued down the ladder—and heard the choppers thumping the air by the time he'd reached the ground. But they were still far enough away he could get undercover.

Yorena flew across the street—a residential street, back here, away from the main street with its merchants—and into a narrow walkway between two old brick apartment buildings.

Bleak ran across the street, making someone in a small Toyota honk at him irritably. He slipped quickly into the shady walkway. A couple of covered garbage cans stood along the passage, but the walkway was neatly kept, broom marks in the dust on the concrete.

He ran through to the next street, coming out between two houses. He had to vault over a short metal-mesh fence, then saw Yorena swoop down into the open back of what looked like an old-fashioned bread delivery truck double-parked next to an old Cadillac; the idling truck, its rear doors standing open, had been painted over, by hand, with a thick coat of gray. He only hesitated a moment, then hurried to the small truck and climbed in the back, closed the door behind him. Kind of regretted closing the door—there was an acrid smell back here, made worse by the hot closeness.

What he was smelling was Yorena and a bum; mostly the bum. Cleaning its wings, Yorena perched facing him on the back of the front passenger-side seat. The man was squatting on the scratched-up white-painted steel floor, behind the driver.

The guy smelled of booze and unwashed clothing. Pretty obvious he'd been in those jeans and that stained blue shirt for a long time. He had rotting sneakers and a three-day growth of red-brown beard and flicking brown eyes and a stub nose and moons of dirt under his fingernails. His hands trembled on his knees as he looked balefully at Bleak from under shaggy red-brown brows.

A spiky corona of short dreadlocks flared over the driver's seat—Shoella put the little truck in gear, hurried it down the street, making her passengers brace on floor and walls; the big raptor rocked with the motion of the vehicle, fluttering her wings.

Bleak sat back against a thin metal wall. "You would be Mr. Coster?"

"That's who I am," the bum said, his voice a slurred rumble. "Who you?"

Bleak ignored the question. He noticed a brown smudge on the floor of the truck. "This a blood spot, back here, Shoella?"

"Yeah." She turned a sharp left so that Bleak had to brace himself. "I had to do a ritual in the back of the truck. Couldn't do it at home, neighbors get funny about it. Had to cut the head off a chicken back there."

"The loas you talk to really care about blood sacrifices?"

"They care about what we expect them to care about. Thousands of years, people kill animals for them, pour drinks for them, dab perfume for them—the loas get to like it. Maybe they eat up a little of that life energy that gets out, when we cut the head off a chicken, I don't know. But, truth to tell, when they get to know you, they don't care you kill the chicken or pig for them, no, *cher darlin'*."

"But you're still cutting off heads."

"Was a loa I didn't know before. What do you care, you're not a vegetarian. You don't think down at the slaughterhouse they cut off heads of animals before they skin 'em for you? Look out the back, you see that helicopter?"

He went to the back window of the truck, squinted up at the sky. "Can't see one. Can't see much though. They had a drone after me."

"Yorena told me. One of those little flying machines with the cameras."

"Yeah. One of those little machines. I shot it down but they had me located, so . . . I guess the chopper was already on its way."

"But I think we lost them. We fittin' to go to a house they don't know."

"I need a drink," Coster said, the way an injured man would say, "Get me to a doctor."

"We got rum at my place for you," Shoella said.

Bleak looked at Coster and thought, *Can this man really tell me anything about my brother? Was a man like that ever really in a position to know anything useful?*

It seemed unlikely. But could Coster simply be hustling Shoella for drinks? For money? And just making stuff up? That wasn't likely.

Hard to put a hustle over on Shoella. Unless she wanted it to happen.

As if sensing he was thinking about her mistress, Yorena cocked her head and looked sullenly at Bleak. And Shoella turned another corner.

EIGHT

I should feel on top of the world here, Gulcher thought. *But I almost feel like I'm back in prison.*

Where he was, really, was in a luxury suite on the top floor of Lucky Lou's Atlantic City Casino. He was lying full dressed on the bed, watching the big-screen, high-definition TV. And seeing his own face, his barefaced mug shot, flickering across it. Good thing he'd grown the neat, carefully clipped black beard. But still—his face was out there, and Jock's too: Watch out for these escapees from prison, believed to be involved in the prison riot that left more than a dozen dead. In prison for second-degree murder, history of drug dealing, fencing, pimping, blah blah blah.

He was feeling down. He wasn't sure if the on-a-high feeling the whisperer had brought him was gone or, like a drug feeling you got used to, just become a dull part of the background of the trip you were on.

He changed the channel. There was what's his name, President Breslin, the old guy who said we *might* just have to do a "later, later" on the general election. Hell, what did Gulcher care? He never voted anyway.

He changed the TV to the Home Shopping Network. Always found this channel comforting. Maybe because his wife, Luella, liked to watch it. He ever found Luella, he was going to have to kill her, just as a matter of honor, but sometimes it was nice to think about the good times they'd had before she met that bearded-weirdo California pot dealer and run off. On TV, a sexy blonde with hair that was artfully sticking up all over her head— like someone had paid a lot of money to make it look messy in a cool way—was selling "Rolex-style" watches. She kept saying she wished she weren't working for the channel, she'd love to buy one of these herself, they were so great and so inexpensive.

"Sure," Gulcher said, out loud. "I'll take two of those and your ass along with 'em."

He'd dipped into the casino women. A couple of the cuter, younger cleaning women had been accommodating. He hadn't needed the whisperer—just the magic of $1,000 to each broad. He had luxury, he had access to all that money in the cash room, nobody ever questioned him, but Gulcher still felt trapped here. He left here, he'd leave the protection of this place. He was hiding out here, but hiding in plain sight. He didn't understand it completely, but he knew he was shielded. At least for now.

"The great power has busted through the weak part in the wall up north," the whisperer had said, when Gulcher lay there, alone in the night, trying to figure it all out. Having access to his mind, it was starting to talk to him in Gulcher's own lingo. "The wall still works, for now anyway, but while it was weakened, the great power came through. You follow? In this place, where the addicts are getting their buzz, the great power finds a safe place to hole up from the spirits of light. He can suck up energy from the addicts,

power it can use to grow, and to keep himself hid. Get it? Some are gonna get sucked dry, but only those no one gives a shit about. *All you have to do is dispose of the bodies.*"

"'All you have to do is dispose of the bodies,'" Gulcher muttered, remembering. "Oh, is that all? Dispose of a pile of bodies." A job he'd delayed, by storing them downstairs. But what bothered him more was the sense that he had no control over any of this. That he was just a pawn, shoved around on some kind of invisible chessboard, by invisible hands, in a game between invisible players. He didn't like it. He had powers he didn't understand. From things he didn't understand. In the old days, there were guns, there was money, there were drugs, there was pussy, and there was hiding what you did from the cops. Those things he understood. But this—

Someone knocked sharply on the door to the suite. Gulcher took his pistol from the bedside table, got up, went to flatten against the wall by the door, gun ready.

"Yeah?"

"Hey, Troy, man, it's me, Jock."

Gulcher relaxed, opened the door. Jock looked a little drunk, and a little wired, both. "You getting high, Jock?"

"What you care if I get high, Gulcher? Shit, we got more important stuff to worry about than do I get high."

Gulcher wasn't sure why he didn't want Jock to get high. He just felt like everything here was balanced on some kind of wire and anything could push it over into chaos and he'd lose all control of it. If he *had* any control of it. He wondered, suddenly, why the whisperer needed him at all, now that this great power had "come through." But it did need him, somehow. Something about "just the right people" in bodies "belonging to the dense layers of this world." Gulcher doubted he'd ever understand it all and he wasn't sure he wanted to.

"So, spit it out, Jock, what's the more important stuff we got to worry about? The cops onto me being here?"

"Not yet. But maybe these people are going to call 'em on us—or maybe call their fucking *paisanos*."

"What people, for fuck's sake?"

"The owners of the casino are here. Luciano Baroni and Ricky Baroni."

"Yeah? I've heard of those pricks. Most casinos, what I see, are owned by Arab guys or Donald Chump or whatever, these days. They're the real owners, huh?"

"What, you didn't know that? I looked it up first time I was in the casino office."

"You're very goddamn efficient, Jock, make somebody a nice secretary. Where are these greasers now?"

Turned out the Baronis were in the basement, in a room off one of those tunnels; in the cash-counting room, talking to the accountants.

Gulcher and Jock found them there in the windowless, low-ceilinged, harshly lit room, standing next to a table stacked with bound bundles of cash. Both of the Baronis were red-faced, the accountants looking sleepy and vague. The accountants were under the whisperer's control, pretty much sleepy and vague whenever they were in the casino.

The older Baroni, with the white hair and the heavy black eyebrows and the jowls, was unbuttoning the jacket of his charcoal-colored silk suit with one hand, as he talked to the accountants. "What do you mean, the new management . . ."

The younger Baroni was holding a cell phone to his ear. "I know Pop told you no bodyguards in the casino, but that's because security here is supposed to be already working for me, but now we need you to get your ass over here—" A bit taller, his hair thick and black and curly, the younger Baroni wore a powder blue suit, replete with a matching blue tie.

Gulcher noticed that Papa Baroni wore a gold-colored ascot with a little pearl pin in the middle of it. "Pop" was taking off his sunglasses with one hand, using them to gesture angrily at the money as he talked to the two accountants. "We make a lot of our money off you Asian guys, crazy about the card rooms, and you're good with numbers, but you're putting me off the whole fucking Chinese race, here, with this. How can you say that the management just got changed and no one consulted us? We're the fucking owners, here. We're—" He broke off, seeing Gulcher. "Who's this?"

"I'm your new management," Gulcher said mildly. "Ron Presley. Board of directors appointed me. Transitional."

The younger Baroni snapped his cell phone shut so vigorously it made a report that caused the accountants to jump a little and look at one another. "Board of directors? They've got no say without us!"

The older Baroni was looking closely at Gulcher and Jock. "I don't normally handle taking out the trash personally," Baroni said, fists clenching at his sides. "Junior, he called someone to do it. But you don't get out of here, right now—I'm gonna do it myself."

"You'll lose a lot of money," Gulcher said patiently, smiling. "There's a misunderstanding here. I'm pretty sure the board thought they'd consulted you."

"I leave town a few weeks, I come back, and a couple of con artists—" The older Baroni broke off, staring. "Where the fuck you get that suit?"

"You don't like it?" Gulcher said. "Maybe I should get an ascot. I'm taken by that ascot, boss. You don't see those much anymore. Gold-colored too."

Jock chuckled at that.

"You making fun of me?" Luciano Baroni's face was beet red. "That suit you're wearing was picked out by me for my head of operations here. It was a gift. I was there when it was tailored. It was part of his fucking bonus!"

"He gave it to me," Gulcher said, shrugging apologetically. "You want to ask him about it, come on. Follow us. He's here — he'll explain the whole thing. Why we're here, everything. Me and Jock, we're just transitional. Helping out here, for a while, really, 'cause your man had some issues."

"Dad," the younger Baroni said, "let's take 'em down now. They're some other fucking . . . organization. Moving in on our shop."

His father looked at Gulcher, licked his lips. Gulcher knew Baroni was a survivor — with an instinct for danger. And Baroni hesitated, sensing the power in Gulcher. Thinking, probably, he'd wait for his muscle to show up.

Gulcher gestured at the door. "We'll go talk to your primary manager — the man you hired. Right this way, gentlemen."

The Baronis looked at one another. Then Pop Baroni nodded. "You walk ahead of us. Don't get cute, we're gonna be looking at your back. My son here's a good shot."

Gulcher made a mock bow and walked out the door, into the underground tunnel. Jock hurrying to catch up. The Baronis followed, a few steps behind.

"We're ready to kick ass . . . just reach out with those other hands," said the whisperer, to Gulcher, somewhere deep in his ear.

But Gulcher just didn't want to do that. Not this time. He wanted to do something *himself.* He wanted to do things in a way he understood — *completely* understood. And there was a kick to this. He could hear the Baronis walking a few strides behind him. They could shoot him in the back anytime they wanted. The adrenaline from this roll of the dice made his heart thump. He liked feeling that again.

As they walked along, Jock leaned over, muttered, "Hope you know what you're doing, Troy."

"Don't call me that, right now. We agreed, I'm Ron Presley,

asshole," Gulcher murmured. He looked back to see the Baronis following with identical scowls on their faces. The junior Baroni looked at him, seemed to be holding up his cell phone. Taking a picture? Lot of good that would do. He turned around again, wondering if they could see the bulge of his gun in his back pocket under the jacket.

"Dad—let's just hold these assholes right here in the hall till our people come. I don't feel good about this," Ricky Baroni said.

"I'll have Stedley send your bodyguards to us in the Special Works room," Gulcher called over his shoulder, not quite looking back as he said it.

"What the fuck is Special Works?" the younger Baroni said. "We got no special works around here."

"Right through here, Mr. Baroni." Gulcher opened the door to Furnace Room One and went through, Jock right behind him.

When the Baronis came in, they stopped, just inside the door, staring at the pile of dried-out bodies. Just what Gulcher had figured they'd do. Too startled by the sight to keep track of Gulcher. So by the time they realized he had his gun out and pointed at them, they couldn't reach for their own pieces.

They just stared, openmouthed, looking back and forth between Gulcher and the desiccated remains.

There were about thirty bodies, currently, stacked like a pyramid. Except for the clothing, they looked a lot like those dried animals you see hanging in Chinatown shops: brown and shrunken to a little more than half size, looking too small for their clothing. They were really superlight too, you could pick one up with a single hand. They were the corpses of people the whisperer had chosen, as especially susceptible. Moloch picked them—or more likely it was the whisperer; Gulcher had worked out that the whisperer was a spirit who worked for Moloch. The whisperer would pick out these gamblers, the kind no one cared about. And the whisperer would wrap himself around them and get them more tweaky obsessed with gambling than they'd ever been, way beyond gambling fever. And they'd keep on and on, and if they ran out of money, somehow credit would miraculously appear. And they'd play on and on even more. Then they'd simply collapse, without a word. And the "great power" that had come through the wall in the north, to use the whisperer's terminology, fed off their spirits as they left their body and became stronger . . . and security would be called, would carry the bodies out, and by the time they got them down here, they'd shriveled to this. Some essential something had been taken out of them. And the bodies burned real good in these furnaces, no problem.

Furnaces. Moloch liked furnaces. Something about people chucking babies in furnaces, for ol' Moloch, thousands of years ago. To please him.

What a guy to be in business with.

The older Baroni was sputtering, "What the hell you do with . . . these people, they . . ."

"Your man Teague's here," Gulcher said. "His ashes anyway. In that furnace. He didn't die like these guys, though. He was kind of resistant, so Stedley took him down."

Jock added, "You wanted to get with him so now's your chance to mix." Jock chuckled, pleased with his own wit.

"Dad—!" the junior Baroni yelped, clutching at a gun.

He never got it out. Gulcher shot them both, two bullets in the body mass, one more each in the head. Pow, pow, pow, and pow—down they went. Kind of a bloody mess compared to the dried-out corpses.

Gun smoke tinted the air blue-gray and made Gulcher cough. "Jock—tell Stedley to get down here, cut these two up, feed 'em in there, in the furnace. And that pile of driftwood too, we got too many backed up there."

"Sure thing, Troy." Jock seemed in awe—and also worried. "You sure that was smart? If they'd been under the whisperer's control . . . I mean, people are gonna look for these guys for sure. They're powerful guys. They were on the phone to their boys."

"We'll deal with their punks the same way."

"Yeah, but, Gulcher—you should've—"

"Jock? Shut up. I feel good now. I'm gonna go have a drink. Save me that ascot and that pearl pin, there."

Gulcher turned around and walked out. Glad to be out of a smoky room piled high with shriveled, mummified gamblers.

And he was sure, just as sure as Jock had been, that he'd made a big goddamn mistake.

SAME DAY, LATE AFTERNOON.

"Sean Bleak was taken," Coster said. "He was alive, not long ago. Probably still is. I need another drink."

They were in the kitchen of a two-bedroom bungalow, Bleak and Shoella and Coster, in Hoboken. Birds chirped from the backyard.

There hadn't been any trouble with cops or helicopters or CCA after Bleak had shot down the drone. The chopper hadn't gotten close enough to use the detector before they'd gotten out of range. But some instinct told Bleak he wasn't safe here. What the danger was, he wasn't certain.

Bleak and Shoella were drinking a licorice-flavored Egyptian tea; Coster, on the other side of the table, was drinking straight white rum from a tumbler. The back door was open to let in fresh air and the sound of the birds. The small kitchen looked like any little, cozy American kitchen in an old house, with its old-fashioned white, curvy-cornered gas stove, and the oak kitchen table. It was like any kitchen except for the African masks on the walls—where other people would have had a ceramic image of a cow. One of the masks, Bleak noticed, was a wood-sculpted vulture head, reminiscent of the thing that had destroyed Bursinksy's friend Gleaman, in River Rat's. Another mask was made of straw, with holes for eyes and wide-open mouth; it seemed to gaze at Bleak with an expression of horrified recognition. Some spirit might be hovering around it, one that would become apparent if Bleak looked at the mask long enough. He looked away.

They hadn't told Coster who Bleak was. He hadn't insisted on knowing. Which made Bleak wonder if he knew already. Shoella had told Coster only that it was important a certain someone hear his story.

Miles Davis played from the stereo in the next room, *Bitches Brew*, and the slinky music seemed to ooze into near-visible animal shapes around the corners of the kitchen.

"You like my place?" Shoella asked Bleak, her tone faintly enticing.

"This where you live?" Bleak said, thinking it odd she was revealing that to Coster. Was she so confident she could control him?

"I got more than one place. But, *oui*. I didn't want to bring him here." She shrugged. "Closest place. I'm tired of running and hiding. I have to be near my center of power or I lose some'tin. And this place is near the water." She looked at Coster. "So you remember, Coster, you make me angry, I will bring a baka loa to eat your brains."

Coster looked at her. "Probably too late for anything to eat my brains, lady."

"I've seen that loa at work," Bleak said. "Not something you want to happen to whatever brains you have left."

Coster nodded ruefully. "Duly noted." He drank about half his rum off. It was his second glass. Seemed unfazed. The alcoholism didn't appear to be an act.

"You have something to tell my friend?" Shoella prompted. "Something we talked about before. There were two boys . . ."

"You said there'd be money," Coster said.

"Shoella," Bleak said, "this guy is pulling a hustle. He's just a drunk trying to get a free ride." He stood up, as if to go. "He doesn't know anything."

Coster looked up at Bleak with red-rimmed eyes. "I know some things. When I look at you, I know you look a hell of a lot like somebody I've met. His name was Sean Bleak. And I know the lady here was asking about my work with an outfit that's pretty interested in finding Sean Bleak's brother. Now, I wonder who that'd be?" Coster made an unpleasant sniggering sound.

So he's made a guess about who I am, Bleak thought. But he didn't see any point in confirming it.

"Shoella," Bleak asked. "You use Yorena? You see into this man's mind?"

Coster didn't seem surprised at the question. Which suggested he might be what he'd told Shoella he was—an ex–CCA agent.

"Looked some," Shoella said. "But it's hard to see anything clear in a drunken mind."

"I got *some* things clear," Coster said. "Sean Bleak and Gabriel Bleak. Sean'd be about your age, now. Saw him a few years ago. And he's kind of like you, pal." Coster pointed a grubby finger at Bleak. "He's a pretty different guy, though, I'd guess, than *you*."

Bleak stared at him. "What happened, and where'd it happen?"

"Where, was Road's End Ranch, out eastern Oregon. South of Bend a ways, and I need more rum."

Bleak felt a shock, hearing those place names. They were dead-on.

Shoella got up, went to a cabinet, found a bottle of Bacardi, and poured some into Coster's glass. Then she put it back in the cabinet. He looked at the cabinet and drank more rum.

"What happened?" Bleak said. "And what was your part in it?" He tried to keep the anger that was bubbling up inside him from spilling into his voice. But it occurred to him that he might have a man sitting in the same room with him who had kidnapped his brother. Or helped kidnap him. If any of it was true.

It was easier, almost more comforting, to simply believe that Sean was dead.

Coster looked at him, and back at his glass. "I was driving the van. I didn't know what they were gonna do on that little trip. It's one of the reasons I . . . left the place."

"You stayed with them long enough to see Sean as an adult," Bleak pointed out. "If it was really him." Not sure he believed any of this yet, despite the correct facts about the ranch, the location, the names. CCA knew where he came from, by now.

Coster sighed. "I left the authority the first time soon after they took the kid. Then I was in military intelligence for a while. That was even more depressing. Then I dropped out of that and worked in insurance for like almost ten years. Drinking too much, but doing the job. Then my wife left me, my son died of a drug OD, and CCA contacted me because, they said, there were new developments, they needed a lot of new staff, and I was already briefed on it and they knew I could handle it, which wasn't true. I couldn't handle it. But I went back. Then the dam started to crack—really cracking big-time—and I started to see ghosts myself and my dead kid was appearing to me there and telling me I was doing wrong and—"

"What do you mean, the dam started to crack?" Shoella said.

"The wall in the north. Isn't that what you people call it? I call it the dam. Anyhow . . . it started to crack a bit before Gabriel here was born. We found a way to trace 'responder signals' from people who reacted to the influx of energy from the Hidden. That's how they found Gabriel and his brother and some others. And they were afraid of that energy, see." Coster's voice was becoming a mumble. "So they started CCA and they started to look for the source. Some documents turned up . . . very old documents. Hundreds of years old. About three hundred."

Coster rubbed his face, seeming confused and exhausted, suddenly, as if he might fall asleep.

"I left again." He went on, after a moment, "That Sean freaked me out. He's a . . . Anyhow I had to skate under the radar, since then. And since I always liked a drink . . ." He said it with a dry-ice sting of irony. "It was easy to slip into skid row, whatever town I was in. Skid row's a good place to hide." His eyelids drooped.

"Someone put you up to getting in touch with us?" Bleak asked, his voice sharp.

Coster brought his head up sharply, blinking at him. "*You people* got in touch with *me.*" He nodded toward Shoella. "*She* found me."

Bleak noticed that Coster hadn't exactly said no about someone putting him up to this. But something else was more troubling.

"You could have told the police there was a kidnapping, if that's what the agency did," Bleak said. Holding the anger barely in check, like obstinately holding the handle of a pot that was too hot, burning his fingers.

"Kidnapping? I wouldn't describe it that way," Coster said. "I mean—we talked to your parents. Told them it was 'administrative custody.' They said they'd fight it no matter what—until we told them, 'You get to keep one kid this way. You fight us, you lose both, and maybe your lives.' What could they do?"

Bleak felt as if he'd been slugged in the stomach. He'd been judging his parents pretty harshly, with their "he was killed in a tractor accident" talk. But what would he have done, in their place?

He wanted rum himself now. He got up and got himself a glass of water, because his mouth felt bone-dry, and to give himself time to think. He drank some water, which tasted of rust, and said, "Coster—you're saying my parents allowed them to take my brother?"

Coster turned the glass. "Like I said. We didn't give them a lot of choice."

It explained a lot. A lot of inexplicable silences; a lot of ellipses in his history. Silences that made a bleak history bleaker. A lot of quiet misery on the part of his mother; the bitter stoicism of his father. Their dismay when they started to realize something was "off" with their remaining son. Their clinging to church.

Bleak's father was dead, six years now, of a heart attack. His mother was still alive but he hadn't been in touch with her for years. Which might be passive aggression on his part, he knew. Angry that they had sent him to that military school; hadn't accepted him as he was.

He should get back in touch with her. Tell her what happened to Sean. If it was true that Sean was alive.

"When was the last time you saw . . . Sean?" Bleak demanded.

Coster shook his head. "That's enough. I want money. I want—"

"Shoella!" A shout from the front of the house. "It's Oliver!"

"We're in the kitchen!" Shoella called.

Oliver appeared in the doorway to the kitchen. Same baseball hat, same baseball jacket. Looked at Coster. Wrinkled his nose. The ferret on his shoulder wrinkled its nose too and ran around to the other shoulder.

"Don't worry about our guest here," Shoella said. "He's . . ." She waved her hand dismissively. "Harmless."

Is he? Bleak wondered.

"I was coming to see you—and I ran into something going on, just a few blocks from here. The guy at the center of it must be one of our people, but I don't know him. . . . Cops and firemen . . ."

"What?" Shoella sat up straight. "Why didn't Yorena tell me? Someone acting out around here. Showing his *especiality*?"

"He sure as hell is. He's at Sol's Restaurant throwing fire imps."

Coster chuckled and waveringly lifted his glass. "Here's to fire imps."

Shoella looked at Bleak. "We got to go see this. I need to know all Shadow people. Best you go too. You're powerful, Gabriel, I might need you."

Bleak didn't like the idea. "It'll attract CCA."

"He's right," Oliver said, raw mistrust showing in his glance at Bleak. "With him along, they could be all over us. Besides—he keeps himself aloof from La'hood. I don't see how we trust him." An undertone of simple jealousy in his voice.

"He's not so aloof—he's here," Shoella pointed out. "I want him there. We may need his power."

"It's a risk. If CCA is still looking for me in Jersey . . ."

"It just started," Shoella put in. "We could be gone before they get there."

Oliver looked exasperated, realizing she'd made her mind up. He had long ago accepted her authority.

Shoella stood up. "I'm protected from CCA now, Gabriel. I got the ancestors protecting me. How you think you get here safe? I talked with the ancestors, and we are safe. Come on—we'll take my little truck. You, Coster—wait here, yes? But I won't have you alone inside my house, I'm sorry. It's a nice day out in the back-yard. There's a garden. Here . . ." She opened the cabinet, gave him the rum bottle. "Take it out back, and this water bottle—we back in maybe thirty minutes. I'm going to lock the house up."

Coster made no objection to being treated like a troublesome stray dog to be locked in the fenced yard. He went meekly in the back, carrying his bottle and cup, and Shoella locked the house's doors.

Oliver and Bleak waited at the gray truck as she locked up the house. As they stood there together, Oliver said softly, bitterly, "I suppose you know that Shoella's in love with you."

Bleak shrugged, wondering why Oliver was bringing this up

now. "Sometimes I thought so. If she is . . . I don't think I'm ready for it."

"I don't think you're *good enough* for it, man," Oliver said bitterly. "She's—" He broke off, as Shoella strode up to them.

They got into the gray truck and she drove them toward the rising column of smoke.

LONG ISLAND. CCA FACILITY 19. About that same time.

"We'll be going north, tonight, Loraine," Helman said. They were waiting in the hall outside Containee Investigation Room 77, waiting for the guards to get Soon Mei settled in the concrete chair. "You recall I mentioned a trip in the offing. In fact"—he smiled mischievously—"we're heading for the north pole."

She blinked. "We skipped the arctic survival class in CCA training. Probably because there isn't one. But if you're serious . . ."

"I am—but actually we're going close to the *magnetic* north pole. First leg will be the base by Goose Bay."

"What? That place in Quebec? I thought the Canadians got it shut down."

"President Breslin talked them out of it. He's so very persuasive." Helman added with satisfaction, "Because they're all afraid of him, of course. You've read Soon Mei's file? Know what she's capable of?"

"I did, yeah. She seems to be authentic."

"You're either authentic or you're not. She is authentic, I assure you. As you will see." He looked at an electronic clipboard he was carrying—no briefcase this time, Soon Mei having no need of "cuing materials" or summoning scepters. "We're going from Goose Bay via special transport. Going far north, to Ellesmere Island—what's left of it. Then up to Mount Eugene."

Loraine shivered, anticipating the cold. She'd been raised

mostly on military bases in California. An "army brat." But she decided she was being childish. "How do I prepare? Do I need special clothing? It's all frozen up there, isn't it?"

"Not this time of year. Loraine"—he lowered his voice—"we've found *the artifact itself*, you know."

"The what?"

"Ah, right, you haven't been fully briefed. Yes, we found it a few months ago. It was referred to in Newton's letters, and the other documents. The partial diagram. I'll show you a summary file. You need to know—because you and I are going to be there to stake our claim on it."

He winked at her. And she thought, *He really is socially clueless.*

"But why me?" she asked. "I don't mean to be uncooperative. General Forsythe assigned me to work with you. But I'm a field agent, not a scientist. If there's an . . . an *artifact*—it's an archaeological question. That's not my strong suit, believe me."

"We want you fully briefed, Loraine. And we want to see how you do up there—we monitored you, medically, during your encounter with Bleak, you know. We've got some very interesting readings."

"Monitored me?"

He ignored her implied question. "Just head to Area Twelve, upstate, get the transport, we'll meet at Goose Bay oh nine hundred tomorrow—"

"Dr. Helman—I don't like being monitored when I don't know about it. I'm willing to volunteer for medical monitoring, but—if I haven't volunteered, it just doesn't seem right. I doubt if it's regulation."

"You shouldn't make knee-jerk pronouncements like 'I don't like being monitored,' my dear. They're absurd, truly they are. You really should stop being so naïve. We're *all* being monitored, one way or another—and if we're under that radar right now, we won't be for long. To object is inherently unpatriotic, since monitoring protects the nation. As for regulations on surveillance, they're all provisional, depending on the needs of the current administration. The president has sent us all notice to that effect. Ah—here we go." The door was opened from the inside by a small, dark man in a black beret and Special Forces uniform.

"Almost ready, Doctor," the soldier said. Sewn on one shoulder was one of the colorful patches that the different military and intelligence projects used to enhance esprit; this one had an image of a knight holding a shield in front of the planet Earth. Below that, in gold, the words SERVING IN SILENCE.

"It's a curious thing," Helman remarked, as they went into Room 77, "how very powerful, and yet how very limited too, the so-called supernatural is."

They were in the familiar concrete room, Loraine and Helman, with the concrete chair, but another person was being strapped into it by two Special Forces escorts. The black berets were stocky, grimly silent Filipinos. This time the ShadowComm containee was a small, vaguely Asiatic-looking woman of about forty. She wore a blue frock and thongs. No makeup. Her short gray-black hair was patchy; she seemed to have cut it out randomly in spots, somehow. Her eyes darted about and her lips moved as she whispered to herself. The suppressor hummed behind her.

"What I mean about the Hidden," Helman said, as he frowned over the electronic clipboard, "is—well, on the one hand we get good results with Soon Mei here. Ghost-Enhanced Surveillance can be very effective. It's one of the reasons we get funded year after year. We've got General Erlich and Swanson threatening our funding if CCA isn't more useful against terrorists—GES did find one terrorist cell for us. But specific information can be difficult to get—the ghosts are individuals themselves . . . and they are almost always befuddled."

Loraine had had a crash course in ghosts, the last few days. She'd been skeptical, then amazed, when she'd seen how much CCA used them. She'd seen video of Ghost-Enhanced Surveillance; had read the files. From what she knew of the metaphysics of ghosts, their erratic usefulness was no surprise. According to the UBE/GES manual, most souls, detached from the body, passed into particular levels of the Hidden, and from there reincarnated, or were drawn into some higher plane. Or into the Wilderness. But earthbound ghosts were souls who clung tenaciously to the material world—they were particularly fixated, neurotic people, who identified with their own little problems and refused to leave them behind. They were too self-obsessed to provide clear information consistently.

Loraine glanced at Soon Mei. The woman twitched in the chair, her lips moving, eyes darting. Seeming indifferent to Helman's remarks.

"Still," Helman said, switching off the suppressor, "Ghost-Enhanced Surveillance can locate people for us—but not just anyone. Those with supernatural powers seem to know when a ghost is shadowing them, and after a brief window they ward the surveillance away. So we shift to technological surveillance, for someone like that. Or we use a special monitor like Orrin Krasnoff. Even someone as powerful as Sean has difficulty tracking some individuals—he has a particular blind spot when it comes to Gabriel Bleak. Krasnoff is really the best we had for direct cognitive projection, but he's going to be useless for a while."

"And—Gabriel Bleak?"

"We have someone working on the Gabriel Bleak contact right now. Let us see what we can find out with Soon Mei—and tomorrow morning, we will head north . . . to see the crack in the dam. And now—Soon Mei . . . you know what to do. If you want your reward this evening."

"I want something better quality," she said, in a creaky, little voice. "And new things to look at, while I . . . while I trippy-trip-trip."

They're giving her drugs, of some kind, Loraine realized.

Helman caught the look on Loraine's face. His lips formed a bent little leer he probably thought was wry. "Oh, yes—addiction has real power over the psyche, Loraine. Indeed, we use many narcotics in our programs here. They are especially useful for someone like our Soon Mei, who likes to 'chase the dragon.'" He didn't seem to care that he was talking about Soon Mei's addiction in front of her, as if she were a lab animal unable to understand. "A mind freed by opiates makes many psychic connections, we find. Often many unwanted connections, it's true. But Soon Mei has a gift for controlling the spirits she meets. Earthbound spirits. Don't you, Soon? She's a sort of hyperskilled spirit medium. And she works best when she's a bit on edge, motivated to focus."

Helman looked at Loraine appraisingly, as if he was trying to decide how she was taking all this.

Loraine thought, *I've got to stop coming across like everything here's a problem for me. It's dangerous.* She nodded in as business-like a way as she could. "I see."

Helman turned to Soon Mei, muttered a few instructions, then went to the wall and dialed down the lights. He opened the narrow overhead shaft but kept a sheet of tinted glass in place so that the light came down murky green.

A full minute more, and ectoplasmic strands descended from the skylight, to stretch probing fingers down into the room within the green shaft of light.

The ectoplasm purled and roiled, in no hurry, like drops of milk spilled in water. Faces formulated from the ectoplasm. The eyes came first, looking fearfully to the left, the right . . . and piercingly into Loraine's heart.

That's how it felt, anyway. When the ghosts looked right at her, they looked not at her face, but into her heart—where she felt a jab of icy needles.

Faces detailed around the eyes, then parts of ethereal bodies formed, usually clothed according to ghostly memories. The crowd of forms never stayed completely in focus; some drawing back from the others in revulsion, others twining around one another in a glutinous dance.

"The time has come, Soon Mei," Helman said. "Send them out to find Harry L. Zelinsky for us. He is in Canada, somewhere in Vancouver, but we don't know exactly where, they keep shifting his safe house."

Zelinsky! Loraine thought. The leader of the opposition to President Breslin. Accused of embezzling—probably framed—he'd fled the country a year before to avoid jail. He still spoke to the American public through the Internet, and Canadian media, though the webs of censorship tightened every day.

Directed by Soon Mei, the ghosts fled up the shaft in search of Zelinsky, and a thought came to Loraine seemingly from nowhere.

Where is my duty, really? Am I really serving my country this way?

AT ALMOST THAT SAME moment, in New Jersey.

Why did I come? Bleak wondered. He stood in a small crowd with Oliver and Shoella.

They watched a perspiring man capering on the sidewalk of a business thoroughfare four blocks from Shoella's house, in front of a burning building. The man was shaking his shoulders like a stripper, laughing and crying at once, silhouetted against the burning inferno that had been Sol's Restaurant. He was a long-haired, thirtysomething man with chipmunk cheeks and a belly that sagged over his wide leather belt and an old INSANE CLOWN POSSE T-shirt. Cheap single-color tattoos decorated his thick, pale arms. He was shaking his arms as if to get something out of them, doing a dance like a child having a tantrum. Sweat splashed when he whipped his head about, and it pasted his long brown hair to his head and neck.

Bleak knew the restaurant, a popular comfort-food family spot, built in the 1950s, with curving pseudo-space-age lines of red panels and curving chrome, Sputnik-shapes projecting from the SOL's sign. Now the low, sweeping building roiled and rumbled with smoke-streamed flame. A window burst out, glass tinkled into the parking lot, glinting with firelight. They could feel the heat of the fire sixty feet away.

Yorena sat on the branch of a small elm nearby. Bleak and Shoella and Oliver and Oliver's ferret—its eyes catching the flames—watched as fire trucks roared up and police cars blocked the area off. Cops were putting up street barriers and telling the small, gaping crowd to stay back, nothing to see here.

A middle-aged woman with dyed-blond hair, wearing a Sol's waitress uniform, stood just in front of Bleak, watching the fire, wringing her hands. "We asked him to leave because he was ranting about how he was a great songwriter and no one appreciated it and they stole his ideas, and we said, 'Quiet down, stop yelling,' and he said he didn't have to, and then he said, 'It's happening to me, finally it's happening,' and he started throwing fire-things around. . . . Oh, Lord, that job was all I had."

"And I don't see much of anything," Bleak said, aside to Shoella, keeping his voice low. "I mean—no 'especialities.'"

Two pale uniformed cops, glistening with sweat themselves, were approaching the capering man, one with a Taser, one with a gun drawn.

"How do you think Sol's got on fire in such a short time?" Oliver insisted.

"I don't know—a firebomb maybe." Bleak was scanning the sky for helicopters or UAV drones. He really shouldn't have come.

A man who had, perhaps, helped kidnap his brother had been right there in front of him. And he'd left him unattended somewhere. Who knew what the guy might be doing? Was he contacting CCA—maybe trying to get more money that way?

Oliver shook his head. "I *saw* it. It wasn't a firebomb."

"I think I'm leaving. We should all go." Bleak wanted to get back and talk to Coster, pay him if necessary.

"That's what he was doing right before the fire started inside," the waitress said. "Throwing himself around like that. I got to go home." But, stricken, she just stood there, staring at the capering man. "How I'm going to pay my . . ."

"Reach out into the Hidden, here," Shoella whispered, to Bleak and Oliver, watching the cops approach the capering man. "You can feel it." She glanced up at Yorena on her perch. "It's something new—he's just gotten this—"

The ferret on Oliver's shoulder stood up on its hind legs, making high-pitched *chi-chi-chi* sounds. And Oliver said, "Yeah. Something's building up . . . about to let go . . . reaching the flash point."

Bleak felt it too. He looked into the Hidden and saw the energies boiling around the capering man . . . as if the man's contortions were bringing it to a boil.

The cops were shouting—and that's when Bleak saw the fire imps.

The sweaty guy in the INSANE CLOWN POSSE T-shirt suddenly stopped moving, stood there in quivering rigidity with his arms held straight out, palms up—and hunkering in his hands were burning tumor-purple creatures, each about the size of a human heart. Probably most people here couldn't see them, as the ShadowComm did: squat, little, purplish fiery mockeries of humanity.

With his heightened sensitivity, Bleak could see the fire-energy drawn down from above; he could see the atmosphere warping around the man's head as he drew energy and spirit-forms from the Hidden; could see the fire imps themselves coming down from overhead somewhere, in their more ghostly forms: like perverse, transparent cupids, descending this shimmering column, diving into the man, rippling out along his arms, emerging more substantially in his hands, without burning his skin.

Hideous, maliciously grinning, little, purple-black homunculi coated in red fire . . . dancing in his hands, and on top of his head, as the man had done on the street.

"Put those things down!" the cop with the Taser shouted. To him it would look like fireballs in the man's hands. He'd be thinking it was some kind of bomb. The cop brandished the Taser . . .

And the long-haired man flung a fire imp like a gas-soaked softball at the cop. The living fireball spun as it hissed through the air, trailing black smoke, to smack into the cop's chest. It *stuck* . . . then sank *into* him. He opened his mouth to scream— and burst into flames from within, shrieking and running, flailing his arms.

The man who'd thrown the fire imp turned and saw the waitress. She was weeping, backing away. He raised an imp that seemed to widen its grin and laugh happily when it realized it was about to be thrown at someone.

The cop with the gun shouted for people to get out of the line of fire—firemen were trying to put out the flames on the sprawled, burning policeman.

The waitress screamed and ran—scurried randomly toward Shoella.

Bleak pulled Oliver and Shoella out of the path of the waitress as the man with the fire imps flung his living fireball after her— which missed the waitress, flashed past them, and struck the small tree where Yorena perched, sinking into its trunk . . . and making the elm explode a split second later, like a grenade of burning splinters. Yorena flapped into the air, to circle overhead screeching angrily. All that remained of the tree was a smoking stump.

If the cops don't do something, Bleak thought, *I'm going to have to try.* He reached into the Hidden.

But the cop with the pistol fired. Two times, three times, the reports ear-ringingly loud; the bullets cracked into the man's head and into his back . . . and the man pitched forward onto his face, the back of his head shot away. Quite dead. And the imps sucked away into nothingness.

Bleak stared at the corpse. A fact he had known for a long time: the supernatural wasn't likely to save you from a gunshot in the head.

He had seen too many good men shot dead in Afghanistan to care when a self-indulgent, murderous neurotic was cut down. But as he hustled away with Shoella and Oliver, he thought, *Shoella was right, that guy was new to this. You could feel it. If it came to him as an adult—how many more like him are out there?*

SHOELLA SAID IT, AS she drove them back to her house. "There's been a change. For a big while, the wall let through just enough for us. Now it's breaking open, opening more, and certain people are being powered up with especialities. From what Yorena and the spirits and Scribbler tell me, it's all bad people. Dangerous people. Crazy, vicious."

"You got to wonder how that happened," Oliver said, sitting beside her, the ferret scuttling agitatedly on his shoulders. "Who's directing the new power that way? Toward people with no real sense of . . . of guidance."

"Maybe they've got guidance," Bleak said. "Maybe it's just the wrong one."

"So," Oliver said, scratching the ferret under its chin to calm it, "that still suggests that someone's deliberately targeting those kind of people."

"So who?" Shoella asked.

Maybe, Bleak thought, *that's something this Coster would know.*

But when they got to Shoella's place, Coster was gone. The yard's gate was left open. No trace of Coster remained but an empty rum bottle.

CHAPTER

NINE

Eighteen hours later, in a Humvee—in the Arctic.

"It was under the permafrost," Dr. Helman said simply. "But the permafrost melted—you know, *global warming*." He emphasized *global warming* wearily. He was up front, beside the driver. That was Morris, the contract engineer, a round-faced Inuit in brown coveralls, sleeves rolled. Morris had a master's in archaeological engineering from the University of Toronto. It seemed to Loraine, when she watched him driving bumpily along, that the Eskimo engineer was having to work at not laughing at them.

Loraine sat behind Helman next to a young U.S. marine holding a carbine across his lap. The marine's expression, she thought, was a clear question: *What the hell am I doing here?*

I don't know much more than he does, Loraine thought. What was *she* doing here, in the Arctic, almost within spitting distance of the magnetic north pole?

She thought about asking them to open the Humvee's windows—the smell of everyone's insect repellent, deployed against the notorious arctic mosquitoes, was sickeningly strong. Her own repellent itched under the collar of her work shirt and at the cuffs of her heavy general-issue military trousers. The bumpy ride didn't help.

The Humvee bumped and fishtailed over the twisty dirt road, between rolling hills covered with low green and purple scrub. To the northwest, the sea off Ellesmere Island was startlingly blue, the kind of nearly black blueness you got when you dumped india ink in water; ice floes littered the horizon like broken Styrofoam.

She looked south, up the lower slopes of Mount Eugene, multicolored and green with lichen and short grasses; up higher, granite outcroppings glittered with ice. "It's on this mountain somewhere?" she asked.

"The dig site, yes, it is," Morris said, nodding, though she'd been talking to Dr. Helman. "Yuh, but not far up it; it's just around the curve a dozen klicks, ay? Was under a glacier but she melted away. Biggest mountain on the United States Range, this one, but we won't be going high up. Just above the lake, there. Still in Quttinirpaaq Park."

"You're keeping the park tourists out, Morris?" Helman asked.

Morris looked surprised. "Tourists? We never had many, almost none now, with the seas rising up, ay? You people south heat up the world, and . . ." He shook his head, knowing better than to risk his paycheck grousing over what couldn't be helped now. "Even the Inuit only come here a few times a year. Ritual ground is underwater, we had to make a new holy place on the slopes above!" After a moment, as he jerked the wheel to fishtail around a curve, he remembered to add, "But if we see any tourists, we'll keep them away from the site. With most of the wildlife gone these days, people mostly came to see where Peary had his camp, and that's all underwater now."

"The whole island will need to be thoroughly secured," Helman said, looking at Loraine in the rearview mirror.

She nodded, because he seemed to expect some response.

They jounced on again for another two miles, following the beveled outline of the mountain, finally coming out of its shadow into eye-bashing sunlight, some of it reflected brightly off a translucent-blue lake a quarter mile below. The lake looked to Loraine like a piece of smirched glass set into a hollow of the mountain, one end streaked with newly disturbed red and brown clay. The cause of the streaky murk was the dig site above the lake, a compound of concrete bunkers encircled by earthworks and hurricane fences topped by antipersonnel wire that glittered with a just-installed brightness.

The road descended two switchback curves, and a few minutes later they passed through the gate in the fence and pulled up in the graveled area near the bunkers. They climbed gratefully out of the Humvee, blinking in the pale sunlight. Arctic mosquitoes dove at them, some of them looking big as dragonflies.

"You put on the insect repellent, I hope, ay?" Morris said to her. "They'll take a bite out of you, fer sure. I use a seal-fat grease but I didn't bring any for you."

It was a little too warm, even for summer in the Arctic. Loraine felt sweat break out on her forehead and, at the same moment, became aware of hungry stares from the two young marines who'd let them in the front gate.

How long have those men been stationed here without a break? she wondered, walking over to the bank of dirt above the lake. She looked down at the lake about sixty feet below; terns circled over it, squawking, their bodies perfectly reflected in the glassy water.

"Right this way, Loraine," said Dr. Helman. "We'll head directly to the dig." He turned toward the marine who'd accompanied them. "Oh—Corporal? We're inside the compound, all is quite secure. You can go into the . . . what do you call the cafeteria here? Get yourself some coffee or . . . whatever you like."

The jug-eared marine nodded briskly. Taking a break was something he understood. "Yes, sir."

When he'd gone, Helman murmured to her, "We'll soon transfer the marines out—we'll have only our own elite black berets here."

Loraine followed Helman and Morris over to the dig site, a shallow pit between the bunkerlike buildings and the drop-off to the lake. Morris talking proudly about the retaining walls, how the archaeologists asked his advice, couldn't get along without him. Not at all snooty, that Dr. Pierce, but that Dr. Koeffel, now, he was a bit of a . . .

They descended a dirt path. Loraine looked down at the dig, estimated it was about a hundred feet across, the artifact just seven feet below the surrounding surface. Just above the dig was a flattened-out dirt terrace supporting four tents. A man in long sleeves and straw sun hat sat at a table in front of the largest tent, looking into a microscope. "That's Dr. Pierce over there, at the microscope," Helman said. "Koeffel is probably in one of the tents poring over the diagrams. Difficult sometimes to drag him away from them."

She only just glanced at the man across the pit; she was drawn to gaze raptly down at the artifact.

"It's been there over three hundred years," Helman was saying. "Using the documents, and other indications, we estimate it was placed here in the year 1709."

The artifact looked to her almost like a miniature Chinese pagoda, undecorated and composed of metal. It seemed made of brass—or was that copper? Could it be copper and still have new-copper sheen, after all this time?

"Did you polish it?"

"No!" Helman seemed delighted with the question. "It looks it though, yes? When I first saw it, I thought it must be a hoax, it can't be ancient, looking like that. But it is."

"How'd they get down through the permafrost, when they

buried it here?" she asked, as they trudged closer to the artifact, a little ahead of Morris.

"An intelligent question," Helman said, patronizing as always. "We've found charcoal in the dig, and the broken heads of iron picks. We believe they brought fuel, melted the frost a layer at a time, used a work gang to dig down a ways, then melted the permafrost some more—quite an elaborate process, with a large crew. There are indications that the crew never made it back. There are bones under rocks in a gulley, nearby. We think they were killed to keep them quiet."

She winced at that. To cross half a world, only to be murdered in this barren place—so far from home. "The artifact . . . it's not very big," Loraine remarked, as they took a switchback on the path, ever closer.

"And what *I* did, you see," Morris interposed rather loudly, "was I used a *particular tool* that moves dirt but at the same time never really risks the artifact. It's very precise—"

"Morris!" Helman interrupted, coming to a stop and turning to him.

The engineer seemed startled. "Yuh?"

"That'll be enough—why don't you go consult with Dr. Pierce on the other side of the site. I understand he wants to set up some kind of weather shelter for the artifact."

"A weather shelter for the . . . Yuh, okay, I was just . . ." Morris stumped off toward the tents, muttering, shaking his head.

Helman gestured for Loraine to follow him, and they descended another loop in the path till they stood just thirty feet above the artifact on a graveled embankment. Helman made a gesture taking in the dig. "There was a nice pocket of clay and primeval sand here, so they didn't have to cut into the stone of the mountain. They wanted the artifact buried, and they wanted it up on the mountain, and they wanted *this side* of the mountain—the artifact had to be within a certain distance of the magnetic north pole."

"But the magnetic north pole shifts around over time, doesn't it?" Loraine asked, staring at the object. Aware of her heart thumping; a thick feeling in her throat, like a difficulty swallowing. And another sensation—a feeling of loss. As if she'd just been cut off from something she hadn't known she was connected to. Things around her seemed unreal; missing some sheen of life that had been there before.

"The magnetic north pole does indeed shift a certain amount, yes, very good, Loraine," Helman said, with his bobblehead nod. "But the magnetic pole stays within a certain elliptical zone, up here, otherwise compasses would never have been of much use, eh? You see?"

"The artifact is only four feet high?"

"Oh, that's just the top of it. We think its center column goes down another thirty-eight feet! It's shaped rather like a wand, with a ziggurat-style top. They probably brought it here in sections."

"How did you know it was here?"

"Newton's *Cryptojournal*, partly. We'd already known there was something anomalous going on in the area—satellite readings of magnetic fields, the unusual charged particles coming up out of the ground here. I'll tell you what has Dr. Koeffel excited, Loraine. *Shall* I tell you?"

Hadn't he just said he would? "Sure. Please." She swiped at a mosquito buzzing too close to her eyes. That odd feeling of disconnection nudged her again. And another feeling like a hand pressing heavily on top of her head.

"Metal analysis suggests that the core of the artifact is from a much earlier era. *Perhaps as far back as thirteen thousand years ago.* Yes, the Lodge had found a more ancient artifact than what you see here—an artifact within the artifact. And that most ancient artifact is within this shell. Koeffel sneers, 'Some would call it Atlantean.' He doesn't want to admit that it *is* from Atlantis. If it wasn't from Atlantis—what civilization was it? There are no markings of known pre-Columbian societies on it. Nothing Native American or First Nations. Nothing Chinese. Nothing Viking. The object is too internally sophisticated for those cultures. No, nor could Newton's Lodge build it, except for some detailing. No. All he did was repair it, set it up. . . . And clearly it's Earth-make— not from some . . ." Helman gestured toward the sky. "You know. Aliens." He chuckled. "No."

"So Isaac Newton brought it here? Personally?"

"Not personally—but he was involved. His people brought it here from Norway, in the early 1700s. Newton—and a faction of the original Rosicrucians, the Lodge of Ten. They learned about it through a series of Sarmoung scrolls found in Athens—which directed them to a remote site in Norway. Magnetic north shifts from time to time, and it had drifted from Norway. There were dark things afoot in the world, in Newton's time—and they thought that if they could repair this artifact, activate it once more, it would protect them. Protect all of humanity, yes? So they brought it here, set it up, and activated it . . . and as a direct result, nearly all magic receded from the world! The artifact you see before you radically changed human history. It's one of *the keys* to history—and yet it's unknown to all but a handful of historians! Who are not permitted to speak of it."

"And . . . it's still working? As a device?"

"It is what creates the 'dam'—the wall in the north, as the ShadowComms say. Yes, it is still working. And thank God for that. It is all that stands between humanity and chaos. It is the great magic-suppressor. The small ones we have at Central Containment are based on it. We've learned to amplify its signal, to intensify it in a small way—though we don't entirely understand it. There are particles emitted by the device we can barely detect and certainly can't quite identify."

"If it's a working machine—what powers it?"

"It appears to take power from the fluctuation of the earth's magnetic field. The artifact transmits its suppression signal uniformly over the world, from here. It uses the magnetic field of the planet as a kind of carrier wave. It continues to put out its signal—but . . . lately, that signal is going out erratically. It is faltering—more. Has been erratic, we suspect, for thirty years. This has created some interesting effects, which we have taken advantage of. But it also creates a great danger—" Helman broke off to slap at a mosquito.

"Faltering more lately—because it was exposed by the dig?"

"That doesn't seem to have affected it—just made it possible for us to get a good look. We assume simple corrosion is reducing its output. We *must* know—we're trying, working feverishly to understand the artifact without taking it apart. So that we can repair it. Because if it stops working entirely . . ." He took a deep breath. "If it stops working, it just might be that the human world will spin out of control."

She looked at him, startled. "You're just . . . guessing that. It couldn't be that bad."

"It's a calculated guess. Newton, and the ancients before him—they knew what they were doing! Newton and the Lodge of Ten discovered that a shift in the poles of the earth would open it up to new planetary influences . . . magic would flood over the earth! Civilization would have descended into chaos! But . . . there is a use for magic. If properly controlled." Helman looked at the sky. "The air out here is really quite bracing. Strange smells." He looked at her, pursing his lips. "Can you feel the energy from the artifact, by the way? Some can."

"I think so. I do feel . . . something out of the ordinary. I'm not such an intuitive person, but . . ." She shook her head, unable to express it.

"You're sensing Newton's Wall of Force itself! We wanted you to get a sense of the"—he waved a hand at the artifact—"the *importance* of what's going on here. The mission of the Lodge of Ten goes on: the suppression of those forces that cripple science, or at least challenge it; forces that threaten to overwhelm reason with the chaos of the so-called supernatural. The mission that made the Enlightenment, the Age of Reason possible. You have an important role to play. You're to be our interface person, our liaison. A bit later. For now, I wanted you to look at this artifact and feel *the awe*, the sense of *purpose* that . . ." Helman broke off, seeing Koeffel striding urgently toward them: a shaggy-haired, hyper-energetic man in a dirty white shirt, thick, dusty glasses. He waved a small archaeological brush, scowling. "Oh, I say, Helman! I want a word with you!"

"Koeffel is coming," Helman said, half whispering to Loraine. "Do not speak of this to him. He knows some things, but . . . very little about CCA. He is almost useless to us now. We're going into a critical new stage of the process."

But her mind was spinning around what he'd said a few moments before. *"You're to be our interface person. Our liaison."*

What had he meant by that?

And before that . . .

"If it stops working, it just might be that the human world will spin out of control."

Quite suddenly, as Dr. Helman walked away from her to intercept Koeffel, she wanted badly to leave this place.

THAT SAME DAY, BUT far to the south. A park, late afternoon, in Brooklyn.

Bleak and Cronin walking along the path. Muddy was running along ahead of them, barking at a maple tree full of chirping blackbirds.

It was funny, Bleak thought, how small city parks were all pretty much the same, with a few old trees and a worn-out baseball field and whatever the fashion in playground climbing toys was—

but you didn't feel "I've seen too many of those parks" the way you did about Starbucks or McDonald's. Each one had its own life; its own markings, like an old man's face. Like Cronin's face.

"I sometimes say, '*Ach*, this boy is crazy,' to you, Gabriel, but I know what you see is real," Cronin said softly.

Muddy was crouched under the maple tree barking at the birds; hundreds of them sang dissonantly in the tree, some perennial blackbird ritual.

"They used to do that sort of thing, those birds, gathering that way to sing together, in the spring, but nature is all confused now," Cronin said, shading his eyes to look up.

"The time may come," Bleak said, "when I have to tell you more about that world—about the Hidden." As he said "the Hidden," Muddy's barking persistence finally dislodged the birds from the tree, so that the whole black flock wheeled around the park, chirping wildly as it went, before returning, taking up their perches on the maple's branches again.

Cronin chuckled sadly and shook his head. "Soon enough, I'll know all about it. I'm old, and not feeling like I hold to this world too well. People think they would want to live forever, but old age helps give us some . . . some appreciation of death."

Bleak looked at him. "Are you sick? I mean . . . is something . . . ?"

Cronin shrugged. "Nothing special."

Bleak suspected Cronin had chosen those words carefully. *Nothing special.* It wasn't exactly lying.

"Why," Cronin asked, "do you have to tell me more about this Hidden of yours?"

Bleak sighed. "There are things happening—a new opening in the north. Things coming through. Danger coming down. Me, I seem to be right in the middle of it, though I don't know why. And it could affect you. And—something else. A man told me my brother might be alive."

Cronin looked at him with arched brows. "Vut is dis?" His accent reappearing in his startlement.

"He might be a kind of permanent guest of the government. And I don't mean prison. Not exactly."

"I see. I *thought* you were upset." Cronin was articulating his English carefully now. "You seemed worried. You know—I think you sometimes try too hard to hide from that hidden world. You use it—but then you turn your back on it."

Bleak looked at him in surprise. How did Cronin know that? He'd never talked about it that much with him. But he was a shrewd old man.

"But when you get closer to that hidden world—as an old man does"—Cronin shrugged—"you see that things in this world mean less, because they are so temporary. The suffering here is bad, people got to try to help. But to take it too seriously? No. Because this is just between then and *there*. The Hidden, what you call it—that is just where the ghosts live for a while. You said that once, yes? It's not . . . what would you say . . . beyond time?"

"No. It's kind of between time and eternity. It's where this world and the next one overlap, I guess. It stores up life energy—seems like it encourages life to find its way out of matter. The more life there is, the more it can encourage." Bleak shrugged, a little embarrassed at explaining anything to Cronin, who was in many ways far more wise. "That's the impression I always got." Though he'd never again managed to contact the being he'd thought of as Mike the Talking Light, he had spoken to lesser spirits, cogent enough to talk, including one that claimed to be the magician Eliphas Levi. And they had told him some things. "But it's also a kind of warehouse for spirits that aren't sorted out."

"So, for them, this thing, the Hidden, is a waiting room. There is great power there, but it is still a waiting room. The *real thing*, the eternal thing, is what is beyond your Hidden. Think on that eternal thing, Gabe, and you will find the strength to fight anything in this world with so much *yetzer ra*. That is what kept us going in the camps. That, and one another. But always: *this too shall pass*. You read the Greeks—what is it Heraclitus says, about the river—you cannot step into the same one twice. It always changes and flows, Gabe. That makes me thirsty, saying that! Now—shall we get a glass of beer? Enough with the *chutzpadik* from me, talking about such things. I know a bar where they will let Muddy come in. Their beer is not as good as mine, but it is still beer. . . . Do you know, I've been arguing with Lev about beer, he says some is kosher, I say it is all kosher—I don't want to shock him by telling him I am not so concerned with kosher—but he says barley, if it has barley, and I say . . ."

THE FOLLOWING MORNING. In a hotel in lower Manhattan.

Bleak lay in bed, in the small room, not quite awake but aware that he was dreaming. And Isaac Preiss, Cronin's son, was speaking to him. Isaac, who had been killed.

In the dream they were walking a patrol together, down a yellow-dirt track between rows of low clay and stone houses, both wearing Kevlar under their Rangers jackets. They were in a small town in Afghanistan, near the border with Pakistan. Isaac was a compact, dark-eyed man with heavy black brows and, usually, a taut, ironic smile—a smile that Bleak later saw in Cronin. Sergeant Bleak was carrying an M4 carbine assault rifle with grenade launcher; Lieutenant Preiss was carrying an M16A2 5.56 mm rifle: lightweight, air-cooled, gas-operated, magazine fed—simple. A desert-yellow LAV-25 trundled along ahead of them, about fifty feet, the gunner swiveling his M242 25 mm chain MG, and Bleak was thinking that it might be better if the vehicle dropped back to provide more cover, intel had Taliban operating within five miles.

It was a cold day, almost sunless, and when you did see the sun, it was a white, heatless orb screened through cloud. The place smelled of stock animals, a smell that Isaac disliked. But Bleak liked it. He'd made friends with a mule owned by a friendly.

Four other Rangers were on patrol, about thirty yards behind. Isaac outranked Bleak but he liked to walk with him, and talk. Mostly it was Isaac who talked, of his father, his cousin—a pretty girl he thought would be good for Bleak to meet, when they were back in the States—and how what had happened to his dad's family had led him to read about World War II as a kid, which led to his thinking about a military career, which led to this. "And what did my dad want me to do? A German Jew, what do you think? He wanted me to study the arts, or be a doctor, one of the two. My mother was horrified, I can tell you, when I joined. My dad understood better, but . . . And you know, the funny thing is, I think I'd have been happier as a doctor. My mother was right. I can't stand it when my mother is right about something, God bless her yenta soul."

Bleak sensed someone watching him, a little behind and to the right, from a small window. He knew it was a man. The man wasn't a friendly, but that didn't mean he was Taliban.

He looked from the man's point of view, seeing himself walking along, about forty feet away, with Isaac—and he didn't see a gun sight or crosshairs in the point of view. Which was encouraging but didn't prove anything. He switched back to his own point of view and thought, *Still, this'd be a good place for an ambush.*

"That's right," Isaac said, with that dry chuckle of his, "it's the same place the ambush happened. You're reliving it—the part that happens about three minutes before the ambush. Us walking along talking. But I'm changing the conversation. The ambush, see, is what your mind returns to first, when you think about me— and so here we are."

"I'll tell the others, we'll spread out, Isaac—"

"Gabe, you're not listening—*this is a dream.* You *can't* stop the ambush. It happened years ago. You've been tormenting yourself because your gifts enabled you to see behind you, to create fields around you to divert shrapnel from the mortar—"

"That's right, that's it, I remember now, they're going to mortar us. Isaac, we have to call the armor back, we have to—"

Isaac dropped his left hand from his weapon, held it loosely in his other hand. "You see, I'm not even fire-ready, here." He put his hand on Bleak's shoulder. His touch felt real, not like a dream. "It's all right. It's just a dream. Maybe this dream is confusing— but I tried some other ways to contact you, couldn't get through. Trying to call you back, really. You keep calling me to the world of time."

"I'm sorry . . ." Bleak felt as if he might start sobbing. Isaac was dead. He didn't want to start sobbing in front of Isaac and the men. "I didn't mean to draw you back."

"Don't worry about it. You're not doing it consciously."

"What's it like, after . . . I mean—I can see into it. But I can't feel what it's like."

"Can't describe it to someone in the temporal world. It's . . . being outside of time. It's much better outside time, Gabriel, believe me. Here in the stream of time, it's like I have to try to dog-paddle in quicksand, to keep my head up."

"Is it really you? Or a 'dream you,' Isaac?"

"It shouldn't be me? Look, it's me, here I am. We only got about a minute before the ambush and I can't stay here in your dream long. I got to get to the point! First, Gabriel, stop blaming yourself . . . for being yourself. You were issued your gifts by the supreme being, so keep them oiled and use them when under fire. Second, tell my dad I'm okay. He's gotten so he doesn't doubt you anymore, he's ready to listen. Third, I'm not permitted to tell you certain things directly, because you might misunderstand and go the wrong direction . . . but I can tell you that your friend is your enemy and your enemy is your friend and love is part of the whole mixture."

"Do you know anything about my brother? What's going on, Isaac? Is he alive? Why are they—"

"Listen—yeah, he's alive, and that was the fourth point, you are in way over your head. There's a thing whose name I don't even want to mention. It's broken through, and your brother is—oh, shit, I took too long, there's no time—or there's too much time—I can't hang on, Gabe—"

A familiar whine, a whistle, warning yells from behind, and Bleak instinctively reached out with his energy field, formed a shield just in time—then the mortar struck and the shrapnel that would have hit an ordinary man spun past him, but he still caught a lot of the shock wave and was thrown against the back wall of the nearest house, bounced to fall on his right side, lying on the ground with his head ringing, and heard the familiar deep-toned chatter of a Kalashnikov. He looked up and saw Isaac, Cronin's son, spinning around, the Kevlar holding, but shrapnel had sliced right through his neck, releasing a jet of dark red. Bleak forced himself to stand, glimpsed bits of Isaac's spine . . . caught the smell of his blood . . .

"Isaac!"

Bleak sat bolt upright, shaking, shouting the name of Cronin's son.

And was back in the hotel room. Fully awake now. Glad to be away from that place. Relieved. And ashamed of the relief. All but one other guy in the foot patrol died that day, killed by mortar strikes and small-arms fire.

Bleak had caught a mujahadeen running with a Kalashnikov—and Bleak shot him dead, no hesitation. Shouting about Isaac, though this man hadn't likely killed Isaac himself, he had no mortar. Bleak had started to walk away. Then someone ran from the nearest house, running up to the dead man, yelling in grief and firing a carbine wildly, one bullet creasing Bleak's side. And Bleak had shot him down too—right through the head. And a moment later he realized the second one was a teenager, probably the dead man's son.

And Bleak had felt ashamed . . . that he felt nothing much about killing the kid.

Then he'd just turned away and headed through the dirt alley, tried to catch the mortarman—and never found him. The LAV-25 found two other Taliban sniping on a roof and shot them to pieces. The house with them.

Bleak had found what was left of his men—three of them ripped up by a direct mortar hit. Mostly just lumps of oozing flesh.

Get up, he ordered himself. *Get the hell out of bed and do something else. And do not have a drink. Don't go back to starting the day drinking.*

Hands still shaking, Bleak got dressed, drank metallic-tasting water from the tap, and went down to buy a street phone.

They were stolen cell phones, usually. But no one would know to listen in to him, on that line, if he used a random cell phone, and he needed to make some calls. He had to earn money. He had to keep busy.

Drinking Turkish coffee at a table near the window, in Ataturk's Coffee Shop on the corner of Avenue B, eating a gooey baklava, blinking in the morning sunlight coming through the flyspecked window . . . Bleak tried to remember the dream. Tried to decide . . .

"First, stop blaming yourself for being yourself. You were issued your gifts by the supreme being, so keep them oiled and use them when under fire. Second, tell my dad I'm okay. He's gotten so he doesn't doubt you anymore, he's ready to listen. Third, I'm not permitted to tell you certain things directly . . . but I can tell you that

your friend is your enemy and your enemy is your friend and love is part of the whole mixture."

Was it just himself talking to himself? Was that just dream psychology—or real advice? Or had it been, actually, Isaac Preiss?

A kind of *taste*, a scentless scent, a feel, went with encountering one of the spirits of the dead in this world. When he thought about it, yeah, that taste had been there. And it had all been too rational, too clearly articulated, to be like a mere dream.

So it had really been Isaac. What had he meant about his brother? About Sean?

"Hey, yo, blood, you wanta buya cell phone?"

Bleak looked up at the tall, skinny black guy in a threadbare New York Knicks fan jersey. He was twitchy, missing a front tooth, had tweak marks on his face and arms, and his eyes were going yellow. Alternating, once a second, between smiling and frowning.

Bleak surprised him by saying, "Yeah—I do wanta buy a cell phone."

"Uh—that right? Forty dollar."

"Ten."

"Thirty."

"Fifteen."

"Twenty lowest I go."

Bleak took a twenty out of a coat pocket, held it up with one hand, kept a grip on it, extending the empty hand. The turfy slapped a small cell phone in Bleak's palm and took the twenty. "You want anything else, chief? I can get you rocks, I can get you yella bag—"

"No, thanks, bro. This cell phone better work, though."

"Worked a minute ago, I was using it all morning. Try it, I stay right here."

Bleak was tempted to try it by calling Wendy. He was lonely;

still feeling hollow, after the dream. He wanted the kind of comfort a woman could offer. She might still be at that number in Queens—maybe she'd digested what had happened by now. But she was probably asleep at this hour. She was a stripper, during the summer; wouldn't be up early.

A stripper with a BA in English, going for her master's. Sexy, good conversation. But he'd spooked her. She'd talked as if she was just fascinated with the supernatural, till he'd exposed her channeler as a charlatan. Wendy hadn't minded that so much, really—it was when he'd said, "You want to see something from the other world . . ." He'd reached into the Hidden—and infused the ghost of a little boy with enough energy that she could see it herself. That had scared her. She'd accused him of dosing her drink. They'd parted uneasily.

Should have known better . . .

He'd never really felt close, really close, to any woman. Intimate, yes, up to a point—but never deeply bonded. Never united. Something was always missing. Something he couldn't quite identify. Just the "it's not her, either" feeling. She was never quite the right one . . . as if he was comparing her to someone he'd never met.

Waste of time to call Wendy. Or any other woman. *Business.* He had a number written down for the Second Chance Bail Bonds outfit that had offered him work. If he was careful, maybe he could get paid without the CCA tracing him. The hot cell phone was the first step.

"You gonna try that phone? I got to go." The turfy was fingering the twenty.

"Hold on. Gonna test it." Bleak called Cronin. The phone was ringing. "Yeah, seems to be working, see you later."

"Hey, yo, blood, you sure you don't want—"

"I'm sure. I don't want to end up selling stolen cell phones on fucking Avenue B, man. Now do yourself a favor and fuck off." And Bleak gave the guy a look that drove him out the door.

"*Ja,* hello?"

"Cronin? It's me. On a phone that should be . . . never mind. You okay? How's Muddy?"

"We're okay. Big thing, you contacting me two days in a row. So? There's something? I'm an old man, I got to pee every two seconds. Can't stay on this phone."

"I won't keep you, I just . . ." Should he really tell him about Isaac? "I wanted to tell you this in person but . . . I don't think I should come around now, until all this . . . stuff . . . is cleared up."

"Tell me what, Gabe?"

"That . . . I had a dream about Isaac. He said to tell you he was okay."

A long silence. "*Ja.* Well. A dream is a dream."

"Not all dreams are just dreams," Bleak said gently.

"Well. Maybe. I got to . . . You're sure? That it was him?"

"I really am. I'm sure."

"You don't try to make a fool of an old man?"

"You think I would?"

"No. Maybe it was a dream, maybe not. But, Gabe—thank you. I know, you maybe don't feel sure you should tell me this. But it's a mitzvah, what you try to do. It's a mitzvah that you try."

"I'll let you go. Give Muddy a hug for me." Bleak cut the connection—and hoped he'd done the right thing.

He got the paper from his pocket and called the bail bonds company. And wondered if calling them was the stupidest thing he'd done all year.

Somewhere overhead, a chopper drummed on the sky.

SAME DAY. NOT MUCH LATER. Sitting in a police station.

"What I get for doing you this favor?" Detective Roseland asked, leaning back in a chair, looking across his desk at Bleak.

"Get?" Bleak mugged surprise. "You owe me!"

"I do? Then maybe I'll buy you a bottle of scotch, or a call girl. Might be safer than doing informational favors for a fucking bounty hunter." Detective Nathan "Rosie" Roseland was about six inches taller than Bleak, a freckled, red-haired plainclothes cop with a prominent nose and small blue eyes and a quirky little mouth. And with big hands that could knock a man flat or exert a precise pressure on a trigger.

"Booze *or* a call girl? What if I want both?"

"It's either-or, you greedy bastard."

"Why is it cops always want to make everything right with a bottle of booze or a hooker?"

"Tends to work. A lot of guys like that superexpensive single malt now. Also we drop charges and fix tickets *if* you can get us a good seat at the Super Bowl."

"I don't need to get you tickets to any-fucking-thing. You owe me."

"Don't keep saying that. What do I owe you for?" A small smile flickered on Roseland's face, as they went through all this. He was enjoying himself.

Bleak found that little smile reassuring. CCA didn't usually work through the cops—and he didn't think an APB was out on him. Not yet. He could tell that Roseland wasn't worried about maybe having to arrest an old friend.

Roseland went on, "I'm supposed to be grateful because you gave me that lunatic from Tonga? He almost killed me, taking him in. Shot me right above the groin, under my fucking vest. Missed the important bits but still . . . it was a major drag."

"That was a big collar for you, Rosie."

"You couldn't get the money from the bondsman on that Tongan guy anyway, be honest."

"Sure I could. Eventually."

They were sitting in Sergeant Roseland's mostly glass booth, a paper-strewn corner office, in a busy Midtown precinct. There was barely enough room for the two of them and the desk between them. Roseland had closed the door because he never knew what Bleak might say and because they'd made some borderline shady deals before. They knew each other from the army; from boot camp, and Rangers school, and then from the VA hospital, after. Roseland had been in Kurdistan; he'd lost a foot to an IED. His new right foot was a pretty efficient microchipped prosthetic. Bleak's wounds had been light—wounds hadn't got Bleak out of the Army. Punching out a second lieutenant had done that. The son of a bitch had held back on the intel that might've saved them from that ambush. Maybe at the behest of a certain Drake Zweig.

"So is it in the backpack, there?" Roseland asked.

Bleak nodded, taking out Coster's empty rum bottle, lifting it out with an index finger inside the opening so he wouldn't smear the outside. He held it up to a table lamp. "See the print, on the rum bottle there? I think that's from the last person to handle it. Guy said his name was Coster. A skid-row lush, currently. Might have a more impressive résumé somewhere in his background."

"Could get me in trouble. And don't say 'you owe me' again. How's Preiss's dad doing?" They'd met Preiss in Rangers' training, after boot camp.

"He's not bad, Rosie. He went through Belsen in the war, as a kid. What's Brooklyn gonna do to him?"

"You'd be surprised. Okay, I'll run this. . . . You want to wait? Might be able to get it lifted quick if my girl Bethany's in the lab."

Bleak waited, alone in Roseland's office. Trying not to wonder if the CCA knew about his connection to Roseland. *Yeah, I got him right here. I'll stall him till you come.*

Paranoia. He'd known Roseland a long time. He didn't think Rosie would play ball with the feds, not on this. Unless he'd been secretly briefed, Roseland didn't know about the CCA nor about Bleak's special abilities—even if he did, Roseland wouldn't hold it against him. He figured Rosie would give him a heads-up, some way. And the detective wasn't keeping anything from him. Bleak usually knew when someone was lying to him. He had the Hidden on his side, an all-pervasive lie detector.

He'd had mixed feelings about Coster, though. Like, the rummy was lying and he wasn't . . . all at once.

"*I didn't kill none of them women.*" A man's voice, speaking to Bleak, coming right out of the air.

Bleak grimaced, recognizing the feeling that came with hearing a ghost. He didn't even turn around. "It's too late to do anything about it," Bleak said, not looking. "You should move on. Head right for the big tunnel, don't pass Go, don't collect two hundred dollars, just go right into the light. It's way too late for anything else."

"*Oh, I know it's too late, pretty much, to save me in this world,*" the ghost said. "*Seeing as I'm dead now.*"

Surprised at hearing common sense from a ghost, Bleak turned around. He could see a man standing in the glass of the office window-wall—it bisected him right down the middle. As if the front half of him were pasted to the glass. He was a chunky, balding white man with a heavy forehead, a crooked nose, a slightly disfigured jaw. U.S. army tattoo on the back of his left hand. He was wearing gray repairman's coveralls, with GREG and ALL BOROUGHS APPLIANCE REPAIRS sewn on the left breast pocket.

"Glad you can hear me," the ghost said. His voice had lost enough of that odd, distant resonance that ghosts usually have that he sounded as if he were just another person talking. "I thought maybe you might. You have the aura of one of those talented people. Hard to find. I went to a bunch of mediums, but they were all fakes. When I find the real deal, they're always too busy to talk to me. So I was trying to get right into it, see. Get you to listen. And here we are, havin' a chin-wag."

"Greg, is it?" Bleak knew he shouldn't be having this conversation. Someone could see him through the windows of the office, talking to no one visible. For a while he'd worn a Bluetooth earpiece, one that didn't actually work, so if he spoke to "no one" in public it looked as if he were talking on a phone. Lots of people around nowadays looked as if they were talking to imaginary people. But he'd left the Bluetooth on his boat. Still, Bleak was bored with waiting and curious about the cogency of this ghost.

"Yeah, Greg Berne," the ghost said. "Spelled *B-e-r-n-e*. You see what they did to my face? Sergeant Chancel beat me up with a nightstick, busted my nose and jaw. Said I tried to jump him in the interrogation room. But it was to get me to confess. Then he bandaged me up and called in the steno lady and said, 'What do you have to say now?' and he was playing with that club, kind of tossing it hand to hand, so what was I gonna do? I figured I could confess and take it back later. But it got in the papers and my wife left me, and my kids wouldn't come to see me on visitors' day. And I got real depressed—always had a hard time with depression anyway—and I hung myself in my cell. Seemed to take forever to strangle with that sheet. Thought I was going to hell, when it was over. But it was just a precinct in Midtown."

"Sergeant Chancel, you said? I've met him," Bleak murmured, thinking. "He's still with NYPD. Why would he do that? They're not usually like that. They're no saints, but—" Bleak shook his head. "They don't pull that rubber-hose stuff much."

"Someone was paying him, is why. I think it was the old man of the guy who killed them ladies. See, I wasn't the only one who went to those houses where they died—there was another suspect, this kid that was doing one of those Mormon walk-around things. Out in Queens, where I had those two assignments. Should never have gone out to Queens. Should know better. Anyway, I figure he'd be going on this Mormon door-to-door, and he'd see these ladies and come back later alone. They placed him at one of the houses. So the cops questioned him. But . . . they focused on me."

"How'd you get picked up?"

"See, I was in two of those houses. Where the women were killed. The company sent me to do warranty repairs on dishwashers in that neighborhood, right? I was seen out there fixin' dishwashers not that long before them ladies were strangled. Tied up and raped. The guy used a condom and they found one, but it never got to evidence. Nobody never tested my DNA or his. I had an idiot for a lawyer. Anyway I didn't know about the condom till after I was dead, I heard somebody asking about it in evidence. Making a joke or something about this thing that coulda saved my life."

Bleak snorted. "You are one glib goddamn ghost. Mostly they're like broken records. You know, if a ghost can think for himself, it means his soul's been reincarnated in the right direction a few times. He's got some good spirit stuff going on. You'd do well in the next world. You should just move on, man."

"But my family still thinks I murdered two women! They think I'm a pervert! I don't want my kids thinking that . . . I keep trying to get someone to listen."

"I can't help you," Bleak said, hoping he sounded firm about it. "Not my wheelhouse, pardner. But, uh . . ." He shrugged. "What was the name of the other suspect?"

"Kyle Braithwaite. College student. His dad is a rich guy, big shot at some Mormon temple out in the boroughs. One of those deals got the angel with the trumpet on the roof."

"I see you got the tattoo."

"Infantry, late in the 'Nam. Just a kid then."

Bleak growled to himself. *Oh, hell.* "I was army too. Sergeant. If I ever hear of anything that could restart the case, I'll pass it on, but honestly, man, it's not very likely, and you'd be better off if you'd just move on, outside time, and—"

He broke off when the door opened and Roseland came in,

looking at him curiously. The ghost backed through the wall, waving good-bye, and was gone.

Bleak was sitting sideways to the door so he put a hand to the ear Roseland couldn't see and said, "Gotta go, talk to you soon, man." He pretended to take a Bluetooth out and put it in his pocket.

"Sitting in my office, chattering away, doing business, probably getting into my booze," Roseland said, sitting down and dropping a folder on the desk.

"I didn't know there was booze in here or I would've. You do the search already?"

"She was between print searches. I got her to lift it and run it right away." He grinned. "I may not look like much but the ladies—they like me."

"Yeah? I bet you said, 'You owe me.'"

"Nah, now I owe her. And she's gonna take it outta my hide too. I know that woman." Roseland opened the folder. "She'll drain me dry. Here's your man, name's Coster all right. Emmerich Coster. He's got clearance for all kinds of things. Seems like he was a former spook because he's got clearance for CIA and . . . some agency they say is so classified they don't even give its name." He shrugged and tossed over the folder.

CCA, Bleak thought, looking over the papers, frowning. A little military service, military intelligence early on. "Marines? Guy drinks like a jarhead, all right."

Roseland laughed. "Don't let my captain hear you say that. You notice there isn't much there about him . . . just the bare essentials. Not much use to you."

"Actually—it's what I wanted to know."

So Coster really did have clearance. Really did have major intel background. So maybe he had been inside at CCA. And maybe Sean was really there.

"Are we even?" Roseland asked, as Bleak took the papers, folded them, stuck them in his little backpack, and stood up.

"Almost." Bleak slung the pack over one shoulder. "I still want the scotch."

"You fuck!"

"Hey—you know a sarge in the department named Chancel?"

The amusement dropped out of Roseland's face. He sighed. "Yeah. A real piece of work. One of those guys who likes to stick broomsticks up people. Probably on the take too. Why?"

"You remember a case about an accused named Greg Berne? Hung himself in your holding?"

Roseland winced. "Too fucking well. What a mess. I guess he saved the state some money though."

"Any thought he might not have been guilty?"

Roseland leaned back in his chair, looked carefully expressionless. "Maybe. Some."

"There a condom with the evidence? A used one, with semen . . . that was never tested?"

"Not that I heard."

"I heard there was. And it wasn't DNA-tested against the other suspect. Kid named Braithwaite."

"You heard that? Where?"

"Uhhhh . . . rumor?"

"Bullshit. Who told you this?"

"I already said, Rosie. Rumor."

"Yeah? Well, it's a cold case. And I don't need enemies. And he's dead anyway."

"It's not that cold. And if the guy that hung himself was innocent—the real asshole is still out there. Anybody been strangled lately?"

"Nah. Come on, Gabe—what's this about?"

"Just heard something. A ghostly little rumor, pard. Talk to you later. And, Rosie—I'll buy the scotch."

Bleak waved good-bye and left before Roseland could ask any-more questions.

Outside, the day was getting hot. Bleak flagged down a yellow cab, took it to the Brooklyn Bridge.

Breezier there, as he walked out on the bridge. He looked down at the water, listened to children laughing as they ran past on the walkway. A cooling wind sang in the steel beams, drew sweat from his forehead.

The cell phone in his pants pocket chimed and shivered against him. He felt a sympathetic shiver—he shouldn't be getting any calls on it, right now. He answered the phone, out of sheer curiosity. "Yeah?"

"Hello?" A boy's voice, maybe a teenager, Hispanic accent. "Is Lupe there?"

"No, this is the guy who bought Lupe's phone. Probably from the guy who stole it."

"Oh, yeah?"

"Yeah—I'm gonna use it a couple times real quick, and then toss it, so when you see Lupe, tell her to have it switched off. Surprising she didn't get to it yet."

"She probably thinks it's in her school locker."

Bleak hung up, and called Shoella. She answered after one ring. "I feel that's our man Bleak calling."

"Shoella—Coster was from the feds, all right, at least in the past."

"You found out? I tried to find out my way, but the ancestors, everyone is blocked out on him—"

"I don't trust him. I'm gonna get out of town but I need some money. I've got a job lined up. When I bring in the skip, I want to send the money to your account, so I can do this without the CCA being all over me. I'll get the money later. You can keep twenty percent."

"I will handle the money for you, and I don't need your twenty percent. You sure your phone is okay?"

"Unless they've identified you."

"No. I have used much power to keep me safe from their eyes. They cannot see me, *cher* darlin'. You do your job, have them send the money to me—and come to me, I will give you your money. They don't know who I am."

Bleak wasn't so sure. But he needed money. He'd take the risk.

He made his other call, to Vince at Second Chance Bail Bonds, then he dropped the phone off the Brooklyn Bridge, into the dark green water far below.

CHAPTER

TEN

Early evening, the same day. On a military transport plane flying over Maine, heading to Long Island.

The big C-119D was noisy and uncomfortable, not even designed for passengers. *I'm freight*, Loraine mused, looking up from her laptop. The plane was mostly used to move armored hydrogen Humvees and small artillery pieces, but the metal floor had grooves where seat supports could be inserted, and seats had been fixed in place, in the echoing whale's belly of the transport; Loraine sat in the front, with a view of the cockpit, the open door showing the two AF pilots, the cloud-mist streaming over the windshield.

She was tired. The plane was drafty and smelled of jet fuel; the trip to the Arctic had tired her out; the revelations on the trip too were a kind of burden to carry. Information that changed the world had a weight of its own. She kept seeing the artifact, in her mind's eye. Dr. Helman had claimed it was all that stood between humanity and chaos.

Helman was sitting on her right, frowningly tapping at a laptop, now and then bobbling his head to himself. On her own laptop she was reviewing the personnel file of a female agent just transferred in, Teresa Caffee; she was supposed to check Caffee out and sign off on her. Any woman was welcome on the team, as far as Loraine was concerned. Only one other woman agent in CCA, in the Washington offices.

She had another window open on the laptop, and she restlessly went back to that page now, to reread a passage from Newton's *Cryptojournal* that Helman had copied to her. The journal had been written in code, which decrypted into Latin, a language Newton sometimes used for scientific treatises; the cryptographer had rendered the Latin into modern English:

> *Those of us who twine the cross with the rose have long kept accounts, books of the damned, where is written what could not happen and yet did. Much is mere fancy, and superstition. Witches said to be witches are rarely witches. But in the secret corners of the Hidden Earth, magic bloats like a Plague blister, and many of the legends of the past were not legend. Visitors from the Farther Place now penetrate freely; fairies and the less fair are nightly upon us. Now we see events conspire to an increase, and swarms will rise from the darkness. Powers come upon those with the Blood; some diabolic, some angelic, but none have a place in the new world of men. If God did not want us to contain this chaos, He would not have given us the means: the artifact of the ancients, which Solomon knew, and to which he added his Seals. But it is older than Solomon; it is older than the pyramids. And the [diagrams?] on the Sarmunna [or, Sarmoung] sheepskin tell us how to set about repairing, recommenc-*

ing its Wall of Force, so that the world is the world of the
mind and not of the heart's darkest impulses.

Loraine shivered and closed the excerpt and went back to the
personnel file, determined to put it out of her mind for a time.
Personnel was busywork, but she was glad to have it. Glad to think
about anything but the artifact, for a time; anything but the heart's
darkest impulses.

Someone came swaying up from the rear of the aircraft, gripping the backs of a seat to keep his footing in the turbulence:
Drake Zweig, in his tight gray suit, tight gray smile on his lipless
mouth. Vigorously rubbing his nose, he stood in front of his assigned seating, to the left of her, then let the plane's motion dump
him into the seat. "Slam dunk!" he said, grinning at her.

She winced. The phrase *slam dunk* was not pleasant to people
working in the American intelligence community.

He buckled himself in, irritating her by leaning over, glancing at her laptop. "You know that pisser back there, it's smaller
than the ones the airlines got. Didn't think they could be made
smaller."

"Uh-huh." She tapped at the laptop, making notes on Agent
Caffee, hoping Zweig would give up talking to her.

"That the file on the new agent?" Zweig asked, craning closer.
"Yeah, she worked with some guy who telepaths with dogs and cats,
for Christ's sake, how useful is that? But I bet you're glad to have
another woman in the agency. Funny there aren't that many—but
then again it figures, what with Forsythe having an attitude."

Loraine glanced at him. "Which attitude?"

"Oh, he doesn't like female agents. Just thinks they're
too . . . they get too emotionally involved. Not coolheaded
enough. Got to be chill-chill-chill, like my kid says, to be able to,
you know, do the necessary."

"You've got children?" She hadn't known that.

Sadness drew over his face like a shade drawn over a bright window. "Yeah. Haven't seen the boy in a while. He kind of flaked out on the family, second he turned eighteen. . . . Anyway"—eager to change the subject—"old Forsythe surprised me, bringing you in. But then maybe it's because of you and that Bleak guy he prizes so much. The whole lure concept . . . I dunno why Bleak's such a big deal. I worked around him along the Pakistan border. Half the time he went out, he'd be the only one to come back. What's that about? Well, maybe not half the time, but still . . . And then he was always giving me shit about my intel sources: 'Not reliable, we could be hurting civilians.' Like that was *his* job. Not a company man, let me tell you. Thinking he could be relied on to work with Sean—"

"Wait—Drake, what did you say about a lure concept? You mean *me*? I'm the—"

"Zweig!" Helman snapped warningly, leaning forward to glare over at Zweig. "You're violating need-to-know."

"Hey, I wasn't going to say anything else." Zweig spread his hands as if to say, *All right, whatever!* And turned his back to Loraine, putting his seat back a little, as if to take a nap, grumbling, "They don't give us any goddamned blankets, even, on these transports. Rather pay my own way and go on a regular commercial flight."

Lure? Loraine thought about demanding to know what that was about. Then decided that this wasn't the time. She'd talk to Helman alone.

"Loraine," Helman said softly. "I have something I'd like you to review. Quite another sort of journal entry."

He handed her a flash stick. "Just insert that into your laptop. The top file in the list . . . I'd just like you apprised. It'll come clearer later. Or perhaps it's not relevant. To tell you the truth I'm not sure. But I wanted one other set of eyes on it. It's from the general's report of his attempt to . . . to reach out to the Wilderness . . . to the Other Side . . . to gain us, well, allies, amongst UBEs. This was done right before we started to see certain manifestations, like the Gulcher case, not long ago. It's not an accident . . . I mean, what happened to Gulcher and . . . this."

Puzzled by his manner—a feeling that he was taking a chance, showing this to her even as he'd warned Zweig not to step outside need-to-know parameters—she clicked the wafer-thin flash stick into her laptop and opened the file.

> CCA EXPERIMENT #351, NOTES
> *This is the seventeenth day in my attempts to use ritual magic to contact the Great Powers beyond the Wall of Force. Admittedly experiments of this nature are controversial in the agency. Erlich and Swanson (increasingly a liability, those two) would have us focus on narrowing the gap in the Wall, and controlling those already activated by the increase in AS energies. But suppose we cannot repair the artifact? We must deal with the new reality, and to that end we will need allies. A threat may become an asset, if we learn to control it.*
>
> *In the course of #E351 I have taken the advice, and some of the formulations, of Eliphas Levi: I have fasted and meditated and honed my mind to single-pointed focus on the summoning. This is how magicians in the past have penetrated Newton's Wall of Force. It can be done, if only passingly. It is like a weak radio signal, coming through the static. But even a weak signal can call a gunship, and a gunship is what we need if we are to overcome our enemies. Today, in Room 32, I felt the sigils as if the insignia, the names, were all coming alive, like creatures in themselves, like that Kabbalistic idea of letters as living things. The ritual markings were glowing and moving*

about and I saw a distant place in my mind's eye. Is the stress, my admittedly obsessive focus, making me imagine things? It's not impossible! But I don't think so.

[Another entry, the following day.]

Eureka! I have seen, I have communicated, I have touched the Great Wrath from Outside, the lord of the Wilderness! In contact with it, I have understood it! We see and think in three dimensions. The fourth-dimensional reality of a UBE is not completely comprehensible to us. But growing up in South Florida, I saw creatures living in lagoons, that also lived outside them, and this is something of that kind: the lagoon is its world; the atmosphere is ours. It can extend part of itself into our world; it can reach through the rift, without quite being here in fullness. It can influence things here. It can send its own version of what, in this world, we call familiars; "independent pseudopods" Dr H calls them, or Formless Familiars; and till now they're theory. But some have been released into our world this day, as a result of my contact with the Great Wrath. It has reached out to our world and we will see those human beings who are congruent with its nature light up with its force. I myself have seen the Great Power reaching for me. I seem to see a circle within a circle, and in that circle is an eye that extends itself, an eye that elongates to contact my forebrain. I drew back, instinctively, in the course of E351 but this time, today, I will not draw back, I will give It access, so that I can learn Its ways, as the Seminole Indians once did with animal spirits. I will be Its means of knowing this world, and in the course of Its knowing, I will know It in turn. Already I have identified It, have learned the name It was called by the ancients:

Moloch!

At first, a giant with the red-eyed head of a bull and a man's body, but all made of hot brass. When I saw him, I heard a slow-thudding drumbeat, and infants screaming in pain, as Moloch reached for me.

And then I saw into him, past the shell imagined by men. I saw his truer form, another being, the single yellow eye within many mouths, mouths that turn one within the next, wheels in wheels.

[The following day's entry had only two lines.]

CCA EXPERIMENT #352, NOTES

Today I am redefined . . . !

That was the end of the file.

"The phrase 'today I am redefined,'" Helman said, just loud enough for her to hear over the background grumbling of the big jet. "It puzzles me—what do you think it means? You've read widely in the occult."

Loraine shrugged. "Hard to say. Makes me think of writing by some of the gnostics. Both notes have that, um, apocalyptic tone. Visionary."

"I see. Well. Probably not a matter for concern." Helman glanced over at Zweig, then leaned a little closer to her. "Close the file. Read the second file, on Troy Gulcher. And then—when you've done that—please give me the flash drive back. Do not save these files to your computer . . . and discuss this with no one else."

Helman didn't say another word on the trip to Long Island. Loraine watched him from the corner of her eye as he took an orange out of his pocket and incised the peel with one extralong thumbnail, exactingly removing it in an unbroken spiral. Then he frowningly ate the orange, section by section, without spilling a drop of juice. Seeming, to Loraine, haunted by something he couldn't quite bring himself to say.

ABOUT THAT TIME, the same evening, Atlantic City.

Gulcher was getting thoroughly sick of the casino. He was even sick of this claustrophobic little room, though it contained ever-growing stacks of money. Jock wanted to pile a van high with that money and just take off. Sooner or later the Baronis' people would come around.

But the whisperer didn't want Gulcher to leave Lucky Lou's Atlantic City Casino.

"Not yet," the whisperer had said to him, last night. *"You're needed right here. To focus through. The Great Power hasn't fed enough yet. Still hungry. We will go to other casinos and take those over too; in other parts of the world. Las Vegas. Europe. All be yours, you wait for it."*

He wasn't going to admit he was scared of the whisperer. And Moloch. But how did you argue with a thing like Moloch — or his whisperer? And Moloch was the only reason he wasn't in prison. But he was going stir-crazy in this place.

"Jock," he said, staring at the piles of money in the counting room, "I can't believe I'm bored with this money, here."

Jock leaned on a table stacked with cash, grinning. He was fucked-up again, looked like. "I'm not bored with it. Sure would like to take it with me though." He reached past the two Chinese guys and took a big, sealed stack of twenties. Tossed it up and caught it.

When would they be able to get out of here? Gulcher tried to call the whisperer, to ask, get some kind of answer. But there was no reply. Hadn't been able to get a response since last night.

"Whisperer," he muttered. "You there?"

Maybe it was gone. Maybe he was free of it. And maybe that was a good thing.

"Boss?" A voice from the air.

Not the whisperer. The whisperer definitely didn't think of Gulcher as "boss." Which worried Gulcher. No, it was Stedley talking on the intercom.

"I hear you, Stedley, what's up?"

"There's federal agents all around the damn place. Surrounding the casino. FBI, ATF, all kinds of guys. State troopers too, did I mention that?"

"Okay—" Gulcher's mouth was dry but he was almost glad. "Don't do nothing yet."

"What do you mean, 'Okay, don't do nothing'?" Jock demanded, throwing the money on the table. His eyes were suddenly wild and he was breathing hard. The bonhomie was gone; the paranoia was back. "You bring these guys here? You tradin' me for some deal, that the idea?"

"Cut that tweaky shit out, Jock, goddammit, and get upstairs and help Stedley. You forget we got the whisperer. What happened is obvious. Those greaser Baroni fucks went missing and they musta told somebody where they were going and somebody infiltrated the place, checked it out. Probably ID'd me. But we got the power to turn their little minds around, all right? Now cool your fucking jets."

Jock was gaping at him, his eyes pinned, but Gulcher just walked away from him, went out to the elevator.

Just before the doors closed, Jock caught up and shoved his way into the elevator, breathing hard.

"Right, okay, we're gonna handle this," Jock muttered, his eyes darting around.

"Goddammit, Jock." Gulcher just shook his head. "Just be quiet . . . I got to contact."

He closed his eyes. Felt the whisperer there. And no response when he called out to it, inside. It had gone into a sullen silence on him.

"What the fuck?" he muttered, as the doors to the elevator opened. He and Jock stepped out into the main poker room: a cavernous space with rows of green felt card tables. All of the tables empty, no players. Stacks of chips still sitting on the felt, in front of the seats. The big television screens over the room showed ESPN, a horse race, and—the front of Lucky Lou's Atlantic City Casino: a newsbreak shot showing rings of cop cars, staties mostly, some vans Gulcher associated with the FBI, all around the casino. And there were the FBI agents, with their cute little jackets and the letters FBI real big across the back. Lots of guns out there too.

"Oh, fuck, Troy," Jock breathed, gaping up at the screen.

He darted frantic looks around the empty room. The rows of slots chattered and buzzed and dinged from the next room, but they could see through the open doors that no one was playing them. "They already got the players out—so that means—"

"Means we're already here," said a man, in an Air Force general's uniform, crossing over to them. His hands were held up as if he were surrendering.

The general was a medium-small guy, with a lot of ribbons on his chest; middle-aged, smiling slightly. He didn't look scared at all. "If you have guns, please don't fire 'em." He had a mild Southern accent, Georgia or Florida. "Look beyond me—you see the sharpshooters, there, among the slot machines?" He paused, half turned, nodded toward the men behind him.

The FBI sharpshooters, four that Gulcher could see, were stepping out into sight—in partial cover from the slot machines. They stood just inside the slot aisles, rifle barrels resting on the warbling, flashing machines, getting a bead on Gulcher and Jock.

"Where's Stedley?" Gulcher asked, for something to say.

Stalling while he tried to contact the whisperer again.

The general lowered his hands, walked slowly, carefully toward them. "Oh, poor, confused Stedley is under arrest. We took him out of the building and the influence he was under simply passed from him. Last thing he remembers is the mornin' you showed up. There was a riot, he says, and then—he woke on up out there, in our custody." The general stopped just out of Gulcher's reach. Clasped his hands in front of him. Smiled gently.

"Yeah, well . . . what do you people want?" Gulcher asked, still stalling. "I got a casino to run, here. We're losing money with this interruption. You got a warrant or what?"

Mentally calling, *Whisperer . . . Moloch . . .*

"Yes, we have a warrant, Mr. Gulcher."

"Oh, shit," Jock said. "Troy—they—"

"Shut up, Jock. Okay, so you think you've ID'd me, General Whosis," Gulcher said.

Whisperer . . . Moloch . . . Need you to step in, this time . . . you there?

"We know exactly who you are, you and your friend here. As for my name, I am General Allan Roger Forsythe. That is, anyway, how I used to be known. And how most people know me. You, sir, you made your mistake when you snuffed out the Baronis. They were part of a big organization. His people knew they were last seen here. And Mr. Baroni's son was smarter than you think. He got a picture of you with his cell phone, sent it to his people, with a little text message: 'Who the fuck is this guy?' Beard and all, one of them recognized you from the news reports. They thought if they bulled in, you'd shoot their bosses—though I expect you've done that already. What did they do, these professional criminals? They called the police! Just one of those little ironies that make life so darn interestin'. Now, the police, they are under instruction to inform all federal agencies if they run across you. And those agencies are under instruction to inform the CCA. We were duly informed—and here we are."

"And what the fuck is the CCA?" Gulcher was aware that Jock was breathing hard, through his mouth.

"I'd rather not explain it all right here. Most of the young men behind me have never heard of it. Maybe none of them have. It's a very special offshoot of our special branches. But believe me—if you come along with me—"

Whisperer . . . Moloch . . .

Forsythe's smile broadened yet somehow became colder. His voice softened. "That won't work, Mr. Gulcher. What you're trying to do."

Gulcher stared. "What'd you say—what I'm trying to do?"

"You called to Moloch," the general said, with unruffled confidence. "I heard you." He smoothed his hair, looking around at the empty poker tables as he spoke. "The Gulcher cat was out of the bag when you killed those men and that image was sent, so . . . the Great Wraith decided to let us take you now. He has ingested a great deal of what he came here for. There was to be *more*, but . . . the timetable too is an issue. Things outside your sphere of awareness have shifted, just this morning—it's been decided he will use you in a different context. Essentially—he sent me to pick you up." The general put his hands in his pockets, rocked casually on his heels as he went on thoughtfully, "I use 'he' because that's how *you* think of the Great Wrath. In fact that entity has no definite gender. Some people see Moloch as a female . . . but Moloch is not so limited."

"Jesus, Troy," Jock breathed, an hysterical whine in his voice. "Oh, Jesus and Mary, they're all around us and now they're in our heads, they can read our minds!"

"What the fuck *are* you?" Gulcher demanded, glowering at the general.

"I am someone without your talents—but with a special relationship to one of the Great Wrath's servants. His benign promise is . . . within me. Always. You are not to mention that, within the confines of the CCA. We don't control everyone there, hence not everyone at the authority can be trusted. Now—the one you call the whisperer has conveyed the Great Wrath's decision. You are to join me. To join forces with us. No longer a loose cannon, but a cannon—lashed to our ship. What do you say to that?"

"I say—"

"I say *fuck you!*" Jock shouted suddenly, the words accompanied by spittle. "*Whatever* the fuck you are!" He reached into his coat, just barely got the gun out before the sharpshooters' bullets slammed into him, made him stagger four steps backward. He fell flat on his back, twitching, already dead.

"I *did* warn him," Forsythe said. "Your friend had very little talent. We can do without him. We'd rather not have to shoot you too. Keep in mind—you won't be going back to prison. You'll be in government custody but . . . it'll be comfortable. And quite interesting, I promise you."

Gulcher looked past Forsythe at the sharpshooters.

And very slowly . . . Gulcher put up his hands. "Fuck it. I'm tired of the noise in this dump. I surrender. Let's go, General."

THE NEXT MORNING. A rooftop in Harlem.

The sun was just breaking above the upper edges of the buildings to the east. Bleak put on a pair of sunglasses and crossed the brownstone's roof to a cornice overlooking the street. He put a booted foot on the cornice and leaned as far forward as he could, taking in the street scene below.

Some blocks south of the rooftop, the Apollo Theatre was still operating, and small shops and soul-food restaurants and old-time record stores bustled on 125th—but much of Harlem had become increasingly gentrified. Rents had doubled, many old brownstone and limestone buildings had gone condo. Chic little bookstore/coffee shops and galleries and crepe shops with small tables on the sidewalk had cropped up, causing longtime residents to shake their heads and mutter in disgust.

But Bleak was in a remoter Harlem, a short distance from the

Harlem River, a relatively untamed neighborhood. A high school across the street, abandoned for lack of funding, was crawling with arcanely psychedelic graffiti. Turfies in sloppy pants and hooded windbreakers, or wearing the new, shiny Slick Up athletic pants, which were finally replacing the low-belt droop, were congregating in clumps next to a tall metal-mesh fence separating the street from the school's cracked and weedy basketball court, where the hoops had long since been pulled off the backboards. Long shadows stretched from fire hydrants and people. A UPS truck rumbled by. There was a line of parked cars, two of them abandoned and burned out. Parked SUVs and vans looked like brightly colored rectangles from up here.

No telling who might be in those vans.

Bleak glanced up at the sky. Choppers out west but none coming his way. A few gulls flashing in the early-morning light. None of the telltale hard glint of camera drones. He felt no one watching him, at that moment.

He hoped he was safe from CCA here. He had made the deal to collar the skip over a phone that couldn't be traced to him; made the arrangement for them to transfer the bounty, the usual 10 percent of the bail bond, to one of Shoella's accounts, when he turned the skip over to NYPD. He was to drop off the perp "at any police precinct." The CCA couldn't be covering them all. He'd sensed puzzlement about his refusal to come to the bail bonds office in person, but they'd made the deal.

"Vince" at Second Chance had told him a private detective had made some inquiries and all he'd come up with was this building, the last place anyone had seen the skip, one Lucille Donella Rhione, wanted on a failure-to-appear. Bleak had seen her mug shot in an e-mail: a bottle-blond, lamp-tanned, scowling woman who, according to the bondsman, "likes to stuff her boobs into stretch-fabric tank tops and her ass into really tight stretchy leggings." She had skipped out after her aunt, the bail "custodian," put up a pile of money. Lucille was said to be in the company of a violence-prone white drug dealer who liked to call himself Gandalf. Nothing else much was known about him, except sometimes he came to this building to pick up crystal, which he sold somewhere in the Bronx. And he carried a gun. His aggressive unpredictability was the reason the private eye had dropped the case. "Said we weren't paying him enough to deal with Gandalf."

Normally Bleak would have hired two or three guys to help him collar the skip. A couple of burly bodyguards to uptown Big Money worked with Bleak in their spare time. But he didn't want them here with the possibility of CCA coming around at any moment. He was going to have to go it alone this time.

Bleak wasn't telepathic, and his precognitive ability was fitful; but everyone who could actively connect with the Hidden had some psychic capacity. His own clairvoyance was fairly minor—his greatest talents lay in manipulation of the Hidden's energy field, and contact with its entities—but when he focused on Lucille Rhione's picture and reached out into the Hidden, he'd got a mental picture of this building. When he'd come to the address he'd been given—there was the building. So the private eye's information had been good: the Hidden seemed to hint the skip was going to be here soon. *Maybe tomorrow.*

Which was now today. But so far he hadn't seen any white people approach the building.

He paced along the cornices, watching the mix down below, watching the skies for drones between times. Waiting. Thinking things through. Remembering the strange shock when he'd had the psychic contact with Agent Sarikosca. Loraine Sarikosca.

Her name was Loraine . . . like a character in an old black-and-white movie. Fascinating sound to it . . . Loraine . . .

Bleak shook his head. Why was he thinking that? What was up with him?

He needed to get bounty, pick up Muddy, and Cronin if he'd go, reclaim his boat, and get out of town for a while. Head south along the coast in the cabin cruiser, out of state. Find some way to contact Sean without giving himself up to CCA.

If Sean was really alive.

Wouldn't he *feel* it, if Sean was alive? He'd never really tried to contact Sean's spirit, assuming the boy had been quickly reincarnated. And he'd shied away from the emotional shock that would go with even trying.

Could he contact him now? But Sean was connected with CCA. If he contacted him now, he'd risk putting them in touch with him.

Could Sean be watching him, psychically, for CCA? No.

He'd sense it . . . probably.

Bleak, like other ShadowComm, had ways of keeping psychic surveillance off. When he used the Hidden, he created a mental pulse of psychic white noise, immediately afterward, that blurred the trace of it. He instinctively kept a kind of psychic camouflage around his own emanation. But it didn't always work. There had been the psychic surveillance that had brought the UAV. *Krasnoff*. And what if—

He never finished the thought. A blond head was bobbing along the sidewalk, below, a woman walking beside a man with a bald head, small, round dark glasses, and a black goatee. The girl in a clinging tank top and stretchy leggings; the guy wore a hoodie, the hood back now, and jeans. Lucille and Gandalf.

Warm to be wearing a hoodie sweatshirt. Kind of funny too that they were out this early, two people in "the life" of drug dealing—and who knew what else.

They walked up to the building, and Bleak drew back, wishing he had his crew with him. This was where he missed them.

There was someone he might use, though. Bleak closed his

eyes and pictured a certain man in repairman's coveralls, with GREG sewed on the breast.

Greg Berne . . . Greg Berne . . .

Greg the Ghost appeared almost immediately; he was there before Bleak opened his eyes to check. He wasn't transparent—but he was suspended a foot over the roof. He had his hands in the pockets of his coveralls.

"Man, you should work for a search-engine company or something," Bleak told him. "You're fast."

"I was just thinking about you, and then I heard you calling," Greg told him. "And here I am. Any news for me?"

"I kind of got a police detective, guy named Roseland, interested in your case. I got a feeling he might look into reopening the whole thing."

"That Mormon kid, Braithwaite—I think he killed someone else," Greg said, gazing out across the city with a kind of dreamy sadness. "I was following him for a while, and then I lost him. . . . Sometimes, see, I gotta go and kinda curl up in the Hidden for a while and, what you call it, recharge . . . and when I came back to where I left him, he was gone. But the paramedics, they was taking a dead girl out on a stretcher, in the same block, and I heard 'em say she was strangled."

"Where was this?"

"Manhattan. East Ninety-fifth and Second Avenue."

"I'll find some way to tell Roseland that murder might be connected to the ones they tried to hang on you."

"Thanks, soldier. But, hey—don't use the words *hang* and *you* around me, makes me feel sick. Considering how I died." Greg wasn't smiling. Wasn't joking.

It was always interesting to Bleak that ghosts could feel sick—even though they had no physical bodies, exactly. "Okay, sorry. So how about doing something for me, Greg?"

"Sure as shit would try, there, Sarge."

"Two people just went into this building . . ." Bleak described them and gave their names. "I need you to tell me where exactly they're going, how many people in the place, what the scene is. If there's a window on a fire escape, and if it's locked."

"I got you. Let me have a look."

Greg sank vertically into the roof, neither slowly nor quickly, as if taking an elevator down.

How do I pull this off? Bleak wondered. It was the woman he needed to take in. But it was the guy he had to worry about. Bleak had a gun with him—he didn't like to even carry them on a skip trace, preferring, as most professionals did, the element of surprise, a couple of burly helpers, and handcuffs. He could maybe use the gun to get the bald Gandalf to surrender, if he got the drop on him—and if the guy resisted, he could knock him cold, then grab the girl and cuff her. He had pepper spray, could use that on her if she struggled. . . . He didn't want to have to throw an energy bullet and ruin his cover.

"Bleak?"

It sounded like a voice coming out of the air, to Bleak, but someone without his gifts would have heard nothing but a sigh on the wind, at most.

"Yeah, Greg, I'm here." Saying it out loud. To the wind.

"They're sitting in a top-floor apartment almost right under you, six oh three. I was in the room, watching 'em. They've been up all night, them two, from what they were saying. So this is like the end of the night for 'em, ya see. They're doing lines of speed. Guy they're buying it from, he don't seem like he wants to use it himself. He just watches them and seems to think they're kinda funny. The girl's missing a couple teeth—them meth heads lose their teeth from the shit. Let's see—oh, yeah, the back window on the fire escape—it's painted shut. Wait, I'm coming up there."

Greg ascended partway into view, up to his waist in the roof.

He brushed at his face. "I always think, when I go through a wall, that I'm gonna get bugs and cobwebs on my face. Course I don't, but—"

"Greg—could you do one more thing for me? I'm going down to the hall outside the apartment. They're getting toasted in there. When they're toasted, they'll pop out of the toaster and come out into the hall. I need to know when they're about to head for the door. You see any guns on them so far?"

"I was looking, the hoodie guy might have one under his sweatshirt in front, but I dunno, Sarge. Couldn't tell for certain."

"Okay. Maybe when he stands up you'd see it."

"You got it. Anything I can do. Meet you down there"—he began to sink into the roof again, saluting, army-style, as he went down—"Sergeant Bleak."

Bleak returned the salute, then went to the roof doorway.

He padded down the stairs to the sixth floor, slipped quietly through the hall to the doorway, passing a small black girl carrying a bag of groceries; the little girl looked at him curiously but hurried past. Bleak found the apartment, the metal door thickly painted in dull red, the number 603 stenciled on it in black. Old jimmy marks scarred the door's lock. He looked at the elevator, which creaked noisily as someone used it, and the stairway, about twenty paces back, and decided they'd probably use the stairway. Tweakers going downstairs were too impatient to wait for a slow old elevator.

"Bleak? You hear me?"

"Yeah," Bleak muttered.

"They're going to the door."

"Just those two, no one going with them?"

"Right. And when the bald guy stood up, I did see a gun in his waistband. Man, I wish I could pick up a baseball bat or something, I'd back you up. I'd—"

"You've done a great job for me, Greg," Bleak murmured softly, hurrying to the stairway. "Nothing else needed."

"He looked kind of bulky, there, Bleak. I was thinking—"

"Quiet, I've got to concentrate," Bleak whispered.

He heard the door open, down the hall behind him, and walked casually into the stairway as if he were on the way out of the building himself. The stairwell was dusty, unevenly lit, graffiti-tagged, and painted the same fleshy beige. He walked down to the next landing, around the stairwell's turn, down two steps . . . and waited.

He heard them coming, Lucille Rhione and her old man. Bleak drew his gun, but didn't put his finger on the trigger. He held the gun like a club—but so he could get to the trigger fast if he needed it—and had the cuffs ready in his left hand.

He had a "this isn't going to go very well" feeling—something that came from the Hidden, not from his own nervousness, and that feeling usually turned out to be right.

They were chattering as they came to the stairwell, started clumping down toward him, the girl saying, "We cash out, we can get a better camera, hire them hos from Georgie's, they'll do a video, we can get that into Skyline distrib—"

My, my, Bleak thought. *Entrepreneurs. In cheap porn.*

And the bald Gandalf, his scalp tattooed with an intricately knotted Celtic symbol, was talking really fast. "Don't be getting too much ahead, I don't know if we're getting outta this, those people got us out of the shit-house set this up, some fucking weirdos, why should I trust them? I got an ounce of shit on me, maybe this is just a fucking setup, maybe it's to get us busted, and Jerry upstairs too, maybe he—"

What does he mean "those people got us out"? Bleak wondered, but it was too late to wonder any more than that, they were coming to his landing, and he was pointing his gun at Gandalf.

"Freeze right there," Bleak said, stepping in closer. "I'm here for Lucille, I have a warrant, she's wanted for failure-to-appear. She's coming with me—"

"Gan-*dalllllf*?" the woman squealed. "They never said he'd be in here with us, like this—"

"It is some kinda fucking setup, they said he wouldn't have a gun," Gandalf chattered, snarling. And pulling his gun as he said it.

Bleak brought his own gun barrel down on Gandalf's bald head—but the guy was hyperalert with methedrine and he jerked back at the last split second, Bleak's gun barrel hitting him glancingly just above the left eye, knocking his sunglasses off, creasing his scalp enough to make blood spurt, but with no solid impact, so that Bleak knew that Gandalf wasn't going down yet.

"Gan-*dalllllf*!" the girl shrieked, scrambling back. "They said he—"

Staggering for balance, Gandalf showed snaggly, yellow teeth in an animal grimace, his eyes looking as steely as the studs piercing his upper lip and brow. He raised his gun, a black Glock nine.

Oh, shit, Bleak thought, as Gandalf raised the gun, *I've got no choice*. Not really even having time to think the words, except *oh, shit*—just realizing it.

He had no time to reach into the Hidden for an energy bullet, or to condense the field, turn the drug dealer's bullet. He had only one option.

His hand found the trigger and he fired directly into the center of that sweatshirt, the middle of Gandalf's chest—Bleak's gun roared, the Rhione woman screamed, and Gandalf was knocked backward with the impact of the shot, slung awkwardly against the iron handrail. The Glock fired, but because Gandalf was off-balance, the shot went wild, ricocheting behind Bleak. The drug dealer's little, round-lensed sunglasses had fallen on the steps. Bleak shifted his stance, kicked the Glock from Gandalf's hand, and swung his own gun at the cowering, crying woman. She scrambled away from him backward. As if he were a horror-movie monster.

"Just come with me, Lucille," Bleak said. "No one's going to hurt you. We'll call an ambulance for—"

"Fucking vulture!" Gandalf snarled, kicking Bleak's left knee, knocking him off-balance.

Bleak started to fall, managed to partly catch himself on the other railing with the heel of his gun hand. He braced and used his left foot to kick the dealer in the face. Felt bone and cartilage crunching.

Gandalf yipped in pain and recoiled. Bleak got his feet under him, realizing that Gandalf had a military-grade bulletproof vest on. Where'd he get it? Not unthinkable a dealer would have one, but they were scarcely "standard issue."

The dealer was clutching his bloodied nose, crimson streaming between his fingers, but he had picked up the Glock with his other hand, was swinging it toward Bleak—grinning bloodily—

Bleak had no choice but to bring his own pistol around and shoot Gandalf in the head. One shot, a single round, in the forehead.

The dealer's head snapped back, his eyes crossed, and he sagged, instantly lifeless.

Lucille Rhione's scream was long and piercing.

"*Fuck.* Okay, well, Lucille, that was self-defense," Bleak added, the words sounding false even to him.

It *was* self-defense, he told himself; he knew he'd be dead if he hadn't done it. He had a strong connection to the After, like everyone who lived with an awareness of the Hidden—but he also had the survival instincts every human being had.

He stood over the dealer's still twitching body. Then realized Lucille was crawling up the stairs, sobbing as she went. Dragging a long-strapped purse along the stairs after her, bump bump bump.

"Hold it, Lucille. I'm sorry I had to shoot your old man, but you've still got to . . ."

She had to do what? Should he let her go? If he turned her in, he'd have to explain about this shooting.

"They're coming," she sobbed. "And they're gonna get your ass and I'll tell 'em you killed him, you fucking pig."

I should have come at the guy from behind, stuck a gun to his head—but the girl might've taken off running.

Then it struck Bleak that she'd said, *They're coming.* And Gandalf had said something about someone getting them "out of the shit-house."

"Who's coming, Lucille?"

But Bleak knew. He could hear the choppers churning the air over the building now.

Lucille was no bail skip. She'd already been in jail. CCA had got her out and used Second Chance Bail Bonds to lure him here . . . and to keep him busy.

"*Lucille, you dumb bitch,*" Gandalf snarled.

The woman climbing the stairs on all fours stopped, lifted her head, like a dog hearing a distant call. "Gandalf?"

Bleak saw him then. Gandalf was standing on the stairs—no, he was floating a foot above the stairs—right next to Lucille Rhione. Looking just as he had in life, except he was missing the gun. But he had his hand held up, pointing at Bleak as if there were a gun in it. He probably thought there was.

Lucille looked around, not seeing him. Her voice rose in pitch. Her lips quivered. "Gan-*dallllllf?*"

She could *hear* her dead boyfriend, Bleak realized—her intuition stimulated by the intensity of the moment—but she couldn't see him.

"*I'm gonna kill you, you fucking bounty vulture!*" the ghost of Gandalf snarled.

"You're a dead guy yourself, man," Bleak pointed out wearily. "You're not in a position to kill anyone."

Should he try the street or try to get away on the roofs? There was one way he might make the roofs work. . . .

"*I was just going to close a major deal, I was getting it all together, I had the shit to pay for everything.*"

"You got some money from CCA, and you bought some dope, and you thought you were going to become the Porn King," Bleak said, starting up the stairs. "But they would have killed you, or gotten rid of you somehow. Probably put you two away in some nut house somewhere. Keep you quiet about this operation. So it wouldn't have worked out, Gandalf, or whatever your name was when you were a living asshole instead of a dead one."

Bleak took two steps at once to get past Lucille—and the snarling ghost leaped at him. Roaring right for his eyes, mouth open, to take a bite of his face.

The way someone else would have tensed the muscles of their stomach to absorb a blow, Bleak intensified the field of the Hidden around himself, and the ghost bounced off, spiraled away, howling, swirled around, started to come back at him.

Then Greg was there, stepping out of the wall—and hit the ghost in the face. Purple sparks flew from the psychic impact, and Gandalf squealed and retreated, whimpering, babbling madly, into a corner.

"Thanks, Greg," Bleak said, hurrying up the stairs. The ghost of Gandalf couldn't really have hurt Bleak—but he could have temporarily blinded him. Tormented him. "I should have listened to you, Greg, you tried to tell me he had some bulkiness about him, should've figured from that there was a vest. Which would have been a clue. Been good if I'd paid attention."

Bleak banged the roof door open, ran out into the bright sunlight. And saw three choppers flying overhead—and two CCA agents climbing onto the roof from a fire escape. One of them he recognized as Drake Zweig.

And nine or ten more were on adjacent roofs. Closing in on him.

ELEVEN

Agent Loraine Sarikosca watched Gabriel Bleak from the adjacent roof. He was crossing to a corner of the roof opposite the agents coming off the fire escape. She saw him look up at the choppers, and at the drone darting between them.

He was about a hundred feet away. He turned to look at her as he ran . . .

To look right at her.

For a moment it was as if he were much closer to her—in that brief glance it felt to her as if he were standing in front of her, the two of them outside of time, gazing at one another in warm curiosity.

Then the contact was broken—and the agents were running at Bleak, shouting, and he was throwing energy bullets at them. One of the men yelled in pain and dropped his gun. The other one ducked the sizzling energy bullet—and Bleak ran past them . . . heading toward another fire escape.

Suppose he was killed, trying to escape? The thought made her clutch up, inside.

She was no longer sure of her footing in CCA. What she'd seen in the north, and the hints Helman had dropped, made her wonder if any of them knew what they were doing. She was still scratching mosquito bites, still tired from the long trip down from the arctic circle, and she'd had only one fitful night's sleep.

The artifact. Nothing seemed to quite make sense, anymore. The implications stretched too far—beyond the limits of human perception. Spying on terrorist cells in Syria seemed simple in comparison.

She shook her head glumly. She had asked Helman if in some way they could bring the suppressor to use on Bleak, and temporarily neutralize his abilities. But the effective range of the suppressor was only about five feet. And getting him within that range in a situation like this—and with a device that required a great deal of energy—was not practical. Not yet.

Helman had another plan for neutralizing Bleak. Sharpshooters with tranquilizer guns were taking up positions nearby. She doubted that was going to work.

The lead agent pursuing Bleak had a handgun out. Not a trank gun. The man aimed it . . . and Bleak snapped an energy bullet at the gun. It struck true and the agent shouted, dropped the gun—its bullets going off. Rounds whizzed, a window broke somewhere.

And Bleak was running full tilt to the rim of the roof.

Loraine caught her breath when she realized that he was running past the fire escape and seemed to be about to leap into empty space between buildings. He couldn't hope to jump the thirty feet, maybe thirty-five, to the next roof. Surely he couldn't cross so wide a gap the way he'd risen over the car in the alley.

"No, don't!" she shouted involuntarily, her heart thumping. Aware that Arnie, standing on her left, was looking curiously at her.

Bleak stepped out into space—

And ran on air, across the space between the two buildings, defying gravity to the next, slightly lower roof. Where no agents had been assigned—because no one thought Bleak could get there. But he could. His bridge reached just far enough.

He'd done it again—some kind of invisible force holding him up, drawn from the Hidden, giving him a bridge to the next roof. It had never occurred to them it could reach so far.

She watched him running across the lower roof—she heard a pop, saw a glint tracking toward Bleak from another roof, to Bleak's left—and saw the projectile turn from him at the last moment, as if it had changed course on its own. A tranquilizer dart. He'd blocked it somehow. Another pop—and this dart too turned away at the last moment.

Then Bleak was rushing down the fire escape of the other building—Loraine noted that he hadn't tried to "walk on air" off the top of the roof, though that would've been faster. Which suggested his power had limits—and he'd probably reached them.

She was already moving as these thoughts came to her; she rushed toward the door to the stairs of the tenement they had set up on, ran ahead of Arnie and the others, taking two and three steps at a time to get down.

Because if CCA got desperate enough, they might order him shot down with real bullets. He couldn't hit every gun trained on him with an energy bullet.

Which meant that Gabriel Bleak's best chance of survival was capture.

This time he wasn't going to get away from her.

I'm not going to let her go this time, Bleak decided. *She can tell me about Sean.*

He was darting across the street, through traffic, with his senses fully alive, using the Hidden to make him hyperaware of the vehicles, the necessary timing. Someone else would probably have been hit. But he slipped between a fast-moving cab and two smaller, frantically honking cars, and the agents coming behind him had to wait till there was room to get through. A drone was watching him, and people in the choppers—he felt someone else watching from a rooftop nearby. Saw himself from above, for a moment, from another point of view . . .

It was *her*.

Then he darted between two tenements, with just room enough between them for a fire escape and trash cans. His boots crunched over chips of plaster and flakes of old paint. He felt it when they'd lost sight of him for a moment. But Bleak knew they'd be on him in seconds. To the right was a door leading into a tenement. It had a padlock on it—the tenement was empty, condemned, scheduled to be torn down. It was the work of a moment to charge the lock with energy, make it burst apart.

Bleak pushed into the dim, small room smelling of mold— once a kitchen. The appliances had been pulled out, their shapes were dimly visible, outlined in brown on the walls. He hurried through, into a dark hallway—made an energy bullet in his hand and held it up for illumination. Heard voices outside. Footsteps.

He came to a cavernous space where two walls had been knocked down; living room, dining room, bedroom, combined into one space. There was a door opposite. He ran to it, used the energy he'd gathered for light to break its lock, and left it slightly ajar. Then he went to the darkest corner of the large room and stood stock-still. He pressed into the corner, reached into the Hidden, and began to weave darkness around himself . . . around his entire body.

You needed a big space for this, and a dim room—he hadn't had either when they'd chased him in Seamus's place—and he had both here. He gathered energies around him that caught light and turned it to the sides. In moments, just as they entered the room, small flashlights flickering in their hands, he'd cocooned himself in darkness.

He couldn't see them; they couldn't see him. If they looked closely at his cocoon of shadow, they'd realize it was unnatural. They'd have him. But the eye tended to slide past it in a dark room.

Bleak knew this wasn't going to work if they had that detector with them. But he'd thrown a monkey wrench in their plans—they hadn't anticipated his getting off that rooftop. Probably figured he couldn't make an air bridge that stretched that far. Chances were they were scattered all over looking for him. Did they all have one of those detectors?

"The son of a bitch came through here."

"We should have brought that Krasnoff character, Arnie."

"Can't trust Krasnoff enough, the doctor says."

"Or one of those detectors."

"They don't work all the time. Some isotope-leakage problem. Just one that's good—and it's with Sarikosca."

"Unit Three? He out there on Sullivan? . . . Yeah, we did. No. He's not in here. You had to have missed him."

"The door's open here—he came through!"

"You hear that, Unit Three? The door's open, looks like he busted the lock. . . . Well, you looked away, then. Maybe he used some trick to get past you."

There was a pause. Bleak felt strength draining from him. He drew energies from the Hidden for his workings—but he needed the strength of his body to direct them. He wasn't sure how much longer he could keep the cocoon of shadow up. Maybe another twenty seconds, at most.

He concentrated to keep it steady—especially when a flicker of light showed through. One of them had swept his flashlight across the dark corner he was in.

"Naw—I'm looking at the room, it's empty, there's nothing to hide behind in here. He's gone out that door somehow. . . . Yeah we've got people checking upstairs too. . . . I'll look but I don't think—"

Footsteps.

"You guys find him up there?"

"That's negative, there's a big metal gate blocking the stairs going up and the lock's on it, hasn't been broken."

"You copy that, Unit Three? He's not upstairs. . . . Okay we're coming out, he had to have slipped past you."

They left the room; Bleak felt them go. He waited as long as he could, then with a sigh of relief he dropped the cocoon of darkness and sank to his knees to rest.

All he had to do now was wait—they'd move on, searching for him.

"Greg?" he whispered. He'd asked the ghost to stick close. "You there?"

"I'm here."

"There's a woman agent—only one I've seen in this crowd. You see her?"

"I do. Black hair? Really cute broad?"

"That's her. . . . Want you to do something for me."

EARLY THAT EVENING, in Brooklyn Heights. Murray grinning at Loraine from the door of his condo as she came wearily up the steps.

"Knew you were coming," he said, opening the screen door. "The cats got up in the window, meowing like crazy. 'She's here!'" He was a plump man with rosy cheeks, big brown shoes, exactly combed short brown hair, a tendency to wear golf shirts with little alligators on them, and creased khaki pants.

The big, old, shingled house had been divided into two condos. Loraine had persuaded Murray to take the one next door.

They shared the garden. She was glad to get home and pick up her cats.

"They're glad to see you," Murray said, smiling. "But I spoil them. I don't think they want to leave me." He was her neighbor and the closest thing she had to a friend in New York, now that Chelsea had gone to Afghanistan. When Loraine had a day off, she and Murray would go to museums together—he loved classical art, and impressionism—and to flower and garden shows. And, now and then, to a musical. "What good is having a gay friend if you don't go to musicals with him?" Murray had asked, one day, bringing her the tickets.

When she was away, he watered her plants and fed her cats. An orange tabby and a Siamese, the cats paced sinuously around her ankles, meowing furiously, rubbing their heads on her.

"They sound like they're mad at me," Loraine said. "They're always mad when I've left them any amount of time. Even though I know they have a great time with Uncle Murray."

"They haven't had their dinner yet, that could be the big issue here."

She let them into her place, and Murray came in for tea. They drank tea, the cats taking turns in her lap, and she talked of everything but what was really on her mind. Asking him about the classes he was taking at the Art Institute of Brooklyn, whether his boyfriend's father was willing to meet him yet; Murray's thoughts about helping her decorate her place. Loraine making herself talk.

"There's something bothering you, girl?" Murray asked, at last, glancing at his gold Rolex watch. A gift from his boyfriend, Ahmed.

If only she could talk to him about it. *Okay, well, I know I told you I work for the State Department, but in fact I work for a spin-off organization and we monitor supernaturally gifted people.*

Not likely. "I'm fine," Loraine said. "Just tired. Diplomatic stuff. People angry on both sides. You get very frustrated. But I can't talk about it, corny as that sounds."

Murray grinned. "Ten-four! Then I'm gonna go and make dinner for Ahmed. He likes you, wouldn't mind at all if you came."

"That's sweet but I just want to veg . . . and think."

" 'Kay." He took his teacup to the sink, washed it out, came back to kiss her on the cheek, and went home to make dinner for his boyfriend.

"Must be nice to have someone to make dinner for," Loraine said, patting Mongy. He yowled with full Siamese dissonance. His full name was Mongkut, named after the Thai king who inspired *The King and I*. The meeting of the values of Western civilization and the exotic culture of the East. Like forcing containment on magic?

She thought, *CCA: The Musical*. She laughed. Then she shook her head sadly. Thinking of the man strapped to the concrete chair.

But what's your excuse?

Loraine looked around and thought that she'd never quite moved in, though she'd been here more than a year. She had one brown leather sofa, a big-screen TV she almost never used, an MP3 player that wasn't hooked up; an old record player purchased at a flea market that *was* hooked up, with vinyl records stacked beside it. Books piled on their sides against the wall, waiting for the bookcase that Murray was going to help her pick out. A Rembrandt print Murray had bought and framed for her over a brass-mantel fireplace. The cream-colored walls seemed sterile and boring. Dusty silk flowers drooped in a crystal vase on her little dining room table, just off the small living room. Her bedroom was even sparser. And the house smelled of used cat litter even though the cats hadn't been here for days.

Loraine sighed and went to check her e-mail. Afraid there might be an order for her to return to work. Maybe they'd caught Bleak. They'd want her there for the interrogation.

No, she thought suddenly. *They haven't caught him. I'd know if they'd caught him.*

Absurd. How would she know that?

Loraine went to her bedroom, trailed by the cats. She sat at the little redwood desk, booted up her computer. She would have to hold at least one cat on her lap while she checked her e-mail. Mongy got there first.

She was hoping for an e-mail from Chelsea, who was close as Loraine had to a best girlfriend. Chelsea was a DIA crypto specialist in Afghanistan. Lately they'd been losing helicopter gunships and Chelsea had been assigned to—

"Hello, Agent Sarikosca," said someone, behind her. A man's voice, familiar, speaking softly.

Where was her purse? Her gun was in it. She realized she'd left it in the living room.

Feeling stiff with fear, Loraine turned slowly in her swivel chair— Mongy on her lap swiveling with her—and caught her breath.

Gabriel Bleak was leaning against the bedroom doorframe, holding her purse up by the strap, with one finger. He wore jeans, boots, a black T-shirt for some rock band, the name largely obscured by the unbuttoned, white overshirt. "Looking for your purse?" he asked lightly. "You left it in the other room. You shouldn't be that far from your gun . . . Loraine."

She swallowed. Feeling strange. "How'd you find me?"

"Oh, you were followed home. By a friend of mine. Since the guy following you is dead, and invisible to most people, you didn't notice you were being followed. He actually sat next to you in the agency car, in the back. Nice guy, name of Greg." Bleak delved through the purse, came up with her pistol. "I'll hold on to this. Just don't want to be shot today. I almost was, earlier, and that was unpleasant enough. You ever been shot?"

She shook her head.

Bleak chuckled grimly. "Ruins your whole day, let me tell

you." He tossed the purse on her bed. "I was looking at some of your records. Mostly old ones. Vinyl. I bet your mother gave them to you."

She nodded numbly. Then shook her head. "My aunt."

"Procol Harum, Cream, the Supremes, Janis Ian, Simon and Garfunkel, Moody Blues, Rolling Stones, Beatles, early Tom Waits . . . some good ones. You listen to any of those? Pretty old-school."

"What do you want?"

"I noticed Joni Mitchell on the record player. Very talented. Never could get into her. I'm more about Polly Jean Harvey."

The cats walked over to him and rubbed against his legs. He smiled. "Animals usually like me." He squatted, to pet the cats with his left hand. Her gun was held loosely in Bleak's right hand. Mongy, the traitor, purred. "In fact they always like me."

I could jump him, she thought. *I could take one step, brace my left foot, kick him on the point of his chin, grab the gun as he goes back.*

But she had read his file. His experience in hand-to-hand combat was undoubted; his alertness was a kind of charge that crackled the air around him.

She decided against it and said, "You routinely break into people's homes? Women alone—that a big thing with you?"

He scratched Mongy under the jaw. "You routinely set up people trying to arrest drug dealers? That a big thing with you? You know I had to shoot that man dead?" He shook his head. "I figure Gandalf was along because it would have looked suspicious if she'd been there alone. And I figure he was supposed to surrender to me, and I'd have been burdened with those two when I took them out of the building, and your people would have closed in and I'd have been pretty hard-pressed to stop them. But you didn't figure on how paranoid he'd get after he tweaked out in that apartment. You can't count on drugged-up people to be your happy little puppets, Agent

Sarikosca." He stood up, looked at her thoughtfully, tossed the gun to his left hand, back to his right. "I hadn't killed anyone since the Rangers. Seeing people die when it's not my doing—that doesn't bother me much. Saw someone shot dead by a cop just the other day. Saw worse about once a week in Afghanistan. But personally stopping someone's path through life, just cutting it off—even an asshole like that . . ." He shook his head. "I don't like to do it unless I'm forced to. Because of where they're headed, afterwards: to the Wilderness. In the afterlife, right? When you've looked into the Wilderness . . ." He shook his head. "Once you've seen that, you like them to have a chance to get their heads right, in this life. Small as that possibility might be. Now that dumb son of a bitch won't have that chance."

What a strange man, she thought, looking at him. Entirely apart from his supernatural abilities. He was angry he'd had to kill Leonard Mearson, the man who'd called himself Gandalf. *He shot him in the head and he's angry at me for it.*

The strangeness was in his eyes too. As if they reflected a light that wasn't there.

And those hands—subtly expressive, gentle with the cats. But he'd used the same hand that was stroking the tabby to shoot a man dead, not much more than an hour ago. And those hands could form orbs of violet fire.

Loraine made herself look away from him. Feeling some of the uncanny attraction she'd felt, on the roof. Remembering the shock of contact when she'd watched him on the surveillance video.

The feelings he conjured in her, just by being there, made it hard to come up with the right course of action. A course she needed badly right now.

"Someone probably saw you coming in here," she said, glancing past him. "They'll call the cops."

He shook his head. Completely unworried. "I was careful."

"And—the man you shot wasn't my 'puppet.' His real name

was Mearson. And he . . . none of that was my plan. I was informed they'd set up a kind of sting to lure you to a particular address. And I was asked to help."

"You weren't much help, though, were you?" He smiled, a relaxed smile . . . but again she had to look away.

"I was supposed to . . . to interface with you after they got you. They were going to surround you, make you surrender. Or, after the tranquilizer darts. . . . After you woke up."

He chuckled. "Tranquilizer darts. Like a wild animal."

"You're *operating* like a wild animal," she said suddenly. "Breaking in here. And you talk about a wilderness—you're in one *out there*, playing with that power. You people—you should be working for your country."

"What happens to people like me who do work for CCA, Agent Sarikosca?" He wasn't looking at her. He was opening the cylinder of her .38. His confidence was irritating.

Bleak emptied the bullets from the gun so they clattered onto the floor. Mongy and Festus started batting the bullets around.

He took a pair of needle-nose pliers from his pocket.

She stared. Was he going to use those pliers on her?

He used them to pull the firing pin from her gun.

"That's the second perfectly good gun that you've ruined," she said.

"You can put the firing pin back in later. And you didn't answer my question, about what happens to ShadowComm people who work for you? We generally never hear from them again."

"I . . . that's classified."

"Things are classified because they're embarrassing to someone." Bleak put the firing pin and the pliers in his pocket and tossed her gun onto the bed beside her purse. "Now, we're going to meet some people. The kind you want to recruit. You and me."

"You're taking me out of here? You're abducting me?"

He shrugged. "Your people are looking for me anyway. I don't have much to lose if I . . . abduct you."

"What if I don't want to go?" Loraine demanded. "What if I scream, throw things through the window?"

"I'm armed, and I've got this too." He formed an energy bullet in his hand, let it glow there for a moment, then closed his hand on it, extinguishing it. When he opened his hand, it was gone.

"And you'd—what? Throw that little ball of light at me and . . . set my hair on fire? Burn me with it?" Loraine shook her head. "I don't think you'd hurt me, Bleak. Not unless it was self-defense." She felt sure of it. But she had no clue how she knew.

Bleak grunted. "You're right. I guess I wouldn't hurt you. But . . . there are other ways." He smiled broadly and spread his hands. "I have 'magic powers,' you remember."

Play along, she thought. *Go with him*. This was a CCA opportunity.

That was the reason, wasn't it, she wanted to go with him? It had nothing to do with the way her pulse raced when he looked at her.

He held her gaze steadily. "You know about a guy named Coster?"

Loraine shrugged. Not wanting to react to the name. "Just that—he used to work for us."

"He's not working for you now?"

"If he was, I wouldn't tell you." She'd heard there was more than one track for luring Bleak. Coster was the other one.

She stood up. "Okay, tough guy, let's go. Maybe—we can negotiate something along the way."

"Negotiate what? My surrender?" He seemed amused.

"It wouldn't be surrender. It'd be recruitment."

"Your recruitment is worse than the army's. And that's going some. You guys have stop-loss?" He chuckled. "Okay, let's go."

As if they understood him, the cats set up a desperate meow-ing. "Oh, okay, sure," Bleak told the cats. "We'll feed you first."

IT WAS JUST SHADING from dusk to darkness. The warm air of the new summer night was like a blanket draped over their shoulders. A blanket they shared.

"So you think we're the oppressive fist of the regime and you're the innocent artists of the supernatural?" Loraine said drily, as they walked down her tree-lined street in Brooklyn Heights. They'd fed the cats, Bleak seeming to take pleasure in spooning out the cat food for them himself.

"Things are rarely so simple," Bleak said, with a wintry smile. "But, yeah—that's the main idea."

She had her purse on a strap over her right shoulder. Bleak was striding along on her left. She could slip her hand in the purse, trigger the "find me" homing beeper she'd been given in case of emergency. But if she did that, the agency would come in force—and she suspected this little trek with Bleak was an opportunity she'd never have again. A chance to peer into the Shadow Com-munity. They might get Bleak, but they might lose a lot more.

Still, he'd broken into her place, and that pissed her off. She stopped. He took another step, then turned to look at her.

"Bleak—you've got your own gun with you. If you're going to shoot me, best shoot me now."

"Do I have to?" He made a *tsk* sound. "Seems like a waste."

"Of a good bullet?"

"Of a good woman. Better than you know."

She snorted. "Oh, thanks, I'll put it on my résumé. Bleak, I mean it—if you're going to try to abduct me, you'll have to shoot me first. But I'm not in the mood to just stand here and passively let you kidnap me. If I go with you, it's got to be my choice."

He surprised her by laughing. "Okay! You're not abducted!

You called my bluff!" He gestured like an old-time aristocrat, rolling his hand magnanimously. "You want to go home, go! You want to call the police or your agency, do it, and I'll split." He paused, looking at her more solemnly. "But I'm hoping you won't do that. I think you should come with me. Without telling anyone about it. There are people for you to meet. You want to learn about us—that's part of your job. So maybe that's what you should do. It makes no sense for me to take you with me. But that's the plan."

"Making no sense is the plan?"

"There, see, you've got me figured out. In a way, making no sense is the plan. I'm hoping you'll see we can be trusted with our freedom. Maybe . . . *maybe* . . . in exchange, we can help your agency. Depending on what you want from us. Working with you people . . . ah, man. We've got mixed feelings. Tell me something." He looked at her with a probing curiosity. He kept his distance—but she felt as if he were touching her face. "You seem . . . like someone with a conscience. You really feel like you belong at CCA?"

The question made her angry and ashamed at once. But she had an answer ready. "You ever hear of a man named Troy Gulcher?"

"Name sounds familiar. Something from the news. A jailbreak?"

"That's right. You don't know him from any other context?"

"If I did—to quote a certain CCA agent—I wouldn't tell you."

"He's one of your kind. Some version, anyway. And he killed a lot of people, using his connection with . . . with the thing you call the Hidden. He's killed prison guards—people with families. Gulcher created a—" She broke off a moment, at a loss for words. "I couldn't tell from the files what it was . . . but it comes across as mass demonic possession. People went mad and killed one another. He used that to get away. And he did something else at a casino in Atlantic City—a lot of people there died." She shook her head. "I don't really understand *how* they died. But Troy Gulcher was mixed up in it. And then there was another man who may have been using magic to start a fire, burn down a restaurant—he killed a police officer."

"Yeah. The fire imps. I know about him. I didn't know him personally. You coming with me or not? We can talk about it on the way."

She hesitated. But she couldn't let the opportunity slip away. "Sure," she said at last. "Let's go." They started down the sidewalk again. *Crossing the Rubicon,* she thought. "Point is, Bleak—how do you rationalize Gulcher? And how about the man who set a cop on fire?"

Bleak frowned and waved dismissively. "Those people aren't part of ShadowComm—not the groups I know. They're not La'hood. They seem to be something new."

"You're claiming your people 'don't use their power for evil'?" Loraine asked skeptically.

"They're not my people. I can't speak for them. I'm not really a part of their community. We have dealings, the ShadowComm and me—and I've known some of them for a long time. The ones I know aren't into violence. They aren't into misusing their talents. Not in any *big* way. Some you might call a bit borderline, but . . . As for this Gulcher, he was picked up in Atlantic City, right? We had a spiritual blackout there."

The phrase *spiritual blackout* interested her. "What's that, exactly?"

"Couldn't *see* there, in the Hidden—like something was covering it up. Some parts especially. So something is hiding that guy from us. Maybe because we're not on the same side as he is."

"You chose a . . . a side?"

"Sort of. And sort of not. Neutrality is good. But you don't want to play ball with anything flat-out evil, either. And some things are flat-out evil."

They fell silent as he turned left toward a subway entrance, and she went calmly along, matching his pace, as if they were old friends.

He said, "Well, here's someone I know." He stopped at a little kiosk next to a newspaper stand. In the kiosk a small, dark, middle-aged woman sold ice cream. She wore a sparkly blue sari and had a little red dot on her forehead and melancholy black eyes. But her eyes lit up when Bleak approached her.

"Mr. Gabriel!" Her accent was southern India. "How good to see you, I don't see you at Grand Central!"

"Of course you don't," he said, smiling. "You moved out of Grand Central."

She shook her head sadly. "Rent was too high for me, there, even so little a shop, that one. But more customers there."

"I just happen to be passing through and here you are. Have to have my rocky road. You still got some?"

"Sure I got some rocky road! One for the lady?"

Bleak turned to Loraine "You like rocky road? Maybe chocolate-chip mint?"

"How'd you know I liked chocolate-chip mint?"

"Just a guess. A scoop of each, Sarojin."

Sarojin made up two ice cream cones. Bleak paid, dropped $2 into the tip box, and chatted with the woman for several minutes as Loraine ate her ice cream and nervously watched the sky.

Some abduction, she thought ruefully.

After a moment she found herself enjoying the ice cream, enjoying Bleak's company the way someone would enjoy the sound of the sea though only half aware of hearing it.

Finishing the ice cream, they walked on toward the subway entrance. They ate companionably, and another thought came to her. "Was that woman—one of yours? ShadowComm?"

He seemed surprised by the question. "No. Just someone I used to buy ice cream from at Grand Central. Kind of a friend of mine." He stopped halfway down the grime-blackened steps. She paused—just like a regular companion who wondered why the other had stopped—and he dabbed at the corner of her mouth with a folded napkin. "You're getting clown makeup from ice cream. There."

They looked at one another for a moment. Then he shrugged and continued down the steps. She went with him.

Loraine felt a powerful impulse to trust Bleak. But that feeling might have a supernatural cause. He might be using his abilities to influence her in some subtle way. The CCA didn't know the full extent of his power.

But she didn't really believe he was "influencing" her—not that way. Somehow . . . she simply trusted him. She felt as if she'd known him for years.

Maybe, she thought, as they walked up to the machine selling subway cards, *it's the other kind of magic.*

Loraine shook her head. *I'm being stupid. Like an adolescent girl.*

It occurred to her that after being with Bleak for only a few minutes she'd already found herself breaking CCA regulations: she'd told him about Gulcher. She hadn't told him everything. But still—she'd blurted classified data to Bleak. And she'd broken situation protocol by not using the beeper; not calling for assistance. Why?

Then she realized that CCA might be coming anyway. Dr. Helman had hinted she was under surveillance. She glanced around—and saw a nondescript van parked nearby, its windows dark. For all she knew they might be sitting in there, watching, right now. A helicopter was flying over—it seemed on its way somewhere. But who knew for sure? It could be them.

Were there listening devices in her apartment? They could have heard some of the conversation she'd had with Bleak.

General Forsythe liked to project cheery comradeship. But

she didn't trust him—and she knew Forsythe didn't trust her. That beeper in her purse itself might be something more. It had been issued to her in-house. They could be using it to listen to her right now.

Loraine made up her mind. She took the beeper out of her purse and dropped it into a trash can.

After they'd walked on a few more steps, she said, "Bleak— we'd better get into the subway—and get out of the area fast." She was a little amazed at herself for saying it. "I mean . . . *really* fast. Otherwise . . . this trip could end up taking you someplace you weren't expecting to go."

TWELVE

That same night. Upstate New York. Special Facility 23.

"It's almost a sad thing, really," General Forsythe was saying, as he and Gulcher walked ahead of the six black berets, the armed guards escorting them into the big, square, concrete courtyard. Their footsteps echoed in the hard-edged, empty space. He didn't immediately explain what was "sad, really."

It was a warm summer evening, gnats and mosquitoes buzzing in the open air above their heads, but there was something chilly about this half acre of courtyard. The high, floodlit concrete walls seemed to suck up the warmth. The glare from the blue-white lights blotted out the stars. The night sky was like a black ceiling.

The courtyard was part of a sprawling, gray, obscurely institutional facility that, to Gulcher, had a "black budget" feel to it. Black budget, because driving up here he'd seen no signs, nothing but a number, and a gate, and razor-wire fence. And armed guards.

"Sad how the yubes need human beings to do their work in this plane of being," Forsythe continued. He sounded to Gulcher like he was acting all the time. Reading lines from a script. "But they can't do that much without people, not in this world. Because this is the world principally designed for embodied humans. Sad they're stuck with human beings to work with."

"Is that right?" Gulcher never wasted any time thinking about what was sad, and what wasn't. What was boring, what was frustrating—*those* were his concerns. He had been both bored and frustrated since surrendering to Forsythe. They'd gone to a federal prison overnight, with the whisperer refusing to respond to him the whole time and Gulcher thinking he was in for hard federal time—but this afternoon he'd been escorted in chains to a military-green bus, most of its windows tinted too dark to see through, with these same unspeaking armed guards, and bused fifty miles north to meet Forsythe here. Just him and the silent marine driver and the six guards on that bus.

Gulcher was having a hard time feeling relieved not to be in prison. He understood prison. But this—it was too much like the stories you heard about extraordinary rendition, or people taken to secret CIA prisons.

Now they stopped in the center of the courtyard, and Gulcher glanced around, thought the courtyard looked disturbingly like some place they stood people against a wall to shoot them.

They sure hadn't hesitated about shooting Jock. *Bang*, down he went. Going to miss that noisy son of a bitch.

My turn now? Were they going to shoot him here? Enough guys with guns were standing right behind him. He tried to ask the whisperer about it—and got a reply, finally, but nothing helpful.

"Hold on, just wait, Greatness is here and Greatness is on its way" was all it would say.

"Ya see," Forsythe went on, "your average yube has to work through humans, most o' the time."

Something about General Forsythe was bothering Gulcher, something that came out of the mysterious place the whisperer came out of. But Gulcher couldn't put his finger on it. And what was this talk of . . .

"Yubes? What's a yube?" Gulcher asked. "That like a noob?"

"No, no. Sorry about the jargon—slang really. Messin' with the acronym. *U-B-Es*—Unconventionally Bodied Entities."

"Oh, okay. Spirits. Elementals. Subtle bodies and stuff. Sure. I read about it in one of Aleister Crowley's books, first stretch I did in state."

"Did you read about it in Crowley! Well, I'll be damned. We had Crowley's spirit in a session with Soon Mei, there." Forsythe nodded toward a nervous, little Asian woman, missing some of her hair, being escorted into the courtyard through a metal door opposite. Her escorts were two guards, a short, heavyset white guard and a tall black one, both with the same corps patches, the same black berets, same nonexpressions. "But Crowley just wanted to whine about things. Didn't care for his situation, inside some big, hungry critter in what they call the Wilderness. Some call it hell, I guess. Old Crowley! He was no use at all. Soon Mei there, though, she's useful. One of the only real mediums we can find. And that peanut-headed fella there, Krasnoff—coming behind her—he's useful as all hell. He's got second sight he can share with you like you were in a movie theater." Forsythe said *theater* like *thee-ate-er*. "It's somethin' to see. And here's our adorable little Billy Blunt."

Billy Blunt, the only one with his hands cuffed, looked to Gulcher like a middle-school kid. A sour-faced, plump little kid of maybe thirteen, with a bowl haircut, gray sweatpants, flip-flops, and a too-small T-shirt emblazoned with BRAINSUCKER in Gothic letters. Brainsucker was a video game, Gulcher remembered, he'd seen an ad for it on TV.

The kid glared at Gulcher and mimed snapping with his teeth, as if he'd like to take a bite out of Gulcher's face. Then he winked and stuck out his tongue.

"Billy there, we've had him almost two years now, bought him from his parents out in Arkansas. They were glad to be shed of him, I can tell you. They tried behavioral therapy, everything, to no avail. Billy liked to set small animals on fire with kerosene, watch 'em run smokin' around the neighborhood. Got the family into some lawsuits. He can do something like you do—he can take control of people, sometimes. Not quite the same way. They tend to die, soon after. Something about blood clots in their brain. He doesn't control spirits to do the possessin'—he kinda steps out of his body and does the possessin' himself. Killed two of our guards. We're hoping he'll be useful . . . eventually."

Right behind Billy was a man who made Gulcher think of one of those old game-show hosts from the 1960s you saw late at night on the Game Channel. He wore funny little glasses and had a contemptuous little smile on his face like he thought everybody else was an idiot. Clearly he was staff around here. He was pushing something that looked like a portable heater, or maybe an air purifier, on a dolly. A long, orange extension cord trailed from the thrumming device, back through the door, and a tiny green light was glowing on it. The dolly, with a waist-high steel handle, made regular squeaking sounds with its wheels, the squeaks reverberating like dolphin noises in the courtyard spaces.

"And that's Dr. Helman with the suppressor. He keeps that little machine pretty close to Billy. The boy might be our most dangerous resident."

"I think that's unlikely, don't you?" said someone, behind them. A soft, teasing voice that sounded like it was coming through clenched teeth.

Gulcher turned around, thinking one of the guards had spoken out of turn.

But it was somebody new. He was a lean, medium-size young

man, with shoulder-length sandy hair, bright blue eyes—and a funny mouth. Kind of a squiggle, that mouth. Like it was struggling to keep its shape. He wore army-style cammies, boots, a khaki shirt, a short military jacket—same jacket the men with black berets had, but without any insignia except that same patch, on the left shoulder, that showed the knight shielding the world. The guy tilted his head a little bit forward, just a little, but you felt like he was going to butt you with it.

"So who the fuck are *you*?" Gulcher didn't like people sneaking up on him.

"Aren't you the rude one," the stranger said, with that squiggly smile, lazily scratching his head—and not sounding offended. "My name's Sean, is all you have to know." He didn't open his mouth much when he spoke. Almost kept his lips shut. "You'd be our new protégé—Mr. Troy Gulcher."

"I'm nobody's *protégé*," Gulcher said.

"He means you're our new student, really," Forsythe said.

"You don't have to say what I mean," Sean said, in the same soft voice. He smiled at Forsythe, then turned to look at Dr. Helman. His look became sleepy, as if he were about to nod off, as he gazed at Helman.

The doctor seemed to trip, would have fallen except he had a grip on the dolly handle. Helman shot a glare at Sean, as he got his feet under him again.

Sean chuckled.

Gulcher watched him—and Sean, aware of the scrutiny, gave his twisty little grin and started to stroll around Gulcher, circling him just out of reach. Walking all the way around so that Gulcher had to turn around to keep an eye on him.

Forsythe looked at Sean with hooded eyes and spoke with an edge in his voice that Gulcher hadn't heard before. "Sean—we need to keep ourselves contained, and directed. We do not wish to waste energy. This man is valuable to me. To all of us." Forsythe had sounded friendlier when he'd warned that the sharpshooters might take Gulcher out.

There was that feeling, again, Gulcher got, looking at Forsythe. Like someone was hiding behind Forsythe, peeking over his shoulder; like something on the Nature Channel—the way a wolf would peer over the stump of a tree. Only there was nothing you could see. Not quite.

"Sure, he's valuable," Sean said, still circling, still looking Gulcher over. "He's another valuable machine, like the rest of us." Said with a hoarse whimsicality through clenched teeth.

Sean ended his circling by standing beside Forsythe, looking toward Billy Blunt. "We're like those cell phone towers that pick up signals and send them on. That's all we are."

"The hell you say," Gulcher snorted.

"Funny you should use that expression," Sean said lightly.

"In certain respects, Sean is right, with his phone-tower analogy," Forsythe said, watching as soldiers set up folding chairs for the three freakish "containees."

Gulcher had heard the word *containees* in an earlier conversation with Forsythe. And he didn't like the sound of it.

He didn't want to be *contained*.

He watched as Dr. Helman moved the suppressor completely out of range of the three containees—and well away from Gulcher. He noticed the guards bringing their guns to bear on the containees when the suppressor was out of range.

"They going to use those guns?" Gulcher asked.

"Not unless they have to," Sean said, his voice barely audible. He reached up and caught a moth in his fingers and slowly crushed it.

"Talented containees," Forsythe went on, "are instruments for other beings to act through—and I suppose you can say it's kinda like being a useful machine. But of course that's what you call your oversimplification."

"I could do this, Forsythe," Sean said. "We don't need him. This Gulcher thing."

Gulcher ground his teeth. This Gulcher *thing*?

"If you could have done it, Sean," Forsythe said vaguely, "you would have. You have . . . other specialties. And sure as the devil it's a process of specialization. We need Mr. Gulcher here for this."

"Could end up a mess," Sean muttered. "But come to think of it, that might be entertaining."

Forsythe shrugged and called, "Are we ready, Dr. Helman?"

"We are!"

"Then, Mr. Gulcher—come over here with me, please." Forsythe led the way to a seven-pointed star, about four feet across, painted in black on the concrete floor. "If you would stand on the mark there . . . thank you. I believe you require no special focusing devices. . . . So if you will simply stand here and"—he lowered his voice, speaking in a tone only Gulcher could hear—"reach out to the Great Power you call the whisperer."

"It hasn't been answering me much lately. Just once and that was . . . almost no answer."

"I believe, for this experiment," Forsythe said confidently, "you will get an answer."

Again Gulcher had that sense of something peering at him from behind Forsythe. Or maybe from inside him. He was beginning to suspect what that might mean.

Gulcher had been briefed, barely, on what he was to do. Now he stood on the appointed spot and looked at the three containees sitting in folding metal chairs with their backs to him. The spotty-headed Asian woman on the left was fidgeting, the Krasnoff guy in the middle was slumped like he was in despair, the fat kid sitting on the right, no longer in handcuffs, was picking his nose with an air of boredom. They sat about forty feet from Gulcher, facing the concrete wall. The soldiers and Dr. Helman had gathered behind

Forsythe. Gulcher was supposed to apply the whisperer to these three losers in the chairs, and do it in a specific way.

It occurred to Gulcher that if he contacted the whisperer, maybe he could get it to obey his wishes again and send influences into Forsythe and the guards and that Sean asshole—Gulcher *really* didn't like that fucker—and get them to take each other out, like at the prison, then he could get out of this place, be on his own again.

"And if you are considering any digression from our agreed-on course of action here, Mr. Gulcher," Forsythe said suddenly, giving him that hooded-eyed look he'd given Sean, "why, it won't work, and we'll be forced to punish you as we punish all problem containees."

The general had shown an ability to look into his mind, Gulcher remembered. Seemed like the old prick was doing it again.

Okay, Gulcher thought, *there's guns all around me, and the whisperer isn't doing what I want it to all the time. But it seems to need me to talk to it here. Maybe I can play along, do something useful for these spooks and get some kind of good deal for myself in return.*

"That'd be fine and dandy, Mr. Gulcher," General Forsythe said, in a more courtly tone, stepping back out of the way.

Gulcher didn't like people getting into his head that way. But he suppressed imagining what he'd like to do about it. And he went to work.

He looked at the back of Krasnoff's head. He focused, calling out, inside, to the whisperer, using the names he'd been given. Wondering for the first time why there was more than one name. *Focus, focus!* The ethereal steam formed; the man-faced serpents wriggled through it. He stretched out his astral hands and the transparent serpents followed . . .

Finally converging on Orrin Krasnoff; making him sit up straight and cry out.

"These containees are difficult for us to control." Forsythe had told him, on the way to the courtyard. "Often they'll do just the opposite of what we want—especially the youngster. Control is what you do, with your . . . special interface. So what we're gonna do, here, Mr. Gulcher, we're gonna use you as a channel for forces that will control these problem containees. You, my friend, are uniquely suited to be of use. There is something Krasnoff does not want to look at. You will control him, make him look into the darkness between the worlds."

Gulcher felt abstract, now, like he wasn't even here. He felt like he was watching from a million miles away, though he saw it all crystal clear up close.

All the while, the energy of psychic invasion built up around him—until, suddenly, it found an outlet through Krasnoff.

Who screamed—and the scream cut off abruptly, stopped by the projection from Krasnoff's open mouth and eyes, the three beams converging on the wall next to the metal door: a circular, swirling image, edged with multicolored sparkles, a projected vision of a place where shapes constructed and deconstructed constantly; where buildings grew out of buildings, like growths of crystal in fast action, clusters of asteroidal shapes that weren't made of stone at all—you could tell, some way, that it was the stuff thoughts were made of—and boiling out of holes in these constructs were nasty shapes chasing others: some, the pursuers, were decidedly demonic, though in some way humanoid; the pursued were vaguely human, but also buglike.

"One perspective on the Wilderness," Sean muttered dismissively, behind. The general hushed him.

Krasnoff writhed, as if trying to escape this vision; as if by projecting it, he was within it.

Then the metal door opened. Three women came through into the courtyard—were pushed through from outside the door, really—wearing identical prison-style, institutional-blue shifts, identically bobbed hair, and blue canvas slippers. The door closed after them with a muted clang. The women huddled together and looked around in confusion.

One of the women was blond, with high cheekbones and small eyes. Russian-looking, to Gulcher, or Ukrainian. The other two, much smaller, looked like they might be from Thailand or Laos, one of those places. They all looked scared but also dulled, and resigned. Like they'd been through a lot before they got here. Gulcher knew the type. They were probably sold women, who'd belonged to brothels. What the Internet news called sex slaves. Eastern Europe and Asia had a great many of them. Probably these spooks had bought some for this experiment.

Gulcher didn't really care. He'd learned not to, a long time ago.

"It's your turn, Billy," Forsythe said.

The Blunt kid was writhing in his seat—then he jumped up and pointed a finger at the blond Eastern European woman . . . and his face went blank. And the blond woman went rigid in response, her back arching, then she sank to her knees beside one of the other women, who shrieked and drew back—but the blond had the shorter of the Asian women by the knees, was gripping her hard, was *biting into the woman's leg* just below the hip.

The girl screamed and pounded on the blonde's head but couldn't get her loose. Blood ran down the Asian woman's quivering leg. The third woman tried to back away, but a guard stepped in and shoved her back in place.

Billy Blunt's jaws made biting, chewing motions. The bitten woman squealed and struggled to escape.

"No, Billy," Forsythe said mildly. "That's not what you were told to do. Now, Gulcher . . . control him. Control Billy, in turn."

Gulcher whispered to the whisperer and gestured, and the steamshapes swirled over Billy . . . and entered him. *Let her go.*

The blond woman Billy was controlling jerked back from the Asian woman, her mouth rimmed in blood. She turned to glare at Forsythe.

The bitten woman struck the other woman resoundingly on the back of the head, knocking her down. The blonde lay stunned—and the wounded woman staggered back, hunched down, clutching her injured leg, murmuring in her own language, rocking back and forth.

The other Asian woman turned and ran—and stopped, suddenly, standing a step away from the swirling image on the wall, caught up, gazing at it, fascinated, gawping . . . then she gasped and her back arched and something ectoplasmic slipped out of the top of her head . . . and the ghostly shape went *into* the image of the Wilderness projected on the wall, as a solid person would step out of the open door of an airplane to fall through the sky. She was staring at the vision of the Wilderness—and she was *in* the image too: her soul, floating along, tumbling, clawing at nothingness. Even as her body stood there shaking with rigidity, ogling at the image of her own soul drifting away.

"This ain't right," Forsythe muttered. "Gulcher—take control of the woman sitting in the chair there, Soon Mei. Bring that woman's soul back. Control!"

Gulcher was having trouble maintaining control over Billy and Krasnoff. But he sent a whispering spirit toward Soon Mei. Felt resistance. Felt it thrust at her . . . then . . . her back went rigid.

And there was an explosion of ghosts.

The apparitions erupted from the swirling circle on the wall, drawn to the patchy-headed little medium sitting in the chair, Soon Mei. Figures of wailing translucent gel were whirling around her— dozens of them becoming scores more, becoming hundreds, lost spirits compacted into a swirling, living vortex; terrified faces, translucent and tormented, all around Soon Mei—who jumped up, screaming, tearing at her hair, running toward the guards, babbling . . .

And one of them, prompted by a gesture from Forsythe, knocked Soon Mei down with a gun butt. She fell onto her side, weeping. The ghosts circled in the air over her, a living ectoplasmic vortex, howling.

Krasnoff was standing, shaking, eyes screwed shut, slapping at his own face.

But the Eastern European woman was up then, blood on her mouth like sick lipstick, crouching, turning toward them, her eyes savage, her blond hair wild—Gulcher's control of Billy, who controlled the woman, incomplete. Gulcher struggled to hold her back.

The armed guards tensed. But Forsythe gestured at them to hold off and shouted, "Gulcher—let them all go, release them!" Gulcher was glad to obey. He was way out of his depth.

As Gulcher released Krasnoff, the image on the wall shrank away, as if swirling down a drain . . . and sucking the eruption of ghosts with it. They were drawn into the drain of the wall and were gone as the image became a pinpoint . . . and vanished.

Krasnoff collapsed, wriggling on the concrete floor. The Asian woman who'd lost her soul in the image crumpled onto the ground. Lay sprawled on her back, staring.

Dead.

Billy, freed from Gulcher's uneven control, started toward Forsythe and Gulcher, raising his hand, the woman with the blood on her mouth stumbling ahead of him, near the sprawled form of Soon Mei.

Billy was sending the blonde to attack them, Gulcher realized.

"Doctor!" Forsythe said sharply. "The boy—the suppressor!"

Helman rushed the dolly with the machine on it between Gulcher and Billy Blunt, and the boy seemed to shiver and shrug . . . and turned away, giving up, when the machine got close.

The blonde sank to her knees, her eyes going blank. She

hugged herself, muttering in some foreign language, near Soon Mei. Who lay there chattering in her own dialect. The surviving woman from Southeast Asia came to sit next to them—some impulse of moral support—weeping and babbling. Three women crying out in three separate languages, voices overlapped and tangled.

The fourth woman, the dead one, just stared emptily at the blackened sky.

Billy sighed loudly and simply sat down on the ground, talking to himself. "This totally like fuckin' sucks, man. I wanta be back in my cell. I got a hella headache, dude."

Gulcher closed his eyes. He felt sick himself. Like someone had injected sludge into his veins. Like he was tainted.

"Well," said Sean, behind him, "there you have it, General. Like I predicted. A goddamned fiasco."

"Not at all," said the general. "I'll admit it was a mite messy—as you predicted. Pressure on Soon Mei created some kind of backlash, opening a doorway we never intended to open. I did not anticipate losing that subject's soul. Billy proved to be more resistant than we supposed. But the *principle* was proven. We had control—and then we lost it. But we made progress. We just need to refine our approach. There were a few damned good moments there, when the one who came through Gulcher controlled Krasnoff—and to some extent, Billy and Soon Mei. The image of the Wilderness showed us the possibility. The mass visitation. We could use that, on purpose, if we wanted to. Send a mass visitation against those who get in our way, and then the Great Wrath will be . . ." Forsythe let the sentence trail off, unfinished.

Gulcher just closed his eyes and wished he could smell something besides blood and fear.

Where the hell have I gotten myself to?

■ ■ ■

Right about that time. Generals Swanson and Erlich. In that same Pentagon office, staring into the same computer surveillance window. But they were looking through another set of cameras, a new vantage on the Containment Authority: the courtyard of Facility 23.

General Erlich toyed with a cup of coffee, untasted and gone cold. "Can we be sure Forsythe doesn't know we're monitoring him like this?"

"I don't think he'd have said some of the things he did, if he knew," General Swanson pointed out, unwrapping a piece of chewing gum. Hard to find Juicy Fruit anymore. Had to order it online. He folded the stick into his mouth, chewed meditatively a moment. "That thing about those who get in their way. Who'd that be? Us maybe? The senators that are down on this project? Foreign enemies? Who? Forsythe knows we're trying to talk the president into closing this thing down."

Erlich frowned. "Does he? Who's told him?"

"He just always seems to know what we talk about with the commander in chief."

Erlich put the coffee cup down on the desk. "I need to see that footage over again. Not sure what I saw. I don't think the cameras picked up everything. Looked like something coming out of the wall. Looks like they've got experimental subjects we never approved. Looks like one of those subjects died. Definitely got a woman going insane, chewing on someone's leg. And that fella Gulcher. You know what he's done? And he's working for us?"

"You know what they'll say about that," Swanson said. "'Might be a son of a bitch, but he's our son of a bitch.'"

"Is he? I'm not sure Forsythe's our son of a bitch. So maybe Gulcher isn't ours either."

"You weren't bothered by that remark, about those who get in his way?"

"Could be talking about the Iranians, for all I know," Erlich said, shrugging.

"What if he meant *us*?"

"You and me?" Erlich took a deep breath and let it out slowly. "Even if he didn't . . . this thing sure looks like it's spinning out of control. Let's look at it again, slow, see what we can see."

ABOUT HALF AN HOUR later, in Manhattan. The same night.

Bleak and Loraine were standing outside an ordinary apartment building in uptown Manhattan, under a softly buzzing streetlight. The apartment building was relatively modern; yellowish plaster, impregnated with little stones, covered the façade. Only one streetlight on the block worked. Maintenance had been shifted to privatization, in most of America, so some neighborhoods kept their streetlights and fire hydrants up, and some wouldn't pay the company fees.

Bleak stood there, waiting, watching the sky. Wondering again if he was doing the right thing, bringing Loraine here.

Doing the right thing? Hell, this could be insanely—*catastrophically*—wrong. The meeting had been Shoella's idea in the first place. With the coming of the detector and that close call on the Jersey dock, Shoella and Oliver had gone to Scribbler, who channeled the words *the recruiter should be recruited*—and he made it clear the "scribble" meant Agent Sarikosca. Loraine.

It was Bleak's idea to bring Loraine to Scribbler. But Bleak was having second thoughts. This woman was an agent of CCA. And the CCA preyed on ShadowComm. And there were ShadowComms in this building. . . .

Shoella had surprised Bleak by agreeing Loraine should come. "*Why we got to be afraid of them all the time?*" Shoella had said. "*If we had someone we could trust—someone who saw we could work on the outside, maybe even help them, on some things, if they trust us to be free while we did it, we could stop hiding.*"

It was a compromise. Some in ShadowComm could choose to

keep their freedom—in exchange for doing some work, at times, for the government . . . *if* Shoella and Bleak could make some kind of diplomatic connection with the government.

If Scribbler's scribbles approved it, on his meeting with her—that'd go a long way to convincing the other ShadowComms. But it would require trusting CCA.

And then there was the other reason Bleak had gone to Loraine—to find out about Sean. If some prototypical form of CCA had abducted his brother, how could he do business with them? For the greater good? But maybe it was the only way to really find Sean.

"We waiting here much longer?" Loraine asked, as an ambulance went warbling by on Second Avenue, headed uptown.

"We're waiting for someone. We can't go inside till she gets here—or I get some other signal to go in. Or to get the hell out of here."

The sidewalks were nearly deserted, though lights burned in the buildings, and hip-hop played from an open window across the street. Bleak watched a bent, white-haired, old woman laboriously pulling a bag of groceries in a small metal cart. Another ten steps and she turned toward a limestone-fronted tenement, maneuvered the cart clankingly down the stone stairs to a basement apartment, descending out of sight.

Loraine looked at the sky. "We shouldn't be out here too long. I don't think we're being surveilled at this point, after changing trains three times, but . . ."

"We won't have to wait long now."

A blue-and-white NYPD patrol car cruised by. Bleak wanted to turn away, hide his face, in case CCA had pulled strings to get an APB out on him. But instead he looked down the street, as if impatient for someone to meet him. Which he didn't have to fake.

The cops looked them over and moved on.

"What worries me," Bleak said in a low voice, when the cops

turned the corner, "is that maybe the cops have Lucille Rhione. Maybe she accused me of being a murderer. Maybe there's an APB out on me—CCA might do it that way. Easiest way to pull me in. Then they get me from the cops."

Loraine shook her head emphatically. "No—we don't want the police bringing you in unless it's way, way necessary. It was a big hassle, with Gulcher, squaring it with all the interested parties. A lot of lies had to be told about where he was going to be—" She broke off, seeming to think she was saying too much; an expression of irritated self-reproach on her face. "Anyway—if the police try to take you, you might be forced to use your gifts. And who knows what might come out in the media. We don't want the general public knowing about that. You could get yourself shot too. You're too valuable to risk to the police."

"If that's true, it's one less thing to worry about. That leaves four hundred other things." Bleak licked his dry lips. It was a warm night. After the fight with Gandalf, the conference with Shoella, then getting Agent Sarikosca here on all those trains, Bleak was hot, tired, and he badly wanted a glass of beer. Maybe a pitcher of beer. The shooting had left him with a clutching feeling; a feeling that was still there. He wasn't much moved by death, especially not the death of a speed dealer. But shooting someone in the head brought back that morning in Afghanistan. Isaac dying, Bleak running to find the mortar, killing another militant because there was no one else to kill . . . then killing the militant's son. Shooting a teenage boy in the head. Yeah, the kid was shooting at him at the time. But the kid was crying with grief as he fired at Bleak. Yelling the Afghan word for "father."

Bleak felt nothing that day. But later . . . the feelings came.

Somehow it was all one thing. Isaac getting killed was of a piece with shooting that kid. As if it were all one shooting.

It didn't help much to know there was life after death. Not when he also knew that people were trying to live out their lives for a reason. The spirit of the young militant he'd shot was probably still wandering in that village. Maybe he should have tried to talk to him, after. But that wouldn't work. Then there was the sheer violence of the thing—right through the head . . . and the blood . . . the smell of blood and shattered brains . . .

Think about something else.

Loraine Sarikosca. Maybe she was an enemy, maybe not. But he liked looking at her; he liked wondering about her. And he felt something extraordinary when they were together. A desire to trust her that he felt to the core of his being. As if he'd known her all his life, and beyond this life. "Okay with you if I call you Loraine?" he asked impulsively. "Calling you Agent Sarikosca . . ." He shook his head. "It's not discreet and . . . the *agent* part gives me the willies."

"Call me Loraine if you want." She glanced at him and looked quickly away. "If you don't mind that I continue to call you Bleak."

Bleak wondered why that was important to her. But all he said was "I was looking at some of your books, before I sprang my visit on you."

"And my records. You're out there poking through my things—"

"Hey—you're detecting me, I'm detecting you. You've got Jane Austen, Fielding. Dickens. O'Brian and Cornwell. I've read those. And the nonfiction. *The Occult* by Colin Wilson. Ouspensky's *A New Model of the Universe*. Some Richard Smoley, some Alice Bailey, Jay Kinney—some Leloup. You're pretty well read in the occult."

She looked down the street. "I had a fascination with the supernatural. When it seemed so far away. So unreachable. Now I feel like . . ."

"Wish it was still . . . Hidden?"

"Sometimes. I'm still not used to seeing it right there in front of me." She looked at him, her eyebrows raised. "I wouldn't think you'd bother with books on the occult, Bleak. Being up to your neck in it."

"I went through a period of trying to understand it better. Wondering what other people understood of it."

"And those books—are they right?"

"Don't you know? You've got all those . . . pets of yours, at CCA."

Her cheeks reddened. "They're not my . . . I don't have that much interaction with them. Tell you the truth, I haven't been with CCA that long. I was . . . I was with another agency before CCA. When I transferred, they put me to work right away. I'm getting kind of a crash course. I'm not exactly sure why they're putting me on . . ." She got that look of being annoyed with herself again. "So—are those books right about the supernatural or not?"

He waved vaguely at the buildings around them. "It's like this island—if you'd never been to Manhattan, and you've just arrived by sea, and went around the island in the sightseeing boat, would you know Manhattan from that? No. You'd have an *impression* of it, though, in some ways. You'd have a sense. But you'd figure a lot of things wrong too. Or—like that story of the blind men and the elephant. Each one of them gets it *partly* right."

He saw she was trying to read the words printed on his T-shirt—he opened his unbuttoned white shirt so she could read it. "Are you in a motorcycle club?" she asked, perplexed by the T-shirt. "The . . . Black Rebel Motorcycle Club?"

"That's a band. I collect rock-band T-shirts. Mostly old bands. Most of them are stored at . . ." He broke off, not wanting to say Cronin's name. "A friend's house."

She peered down the empty street. "You don't want to tell me who we're going to meet here?"

"Someone I trust who . . . has gifts. A certain woman. And someone we call Scribbler, who uses automatic writing, to get insights. Psychic insights. He doesn't always know what the 'scribbles' mean. It always turns out to be meaningful though. Sometimes it sees the future. Sometimes it sees things we can't see in the present. Let's leave it at that."

She pushed at a flattened beer can with the toe of her shoe, her tone way too casual as she said, "On the subway you asked about someone at CCA. I didn't answer. There's probably not much I can tell you. But maybe you should ask me the question anyway."

Bleak chuckled. "Sure, so you can learn something from the question. But I'll play. What do you know about Sean Bleak? I heard a story from one of your people—or he used to be one of your people—that Sean was . . ." He found it hard to actually get the words out. "That he was there. Alive. At one of your facilities, I guess. Being used for something."

Loraine seemed relieved. "I can tell you that I've heard of someone named *Sean* there, who seems to be important to . . . to my superiors. But I've never met him. I'm *supposed* to meet him—it hasn't happened yet. I don't know his last name. I can only read the files they give me. Some files are 'need to know.'" She frowned, as if she'd said too much again. Then seemed to shrug it away. "Sean *Bleak*? He's a relative?"

"If it's him . . . he was my brother. Fraternal twin. Or . . . he *is* my brother. I don't know which. I find it hard to believe he's . . ." Bleak shook his head. "Too long a story for right now."

He heard a discordantly unfriendly squawk and looked up to see Yorena circling overhead. "Here comes one animal that doesn't like me. Only it's not exactly an animal, really. You see it up there? Probably means her mistress is about to arrive."

A yellow cab turned onto the street. The cabbie, wearing a turban, pulled up nearby, next to a fire hydrant. Shoella paid him and got out, and as the cab drove away, she stood there, a long moment, scowlingly looking Loraine over. As if she wanted Loraine to know she didn't trust her.

Maybe that's good instincts, Bleak thought. *Simple street smarts. I shouldn't be this friendly with Agent Sarikosca either.*

Yorena flapped down—making Loraine take a quick step backward in mild alarm—and settled on Shoella's right shoulder.

"I'm Loraine." Smiling slightly at Shoella. "Loraine Sarikosca."

Shoella didn't answer. Finally she said, turning to Bleak, "The *bon Dieu* knows if we do right. If she's coming, bring her upstairs, *cher* darlin'."

She twitched the big, dark red bird off her shoulder, and the familiar leaped into the air, to flap raucously overhead. "Yorena, you wait on the roof, I call you soon. Scribbler, he don't want you in there."

Shoella watched the bird fly off, then turned to look at Loraine. "But you—I suppose you got to come in."

THIRTEEN

His real name was Conrad Pflug. He lived in a two-bedroom apartment whose only visible furnishing was the sofa bed in his living room and a coffee table. The coffee table was his center of operations. Scribbler was a compulsive pack rat, and the rest of the apartment was taken up with overpacked cardboard boxes, and newspapers and magazines, fussily stacked. He was only midthirties, but looked older; a small, colorless, balding, wizened man with eyes crowded together above a long, narrow stroke of nose; dark red lips, weak chin. He invariably wore a long-sleeved black shirt, black slacks, black slippers. If he wore anything but black, he'd find himself scribbling on the fabric.

Scribbler rarely went out. Maybe, Bleak thought, as they pressed through the narrow passage between boxes, Conrad Pflug stayed indoors because when he did go out, he would inevitably come back with something scavenged from the street for which he had no more room. He lived on a small annuity, and donations from people who came for his precognitive scribblings.

Most psychics were frauds. Most who predicted the future couldn't accurately predict their own grocery list. But Scribbler was different. He was ShadowComm, and quiet about his ability, which had repeatedly proved itself. If you could interpret Scribbler's automatic writing, you got value for your money.

Groceries and medicines could be delivered to Conrad Pflug, but Scribbler had to go out for pens, the right sort of ink pens. He needed a great many of them.

Scribbler led the way from his front door, followed by Shoella, Bleak, and Loraine, edging along sideways between walls of cardboard boxes stacked to the ceiling on both sides of the dingily lit hallway; the old synthetic carpet, badly worn, was the same color as the boxes.

What was in the boxes? Bleak had no idea. Odds and ends collected from the street, he supposed, on Scribbler's increasingly rare forays out. What was *on* the boxes, though, intrigued the eye: scribbles, every square inch of cardboard covered with words, closely written cursive, mostly in black, sometimes blue, rarely in red; some of the scribbles on the boxes couldn't quite be read as words—but seemed to want to *become* words.

Scribbler took his guests through a doorway covered by a shabby brown curtain, into what had been a living room. It was now a musty cave of stacked boxes and square-edged columns of mildewed, yellowing magazines bound with string in blocks of exactly twenty issues. The window onto the street was completely covered up by boxes—Bleak only knew the window must be there because this room was at the front of the building. The room's single light, on the coffee table, was from a lamp with a white shade that had been covered in scribbles, mostly in black ink. Here and there on the shade was a red-ink scribble, and the light seemed to make the red ink phrases stand out. Bleak picked out one in red ink: *Breslin hemmed in.* Did that refer to President Breslin?

The cluttered coffee table was wedged in front of the black-draped sofa bed. Somewhere an air conditioner worked wheezily, just enough to keep the apartment from being dangerously hot. Scribbler lived in fear of the fire marshal seeing his place.

He lived in fear of other things too: about twenty prescription-medicine bottles were on a small tray in the corner of the coffee table. Under the clutter, the coffee table was also covered with a black cloth, for the same reason that Scribbler wore black. His graphomania.

Among coffee cups, empty wrappers for energy bars, and cookies—Scribbler ate almost nothing but one or two energy bars a day, and Oreo cookies—writing implements in mason jars shared the table with a long roll of white wrapping paper. Most of the pens were the cheap plastic, three-way sort, each pen with three different colors, red, blue, and black, depending on which button you pushed.

Scribbler eased himself onto the edge of the sofa bed, blinking in the cone of light from the lamp. He carefully selected a pen from a jar with his left hand—a pen apparently identical to the others. "This one ought to be good." His voice was very New York, and he tended to crowd the words together.

Bleak and Shoella and Loraine stood awkwardly nearby, squeezed like pens into the small floor space.

"My name is Loraine Sarikosca," Loraine said suddenly, perhaps hoping for his name in return. "I am here to just . . . offer the possibility of friendship and . . ." Her voice trailed off. As if she were wondering, herself, what she was offering.

Scribbler flicked a look at her, then looked quickly away, as if abashed—he couldn't bear eye contact, Bleak knew. Some form of Asperger's. "I *know* your name. It's in there." Scribbler nodded his head at a large plastic paint bucket tucked against a high stack of *People* magazines; the faces of celebrities on the top magazine were covered with scribbles. The bucket he pointed out was packed with other rolls of paper, standing on end—all covered with scribbles.

"I see, well, I . . ." Loraine coughed and rubbed a watering eye. Stifled a sneeze. "Sorry. I've got allergies."

"It's the dust in here," Scribbler said, the words tumbling over one another. *Itsadustnhere.* "An' the little mites what live on the dust, and the paper fleas. When the air conditioner's off, you can hear the paper fleas *ticketyticking* around." He seemed delighted by the idea and gave a grimacing grin at no one in particular; his teeth were edged in black.

"Where's Oliver?" Bleak asked.

"Said he didn't wanna come." *Saidhedidnwannacome.* "Changed his mind. Said he wasn't going to trust no one from CCA, said they don't believe in neutral ground."

"I believe in it," Loraine said, sniffling.

Bleak glanced at Loraine. She was standing over by the lamp, and he could see the dust in the air around her in the smaller, inverted cone of lamplight from the coffee table. Was Oliver right? This whole encounter with Loraine was counterintuitive. But Shoella's work with Scribbler had convinced her that Agent Sarikosca was a *"bridge to a secret that could liberate us, and it's worth the risk."*

"Let's get this done, let's get this done, it's too crowded in here," Scribbler said, his long, slim, trembling, white fingers becoming one with the pen, rolling it from finger to finger and back to a writing grip. The others stood with their backs close to stacks of boxes and magazines—there was no place to comfortably sit—and they watched him as he turned almost sideways to the coffee table and with his right hand pulled an old Parker Brothers Ouija board from under the sofa bed, set it on his lap, pulled on the roll of paper so it unreeled onto the Ouija board. It acted as his writing desk.

"A Ouija board?" Loraine murmured, surprised. "Does that signify anything? I mean traditionally it—"

"Fool," Shoella interrupted, "sure it signify something—that Scribbler man has a sense of humor."

"Quiet," Scribbler snapped. When he'd got the paper arranged just so, he reached into the clutter on the coffee table and drew a black sleeping mask from under an Oreo wrapper. He pulled it over his eyes, with a single practiced motion, so that he was blindfolded. He murmured, "Where is my friend? Where is Conrad's friend? Speak through me, my friend. Where is . . ." He broke off—and immediately began scribbling on the roll of paper with his left hand, dragging it slowly past him with his right so that, turned as he was, the ribbon of written-on paper piled up on the floor by his feet. The pen moved with remarkable speed, with dexterous exactitude, straight across the page as if following ruled lines—without having any. The cursive scribbling was difficult to read but almost beautiful, appearing like the lines on a seismograph recording vibrations in the earth. Which is what it was, in a way, only it recorded vibrations in the Hidden, the unseen cloak of the earth.

The words used up most of the sixteen-inch width of the wrapping paper, and they ran together, in one continuous flow per line, so far only in black ink. A little space between letters indicated separate words. He filled up inch after inch of paper as the seconds passed. He could fill up reams this way. Scribbler had a special ritual, Bleak knew, for getting rid of old "scrolls," which he performed each full moon. It was the only thing he willingly got rid of.

Scribbler scribbled for several minutes. His thumb only clicked the pen once, making a single line blue instead of black; then returning to black ink. He knew which button to press for red or blue or black, though his eyes were covered.

Bleak edged around to Scribbler's left, craned to try to read the newest scribbles:

> . . . *Chicano poet memoirist Rodriguez calling the recent devastation the most terrifying indoor weather to defer to the cynical and to just assume that beneath the veneer the world is made up of predators and prey and all you can hope for is a kind of break in the isolation in attempts to envision the worst of our world indentured epiphany lost in these moments and you always lose something but come out on the other side having always felt a kind of entelechy to be drawn on . . .*

It was nonsense, for the most part. Still, Bleak suspected it meant something, from some perspective in the Hidden.

Scribbler scrivened on. After writing the words "wildly experimental scenes in those days," without any apparent pause in writing, he clicked on the red ink and started writing in something more like sentences, and Bleak paid close attention to the words scribbled in red, which started with "and emerged from opposite ends."

> . . . *always felt a kind of entelechy to be drawn on, that's what happens in the other end, a dismaying social consequence, wildly experimental scenes in those days and emerged from opposite ends of the world, the stony and the starry, Gabriel and Loraine, and she draws him and another draws her to draw him to them, where Sean awaits to lock minds with Gabriel. One will lock hearts, the other would lock minds. Loraine does not know that you can trust her but you can. It is like thinking you cannot trust your own left hand. In your right hand you hold her despair and if you make a fist you destroy it and the glass egg breaks and hope melts free to run between your*

fingers to take a shape of its own determination. Shoella's heart stands in the way, Shoella's heart is the doorway to be broken, though Yorena frowns from dark clouds in the place of ancestors. Loraine is beyond the doorway for Gabriel, arms an entrance, Loraine and Gabriel like puzzle pieces made to fit. Sean seeks Gabriel as an anaconda seeks the sleeping child. The President is afraid, Breslin is afraid of the man within the man who stands on his right, and the crack in the wall lets the Great Wrath through, who darkens like ink in the water those he would conceal, and yet move toward Facility 23 and find the liberating truth on the way to the North, there in the North tragedy mates with triumph and the Ten shrink to the new Ten and she must return to them alone for now for they seek her nearby but she will not knowingly draw them to me and we must do that which we would never do, we must trust Loraine this time and always so long as it is her will who guides her and sometimes they're psychopaths but most of the time people rationalize everything they do, that is what keeps us trapped in who we are, our rationales, the constructions we make to justify our behavior are our destiny . . .

Scribbler had returned to using black ink with "and sometimes they're psychopaths," and that was the end of the oracle's message.

Staring at a sentence in red, Bleak felt a surprising embarrassment of exposure. Like something he'd felt in a dream of riding a subway—and suddenly realizing he was riding it stark naked.

Shoella's heart is the doorway to be broken, though Yorena frowns from dark clouds in the place of ancestors. Loraine is beyond the doorway for Gabriel, arms an entrance, Loraine and Gabriel like puzzle pieces made to fit.

Bleak shook his head. *Like puzzle pieces made to fit?* He didn't know the meaning for certain quite yet—but he suspected it. He'd come to expect irony from life.

Scribbler filled another four lines with cryptic black script, then abruptly dropped the pen, swept the blindfold off, and set to massaging his left hand with his right, chewing his lower lip. "Hurts. Hurts like a bitchy old lady. Speakin' of bitchy old ladies, wish my mama was alive, she used to massage my hands."

"I'll massage it for you," Loraine said, with calm assurance. She sat on the arm of the sofa bed, took his left hand between hers, and began to massage it.

Both Bleak and Shoella stared in astonishment—they expected Scribbler to jerk his hand away from her.

But he let her massage his fingers for a couple of minutes, though he wouldn't look at her. His face blissed-out like a dog getting its belly rubbed.

Bleak waited for Loraine to ask for something in exchange for the intimacy. An interpretation. An appointment, perhaps, with CCA. But she said nothing. And after all, Bleak supposed, if Loraine chose to, she could simply make a phone call and CCA would storm this place and drag Scribbler away.

He was sure she wouldn't do that, though. Because Scribbler always knew. He was always right. And he had let her come here. He knew, somehow, that she would not betray him, though it was her job to do so.

Unless, for once, Scribbler was wrong.

Bleak looked again at the scribbles in red. The part at the end . . .

. . . *and she must return to them alone for now for they seek her nearby but she will not knowingly draw them to me and we must do that which we would never do, we must trust Loraine this time and always so long as it is her will who guides her . . .*

Bleak noticed the phrase *will not knowingly draw them to me.*

And he noticed that as Loraine rubbed Scribbler's hand, she was looking at what he'd written, in red, as if trying to memorize it.

She was still an agent of CCA.

At last Loraine drew her hands back and stood up. "Is that any better?"

Scribbler still wouldn't look at her. But he said, "Yeah. Thank you. Loraine. My name is Conrad, by the way."

"Conrad." She nodded.

"But I still have to charge somebody for the words. It's a rule. You can't take it with you unless you pay. Whoever takes the red page has to pay." He ran his left hand over the scroll; over the words in red, as if his hand were counting. Never looking right at it. "That's two hundred eighty-six words. At one dollar a word that's two hundred eighty-six dollars."

"I'll pay it," Loraine said. "Can I write a check or—"

"*I* will pay it!" Shoella interrupted loudly, taking folding money from a pocket. "I have that much. The one who pays takes the paper." She scowled at Loraine. "You will not take it. You have seen it, that is enough. I had to have you here—Scribbler said so. The ancestors advised it. But I don't have to give you the paper."

"But . . . you have to give me the two hundred eighty-six dollars," Scribbler reminded her.

OUTSIDE, SHOELLA, BLEAK, AND Loraine paused on the front steps to look for a CCA chopper or a spy drone because the words in red said *they seek her nearby.* But if they were nearby, they were well hidden.

Yorena flew down from above and settled on Shoella's left shoulder. Shoella scratched the back of the familiar's neck and said to Loraine, "I had to see you two together, and I had to bring us into a room with Scribbler, to get his Sight, and . . . Gabriel and I will discuss it. Someplace else. Alone." She touched her blouse, where she'd tucked away the folded, red-inked paper torn from Scribbler's scroll.

Shoella glared up at the one working streetlight as if that's what she was mad at, streetlights. But Yorena seemed to glare at Loraine. Who exactly *was* Shoella angry at? Bleak wondered. Hadn't this been her idea? Hadn't she been talking about working with CCA, if they could retain their freedom? "Shoella—" He waited as a police car and then another sirened by on the avenue, going downtown, followed by the whine of an electric bus. "You feel like you can interpret the writing he gave us?"

"Later. She . . ." Shoella nodded at Loraine. "She doesn't have to hear. She only had to be there with us when he did it."

Bleak looked curiously at Loraine. "What made you rub Scribbler's hand like that? I've never seen him let anyone else touch him."

"Why?" Shoella snorted. "So she could read what he wrote."

Loraine shook her head. "I'm sure he'd have shown me anyway. I just wanted to." She took a long, slow breath, frowning in thought. "I don't know. I just felt like he needed it. I felt sorry for him. Like he'd gotten close to me in some way and looked into me and when he did . . . I don't know how to say it."

Bleak nodded. This woman could surprise him. Which was something he liked.

"I don't want to spend any more time around this woman," Shoella snapped. Not looking at Loraine as she said it.

Why this desire in Shoella to get away from Loraine? Bleak wondered. Was it jealousy—or mistrust because she was CCA?

The look in Shoella's eyes suggested it was something personal. As if she too suspected a bond between Bleak and Loraine. An extraordinary bond.

He seemed to hear Oliver's bitter voice again: *"I suppose you know that Shoella's in love with you."*

"I'll be going soon, Shoella," Loraine said, in a low voice.

"Bleak—what did it mean . . . what it said about me, and you? I didn't exactly . . . follow."

Bleak pretended to be interested in looking at Yorena. "I don't know for sure. It appears you and I are connected in some way. Linked somehow. But I don't know how. Not yet." He had a suspicion, though. And the suspicion renewed that feeling of embarrassment. Of feeling naked.

Loraine nodded quickly, as if glad to have put the question behind her. "And—what did the . . . the *divination* mean, 'the President is afraid of the man within the man'? And what is the Great Wrath?"

"I don't know that either. Eventually it'll show itself to us, as the facts start to unfold. I do know that this oracle often tends to be surprisingly literal."

"By this oracle—you mean, um, Conrad?"

"No, he's just a medium for the message. Just the transmitter. We say, 'Scribbler says this,' but we don't mean it's really him saying it. His vocabulary doesn't even extend to a lot of the words he writes." Bleak paused, thinking about how to explain it. Feeling a breeze off the East River. It smelled of the river's living murk. "No, the oracle is an entity in the Hidden that is trying to help, but it has to do it indirectly. It doesn't seem to make sense when the oracle speaks because you aren't caught up to the truth yet. That's something you find out later—then you see what it meant. But I could guess at one thing—if it says 'a man within the man' about someone around President Breslin—it's talking about some kind of diabolic influence."

Loraine's eyes widened. "Diabolic influence. Around the president?"

Shoella said sharply, "Evil souls like to be with evil souls." She gave Loraine a look that conveyed matter-of-fact hatred as effectively as a hard slap to the face. "The president approved your Central Containment Authority. I know what your people have done to my people." Shoella seemed to loom over Loraine as she spoke, her voice becoming a hiss. "I should tie you to a roof and let Yorena eat your eyes. I should call the baka who eats minds—and I should say, 'Feed on her!' But"—Shoella made a gesture of exasperation and drew back from Loraine—"you are to be of use, some kind of bridge, this the oracle says, so I got to bring you here . . . and let you walk away." Adding, her voice barely audible, "Though you are sure to betray me."

Loraine remained outwardly unmoved, watching Shoella closely during the diatribe but not showing any fear, and not arguing.

"Sarikosca here won't betray us," Bleak said. "Scribbler would have warned us. The Hidden seems to say she won't. Seems to say we should trust her. I know it doesn't make sense—but . . ."

He turned to Loraine—and for a moment, when she looked back, he felt an electric connection between them. He felt a stirring, a pull. Then, lips parted as if she were catching her breath, Loraine looked quickly away. "But she won't betray us," he said again.

"I didn't mean she will betray me like that," Shoella said softly. She turned to him, adding more forcefully, "Now, Bleak, you come with me. We need to talk. And she must go."

Loraine turned to Bleak, their gazes intersected again, and though her face was impassive he saw, quite clearly, the depth of emotion in her eyes. "I . . . had better go anyway," she said. "I'm not going to tell anyone about Scribbler. Or Shoella. I will talk to them about the possibility that CCA could be in a different kind of . . . of relationship with ShadowComm. A new deal."

"You could answer some questions, yourself," Bleak said, holding her gaze. Not letting her go just yet. "What is happening in the north? Where does the wall come from? What's happening to it?"

"I can't tell you those things. I took an oath."

"How about Facility Twenty-three? It was in the red scribble.

That sounds like it'd refer to something of yours—something belonging to CCA."

She looked at the sidewalk. "It is CCA's, yes. I haven't been there yet. It's their most clandestine facility."

"That where the ShadowComms go?"

She didn't deny it. "Not just there. But Twenty-three is one of the most . . ." She shrugged. "Like I say, I haven't been admitted there yet."

"But you know who's there?" Bleak took a step closer to her. Could feel the aura of life around her; could feel the outer edges of her mind as if feeling the static electricity in a cat's fur. He realized, all of a sudden, that he wanted to take her in his arms.

But if he did, she would probably draw back from him—and Shoella might do anything. Might try to kill them both.

Still, Loraine tolerated him, standing so close; she looked up into his face. And he asked her softly, "Is Sean there? Is my brother in Facility Twenty-three?" He knew, somehow, with the two of them so near each other, that she couldn't keep herself from answering. But he didn't know exactly why that was.

She swallowed. Then nodded. "I think he probably is."

They were standing so close . . . he could almost—

"Gabriel," Shoella said, her voice husky with warning.

Loraine stepped decisively back. Then she forced a thin smile, a parting nod. "I'll be in touch. I have to go . . . they'll be looking for me." She fished in her purse, found a business card and a pen, wrote a number on the back of the card. "That's my personal cell phone." She gave it to Bleak and turned to walk away, toward the west.

Yorena squawked, and Shoella glanced at the creature in irritation. "Shut up. You don't know that. You don't know anything. It might go any way at all."

Bleak glanced at the familiar. "What did Yorena say?"

"Lies. Yorena's very emotional. Very pessimistic. Nothing to repeat." Shoella looked in a pocket for a cell phone. "I'll call a cab."

He turned and watched Loraine walk away. He felt a tearing inside. A completely irrational feeling. *All this is irrational. Trusting her. Feeling this way as she walks away. Makes no sense.*

"Maybe Yorena is right," Shoella said softly, watching Loraine narrowly. "Maybe I am making a big mistake, letting her go. I could send Yorena after her, Gabriel. One quick clawing at the woman's neck, in the right spot, tear that big vein, she would probably die."

Bleak looked at Shoella in dull shock. Finally he said, "You've got better judgment than that, Shoella. That woman won't betray us."

Shoella just shook her head in sullen disgust. Bleak stared after Loraine, then put the card in his wallet, thinking that something monumental, something key and important, had happened tonight . . . and he had no idea, exactly, what it was.

And when Loraine walked away, he felt something else: a sinking inside him, a lost feeling, a groping in darkness . . . as if he were suddenly missing some precious part of himself.

In your right hand you hold her despair . . .

FOURTEEN

lmost two hours later. Upstate New York. A warm and sticky night. Just outside Facility 23.

Dying oaks, crumbling inwardly from a blight, stretched out their branches alongside the access road with lugubrious crookedness. As the young soldier drove her up to the facility gate, Loraine told herself there was nothing special, outwardly, about the facility. Surrounded by razor wire, floodlights, and cameras on steel poles, it was just another sprawling, generic government structure, with a cryptic sign but no clear markings. But there was something about it . . .

The air conditioner in the government car was broken; the driver had apologized, but there was no time to go to the motor pool for another—she'd received a cell phone call from Dr. Helman summoning her here within minutes of leaving Bleak. Sweat gathered on her brow and blew away in the air washing through the car's open windows. Her clothes chafed her, under the armpits, and at her collar. The young Special Forces driver, a stocky white man in a uniform and black beret, had hardly spoken since she'd got in beside him.

She stared at the bland façade of Facility 23, thinking, *Sean Bleak is in there somewhere.* In a place that hummed with frightened desperation.

Now what brought that on? she thought. But since her first encounter with Bleak, she'd felt more intuitive, more sensitive, than she ever had before.

She pondered her sense of deep but indescribable connection to Gabriel Bleak. She'd felt him watching her as she walked away, down Ninety-fifth Street. Felt it as clearly as you'd feel a cool breeze on the back of your neck.

Maybe all this exposure to the supernatural had her imagining things. Seeing Krasnoff project his visions; seeing Soon Mei open the Hidden. Glimpsing her fate scribbled in red ink. She was seeing the unearthly everywhere.

No—it was more as if her boundaries had been fractured. Her assumptions about reality had flown to pieces. It was as if hidden doors, secret passages, were everywhere, no matter where you went. As if she had been walking down the corridor of life looking for a door where the walls looked blank, then she'd discovered the doors *were there* all the time. They were simply invisible, until you learned to see them. She was starting to sense things she'd never sensed before.

And her newly kindled intuition told her that Facility 23 was one big bad omen.

Deal with it, she thought, as the sedan drove through the gate to the first checkpoint. The driver spoke to the guards, flashlight beams made Loraine blink, then the car was waved on. It drove along a narrow asphalt road around the building to stop at a nondescript gray metal door in a big, otherwise featureless concrete wall in the back.

The gray metal door opened, as she got out of the car, and Dr. Helman was waiting for her in its rectangle of cold light, bobblehead nodding. "I apologize in advance," Helman said, as she walked up to the building's back door. "I should let you read the file of the man you're about to meet, first. But there isn't time. Events press. Time grows short. You must meet him now."

She followed him into a building, and down a corridor—for much of its length a blank, doorless corridor, like so many others she'd walked through—Loraine thinking it strange Helman hadn't mentioned her meeting with Bleak. Maybe they didn't have her under surveillance after all. Not all the time. But there was another possibility. . . .

SHE KNEW IT WAS him, before Helman introduced the man sitting at the table: "This is Sean Bleak. Sean, Agent Sarikosca."

They were in a small, windowless conference room with a large flat-screen TV at one end; a glossy pine-finish, oval conference table with a few chairs, concrete walls painted light green. An opaque glass hemisphere in the center of the ceiling probably held a surveillance camera. Just outside the open door were two guards, alert to a call from Helman. Apparently Helman didn't trust Sean.

"I don't want to call her Agent Sarikosca," Sean said as she sat across from him. A peculiar, twisted little smile as he said it; a pettish, whispery voice; ice-chip blue eyes. Long sandy hair. He wore a paramilitary outfit. On him it looked almost like the clothing of an inmate in a military prison.

Not an identical twin. But much like Gabriel Bleak—and very much unlike him.

"You'll call her what protocol demands, Sean," Helman told him, sitting at the end of the table, frowning over a complicated remote control. "General Forsythe wants a structured environment for you. Your privileges are contingent on staying within that structure. That means following protocol."

Sean chuckled at that; eyes flicking at Helman with barely concealed contempt. "You invoke Forsythe's name to keep me in line." She noticed he had a way of talking with his mouth nearly shut. "You know he's special; that he's the one I respect. But don't pretend I've got any real freedom." Sean looked at Loraine, added hastily, "Not that I don't ever leave this place. I've been in places like this most of my life—but there were other places too." It seemed important to him to tell her that he was more than some lab rat, here. "There was a place up in the mountains, in the trees. I had a nanny, she was a good old girl. I had a tutor who was kind of like a dad to me. In a sort of way. I had play dates with kids, for a while. Till that got weird. I even got taken to Disney World one time. I've got the latest game consoles. Lately I go on what they like to call virtual excursions. We've got some pretty good VR gear. And I've had women—"

"Sean!" Helman snapped. "Have some respect for the agent."

"But it's true—I've had women! Brought in special. Kind of like the ones you'll see here on the TV tonight. That what we're going to see, Dr. Helman? That experiment with Gulcher?"

"Yes, yes."

One other thing was in the room. She hadn't seen it till Sean leaned forward. It was behind him: a suppressor, plugged in and turned on.

Feeling pity for Sean, thinking he had been raised in places like this and there was no telling what he'd been through, Loraine impulsively said, "You can call me Loraine, Sean, if you like."

"Thank you, *Loraine*," he said, studying her. He smiled, suddenly, briefly showing yellowed teeth, as if he remembered that it was good to smile broadly but wasn't quite sure how to do it.

Helman used the remote to turn on the television and clicked through a menu till he got a window on the screen that said PRE-

PARED MATERIAL. "Here we go. This is . . ." He turned to Loraine, putting on an expression of solemnity. "Well—perhaps I should prepare you."

It was funny how socially artificial both of these men seemed, Loraine decided. In different ways, each seemed strikingly insincere. As if they'd learned to interact with people the way a clumsy man learned to dance—by rote.

"Why don't you turn that suppressor off, Helman," Sean said suddenly. "You don't need it. And I could show Loraine some things."

"No, not this time; I don't think so, Sean," Helman said, with asperity. "I wish to tell her . . ." He leaned toward Loraine, his manner grave, weighty. "You've seen some hard things, Loraine. Your duty has taken you to some dangerous places. You saw women you'd recruited taken into custody in Syria—and there was nothing you could do for them. You saw a suicide bomb attack in Kabul. You were involved in the debriefing on the Miami attack. You know what the terrorists did there. That is what we're up against—a brutally unstable world." Helman gently rapped the table to emphasize the next sentence. "We cannot afford to be concerned with every fallen sparrow! We must be willing to do *whatever is necessary*! Power like this, potential of the kind the CCA contains, and directs . . . we cannot risk losing control of it. It's like the Manhattan Project in the last century. Sometimes the testing is dangerous. People die. We need to know that you're . . . capable of dealing with the harsh realities."

Loraine shrugged. "It's all been harsh reality, Doctor." She wasn't thinking of Syria, though that had been bad enough. She was thinking of Krasnoff—and Sean Bleak, sitting across from her. It seemed likely he'd been pried from his parents' hands, raised in an institutional setting. She'd had to work hard on accepting that kind of reality at CCA.

"To be sure," Helman said. "But what I am going to show you

may shock you anyway. We run tremendous risks here—and to protect the country we must test the forces we work with. Test them on people, on human beings. You must have a spine of steel to proceed with us, Loraine. And if you don't—well." He glanced at Sean. "One way or another . . . we will have your help."

That one startled her. *One way or another?*

"I've had women," Sean said suddenly, out of left field, almost leering at Loraine, "but nobody with your class."

"I'm here as a federal agent, Sean," Loraine said, forcing herself to smile politely—but feeling her skin crawl. "Let's keep this professional."

"Professional?" Sean's eyes looked shiny, as if he were close to tears. His mouth compressed. When he spoke, it was through clenched teeth, and hard to make out. "What profession do *I* have?"

It came to her that Sean was stuck in adolescence. He had his brother's penetrating eyes—and a sense about him, as with his brother, that he was always aware of something you couldn't see. Even with the suppressor in the room Sean knew the Hidden was there, in ways she couldn't.

But he was so different from Gabriel Bleak. Gabriel had a still, strong center to him. You felt that he was ready for anything. You knew you could trust him. He might hold things back, but he wouldn't want to lie to you. It would be unnatural to him.

But his brother, she suspected, might say anything to get what he wanted. Sean was damaged—and there was no telling how deep the damage went.

"Your profession, Sean, is to serve the United States of America by helping it control UBEs," Helman said, using the remote control again, fast-forwarding. Images flickered by on the television screen, too fast to make out. "You even get paid for it, every month. Sometimes you spend the money."

Sean sniffed. "Spend the money! EBay purchases. Amazon. Once a month I get to have a bottle of wine." He sniffed in disgust. "The occasional hired girl. It's how they manage me . . . *control* me."

The images on the screen slowed, became recognizable: a concrete courtyard, a view from high on a wall, and to one side was General Forsythe with a man she didn't recognize at first, and a group of armed black berets. The man with Forsythe turned, his face caught the light, and she recognized him. "Troy Gulcher!" she blurted.

"Very good," Sean said, with a kind of nerdy irony. "Our man Gulcher. Who's been bitching continuously since he got here."

She saw that Gulcher, in the video, had no restraints, no cuffs. That he was standing with Forsythe in a friendly way. She realized that Gulcher was not just contained—but recruited. *A man like that. A murderer.* Was she really supposed to work beside him?

Doors opened, in the courtyard. People came through, accompanied by more guards. She recognized Helman, Soon Mei, Krasnoff—and someone she didn't know.

"Who is that child? He's got cuffs on!"

"That is just one of the difficult elements I was warning you about," Helman said. "William John Blunt. Billy Blunt. We purchased him from his parents—"

"You *purchased* him?"

"Yes. We arranged for them to report him missing and gave them a substantial fee. They were quite happy with the arrangement. He is a casebook psychopath—they were quite afraid of him. He was starting to use his abilities on them. Just coming into them fully, then. He's quite a little government secret. Top secret, as you might imagine."

"Like me," Sean said ruefully. "But uglier and not so talented. Can't play a first-person shooter to save his little ass."

"Yes, indeed, just as you say," Helman said distractedly, watching the screen. "There . . . you see something interesting . . . Krasnoff is now projecting his vision."

"I don't see it," she murmured. She could see the light projecting from Krasnoff's eyes and mouth—and a circle on the wall, sparkling around the edges. Nothing inside the circle but concrete wall.

"Exactly so," Helman said, with an expert's excitement. "It doesn't show up on this video. Other visions of his have shown up, rather fuzzily. But not this."

"It's because it's the Wilderness," Sean said matter-of-factly. "They don't want you making pictures of them."

Loraine was peripherally aware that Sean was looking at her. Specifically, at her breasts. Which was something else he had in common with Helman.

"Now these girls . . ."

Then Loraine went rigid in her seat as it played out: The three women in blue prison shifts brought in. One of them somehow being influenced by Billy Blunt to attack another. Blood flowing. The woman being attacked with teeth and fingers. Soon Mei summoning ghosts—seen only murkily on the video. Madness— possession. The boy in the midst of it . . .

Loraine forced herself to watch—sure that if she came off as if she couldn't handle it, she'd be in danger of "containment" herself. They wouldn't take any chances. She'd have to pretend to accept this.

But she *couldn't* accept it, not really. Not seeing a boy purchased from his parents. Three women held prisoner to be used as experimental subjects. Women deliberately subjected to possession, violence.

Deep down inside, Loraine knew she'd changed sides. She could pretend she hadn't, for a while. But she couldn't really be part of this.

And that was it—she had pivoted, internally. She'd shifted the center of gravity of her loyalties. She was still a loyal American. But she was no longer loyal to CCA.

Then the courtyard footage was over. She stared at the blank television screen.

"I could have called something to take control—something better than that idiot kid," Sean was saying.

Loraine realized that Dr. Helman was watching her closely. "This is a kind of initiation for you, Loraine—almost in the ancient sense of the word. But—the initiated can't always bear the initiation."

She had to keep up the façade. She managed a faint smile. "You were right, Doctor," she said calmly. "It's shocking stuff. But I can . . . see the potential."

"Can you?" Helman looked at her skeptically. "If we could control people with talents like Krasnoff and Soon Mei and Billy, in the outside world . . ."

"Anybody's name left off that list?" Sean muttered bitterly.

Helman pretended not to hear. "We can't control them *efficiently*, as it stands. We need to establish real, reliable power over them—that's what we were trying to do, through Gulcher . . . and other possibilities. To control these ShadowComm types—but also so-called spirits that may be of use. You see, those UBEs who could be of use in . . . in offensive capabilities . . . they do not cooperate with one another. Or consistently with us. They're rather savage. But we believe they can be forced to cooperate with much greater control. We believe that Gabriel Bleak will give us the means."

She looked at him. "Gabriel Bleak?"

"Yes. That's why we've been pursuing him in particular. Oh, yes, we know you met with him today. We lost track of you once you got on the subway—but we weren't trying very hard to keep up. We don't want him to be too suspicious—too wary. We've been readying you for interaction with him, for some time now. For special work with Gabriel Bleak. We hoped to simply capture him, first. He's proven remarkably elusive. But a special sort of recruitment . . . that might work too. Might perhaps yield better results. We have people already preparing the ground."

"So—" She licked her lips. She really wanted a drink of water. "So you would be willing to work with the Shadow Community on its own terms? To let them work independently, in the field, under assignment? Bleak—Gabriel Bleak—was willing to consider it."

Sean chuckled; Helman's head bobbled with amusement. "Ha-ha, well, we would not allow that, no, no, not as such. But we want them to *think* we might do that, in the short term. In the long term, we'll need to have most of them in constant containment. Except for a very few special individuals. In time, Sean here, and Gabriel Bleak, selected others, may be allowed to work in the outside world. But we have to create certain *control precedents* first. *You*, Loraine—you are one of those precedents. You and Gabriel Bleak are, to use the old-fashioned term, soul mates."

"We're *what*?" She actually rocked back in her chair.

"So that's what they mean by *taken aback*!" Sean said, amused. "Yeah, Loraine—you're fated to be mated with my brother." He added sullenly, "Like he hasn't had all the luck already."

"It's not as if you're 'soul mates' in the sense of two people who merely feel comfortable together," Helman said. "*True* soul mates are fairly rare. They are souls that were *created at the same instant*, a symmetrical cocreation, for a special kind of union. They're not created merely for romantic reasons, you know. It has something to do with creating a ripple effect from the symmetry of putting them together—soul mates send out a 'harmonic transmission,' when they unite. Helping, supposedly, to bring more harmony to the world."

"See, now you're getting all pompous and erudite and shit," Sean said, rolling his eyes.

Helman seemed to control his temper, then went on, "Now, with Gabriel Bleak—our profile suggests that deep down he's a very romantic man. He's lonely. And we believe he's already unconsciously enamored of you. As he's your soul mate, and you his—he really cannot help falling in love with you. At first it might be hard to get him to admit that—"

"Have to get him hard before he admits it," Sean said, grinning around clenched yellow teeth.

Helman sighed and shot Sean a look of irritation. Which Loraine thought was ironic, considering Helman's own arrested-adolescent behavior. Could be that Helman was a kind of warped role model for Sean.

Helman looked earnestly back at Loraine. "We don't believe Gabriel Bleak will work with us willingly without you on board. And we need him to be genuinely on our side. There's something very specific we need him to do. And for you—though he may not know it yet—he would do *anything*."

"Bleak and I hardly know each other. I find it hard to believe that . . . that he and I are . . . 'soul mates.' Find it hard to believe in soul mates at all."

"Nevertheless, it is the case. Soul mates are just one of those oddities of metaphysics. But believe me, they are quite real. But we use the term in a higher sense than the usual sentimentality."

Soul mates. She'd thought the idea childish, improbable, before. But there was something beautiful, really, in this higher kind of soul mates, she decided. Souls "created at the same instant, a symmetrical cocreation, for a special kind of union." And CCA had perverted that beauty—used it for their own sick little agenda.

What had Zweig called it? The "lure concept." That's what she was—a lure. To get Bleak here—to containment.

Keeping impassive, she asked, "What is it you need Bleak to do for you . . . specifically?"

"He's got to work with me," Sean said. "Do a dual magicking with me."

"A . . . a what?" she asked numbly. Trying not to sit there with her mouth hanging open. *Soul mates.*

"A certain ritual."

"There is great power," Helman put in, "when you put the Bleak brothers together. So we're told. They represent two ends of one metaphysical pole. Bring them together, in the same working, and we can bring under our control a certain entity who will, in turn, control all the ShadowComms we can locate. Gulcher was just a temporary expedient. This . . . other entity will make it possible for us to bring about a basic and much needed change in our society. We cannot go on like this, you know, with the world so dangerous, so unstable. For a start, the president is planning to suspend elections, a couple years from now."

Loraine was not as shocked as she thought she'd be. "So that rumor is true."

"It'll be necessary for a time. An . . . indefinite time. You see—"

"Hey, Doc," Sean said, looking at Helman suddenly with a sneering triumph. "You're gettin' way past 'need to know.'"

Helman scowled, not liking to be brought up short by Sean. But he nodded reluctantly. "I suppose you're right. There'll be time for that later. The general will decide when."

Loraine took a long breath, trying to center herself. She couldn't let them know how all this made her feel. Especially the part about the president's plans. *I'm supposed to be loyal to the president—when loyalty is actually treason.*

But she nodded, locking eyes with Helman, trying to sound as if she believed what she was saying. As if she didn't privately believe that Dr. Helman was insane. "If the president thinks that this change is necessary for the safety and stability of the country then"—she shrugged—"I've taken an oath: I serve at the pleasure of the president."

"Must be good to be president," Sean said. "With you serving at his pleasure."

Helman winced. Loraine simply stood up and said, "I've given you my answer, Doctor. I'm tired and it's a long trip back to Brooklyn Heights."

"Actually"—it was General Forsythe, standing in the doorway—"I reckon you won't be going back to Brooklyn Heights tonight." Forsythe stood there with his hands casually in his pockets; smiling apologetically. And seeming just as fundamentally insincere as Helman and Sean. "I'm sorry, by the way, that I missed the meeting, turning up at the last moment here like this. I had a kind of a set-to with Mr. Gulcher. Discipline issue."

"I . . . didn't come prepared to stay overnight. I need to clean up, get some rest—"

"Oh, we have rooms for officers and government visitors here, you can use one of those. They're a bit dormlike but comfortable enough. I've already sent for your necessities. Your things will be here any minute."

She stared. "You sent someone to rifle through my apartment? That really wasn't necessary, General."

He shrugged. His vaguely apologetic look didn't waver. "We've got a state of national emergency coming up here, Agent Sarikosca." The regret dropped from his face. She saw him, suddenly, as he really was. A cold-eyed slug of a man capable of doing anything to anyone. "This is no time to think like a suburban housewife."

That one felt like a slap in the face. But she had to ask: "My cats . . . ?"

He snorted impatiently. "We can have them put down for you. You'll be here for a long time, I expect. You'll want to cancel your lease."

"Cancel my . . . How long will I be here?"

"Oh—you'll be here at Facility Twenty-three indefinitely, Agent Sarikosca. Unless we need you to bring Bleak to us—and then, perhaps, we'll cast that fishin' line in the water. But the bait will be firmly on the hook. You won't be going anywhere we don't want you to go. And now—I believe there is a debriefing we need to get ourselves to. There is a good deal, I reckon, you haven't told us about Gabriel Bleak." The two black berets in the hall stepped into view, then, behind him, looking at her coolly, without pointing their weapons at her. But making their purpose clear. And Forsythe told her, "Come right this way, please."

GULCHER SAT ON THE edge of the small bed, looking around at the tiny room they'd given him. Superficially, it was more comfortable than a jail cell. But it was still locked from the outside.

"Fucking college dorm room," he muttered. "But they don't lock those kids in." He should be asleep. He was tired, and frustrated. The whisperer wouldn't say much to him. He could sense the ethereal familiars around, but they weren't responsive to him. Forsythe was interfering some way. Gulcher could sense a connection.

A knock on the door. "Yeah, come in, as if I have a fucking choice!"

The door unlocked, and Dr. Helman was there, carrying two tiny liquor bottles, as if from a minibar. Helman's head bobbled. "Mr. Gulcher? Can I have a word? And the use of a couple of glasses?"

What was this all about? "Sure. Glasses over by that dinky-ass little sink there."

Helman closed the door behind him, busied himself at the sink, pouring the drinks. "Water in yours?"

"Hell no, I want to taste it. That all you've brought?"

"It is, I'm afraid, all I could scrounge. I thought—bourbon?"

"Yeah."

"I'll have the brandy. Here you go." He handed Gulcher the glass with a little more than a finger of amber fluid in it and actually clinked it with his own.

"Chin-chin!" Helman said, taking the merest sip.

Gulcher snorted. "Whatever. Sit down." He nodded toward a small chair at the small desk.

Helman sat, cradling the glass in both hands. Sipping the bourbon, Gulcher noticed that despite the hour, Helman still wore his suit jacket and the tie with the flowers painted on it.

Helman sighed. "I am a man of the world. I'm sure it's evident. Yet when it comes to the ladies, I find myself tongue-tied. Loraine Sarikosca is here. I don't know as you've met her. A handsome woman. Perhaps a tad young for me. She's not happy with her current situation—she's under restrictions."

"I know the feeling."

"Ah, yes. Oh, you'll be given much more latitude when we have what the general calls 'full control.' And when your loyalty has been tested. But until then . . . at any rate, I, ah . . . well, you seem a vigorous sort of man, who doubtless has had women in his time. I mean—the ones you had, who . . . that is, I don't mean to imply—"

"The ones I didn't pay for, or force?"

"As I said, I meant no offense—"

"It's all right. I'm a con, you rack up a lot of run-ins with the heat, you get to expect people to have, you know, assumptions and shit. I prefer my women voluntary. And I've had plenty of girlfriends."

"So . . . with a woman who's a professional—"

"She's a whore?"

"Not that kind of professional, Mr. Gulcher. Troy . . . I mean, she's a member of a *profession*, she's a federal agent, she's . . . not someone to be trifled with. How would one . . . Well, I was thinking of knocking on her door this very evening. She might be lonely, here."

"She give you any indication she thinks of you that way?"

"Ah—not as such. No."

"Then she probably doesn't. Figures you for too old for her. And she's not going to be in the mood, when she's already feeling trapped, for Christ's sake. Hey, Doc?" Gulcher paused to drink off half his bourbon. Too bad there was only this one baby bottle. "I'm a little, what you might say, *skeptical*, that advice about women is the only reason you're here."

Helman chewed his lower lip, glanced nervously at the door. "Very perceptive. Yes, there is something else. I hesitate to discuss it. What—yes, let's put it this way—what was your impression of the event in the courtyard? With Billy Blunt, the others. Forsythe supervising."

Gulcher didn't enjoy thinking about it. He didn't like anyone else having the ability to take control of people. What if it happened to him next? He shrugged. "Gave me a feeling you people could lose control of this thing. What do I know, I'm no expert. But for one thing—that Forsythe's got something else going on. He's got his own agenda. Only it's not his. That thing that's in him—something ain't human, in there."

Helman looked pale. Drank a little more brandy. "What do you mean, he ain't . . . isn't human?"

"With that mind reading of his. You notice that? And it's not like he's . . . you know, got a talent, like I do. It's something else. It's like it's not *him* reading the minds."

"Ah. Yes. I have been wondering about that myself." Helman made his brandy swirl in the glass. "Forsythe was the first one in our research department to do what he called 'direct outreach' to the . . . the After. Specifically—to entities in what the Shadow Community likes to call the Wilderness. The part of the Hidden that's kept back from close interaction with our world, in normal conditions. The general bridged that gap—and he says he was rewarded with a certain 'extraordinary sensitivity.' Which we perceive as mind reading. But . . . I'm not sure that's the whole story."

"That what he calls it? 'Sensitivity'?" It occurred to Gulcher that the more he knew about what was going on, the more options he had. Just like in jail. Know when they trucked out the laundry—and you might be able to go with it. "So what was this 'outreach' of his?"

"Ritual magic. He was the first to do it, that I'm aware of, in CCA. He has a special room that he performed it in."

"And he sorta *changed*, after he did that ritual stuff—right?"

Helman blinked, opening his mouth to reply. Then he shut it. Seemed to think for a moment. "I suppose that's true. Not too obviously. But it shows, at times. He's changed. As I said—if it is merely enhanced psychic sensitivity—"

Gulcher made eye contact with Helman and shook his head. "No. And I don't think I'm telling you anything you're not already guessing. You're asking me because I help that kind of takeover happen. So you figure I'd know for sure. I don't. But I can make a good guess. And I'd guess your Forsythe ain't Forsythe anymore. He's only General Forsythe on the outside."

"You're saying—he's a victim of neurological redirection by an Unconventionally Bodied Predatory Entity?"

"And what the hell's that mean?"

"The conventional term is . . . *possessed*." Helman looked nervously at the door.

"*Possessed?* I wouldn't use that term. That's like you're talking demons. I've seen some things, since I got this power. You know what it's more like? When I was a kid, I lived in a shitty part of Philadelphia. Then they started building a shopping center in there. We figured that'd make things better. My old man opened a car-supplies store in this shopping center—and then some wiseguys came around, the whole operation got taken over. Pretty soon they were asking twice the rents, and protection too. They were from the Florida mob, these guys. That's what you got here in your CCA now. These aren't, what you call them, devils. Oh, people took 'em for gods and devils once. But these are—just things that ain't human. They're from *outside*. They're—what's that term you use, UB something?"

"Ah. Unconventionally Bodied Entities. UBEs. Or UBPE in the case of some of the more aggressive individuals."

"Well, you got that right, seems to me. That's what they are. They've got an agenda, that's all. Like any other hustler. They're moving into your operation, pretending it's still what you say it is—but just like that shopping center, pal, it ain't what it seems. Not no more. They got their chance when your General Forsythe stuck his nose too far into their world, and I figure they used him to come partway over here. And they're gonna use your operation to make things safe for them once they're here. Because there's cops, over here, too. I mean, you know, spirit cops. And these hustlers that are pushing the general around, they need to protect themselves from that. And you guys, you're providing their, what you call it—their camouflage. The mob from the other side is moving in, and the general, now—he's one of them."

Helman looked at Gulcher blankly. "Oh, no. I don't believe it could be quite so . . . so dire. That we're being used so . . ." Helman shook his head, drained his glass, set it down on the desk, and stood up. Seeming hostile to Gulcher, now, in a passive-aggressive way. "Well. I'll take your . . . your *opinion* under consideration. . . . And thank you for the advice on the fairer sex. Good evening."

Just like that, boom, he walked out. Locking the door behind him. Gulcher chuckled, thinking, *He's been wondering the same thing. Wanted me to tell him it wasn't so. Doesn't like hearing that what he's scared of just might be real.*

"I know the feeling," Gulcher said aloud. He drank the last piddly little drops of bourbon, adding, "I sure know that feeling."

■ ■ ■

At about the same time. Embedded in the sticky New Jersey night.

"Greg? You there?" Bleak called—both in his mind and out loud. He was sitting at the kitchen table in Shoella's house, waiting for her. She'd been closeted with the loas in her summoning room for two hours. Bleak had got tired of puzzling over the Scribbler document.

He had reached out to Greg the Ghost through the Hidden; had felt him responding, hearing his name called from the shadows within shadows. But the voice was faint, the ghost seeming distant, unable to get through.

Bleak tried again, his eyes focused on a blank spot in the wall. "Greg Berne . . . it's Bleak . . . come to me." The off-white wall seemed to ripple, becoming a blizzard—all one color but with depth, something you could walk into. A tiny little dark figure was there, in the apparent blizzard—at first Bleak thought it might be a housefly walking down the wall. Then it came into focus, growing, as if someone were walking toward him in a snowfall. Closer . . .

And he stepped out of the rippling wall, to stand before Bleak in the kitchen, floating there, really, about a foot off the floor. Greg the Ghost.

"You got something needs fixing here?" Greg asked, looking around vaguely. "Somebody call me?"

"Greg? It's Gabriel Bleak. Remember?"

"My wife . . . you know she was banging someone else?"

"No, Greg, I didn't know that." Bleak had a bad feeling about this. "Greg—you've been wandering around in this plane too long. You're starting to forget your mission. You're starting to forget basic things. You need to move on, man. And you can. I spoke to Roseland."

The ghost looked at Bleak, frowning—then his eyes focused, and he nodded. "Bleak! Gabriel Bleak! I remember. Roseland the detective. To clear my name!"

"With luck—it will be cleared. I told Roseland that I had information that Mormon kid was in the neighborhood where that new murder was. They found DNA evidence there—they're testing him. And comparing with the DNA in that condom. They've already got a sort of confession out of him, though they can't use it, exactly—but the DNA will cinch it. Your family will be informed. Roseland promised. It'll be all over the news too. You can move on, Greg."

The ghost nodded sadly. No smile, but a new light gleamed in his eyes. "That's the good news. Bad news is, I hung myself, and I'm dead."

"You've done penance already. Move on, Greg."

"I gotta tell you—there's a kind of bubble around this house you're in. Making it hard to get through. It's kinda like you're in another world completely, Bleak. Somebody's hemming you in."

Bleak had sensed energy fields shifting around him—but the Hidden had its tides, its currents, its sea changes. He'd thought it was something like that. "Must be Shoella. Her summoning."

Greg tried to rub his eyes—then realized he couldn't feel it. "Feel myself less and less . . . So my kids will get the word, right?"

"They will."

"Then I'm going . . . and I ain't comin' back. But, Bleak, be really fucking careful. I saw something that don't have any kinda real shape, around here, watching you. It's changing its shape all the time. And it's angry at you . . . and . . ." Greg was starting to recede, back into the wall—into the psychic distance. Getting smaller, rippling. "I saw it in the Hidden—that there's something close to you that wants to trap you . . . and something else that hates you and they're not far away. . . . I'd stay and help but I've been getting confused and . . ." Smaller, smaller. Like a housefly. Hard to hear the fading voice as Greg went on, voice phasing in and out of audibility. "It wants to make you some kinda slave . . . and . . . you won't be you anymore . . . that's the feeling I get . . . thanks for all . . . your . . ."

Gone.

"Gabriel?" Shoella calling, from down the hall.

Greg's warning ringing in his mind, Bleak got up and went to find her. Her bedroom door was open. Candlelight wavered the room's shadows. There was a smell of incense—roses and some unknown musk. He stepped through the doorway and saw Shoella kneeling, facing the door. She was completely nude, yellow candlelight highlighting her dark skin. She was kneeling on an animal skin—a cougar pelt, its outer edges sewn with black feathers.

Bleak had never seen her naked before—had never seen the tattoos on her breasts, dark blue ink designs, like barbed wire, spiraling toward the nipples.

Candle glow replicated in her eyes as she gazed up at him. "Sit with me," she said.

He had thought they were going to talk about Scribbler's divinations. The scrivening in red ink. But she had some other agenda. He could feel it in the room.

Yorena was there too; the big birdlike familiar was perched on a world globe set up in a far corner. Eyes glittering as she watched him.

Bleak couldn't see much else in the room, outside the circle of candlelight. Just the outlines of masks on the wall; the old, mahogany-framed bed.

Shoella held a carved wooden goblet up to him. It brimmed with a dark liquid. "Honor me by drinking."

"What is it?" he asked, coming closer, taking the goblet.

"Honor me by drinking," she repeated.

The moment seemed steeped in ritual; she was an ally. He rarely needed ritual magic. But she used it, and he could not disrespect it. So Gabriel Bleak drank.

At first he tasted only sweet red wine, and, he thought, salt. But that might be a little blood, making the salty taste, mixed in the wine. Then something else, something bitter. Very bitter.

He stopped drinking, but it was too late—he felt, almost immediately, that he was slipping into an altered state. Had she introduced a loa into the drink? Some entity infused in the liquid?

But as he squatted by the candle, handing her back the wooden goblet—from which she drank, in turn—he decided that it was something else. It was a druggy feeling.

The walls of the room fell away. There was just the candlelight, seeming to replicate itself into a continuum of candle flames, each flame infinitely repeated within the next, each encompassing the others.

Shoella reached behind her and touched a switch. Music came on, drums and Jamaican voices in words he couldn't quite make out. But he could see the notes, a blood-red and sulfuryellow stars, dancing in the air as they were sung. And then she was standing beside him, taking his hands, drawing him to his feet, and peeling the clothes from him.

She was so slender, so long and willowy and burnished and warm, her body elongated like a modern sculpture.

She drew him by the hand toward the bed. As they lay down, he thought, *This is some form of enchantment.*

But he was a man, caught up in the feeling of her skin against his, their sweat running together in the warm room, as she drew him on top of her; the imperative rising at his groin. He seemed to hear Jim Morrison singing about his mojo rising; Morrison in the darkness, nodding at him, then melting into the cloud that was Bleak's feeling, every sensation pillowy soft except the hard part that she drew into herself, a deep piercing between her legs, as she drew his tongue into her mouth, as she entwined him with her long arms and legs, murmuring incantations in his ear in a language . . .

A language he didn't quite recognize.

And the thought came to him that if he ever wanted to be a Great Magus, he was not going to achieve it this way, by allowing himself to be drugged and bedded, without it being his True Will.

But right now, he decided, coupling with Shoella *was* his True Will. He melted against her; he shattered himself against her, and the wave rose up again, and he was once more crashing against her . . . in a midnight sea.

GABRIEL BLEAK WOKE TO see silvery light coming through the slit in the curtain over the bedroom window. *Must be dawn.*

A powerful restlessness surged up in him. He considered taking Shoella again—she lay beside him, arms and legs splayed. She was deeply asleep, but he knew she would not deny him.

Instead he sat up, swiveled to sit on the edge of the bed, his brain percussing in his skull with the motion. The sensations of his limbs, his bare feet on the floor, seemed to whip around, as if trying to escape, before suddenly snapping back where they should be in his body, with an audible click.

"What was *in* that shit," he muttered, standing to walk wobblingly out the bedroom door, barefoot and naked down the hall to the kitchen. He was terribly thirsty, badly needing a long drink of water. The kitchen was brighter, the light hurting his eyes. He found a glass, turned the spigot at the sink—nothing came out. "Shoella!" he called hoarsely. "Something wrong with your water."

Then he became aware of a shushing sound; a gurgling, splashing. Water. But the sound was coming from outside.

He went to the open back door, and looked. And saw that Shoella's backyard was gone. In fact . . .

The whole neighborhood was gone.

In its place was a tropical forest: a verdant hillside, columned by kapok trees and kauri and cathedral fig, canopied by foliage but flecked brightly with bird-of-paradise flowers and flowered lianas and purple orchids and shafts of golden sunlight. Just forty paces outside the back door a small, silver-white waterfall tumbled in slow motion, falling twenty-five feet into a dark green pool. Parrots, bright red and dark green, fluttered in the ancient, gnarled trees.

A rustling to his left. He looked and saw a small deerlike animal—nothing native to North America—with tiny, fuzzy antlers, long ears, exquisite little hooves. It stepped delicately out of the shady underbrush and stopped to look at him with large, brown, mildly curious eyes. It was completely unconcerned. It turned its attention to the little pool under the waterfall, dipped its head to drink.

Okay, he thought. *I'm still asleep, and dreaming.* But the thirst he felt seemed quite real. *Go along with the dream. Drink from the waterfall. See what happens.*

Nakedness couldn't matter here, so Bleak stepped outside the back door and walked along a thin path through knee-high, spearlike grass, his bare feet treading warm red clay. He looked for some remnant of the fences that should be here, the other houses either side of Shoella's. No fence, no houses. No power lines, no people. Nothing but forest.

He came to the waterfall, found himself staring in fascination at its silvery tumbling. He seemed to see each silvery, crystalline drop individually; and at the same time he saw them all at once, in galactic splendor. It was heartbreakingly beautiful.

But something, here, was watching him; something in the trees, the grass, the air itself. Watching.

He looked around—and saw no one. In particular.

Bleak moved closer to the waterfall, stepped out on a warm boulder at the edge of the pool, braced himself with a hand on the

mossy hillside, leaned over, plunged his face into the cascade —
and drank.

The water sent a stroke of illuminating energy through his
body with the first swallow. Straightening up, wiping his mouth,
he felt twice the man he'd been a moment before.

"Not such a bad dream," he said.

"It's no dream," Shoella said, walking up behind him. "This is
real. It is a world outside of time, *cher* darlin'."

"Is it? You know, I don't think we're in Hoboken anymore,"
Bleak said, looking around at the place's tropical growth, its verdant beauty.

"No," Shoella said, laughing. "This is not Hoboken."

FIFTEEN

The next morning. In Facility 23.

Loraine was propped up on her bunk in the small, windowless, dorm-style room, a cup of coffee on the night table beside her, poring over what she'd written in a notebook the night before.

She'd slept in her clothes. An overwhelming feeling of vulnerability had made her unwilling to undress. Maybe because of Forsythe—or Sean.

And maybe she shouldn't have written out Scribbler's message. Suppose Helman or Forsythe got hold of it? She didn't want them to know about Scribbler, nor get any help from his divination.

But Loraine felt it was important to transcribe the message so she could think about it, try to interpret it. Work out what the words meant for her and Bleak—and for the United States. She could destroy the pages before anyone else saw them. She would wet them, shred them in her fingers, flush them down the toilet.

She had written out most of what Scribbler had channeled—the parts scribbled in red ink. Her photographic memory had served her well, she decided. It seemed right.

Her eyes kept returning to one line in particular.

Loraine is beyond the doorway for Gabriel, arms an entrance, Loraine and Gabriel like puzzle pieces made to fit.

Like puzzle pieces made to fit. Soul mates? Two souls created at the same moment, symmetrical to one another, complementary opposites destined to search for one another—and eventually unite. It would explain the strong emotions that came over her when she was around Bleak.

The thought made her heart pound. *Gabriel Bleak.*

She shook her head, amused at herself.

But if it was true—it was appalling. *Everything's been decided for me.* And if he was in fact her soul mate, now that she knew it, how could she ever have a relationship with any man besides Bleak? She would always know that the "someone else" was not her "intended," in the truest sense. She might be destined to be alone because there was every chance Scribbler's "puzzle pieces made to fit" would not be fitted.

Now that she knew what CCA was planning, she couldn't work with them—not really. She could only stall them and wait her chance to get away. And that meant she should stay away from Gabriel Bleak—for his sake. If she got together with him, she was playing CCA's game. Besides, the idea of someone like her, hooking up with . . . someone like Bleak. A ShadowComm. A man from the supernatural underground . . . Absurd. Almost like a CIA agent falling for Che Guevara.

When Forsythe debriefed her about the "abduction" by Gabriel Bleak, she'd told him Bleak and the woman Shoella would consider brokering a deal between CCA and ShadowComm, allowing the Shadow Community to remain free. She had skirted talking about Scribbler and given as little information on Shoella as possible. But she didn't think Forsythe was going to leave it that way.

She looked at the notebook, wondering . . .

. . . *Breslin is afraid of the man within the man who stands on his right, and the crack in the wall lets the Great Wrath through, who darkens like ink in the water those he would conceal, and yet move toward Facility 23 and find the liberating truth on the way to the North* . . .

The man within the man who stands on his right. An image came to her mind, a photo she'd seen in a CCA office: Forsythe with President Breslin, both men smiling for the camera. General Forsythe standing on Breslin's right.

Was Forsythe "the man within the man" Breslin was afraid of? Why "a man within a man"?

. . . *and yet move toward Facility 23* . . .

She had done that—she'd moved right *into* Facility 23.

Was she *supposed* to be here? Could it be that she was *intended* to bring Bleak here—but not for Forsythe's reasons. Not for Helman. Not for Sean.

But for something better—by whatever wanted her and Bleak together.

Gabriel Bleak was resourceful, unpredictable, perhaps more powerful than even he suspected. Bringing him here might be like tossing a wrench into the CCA machine.

But if she was considering that—was it really for strategic reasons? Or did she want to bring Bleak here for herself?

A knock at the door. It was a shave-and-a-haircut knock, without the two bits. She swallowed, but made herself call out calmly, "Who is it?"

"Drake Zweig. Got a package for ya."

Zweig? Ugh. If it had to be someone from her team, she wished it could be Arnie.

Loraine got up, hid the notebook under her mattress, ruefully thinking, *Brilliant job of concealment, Agent Sarikosca.* It occurred to her to wonder, as she went to open the door, if the room was camera-live. Where would the surveillance cam be? The light fixture?

She unlocked the door. Zweig was in the hall, with Loraine's overnight bag in his hands. He looked exactly as she'd last seen him. "Got your clothes here, from your place."

He'd been rooting around in her apartment, then. Her clothes. Had they gotten into her laptop? Nothing there would get her in trouble. She just didn't like to think of Zweig chortling over it.

Loraine took the bag. "Thanks, Zweig."

He just stood there, looking at her, cracking the knuckles on those big hands. She could almost see the wheels turning in his head.

"What's the team working on?" she asked, when she realized he wasn't going to just go away.

"Oh, they're monitoring Coster, and . . . well, I'll have to check with the General before I talk about it. I'm not sure where your clearance is right now."

She felt a chill. "What's that supposed to mean?"

"Seemed to be some question about it. Got everything you could need in that bag there."

"Thanks," she said sourly. "Did you see my cats?" If they'd hurt those cats . . .

"I was gonna take them to the pound, like the general said, but that poof that lives next door came over, when I was trying to grab them, and they ran up to him so he picked them up and wouldn't give them to me. Said over his dead body. I was tempted to accommodate him. But what the hell, let him deal with that little loose end."

Loraine felt like slapping him. Instead she said, as impassively as she could, "Uh-huh. So you hear anything about how long I'm supposed to remain on-site here?"

"Indefinitely, is what I heard. You know, I've got a bottle of bourbon in my—"

She closed the door in his face and went to the bed to unpack her overnight bag. It contained a pants suit she almost never wore, a dress she'd worn to work once, a few other more or less random items, her travel toiletries kit, and some of her underwear, crumpled up at the bottom.

Like he'd gotten at those first. Zweig, fingering her underwear. She was surprised he hadn't put her vibrator in the bag too.

She got undressed, showered, put on the rumpled flat-black pants suit, white blouse. Decided the jacket was too wrinkly. She was just brushing her hair when another, sharper knock came at the door.

She opened it, knowing, somehow, that it was Forsythe. The general wasn't wearing his uniform. He wore khaki pants, a turtle-neck sweatshirt. The sleeves were pulled back, showing beefy forearms. Behind him stood those same two black berets, looking calm but watchful, submachine guns in their hands. Not pointed at anyone. But ready.

Forsythe said, "If I may."

Not waiting to see if he might, he started through the door, his bulk making her step back to keep from being trampled. She stood with the backs of her knees against the small bed. He looked her up and down, even leaning to look behind her. Not lascivi-ously, but looking for something. "She doesn't seem to be armed," he said, half-turned, talking to the soldiers. "Wait outside."

One of the soldiers nodded, reached over, and closed the door from the outside. She was alone in the room with General Forsythe.

He stood there a moment, audibly breathing, looking at her. Loraine felt as if something was pushing against her forehead, though he hadn't touched her.

"General, is there—"

"Sarikosca, you've been holding out on us. Last night, you kept things back."

She shrugged. She wondered if he could hear her heart thudding—it seemed loud enough to hear in the hallway. "I hit the broad strokes, General. I wasn't as detailed as I might have been. I was tired last night."

Forsythe acted as if he hadn't heard. "I knew at the time you were keeping something back but I was pressed for time. Something to see to. Now. Let us see if we can get caught up."

He grabbed her shoulders and dragged her close. His breath smelled like hot iron. She struggled to pull away—but this was the strongest grip she'd ever felt. It was as if something else was holding her too, keeping her from breaking free. Like the muscular paralysis that comes from an electrical shock.

He pushed his forehead against hers, hard enough that it hurt. She could feel the bone of his skull, grinding on the bone of her brow, the skin seeming barely there at all. "General—this is not necessary!"

"*Silence*," he hissed, and she felt his spittle on her face. "Let me in! You are more difficult than Gulcher. Your thoughts are guarded. You are inward. But . . ."

Loraine felt something pushing through her forehead.

Some part of her knew it wasn't physical—not the kind of physicality that body and bone had. The phrase *unconventionally bodied* came to her. It was a probing from something like that. From Forsythe—and from something else that came through Forsythe.

. . . *Breslin is afraid of the man within the man who stands on his right* . . .

Loraine knew, then. She was certain. That General Forsythe was no longer General Forsythe. For perhaps a long time now, he had been taken over by something inhuman.

Then the entity that was pressing into her forehead showed itself to her inner eye. She was staring into the mouth of a lamprey, a circular mouth with teeth all around, and another circle of teeth within those—and another within those. Inside the innermost ring was something like a polyp, but one that could stretch out, and on the end of the polyp there was an eye, a mucus-colored eye with a black iris, and this eye was rushing toward her, toward the center of her being, pushing into her mind to stare around at her inmost thoughts. It was a rape of the mind; it was a deep, bottomless violation, a stabbingly painful violation, a cold, cutting agony that plunged into the center of her, ripping into her living soul.

She had seen some bad things—pieces of still-bleeding bodies after the bomb attack in Kabul.

But she hadn't lost control at that.

Loraine believed a woman should be as strong as any man—and she was stronger than most men.

But now . . . but this time . . .

Loraine screamed.

SOMEWHERE. OUTSIDE OF TIME.

A warm day—but not too hot, or humid. The air seemed to wrap around them with a velvety, pristine embrace. Truly it was not Hoboken.

It seemed to Gabriel Bleak that they had been walking for almost two miles. He and Shoella—dressed now, in the clothes they'd worn yesterday—were following a path made by forest creatures, along the bottom of the valley that meandered through the jungled hills. They passed through bands of mist that sparkled in shafts of sunlight; they crossed singing brooks and walked through sudden meadows of tropical flowers droning with bees that never threatened. Occasionally they saw termite mounds taller than a man, looking like models of dried-out hills pocked with tiny caves; they saw a leopard, with a small deer sagging from its jaws, in the crook of a broad-trunked baobab tree. Its muzzle red with feeding, the leopard looked at them with only placid curiosity as they passed—and Bleak could have sworn he heard it purring. They saw a large black buzzard feeding on a dead water buffalo; it ducked its naked red head under its wing, as if in obeisance to them. Flamingos quivering with pink light watched them pass close by and never fluttered in alarm.

And all the time, Bleak felt something, someone, watching.

They paused to eat from two fruit trees; mangoes and guavas, perfectly ripe and tasting as if they were infused with the sunlight—the sunlight that was warming, comforting, but never too hot. They passed through a meadow of fragrant, yellow flowers, like little hands opening to the sun. Beyond the meadow the path ended at a large pond at the base of a hill. Here a stand of gnarled cypresses encircled the pond, which was fed by another, higher waterfall. The thin cascade showed a shoulder of emerald green before tumbling in white lights from a beetling, mossy hillside. Glimmering gold-mottled fish luxuriated under the lily pads in the clear water of the pool. The lichened stones flanking the top of the waterfall seemed the worn, carved remnants of an ancient civilization that had never actually existed.

"Shall we swim?" Shoella suggested.

"Is it safe?" Bleak said vaguely, shading his eyes to look into the pool. Still stunned by all this. "Could be . . . I don't know . . . piranha in there or . . ."

Shoella leaned against him, caressed his cheek. "You haven't noticed that nothing here does us harm, *cher* darlin'? There are no mosquitoes—or if there are, they will not bite us. The bees, they don't sting us. It is the ideal place of the ancestors, with all its pleasures, its shady places and water and food, and none of its harm, not for us. You could embrace that leopard we passed— she would not harm you. And me, I would not harm you." She grinned. "You could embrace me here on the grass by the pond."

Bleak drew away from her and squatted to trail his fingers in the water. He had gone on the long walk to make the drug wear off—and to see if this world ended, like a stage set; like a ride at an amusement park. The walk had worked to clear his mind. "This just goes on and on, this world?"

"Yes. The gods created it for us. To go on and on." After a moment she said, "You're angry."

"You drugged me. I don't take drugs, Shoella. I tried them a couple times. They make me imagine the Hidden where it isn't, or miss it where it is. I only make mistakes on drugs."

"This drug was something . . . *special.* Because—I didn't think I could get my chance any other way. It did not harm you—just a certain shaman's mixture. Some seeds from Hawaii, some bark from Haiti, some other things. It was only meant to bring us together."

"You had only to ask. A couple of glasses of beer and a kiss would have worked, Shoella. In fact you could have left out the beer."

She seemed genuinely surprised. "Truly? Years I felt this way—and you gave me no sign. I thought you wanted that Sarikosca woman, and if I was to have you . . ."

"I barely know her. Of course you're attractive to me, Shoella. I didn't know if it was wise for us to get together, so I didn't push it. I don't like being pushed *into* it—not the way you did it. If you'd just—"

"I'm sorry, *cher* darlin'. To push you. But . . . there is something else you should know." She sat down by him, looked at him tenderly, spoke to him gently—but he felt she was talking to him like a perverse kindergarten teacher to a little boy. "I did not bring you here only to keep you away from her—yes, this was in my mind, but there was more. I have cast the bones and splashed the blood; I have listened to the growls of the great powers. The ancestors tell me *I must mate, and it must be this year.* And I must produce a child! This child"—she pressed her belly—"she is to be my great destiny! And I feel—I see it in the Hidden—*that you are the man* to make this child with me! I cannot follow my path as a priestess until I do this, Gabe. Life is ritual, my darlin'. If we make love, this is an invocation; if we make a baby, this is to please the powers of the Hidden. . . . And to do this, I must have you to myself. No one else may have you. Here we are safe, Gabe—safe from the devils at CCA, safe from that pale little liar who looks at you with big eyes and her lips parted . . . safe!"

"This is all to please your ancestors? And what makes you think those powers are the ones I want to please?" Bleak asked.

"Not just to please them—to weave a great destiny!" She took both his hands in hers; tried to clasp his gaze with hers, leaning toward him urgently. "The beginning of a magical dynasty, *cher* darlin'! What could be more *merveilleux*!"

Bleak snorted and shook his head, drew his hands away. "And I was selected . . . for breeding?"

"Not only this! To be the high priest beside the priestess! Oh, Gabriel, you must know I love you. Have loved you since I first saw you, my *cher* darlin'! So I brought you to paradise."

"Paradise." He glanced around at the lovely, womblike tropical forest. A seductive place. But paradise? "Meaning what exactly? Where are we?"

She shrugged. "A . . . *world*. We can give it a name. A 'demi-world' some say, but also a real world." She stretched her legs out, put her feet in the water, splashed it softly. "Magicians know these places. Many a sorcerer, many a sorceress, they create one such, and live there, in their own demiworld. It is . . . a *pocket* world, you might say." She stood, walked a few paces up the bank, picked a purple-red orchid, growing from the base of a cypress that grew in the shallows, and brought it back to him. "Look! Perfect in every detail! *Fait* by the"—she tapped her head—"and magic. And a person can live there forever. And *not die*, no never die, in such a place. The wearing down of time, it is not here! It is between the universes and safe—made of the things of this world, and . . . oh, only the *bon Dieu* knows. Someday we will feel it right to return to the world of our birth. But until then—I know we can be happy here!"

He shook his head. "You brought your whole house and just dropped it here? Is there a witch under it?"

She laughed softly, tossing the orchid in the pool so it floated in its own dimple, the blossom reflected in the clear water. "It is only a copy of my house. But you and I—we came here entire. We are not here only in our minds. Our bodies are here, our souls, all of us. Forever, until forever is too much—and then we go back. But now, you and me, *cher* darlin' Gabe. Here you are safe with me."

He looked at her. "You keep saying 'safe.'"

"Yes. Our enemies were coming for us, Gabe. This place"—she gestured at the world around them—"they cannot come to." She plucked another orchid.

He wasn't convinced that no one else could come here. He suspected her of using magic that she had stumbled upon—and didn't fully understand.

A thought came to him. "Where is Yorena? I haven't seen your familiar. Unless it was that buzzard."

"That . . . no! Yorena—" Her expression became guarded. "I chose not to bring Yorena. I want only you and I."

Strange, Bleak thought. She was never far from Yorena, and vice versa. "Shoella—do you respect me?"

She looked at him in open surprise. "Of course—*bien sûr!*"

"If you respect me as a magus—as a worker in the Hidden— you know I cannot stay here, if I'm . . . if someone else makes the decision. That would make me passive, a shrunken man."

She laughed. "You could never be shrunken!"

"Then give me time to think. To feel this place out and understand it. Leave me alone for a while. I suppose I can find my way back to the house."

She frowned. But she nodded. "Just picture it in your mind, and look for a path. The path will lead back to the house."

Shoella shredded the orchid with a sudden motion of her long fingers, tears gleaming in her eyes. She turned and stalked away, then, back along the path they'd come.

Bleak sat down on the grassy bank, watching the fish dart at the bits of shredded orchid petal. *Just picture it in your mind, and look for a path. The path will lead back to the house.*

So this place, this "demiworld," was responsive—strongly responsive—to the mind of the sorcerer. That had implications.

He had never been to any world but his own before—not in this lifetime—and wasn't sure if the Hidden worked by the same principles here. But he knew the invisible field of living force was there, knew that those same energies, the same potential, the field of the Hidden, was all around him, in this world. He had felt it, since waking here, the way someone else would feel the ground underfoot. You didn't doubt the ground. Until, he reminded himself, an earthquake came.

He needed to know. Could he access the Hidden, here, the way he had in his world?

Bleak closed his eyes and looked, with the other kind of seeing.

He saw the forest, around him, the cliff and the waterfall, the whole demiworld, as if it were in photo-negative, its lines etched in luminous purple. Then he made out living energy, seething, rising and falling, between each object, each plant and rock, each blade of grass. When he looked at it, it responded to his attention, pulsing brighter.

So the Hidden was available to him, here—it had a different character, but any world had its own Hidden.

He opened his eyes and saw Shoella's world around him, saw

it anew—as lines of force, shaped into foliage, into earth and rock and sky. He searched, looking for the entity he sensed behind the veil of this world. The lines of force shivered, converged, and re-shaped . . . into Yorena.

The bird looked bigger than ever—big as a man. She spread her wings and hovered there, not flapping them, just hanging in the air in front of him, defying gravity, like an emblem on a flag.

"No," Bleak said. "That's not you, is it, Yorena?" He could sense this was a false image; an external. A mask.

He used his ability to draw on the power of the Hidden—and evaporated the veil of appearance.

Yorena's wings stretched out, changing shape. The familiar's eyes altered shape too; her beak became smaller and formed into a nose. The bird-head developed a mouth, a chin . . . feathers became clothing . . .

A man, now, hovered there where Yorena had been. Revealed, exposed—and staring impudently at him.

The man was suspended in the air, about three feet over the middle of the pond, with the waterfall as spectacular backdrop. He looked vaguely familiar, though Bleak didn't immediately know him.

The man was young. He had a military jacket, cammie shirt under it, khaki pants, boots. Long brown hair. His eyes . . .

"Sean . . . ?" Bleak said, jumping to his feet.

"Surprised you recognize me!" Sean chuckled, drifting slowly toward him, across the water, like someone on a moving sidewalk at the airport. Looking that bored too. "You were aware of me, the whole time, Gabriel. But you couldn't deal with it. Kept hiding from that part of the Hidden, funnily enough."

Sean had reached the grassy bank, floated not quite within reach, a few feet higher than his brother, Gabriel—so that he could look down on him.

"Sean . . . you're really here?"

"Not exactly. Shoella only just realized, a short time ago, back on Earth, that Yorena was no longer Yorena. Seems to me familiars are just a kind of idea that takes on form and function. They're part of our own minds, like a computer program, that we put out to run in the Hidden. Easy enough for someone with my gifts to capture her familiar and destroy its inner nature. Set my own mind inside it. Make it my little spiritual UAV, a little supernatural drone, to watch you and her! Follow you here. Could have had you earlier—I waited too long, listening in, that night at the Battery. Should have called in the troops to take you in right there. Lost track of you for a while. You're good at creating a chaotic energy cloud around you, to muddy the waters. Been doing it so long you hardly know you're doing it. You slipped away—we set you up with that skip-trace job . . . and presto! You slipped away again! How'd you do that, by the way?"

"Probably shouldn't tell you that," Bleak mumbled. Amazed to be talking to his lost brother. Feeling almost numb.

"Why not tell me? We're not enemies, Gabriel! We're brothers! It's all been a stupid misunderstanding! We are to be allies. We've even got the girl, she's waiting for you. The girl you're *intended* to have. Not this exiled voodoo priestess you're tangled up with. No—your soul mate, for God's sake, Gabe! The real deal! The *true soul mate!*"

"Loraine . . ."

"That's right. You felt it. You suspected. I confirmed it for myself, talking to the Powers—and now you know it. That's what she is: your soul mate—and we've got her! She wants you to come and help us, Gabriel."

"If she does . . . it's because she's CCA. Indoctrinated. Doesn't know any better." After a moment he added sadly, "Like you, Sean."

"Oh, I know what I'm doing! I'm on the inside, Gabe, you're on the outside—so you should be guided by me. You've got to trust someone sometime!" Sean grinned crookedly. "You and I are like oxygen and fire, Brother. Bring us together"—he raised his hand and fire seemed to leap from the sun overhead, to become a roaring flame in the air above him—"and the fire grows!" He turned and made a throwing motion, down into the pool of water, and the fire in the air formed into a ball and shot down to crash like a meteor into a sea, so that a pillar of water surged up, widened into the shape of a ten-foot-high mushroom cloud, boiling and seething in a nuclear explosion, the fire glowing in its heart. "We're like uranium and the atom splitter! Bring us together and the power of the sun is set free!" Sean dismissed the water and it fell back into the waterfall pool, the fire going out with a hiss. Turning toward Bleak, he went on, "You get it? I don't think you do—God, look at your face! Well. I don't like having to collaborate with you much, myself. Wish I didn't need you. I mean, shit—you've had so much already! You got to stay with our parents. Had freedom out in the world. Adventure . . . women . . . And what have I had? I've been a prisoner. Been close to escaping too."

Sean paused, looked up at a small flock of parrots flying by overhead. His voice became low and earnest. "Then Forsythe came along, changed all that for me." He looked fiercely down at his brother. "You'll see why—if you come with me. The hell away from this half-world. Come to CCA, Gabriel—and you can have Loraine!" Adding bitterly, "You can have the person who completes you. Something I'll never have. I've had that revealed to me too. But *you* can have it—what everyone yearns for! True love. Completion. Peace. Only, brother, if you want it—you've got to cooperate with us. We're going to change the balance of power of the whole world. And there'll be something for your brother in this: *I'll have real freedom for the first time.*"

"Yeah? How, exactly, does this come about, Sean?" Bleak asked. Thinking that Sean had a grimace, when he talked, that looked like his attempt to smile. And he always seemed to have his teeth almost clenched. Even though this wasn't him—was some kind of magical projection of him—it was probably how he looked in life.

"How? I'll tell you, Gabe. We . . . Forsythe, CCA, and I, all of us . . . we'll *stop all magic*, except the magic that *we* control! Imagine it! A *monopoly on magic!* And that means that the country will be safe, for the first time. That's what gets Helman and Breslin wet. No one would dare to threaten America if we had *all the magic*. The artifact in the north—the thing that makes that cracked Wall of Force—it'll seal up the cracks. But you and I, *we'll be on the other side of the wall*. You know—figuratively speaking." Sean made an elaborate shrug, flipping his hand. "Main thing is, long-lost bro of mine, we'll have the full power of the Hidden! Only, we won't have enough power, working alone—not for what's needed. No, see, to do this, to extend control over whole armies, we've got to have an ally. An Unconventionally Bodied Entity—a more powerful one than you've ever encountered. A *Great Power*. All the big magic is done through working with the Great Powers, the real lords of the Hidden."

"An ally. Would that be—the Great Wrath?"

"Very good! You were paying attention to what your Scribbler scribbled! Don't look so startled—we've got Scribbler in custody. Your woman buckled, first time Forsythe rammed her mind. Forsythe saw your Scribbler in her thoughts, found her notebook where she'd copied down the lines in red."

"What's going to happen to Scribbler now?" Bleak asked. Feeling sick, thinking of someone as fragile as Scribbler in the hands of the CCA.

"He'll become one of us, that's all. A recruit. He's *fine*, don't worry about him. Don't worry about your precious darling Agent Sarikosca either. Worry about us! You and me! We've got to work together—meaning you come back with me. You'll just vegetate if you stay in this place."

"I've felt you watching since I got here," Bleak said musingly. "Did *you* create this place?"

"No—Shoella created it, just as she said, as a way of trying to get away from us. And to keep you isolated so she can use you for her little agenda. She was supposed to be working with us—we had her set up to bring you in, through Coster. He's not entirely the drunk he seems to be. He was supposed to tempt you to come looking for me. But he did manage to make a bridge to Shoella. Planted a little magical charm I had worked up—and made it possible for me to take over Yorena."

Sean floated down to the bank, walked back and forth—almost strutting as he talked. Bleak noticed Sean, in this world, had no shadow.

It seemed to Bleak that Sean was boasting to him the way a little boy would boast to his father of something he'd done in school sports. "Then *I* talked to Shoella through the Yorena guise. She was angry at you because you just weren't taking her *hints*—and we told her that if she got you for us, her ShadowComm people could be free." He smirked, enjoying the lie they'd told her. "Offered her something else. Told her that you would become hers! We'd basically give you to her! But"—he spread his hands, cocked his head—"something about that Scribbler session changed her point of view." He grinned crookedly. "Shoella figured out the soul mate thing. She knew if you went to CCA, you'd be with her rival. That if you were with Loraine, any length of time, you'd never leave her—never could leave a soul mate. So she brought you here." Sean gestured at the gorgeous junglescape around them. "Thought she was clever." He made a dismissive gesture and grimaced—a grin with clenched teeth. "She has the talisman for the summoning—transported the two of you here. But . . . too bad for her! She didn't think I could follow but I came right along in the psychic slipstream." He shrugged, very devil-may-care. "When you've got it, flaunt it."

When you've got it, flaunt it? What old movie had Sean taken that from?

"Well, Gabe? You coming with me? It's all waiting for you."

"I don't think so, Sean. At least not till you answer some questions." Bleak felt close to tears, seeing his brother like this: a resentful, predatory liar. Too socially naïve to hide his real intentions. Hostility showing nakedly on his face.

"Questions." Sean snorted dismissively. "Like what?"

"Tell me about your . . . your talents. Like shape changing—to become something like Yorena?"

"Yeah. I can do what you can do—and I can do *more*. I can alter my spirit form—I can *possess*. That's a valuable ally, right? And I can open a path between worlds! I can take you out of this demiworld—this prison of love! You know you can't stay here with Shoella—you can't trust her! She drugged you, kidnapped you here. . . . You don't want to stay with her—and she can't go with us. That's the sacrifice she made. This world emanates from her—she's part of it now. . . . Hard to pull her out of it and keep her alive."

Bleak's mouth was papery dry. Reeling inwardly with shock at all this, he hunkered for a moment, to scoop water from the pond—it would be safe to drink from, in this world—and to take a moment to deal with meeting his brother again . . . and with what he'd said about Shoella. Had she really been playing him against CCA?

"I made you an offer, Gabriel," Sean said. "You going to help your brother—or not?"

Stalling, Bleak straightened up, wiped his mouth. "There a guy named Gulcher you're working with?"

Sean tilted his head, looked at him with narrowed eyes. Then he levitated into the air, rotating slowly, arms outspread, making a whirlpool in the water beneath him. Despite reacting to him, the water did not reflect him. "Yeah," he said, as he whirled slowly over the water, like a slow-motion ballet dancer. "We've got a little meeting with the Joint Chiefs of Staff planned. Gulcher's going to help us with that."

Bleak wondered if he too could fly, move objects about, in this world. He suspected flying wouldn't be possible because he was here in his physical body; Sean was here as an astral body.

"You know Gulcher's a mass murderer, Sean?"

Sean stopped spinning, stabbed an accusing finger. "And *you* fought in a war! Killed quite a number of people yourself. You shot a teenage boy once, in Afghanistan."

Bleak felt punched in the stomach, hearing that from Sean. But he said, "He was part of a team that killed my best friend. And he was trying to shoot me."

"I know—absolutely! You did what you had to. Gulcher figured he did what he had to do—to get out of where he was. And that's all we're doing at CCA, Gabriel! What we have to do. Even if it means working with losers like Gulcher."

Looking at Sean, Bleak had a sinking feeling there wasn't much left of the boy who'd been abducted from a ranch in Oregon. There was a man with special DNA, extraordinary talents—and inside that man was a disfigured little soul. That was all that was left of his brother. An imp where there should be a man. It was what CCA had made of him, with confinement and testing and isolation and "training," all these years. It hurt to see it; hurt even more to feel it.

"Sean . . ." There was so much to say. He didn't know where to start. "Sean, I'm sorry about what happened to you. From what I can find out, they didn't give our parents much choice."

The façade of brotherly fondness dropped away from Sean. He loomed in midair, staring down at Bleak. "They chose you over me. 'Sure, take that one, we'll keep this one.'"

"I can't blame you for thinking that. But I don't think it was that way. Mom never got over it. She just retreated into her shell.

They both got Bible-crazy. And that was a reaction to losing you."

Sean snorted. "Yeah? They told people I was dead! But I did okay without you and them—I adapted! I made them give me things, at CCA! I showed my worth . . . and now I'm on top of it." And he bobbed ten feet higher in the air, for emphasis.

"Sean—you know about Stockholm syndrome? You get kid-napped—and you adapt by identifying with your captor?"

"So that's going to be your attitude! Patronizing, condescending. Disrespecting me."

"Sean—"

"I can take you back. You coming back with me or not?"

"No. Not right now. I don't trust them."

"I can stop you from *ever leaving here*! I can change the char-acter of this place! I can make it so it's definitely *not* paradise. Heaven can become hell! You know how? I can *bring things here*. You going to make me do that?"

"Sean, let's just . . . start over. Why don't you come with *me*? We can go back to earth—but we'll stay the hell away from the Central Containment Authority. Who wants to be centrally con-tained, or contained any other way?"

"You don't understand. I'm the one who's doing the contain-ing—the controlling!"

"They've manipulated you into believing that."

"You're putting me down again! You deny my power!" Sean spread his arms, beginning to change. "Look at me and deny this, asshole!"

Sean joined his outstretched arms up over his head, as if aim-ing himself into the sky—but suddenly Sean Bleak's whole body spiked downward, feetfirst into the pool of water, into the mud under it, vanishing, all at once, into water and murk, gone from his brother's sight. A geyser of water rising and falling away, a swirl of diffuse mud, was the only evidence, for the moment, that he'd been there.

"Uh-oh," Bleak said, backing away. Already beginning to draw on the energy of the Hidden.

The ground shook. There was a count of three: Sean's voice, booming sourcelessly, from all around.

"One! Two! THREE!"

And on *three*, the spot in the water where Sean had disappeared erupted outwardly with a visible shock wave, an explosion of water and mud and shredded plants that made Bleak stagger; a shock wave that continued outward into the cypresses around the pool, making them bend and crack and splinter, one of the more slender trees uprooting, falling backward. A stench clung to the air, and a black cloud formed over the pool, starting small but quickly growing, a miniature thundercloud just fifty feet up that spread, extending tentacles of itself into the surrounding forest, crackling within like distant heat lightning. Then the electrical charge built up unbearably—and let go in the form of a crooked, branchy stroke of red-yellow lightning that smashed down into the pool, churning it with foam and sparkling it with electric death. Fish died and bobbed up, pale bellies turned to the darkening sky. The electricity crackled through the ground—right at Gabriel Bleak.

And as Sean's baleful influences struck, Gabriel Bleak hardened the energy he'd drawn from the Hidden into a field of repulsion, a cocoon of light. The assault struck the shield of light and dissipated—into the surrounding forest.

For a moment, an apparition formed, a shape of mist and smoke and dust—Sean's head, big as a dragon's, with a crocodile's jaws and eyes of polished obsidian. It reared over Bleak, its jaws agape. He saw Sean—the *child* Sean—replicated there in the crocodilian apparition's shiny black eyes, as if Sean were trapped in the obsidian, shouting with fury. *"No one's going to pretend I'm not around, not ever again!"*

"Sean. This was not the course we agreed on," boomed another voice, from somewhere else entirely. A guttural voice, with a faint Deep South accent, Bleak did not recognize. **"We need him alive."**

"He won't come to us your way, General!" Sean roared. *"It's better to crush him than to let him run free!"*

And the energies slammed at Gabriel Bleak again—and Bleak strove to hold them back, afraid he couldn't continue much longer, feeling the pressure more with each second.

It was beginning to hurt, as the charge increased air pressure around him; he was beginning to feel his ribs close to cracking, despite the cushion of protective energy.

"You're letting your boyish resentment get the best of you. He will come to us. I withdraw you. Come."

Then came a whining roar of frustration, the force of the roar bursting the crocodilian apparition from within . . . so that it blew up—and drifted into smoke and mist, which blew away . . . into the forest.

Bleak sank to his knees, resting, immensely relieved.

Then the jungle was silent for three long seconds. One, two, three. And a whisper came, close to Bleak's right ear. Sean's voice.

"Gabriel. I'm opening a way to Shoella's world, from the Wilderness. You won't want to stay here any longer. Don't trust that crazy bitch. She's been way over the edge for a long time. Let them have her. . . . You can't stay here, I've opened the way for predators from the Wilderness. You'll have to leave! I'm going to go. . . . You'll find your way to us. . . . The general might not know . . ."

"Sean . . . wait!"

But a wind rose—and he felt Sean sweeping away with the wind; felt his brother withdrawn from the jungle paradise, making the leaves flash their paler undersides, the grass giving one long wave, the trees swaying with his departure.

And the demiworld fell into a sullen quiet.

Bleak sighed. Then he got to his feet, took a deep breath, and turned to hurry back to Shoella's house.

But as he went, with each step he was a little more aware of Shoella's world growing dark within itself; it curdled; it began to rot; it sickened, like a woman with a tropical fever. The air grew close and heavy around him; the sun glared, growing hotter, the ground trembled, so that every few steps he stumbled. He heard a thundering and turned to see a great plume of black smoke rising in the distance—a volcano. He hurried on—but before long volcanic ash was falling around him, thick and choking. The sky was blackening with it. The path was hard to see, and the grass, it seemed to him, was twisting to conceal the way. He visualized the house, as Shoella had told him, and the path reluctantly opened up again, just the merest thread. He plunged along it, coughing, realizing that the protection had been lifted. This was no longer paradise—he was no longer safe from this jungle.

The forest rustled—a large striped antelope ran in terror from a grove of trees on Bleak's left, pursued by hyenas. Seven hyenas, ululating hungrily, tearing at the antelope as it went, making blood spray. Only their bloodlust for the animal, he knew, kept them from going after him.

The trees swayed in a rising wind . . . ash swirled red around the glaring sun. The face of a three-eyed demon formed from swirling ash—and watched him from on high.

"I'm opening a way to Shoella's world, from the Wilderness."

Then he saw the house, up ahead. He ran toward the back door, shouting for Shoella over the rumbling of the unearthly earth. He saw the waterfall running red—with blood? No, it was dissolved red clay, but it looked like a waterfall of blood, blackening now with ash. A eucalyptus tree swayed, shivered—and fell across a corner of the house, and he heard Shoella shout in fear. The back door was skewed now, the rectangle geometrically distorted with the impact of the tree on the frame of the house.

Bleak rushed through the skewed doorway, coughing, into the kitchen; blinking away black snow, stumbling down the hall, shouting her name. The living room was crushed—the bedroom looked intact.

He found her in the bedroom kneeling on the cracking floor. She'd opened up loose floorboards, under that North African rug, had taken a talisman of brass and hair and glass from its hiding place, gripped it in the long, slim fingers of her right hand. She held it up to him, her mouth quivering, her eyes streaming tears. "Take this in your hand!" Shoella shouted, over the growing rumble.

"Sean—he did this—he said you knew, that you were with them—"

"I know—just take it! And *laissez les bons temps rouler.*"

He took the talisman, not understanding at first what it meant to her—and realized then that the talisman had guided them here. She shouted certain words in another language.

"No, Shoella!"

But it was too late, blackness washed over him, then he was falling through a red-streaked vortex.

The demiworld was gone—and Bleak was spinning through the center of a tornado that whipped and rippled through space itself. He glimpsed faces flashing by—but one slowed and approached, to race along beside him, murmuring to him—the Talking Light he'd seen as a boy.

"*Now I will guide you to The Other . . . the one who completes you,*" said the spirit of light, its voice resounding in his mind. "*As close to her as I can take you. They have protections, you will have to cross their barriers. But you will be close.*"

"Shoella!" Bleak yelled. Out loud—or in his mind? Where was his body? He wasn't sure. "We have to help her!"

"*Shoella is beyond my help. She is trapped in her imagining, a world coupled with your brother's vision. But you I may* guide. . . . *Find The Other and heal her. . . . Look for my guidance inwardly.*"

Then the spirit of light was gone and Bleak could see nothing but the colorless vortex; he felt a tremendous force spinning him around ever faster, spinning him like in a cyclotron, and he felt gravity build up in him, but instead of crushing him it stretched him out, as if he were a man of rubber; his body stretched out to an infinite wire—which suddenly snapped like a broken violin string.

Snap, and he was propelled by the recoil into . . .

The atmosphere of the planet Earth. Clouds poured by him; a passenger jet was there and gone in a second. A passing crackle of lightning. The lights of cars on a nighttime highway far below . . .

Down. Slowly, turning like a falling leaf as he descended. His body taking its old shape again. Approaching the solid ground and . . .

Impact—not bone-breaking hard, but the breath was knocked out of him.

And he was back. He was lying on the ground, facedown. Back in the world he'd grown up in.

Bleak lay there a few long, stammering breaths, letting his heart quiet, his breathing return to normal.

Then, the talisman in his hand, he stood up and looked around.

It appeared to be early afternoon. He was in a copse of dying oaks. He was standing on dry, dead leaves. About a hundred feet away was a sprawling concrete building surrounded by razor wire.

A sign said FACILITY 23.

CHAPTER

SIXTEEN

Facility 23. That moment.

Loraine sat alone in the cafeteria, drinking coffee. She was aware that the two guards who'd escorted her were still leaning against the wall behind her, weapons cradled in their arms. Bored but watching.

She had finally slept a bit after the facility nurse had given her a sleeping pill. The nightmares had been persistent. But she felt better now than she had last night. The feeling of having been mentally violated was receding, though she still felt a dull ache, right through her.

She'd been trained for tough interrogations; she'd been trained to withstand torture, to think of it as an accident, like breaking your leg; to not get emotionally identified with it. She was trained to deal with it as much as anyone could be.

But when Loraine thought of that eye-tipped tendril, jabbing into her forehead . . .

Her stomach curled up inside her like a child shrinking away from a beating.

She heard footsteps behind her and froze, afraid it was Forsythe again. After a moment she smelled an aftershave she recognized, a honeysuckle smell, and she relaxed a little. "Dr. Helman."

"Loraine, would you come with me, please? Oh, and—gentlemen, you may stand down."

She turned and saw that, beyond Helman, the two black berets were approaching—the two who'd escorted the women into that courtyard.

"Sir," the scowling one said, "General Forsythe—"

"No need for you to come along, Corporal." Helman was trying to sound commanding but his voice was a bit shrill, his hands trembling. He seemed to realize this and put his hands too casually into his coat pockets. The coat was rumpled, as if he hadn't changed out of it, and dark smudges were under his eyes. "You may check with the general if you like. But it seems pointless—I've had full authority here all this time."

The guards stared, but didn't try to stop them when Loraine followed Dr. Helman out of the cafeteria. She and Helman walked in silence down the hall—toward Building 4, Containment. Was he going to lock her up?

"You look as if you had as rough a night as I did," she said. Trying to remind him that they were caught up in CCA together.

"Certain things . . ." His voice was almost a whisper. He looked over his shoulder before he went on. "Certain things have come to my attention. I'm a bit alarmed. I'm afraid we may be in danger of . . . digressing from our real purpose, here. We've just lost two containees. And the manner in which . . ." He broke off, shaking his head. "You'll see."

They passed through a metal door, overseen by a whirring camera, into Building 4. A yawning black-haired woman, a medic, was chatting with two black berets at the administration desk. "No need, no need," Helman said, waving them away impatiently, when one of them started toward him.

He led Loraine down a side corridor, to a door marked 17-B3. He took a small device like an automatic car-door opener from his pocket, pointed it at the lock, and the door clicked, stood slightly open. Immediately, Loraine caught the familiar smell of a dead body, from inside.

He held the door open. "An unpleasant sight, I'm afraid."

She stepped into the room . . . and found Conrad Pflug, Scribbler, sitting on his bunk, his back against the wall in the corner.

And quite dead.

His arms were limp, palms turned upward, wrists messily torn open. A red-ink pen was still stuck halfway into the wound of his left arm—he'd used it to gouge open his veins, with such force she could see torn tendons. Scribbler's bulging, unblinking eyes stared into hers. The smell of death was in the room, sweet and ugly.

Loraine felt sick with sadness, looking at him.

"I haven't shown this to anyone else," Helman said dully. "I have my reasons." He sighed. "Conrad was already quite agitated. Threatening suicide. Really could not bear confinement here. Then Forsythe went in to interrogate him. I believe the general used the same methods on you. And . . . well, this is the result. You were stronger than Scribbler. What I really wanted to show you was this—on the wall here."

Lines were written at a steep angle down the wall in shaky, thin, red ballpoint ink . . . mixed with something else.

"I gave him the red pen . . . and some paper. Hoping he might prophesy for us. He chose to write on the walls . . . in his own blood, as he was dying."

Most of the lines were illegible. All she could make out clearly was *the door stands cracked, chain still holds. Hand in a puppet reaches through. Helman obsolete. Outliving his usefulness. When he dies, the President taken puppeteer has two hands . . . the Wil-*

derness howls . . . CCA is a wasp nest in the walls . . . Sean Bleak and Forsythe will . . .

There was one more line—but she couldn't quite read it. Was it *tear down the wall?*

"It sounds . . . like you might be at risk, Doctor," Loraine said. Thinking, through her distress, that this might be a chance to forge an alliance with Helman.

"Without doubt." Helman's voice seemed slightly bleary, as if he'd been drinking. "Gulcher warned me too. And . . . there have been other indications. I had a session with Krasnoff this morning—he tried to warn me. Said he *saw* things. Warned me about Forsythe. Krasnoff said a curious thing—that he was warning me because he didn't hate the USA! Come along."

She was grateful to leave the cell. It reeked of death.

Helman relocked it, and they went three doors down. She walked along, still feeling sick. Remembering when she'd massaged Scribbler's hand. What a vulnerable little man he'd seemed. Eager to be of use. But most of the time simply wanting to be left alone . . . and he ended up here, tearing at his wrists with a red pen.

Dr. Helman opened room 20-B3. Krasnoff was lying in a fetal position, in a puddle of blood on the floor. His wrists had been raggedly ripped open—the ends of bedsprings had been used. It must have taken a while.

"Oh, God," she muttered, her gorge rising.

"Nothing else to see in there," Helman murmured sadly, closing the door. "I'm told Forsythe took Billy Blunt in there, just after I left. I believe he induced Krasnoff to kill himself. Because he was aware that Krasnoff had warned me about what Forsythe had become . . . didn't want him talking to anyone else."

"Are there others killed this way?" Loraine asked, feeling shaky.

"Not that I know of. But come along."

They left Building 4, and passed through a windowless passage between buildings. In Building 3, he opened another door for her, Room 32, and escorted her inside.

The medium-small room was barren of furniture. Intricate magical symbols, geometric and calligraphic sigils, marked the gray-painted walls, ceiling, and floor, in black, red, and silver.

Helman looked broodingly around. "This was Forsythe's project—this room. He spent years researching the symbols, the rituals. He went far outside our protocols to do it. He decided that to really get control of the country, we needed access to the most powerful entities in the Hidden. We could learn to control them . . . perhaps through ShadowComm."

Looking around at the symbols on the walls, the floor, Loraine felt a distinct inner pinching. What had happened here? She remembered the experiment notations Helman had shown her on the transport plane.

"I knew Forsythe 'when,'" Helman went on, chuckling, tracing one of the diagrams on the wall with an index finger. "His uncle Seymour had run MK Omega's remote-viewing project. Patriot Act surveillance turned up more and more evidence of the Shadow Community—I was working in Special Interrogations for the CIA and came upon the ShadowComm files. It was data collected by an earlier paranormal-control program—the beginnings of CCA, though it was called something different then. They'd found Gabriel Bleak's family—and the boy they took to a special Remote Viewer facility. Sean Bleak. And what incredible potential there was in those files! We imagined what real control of magic could do for this country . . . especially in protecting us from terrorism. I took it to Forsythe, and together we pitched CCA to the Pentagon's Domestic Defense branch, and we got a pretty decent budget . . . And after the terrorist attack on Miami our budget doubled."

Helman seemed to be trying to understand, himself, how he'd

come to this. "And when we found the artifact in the north—oh, my dear, it presented intriguing possibilities. We could have the power of magic—*but restrict it so no one else had it*. I thought it might be best done electronically—give selected ShadowComm recruits a device that electronically sheltered them from the artifact. Forsythe had another plan—the specialized use of Unconventionally Bodied allies. A plan which I'm only just beginning to grasp fully. I *thought* I understood it." He shook his head. "I was for it when you and I had that little conference, where you met Sean, but . . . ah, well."

Helman walked to the center of the room, squatted by a pentagram etched in silver on the floor, touching the lines wonderingly with the tips of his fingers. "Some of the Joint Chiefs argued for just repairing the artifact and reburying it. Those two thorns in our side, Erlich and Swanson, kept at us. But Forsythe had the ear of the president. Forsythe knew Breslin was headed for disaster, next election. So Forsythe suggested that the president might not have to have another election. And Breslin agreed. He made some deals, *tripled* our budget, gave us new access. Time to give the country a new direction."

"Not just a temporary suspension of elections? President-for-life?"

"Yes. His philosophy of governance was ours. Strict social control. But without military backing, president-for-life can't be done. They're an authoritarian bunch at the Pentagon—but most of them are quite sentimental about our so-called democracy. I felt we had to turn the corner, leave the old style of government behind, to make sure America was really safe. I had family who died in Miami. Oh, yes. To me, a truly controlled society seemed like a wonderful chance to close up every rat-hole terrorists could use to get in the country, you see. We could use magic to close those rat-holes—and to give us the power to counterbalance the military. To control people like Erlich and Swanson, through

Gulcher . . . so that the military would not oppose Breslin's new role."

"As *dictator*." She couldn't keep the disgust out of her voice.

"It really has such an unsavory sound when you say it! Well—we didn't have enough influence, enough power, to pull off a real coup. Not militarily. But magically! We might do it that way. It was exciting—a chance to remake the world!" Helman stood up. "But it's tainted now, all tainted. General Forsythe is under the *complete control* of a UBE—I'm convinced of it. It was his idea, after he engaged in the contact rituals in this room, to bring the elements together for the Opening ritual. But now I see it wasn't in fact *his* idea at all. It seems he's been . . . been *taken over* by something, by this thing he calls the Great Wrath, what the Tradition calls Moloch." Helman grimaced, shook his head. "Whatever its agenda really is, it's not the interests of the United States of America."

Loraine heard herself laughing softly, bitterly. "Really. You think? 'Not in the interests of the USA.' You thought you could *work with* the thing that looked into my mind? I looked *back* at 'Moloch,' Dr. Helman. I looked into that abyss. That thing has no thought of working with you. Or anyone else! Any more than you care what a chicken has on its mind before you order it slaughtered and fried." She took a long, ragged breath. Forced away the memory of the lamprey mouths, the probing eye . . .

"Yes." His voice was hoarse. "I believe you're right, my dear. You know," he added dreamily, "in ancient times, Moloch demanded of his worshippers that they place their firstborn child into the heated brass hands of his idol . . . and the child burned alive there, as enormous drums beat so the parents would not have to hear their infant's screams. Yes. I have been . . . naïve." He turned her a heavy-lidded, feverish look, like that of a man sleepwalking through a nightmare. "Something to tell you . . . shouldn't be telling you this, Loraine. But—Forsythe saw your real feelings, in your mind—in your little session with Forsythe. He will not"—Helman yawned, rubbed his eyes—"not let you leave here alive. Remember that." He shook himself, straightened, seemed to rally, looking at her more forcefully. "You *need* me—and I need someone I can work with. To stop Forsythe before he gives everything we've worked for . . . to that *thing*. Before he . . . who knows? . . . gives our infants to burn in Moloch's hands."

"You want to stop him—now?" She couldn't help needling him in her bitterness. "Now that you're rethinking treason?"

He was faintly surprised. "Treason? I didn't see it as treason. I thought of it as the ultimate loyalty. But . . . Forsythe knows I've changed my mind . . . that I oppose the Opening." He stared into space—and shrugged. "It appears that if I don't get out in time, I'm going to die here. Right here in this building. Look." He opened his coat, showing a small automatic pistol in a rather petite shoulder holster. "Rarely carry them. But I've brought the .25 along—since I found the bodies." He sighed. "Doubt I could hit much with it."

"You've suspected for a while. The report you showed me— Forsythe's account . . ."

"I suspected. But I made up my mind that I was wrong— because being right meant the entire project had gone to hell. So I talked myself into believing that Forsythe's agenda was exactly as he said it was. Only—having talked to Gulcher and having seen what I have seen, and now the murders of Krasnoff and Pflug, valuable containees . . . I knew. It's more than a suspicion now." He yawned. "I feel sleepy. Isn't that odd? With all that's happened?"

She was thinking about something he'd said. *"Bring the elements together for the Opening ritual."*

It all came together for her then, with what he'd said in the conference room, that day. *"A special work with Gabriel Bleak."* Helman had told her. "Sean and Gabriel Bleak. The elements for the ritual!"

Helman nodded. "Yes. To bring Moloch."

"But the artifact . . ."

"We need the artifact—even Moloch needs it, once he's here. It has weakened its output enough that he can come partway into our world—think of it as a crack in the hull of a ship. A giant squid reaches through the crack—one tentacle, controlling Forsythe. Two, controlling Gulcher—though not as directly. Then three: third tentacle shows itself with influences here—like Gulcher, all that he's done—and that man in New Jersey, flinging fire about. A whole darker kind of ShadowComm, prompted by Moloch. But Forsythe wanted to use the Bleak brothers to open it the rest of the way . . . to let the whole beast in. And he wants to use the Wall of Force—to close that opening behind it. Keep the other entities out . . . *so it can control our world alone.* No help from the spirits of light, no competition from other demons. That which has kept it at bay—will then keep it strong. I must move about, try to wake up a bit." Helman stretched, like a man getting out of bed, then began to walk wobblingly back and forth in the small space, so that she had to retreat to a corner to get out of his way. "I had been told that this Moloch entity would be controlled by Gulcher. Ironic, since clearly it has a great influence over him. But of course Moloch will allow no control over it at all." Helman's voice had started to fade as if he were slipping into a reverie.

"Suppose we went to General Erlich, and to Congress . . . would you testify about all this? I mean—in a closed session?"

"Oh . . . if the chance comes. If it . . . but I'm beginning to feel . . . that it won't . . . that all my chances are over . . ." The words just trailed off.

Then he crossed to the door and pointed the controller at it, and the door clicked within itself.

"Are you locking someone out—or me in?"

He looked at the controller in confusion. "I'm not precisely sure . . . why I did that. But the door is locked . . . can only be unlocked with another . . ." His voice faded again and he leaned against a wall, loosening his tie with one hand, sinking down to sit in a corner. "Do you know what I really wanted to go into, as a career?"

She looked at the door. Was it really locked from the inside? "No—what?"

"Horticulture. My father, you see—he had a large nursery. Raised flowers, of all kinds, for florists. And I rather liked it. It's why I wear those ties, with the flowers on them, hand-painted, you know. But father was ambitious for me. He pushed me to use my talents 'for the greater good'—go into government research. And then I drifted into . . . intelligence . . . I . . ." He seemed decidedly dreamy now. Adding wistfully, "I wonder if I should have stuck with . . . raising flowers."

She went and tried the door. Locked. "Dr. Helman? Why did you lock the door?"

"To tell you the truth . . . I don't know. I felt under a sort of . . . compulsion to do it . . . and I'm so tired . . . I only wish . . . to sit here and . . ."

Then his eyes became glassy, and he stared silently off into space.

"Give me the door opener you used. Will you please? Doctor?"

He opened his hand. There it was. She took it, turned to unlock the door. "It won't work, now," he said. "The door won't open."

And it didn't.

"You people keep telling me I'm lucky to be here," Gulcher growled. "Like I'm—what does Helman say?—'empowered' by CCA. But *trapped* is more like it."

They were in the windowless conference room, the same one

that Dr. Helman and Sean and Loraine had used, Gulcher sitting at the table, a suppressor thrumming behind him, Forsythe standing.

"It's what ya call a matter of perspective," Forsythe said. "Now—I'm going to bring in our guests. When we turn off the suppressor, don't you allow yourself to be distracted by the surge in connectivity. You've gotta focus. So far, I can't do much to help. It's up to you and Billy."

So far. Gulcher wondered what he meant by that. But aloud he said, "We got to have that sick little kid in on this? I don't like the smell of him."

"You bet 'we got to,'" Forsythe said, winking. Just like a human being would. "That little dickens is my pride and joy."

A beeping sounded, and Forsythe checked a PDA. "Ah— they're here. Hold yourself good and quiet, there, Troy, till we've got them in hand."

A minute later two generals in full uniform came in. The stocky one, General Erlich, according to his name tag, had thin white hair, a comb-over, a bulldog face, was maybe sixty; the taller, stooped one, General Swanson, had a craggy face, the kind of guy with hair growing out of his nose and ears. Both of them glanced at Gulcher as if they didn't like the look of him, though he was cleaned up and wearing a white formal shirt and some slick trousers. Behind the generals came Drake Zweig, their escort; Zweig seemed to be sucking food out of his teeth as he came—maybe just ate his lunch. Which reminded Gulcher he hadn't had any yet. But his stomach was flighty, nervous. With the suppressor on, he wasn't sure where he stood. But he knew he was going to look for a chance to use his power in some way these bastards didn't expect. And he knew it could all go sideways. Bringing that kid Billy in here was dealing a wild card. "He'll be there just to make sure," Forsythe had said, earlier. One of them would control Swanson, the other Erlich. Both an experiment and a method for getting rid of "obstacles," Forsythe said. Killing two birds with one stone.

Only, the stones in this place could fly around in the air and come back to smash out your damn brains. And all Gulcher wanted was to find a way out of CCA.

"All this," Erlich said, in a gravelly voice, "is a waste of time, Forsythe." He strolled into the room, hands in his pockets, looking around dubiously. "A conference room. Very impressive. You haven't even got coffee here for us? I sure could use a cup of coffee."

"Oh, there'll be coffee after, General Erlich, if you still feel like it," Forsythe said, with a sharklike grin. "This won't take long."

Swanson's cynical gaze took in Gulcher. "Don't I know this man's face? I can't place it."

"I'll include that in the briefing as soon as the rest of our team gets here for the demonstration."

"I don't care what you can demonstrate," Erlich said, looking exasperated. "We're out of our depth—all of us. You too, Forsythe. This is a work for theologians, not scientists. Newton knew what he was doing."

"If I thought it could be controlled," Swanson put in, his voice nasal, Bostonian, "I would consider it. For a while we thought—maybe. But now—I don't think it's doable. It's like herding cats. Black cats. It's not quantifiable. Whatever it is you think you can demonstrate today is not going to change our minds, Forsythe. It could be spectacular and it wouldn't matter. If we have anything to say about it, we're going to shut CCA down."

"That is, in fact, why you're here," Forsythe said. "You see, we need just a little more time—we can't have you take that time away from us."

"So you think you can persuade us with a magic trick?" Erlich asked, snorting.

The door opened and Billy Blunt came in, looking around, with his mouth open, a finger in one nostril. He still wore the BRAINSUCKER T-shirt—and smelled as if he'd never washed it. The two black berets who had escorted him here stood uncertainly in the doorway.

"You fellas just wait down the hall, in the cafeteria," Forsythe said.

"Sir? This kid—"

"Don't worry." Forsythe patted the suppressor. "We've got it under control. Go ahead."

They closed the door from the outside. Gulcher was glad they were gone. Those little machine guns they carried made him nervous—in their hands. Sure like to get hold of one.

"Now," Forsythe said, "let's have a chin-wag. I'll start us off—I have some questions to ask you about the defenses at the Pentagon."

"What?" Erlich seemed startled. "Why would you ask us about that? And why would we talk about it here in front of . . . this odious child and"—he nodded at Gulcher—"and whoever this man is."

"Why—I'll need the information later for a smoother transition, when I take over the Pentagon, gentlemen." Forsythe's grin was now perfectly raffish.

Erlich and Swanson glanced at one another. "You're out of your mind, Forsythe," Swanson said.

"Sounds that way, I know. First—let's squeeze the information out of you. Then—we video one of you killing the other. The video will be mostly for our own study. And for my amusement. I thought we might have you strangle General Erlich."

"The devil you say!" Swanson spat, starting for the door.

Forsythe switched off the suppressor—and nodded to Gulcher. Who spoke a name and reached out.

And Swanson stopped in his tracks.

THE SUN WAS HIGH overhead, burning the back of his neck. The shadows were shrunken.

And she was near. Bleak could feel it. She was in that building.

He could still change his mind. He could get up—and walk away from this. That'd be the smart thing to do. Going into the lion's den to rescue Loraine . . . when he wasn't even sure she wanted to be rescued.

Bleak grimaced. Coming here to find her had a grating feeling of compulsion about it. Seemed connected to their status as "soul mates." Not so much in the romantic sense—but in the esoteric sense. Something *destined*, something he was *shaped for* at birth. Like astrology but without wiggle room. *Compulsion.*

Supposedly, it was his destiny—but going with compulsion went against his grain. One reason he and the army hadn't been a good fit.

He suspected he was being *used* by something. By someone. By "Mike the Light," and the other spirits of light. Entities who'd had precious little time for him over the years—who'd held aloof. Suddenly he was supposed to do their bidding.

But you had to serve somebody, as the song said. In the end, you had to choose sides. The smart thing to do wasn't always the *wise* thing to do.

And there was something else. He looked inside himself, and finally, he had to admit it: he really, *really* wanted to see Loraine Sarikosca again. Even if it meant risking his life.

Bleak sighed—and made up his mind.

Lying flat in the dry, yellow grass around the black trunks of the dying oaks, Bleak looked over the facility, its fence about sixty feet away. What was the best way to get in?

He heard a rumble of engine noise approaching, and three soldiers in black berets—two Hispanic and one gangly white one—came riding along the other side of the high, razor-topped steel fence in something like a golf cart, but painted in military camouflage colors. They were all armed, and not with golf clubs.

Special Forces. Could be alert for Gabriel Bleak. Not good.

Bleak waited, motionless, till they'd ridden past. He considered the security camera mounted on a pole over the gate. Whirring back and forth, it was aimed along the entrance road. Was probably motion sensitive enough to swivel his way if he got close.

When he was sure the men in the cart were gone around the corner of the front facility building, he stood up, balling an energy bullet in his right hand, winding up like a pitcher as he ran toward the camera. It was turned away from him just then—he had to hit it before it swiveled back. He fixed his attention on it and threw the energy bullet, a purple-violet meteor that sizzled through the air and struck the camera square. The camera's aluminum cowling blackened; the lens cracked; sparks shed from its wiring; and it stopped moving.

Bleak smiled, thinking he should really get back onto a softball team. If he survived.

He walked up to the metal gate in the fence, reached out to transfer explosive energy into its locks . . . then stopped his hand an inch from the steel mesh. He could sense the electrical power radiating through the metal. And dead birds, two crows and a finch, were lying on the ground nearby.

Bleak stepped back and thought that, anyway, if he broke the lock, it might well set off an alarm. There was another way.

He backed up twenty feet and drew energy from the Hidden. He formed the ramp in the air and reified it, made it dear in his mind—which made it more defined in the air.

And then Bleak ran for the fence. Felt the lift almost immediately, as he ran up the invisible ramp, up, up, and over the fence, jumping down to hit the asphalt on the balls of his feet, as the energy of the ramp drained away behind him.

He ran toward the nearest door—then saw a camera over it, swiveling toward him. Was there a more discreet way in?

Bleak dodged left, around a corner—and immediately encountered the three soldiers, about ten yards off, coming back in the cammied "golf cart," looking bored . . . till they spotted him.

He was already forming energy bullets in both hands, and as the guards screeched their little vehicle to a halt, sideways to him, jumping out and swinging their weapons his way, Bleak flung the energy bullets overhand, left and right, forming two more the instant he let go of the first ones.

The four energy bullets sizzled through the air, right to their marks: the soldiers' guns, and the cart. The men yelled, their hands burnt, and flung the guns away; bullets exploded in the fallen guns and whined along the ground nearby; Bleak's fourth energy bullet striking the cart's electrical engine—it gushed smoke and sparks. That was for show, to keep them confused while he turned, making a stairway in the air with compressed energy, running up it before it was quite fully formed so that he had to create steps ahead of him as he went . . . up, and onto the roof of the building.

The soldiers were shouting into communicators, their voices distant from up here as Bleak ran clatteringly across the metal-sheathed roof to the other side—found himself looking down into a courtyard between several buildings. He knelt, took hold of the edge of the roof, lowered himself, and dropped into the empty concrete courtyard, turning to run immediately to the nearest door. An alarm was yipping somewhere.

He put his hand on the metal over the door's lock, focused energy, and its works burst apart. The door sprang open. He looked through—an empty corridor.

Loraine. Loraine Sarikosca . . .

Picturing her. Extending his senses into the Hidden. His intuitive sensitivity coupled with his esoteric connection to her should be enough to guide him.

There—he felt her to the right.

Bleak ran along the corridor . . . and stopped dead, seeing Conrad Pflug standing there in front of him at the end of the hall a few strides away. Scribbler. And Bleak knew immediately that this was a ghost.

That Scribbler was dead.

A clue to his death was his wrists—both of them ripped open. He thought of stigmata.

"If you go to her now," Scribbler said blandly, "we may lose our only allies. There is no time."

He reached out with a finger and wrote in the air, and the letters appeared, backward to Bleak, in red. He was able to read it backward, mentally translating:

Find the Gulcher and the Blunt and the three generals, behind you.

Then Scribbler closed his eyes, his face screwing up in pain. "Can't stay . . . I'm going to the After. Maybe I can just leave a little bit of . . ."

Then he dissolved, shimmering away.

Bleak thought—*What should I do?*

Should he be guided by Scribbler . . . or look for Loraine?

SEVENTEEN

leak heard shouting, running footsteps, around the corner ahead—and Loraine was that way. He turned reluctantly back. He would have to trust Scribbler.

A startling rattle of gunfire behind him—bullets pocked the wall to his left. Then he'd turned right, around a corner. A short corridor, and up ahead it turned left again.

As he ran, Bleak threw an energy bullet into an overhead light. The bulb shattered from within, and this short stretch of corridor went dark. He turned, threw a larger ball of energy at the floor by the corner where the black berets were rushing up—the floor tiles shattered, the corner edge of the wall blew apart, and the pursuing men yelled and backed up. Bleak closed his eyes, huddling into the darkest spot in the corridor. The alarm was still blaring.

"Whoa—some kind of grenade!" one of them yelled. "Hold on—we can call unit two to trap him—"

"That wasn't a damn grenade, man—let's just rush him!"

Bleak was forming the cocoon of darkness in the corner, under the darkened light. He'd just enclosed himself when the black-beret guards looked around the corner . . . and saw no one.

He heard them run past him, clattering down the corridor. He waited a four count, then dropped the cocoon of darkness. He was alone—but it wouldn't last. He started down the corridor, jogging along, the alarm louder with each step—and saw a circuit box near the ceiling, marked ALARM. He sent an energy bullet into it and the alarm shut off. Another twenty paces—and a corridor led left, into a series of locked doors, and right into a structure like a covered bridge to another building.

Words scribbled themselves luminously on the floor just in front of him:

Turn right.

A surveillance camera looked down the hallway. If he destroyed it, the feed would go blank—they'd know where he was. He ignored the camera and ran down the wooden-walled passage, through double metal doors into another building. Glanced at the floor . . .

Right again then left.

He hurried right, then left . . . and heard men shouting behind him. They'd almost found him again.

He stopped at a closed door painted a dull green—with Scribbler's red handwriting luminous across it:

This is it.

As the words faded out, Bleak formed an energy bullet in his right hand, opened the door with his left, and stepped through— and time seemed to slow, for a moment, as he took in the crowded conference room.

He saw four men and a young boy. Three of the men, on Bleak's right, wore military uniforms—all three at a general's rank.

The man in the white shirt, with the slash-mark eyebrows and short beard, was standing next to the kid, on Bleak's left.

Gulcher, Bleak thought, intensifying the energy bullet in his hand. *This is what Scribbler meant.*

Gulcher and the boy were focused in concentration on the odd tableau in front of him in which one of the generals, a tall man with a craggy face, was *strangling* the shorter one, who was on his knees, face red and bloating, passively allowing it to happen.

And the third general was humming tunelessly to himself as he documented the whole thing with a small digital movie camera. His ID badge read FORSYTHE.

The strangling continued. The man's face was purpling, swelling. Bleak recognized the strangler—General Swanson. One of the Joint Chiefs—strangling another general. Apparently for the amusement of Forsythe—whom Bleak knew, by reputation, as the head of the CCA.

Forsythe was just lowering the camera, turning to look at Bleak. Who tried to decide what to do with the energy bullet beginning to burn his hand.

"Ain't this funny," the chubby kid said, to himself, staring at the two men, the strangler and the strangled. The boy's T-shirt, Bleak noticed, read BRAINSUCKER. The boy's hands were clenching, though there was nothing in them, as if he were doing the strangling himself.

The kid was controlling the strangler, Bleak guessed. Gulcher was controlling the strangled man.

Bleak threw the energy bullet instinctively—it exploded with a strobelike flash in the air just in front of the boy and Gulcher. Both of them threw their hands up to protect their eyes, concentration broken.

General Swanson gave out a cry of relief and outrage, jerking his hands away from the other man. Wasn't the kneeling man General Erlich? From the Joint Chiefs? Erlich collapsed onto the floor, wheezing, clutching at his neck.

"Whatever's going on here," Bleak said, "it can't be good. Let's give it a rest, what do you say—"

He began to form another energy bullet in the hand he held against his right side.

Forsythe turned, smiling coldly, to Bleak. "I suppose we have enough on video, after all. I can erase the last few seconds. Drake?" He set the camera on the conference table.

And someone stepped out to press the muzzle of a pistol to the left side of Bleak's neck.

Bleak realized that he'd unconsciously sensed the man all along, hiding behind the door—but the perverse tableau had held him fascinated. He'd become careless.

"Bleak!" the man said gleefully. "Remember me? Zweig? From Kabul? It's been a while! Where you been keepin' yourself?"

"Zweig. Yeah. I remember. Long time," Bleak said, intensifying the energy bullet in his right hand.

"Zweig," Forsythe said. "He's playing with fire again."

"You dissolve that little glow-ball in your hand, there, Bleak," Zweig said, "or I'll pull the trigger. We're talking safety off, finger already squeezin'. Just make that thing go away and don't even breathe deep."

Bleak felt the metal chill of the gun muzzle jab harder into his neck.

"*Now*, Bleak!"

Could he move aside, hit the gun with an energy bullet before Zweig shot him?

Not a chance. He closed his fingers, extinguishing the ovoid of violet light, held up his hand to show it was empty.

General Swanson had taken off his coat, folded it and put it under Erlich's head. "What have you made me do! Oh, Jesus. He's in a bad way."

"I . . . ," Erlich said hoarsely. "I'm still . . . not getting much air."

"His windpipe is crushed. He needs help!" Swanson said.

"My eyes," the boy said, blinking, whining. "That flash hurt my eyes."

Gulcher, rubbing one eye, was squinting around at the others. Seeming to loathe everyone equally.

"This is not the room I expected you to go to, Bleak," Forsythe was saying, looking critically at Gulcher and the boy. "Loraine Sarikosca is in another room entirely. But we can make this work. Zweig will escort you to her. Room Thirty-two."

Swanson glowered up at Forsythe. "Recording this. You were recording it—going to claim it was surveillance footage? That I went mad and killed Swanson?"

"Oh, I wouldn't say so, no. The video is for our own research reference. What you call in-house documentation. No, we plan to simply dump your bodies somewhere interestin'." Forsythe made a dismissive gesture with his hand—a kind of false modesty. "We'll have you destroy yourself after you're done with Erlich. We'll leave evidence suggesting you were driven to murder and suicide by the very forces that we must be free to stop—your death will be proof that CCA is needed! Ingenious? Yes. Forsythe has an ingenious mind. He's a marvelous resource."

Bleak noted Forsythe speaking of himself in the third person. He'd suspected from the moment he'd first seen him that the general was under a dark influence; was controlled by an Outsider. He could feel the energy trail, in the Hidden, leading into the After; into the Outside . . . and into the Wilderness.

"And we will now conclude our business," Forsythe said firmly. "If my proxies here have recovered. Gulcher? How are you feeling?"

Gulcher just snorted and shook his head.

"I just want to point something out, gentlemen, if I might," Bleak said mildly, while looking up at the overhead light. He focused the energy field in the room as he spoke. It was harder to funnel an energy bullet at a target by simply looking at it. But given a little more time. "Sean told me you need me. So if you shoot me through the neck, as Zweig proposes to do if I move, I don't think I'll be of much use to you. I think the gun is a bluff."

"Try me!" Zweig growled. "I always despised you, Bleak, you smug son of a bitch! You came back when better men went down."

"You didn't like my coming back," Bleak interrupted, staring at the ceiling light, "because I was alive to tell people your intelligence was no good."

Having a harder time focusing now. Zweig had stirred the anger, the old feelings. The day Isaac died.

The light, the light . . . the cocoon of darkness . . .

"Anyway," Bleak went on, "I just wanted to establish that this might not be a time to do anything rash, Drake. Go for the good intel this once: ask Forsythe there."

"General?" Zweig said, looking away from Bleak—just as darkness began to weave itself around him. "Whatever he's good for—it's not worth it."

Forsythe frowned. "Bleak? What are you . . . ?"

Then the overhead light shattered, and the windowless room fell into darkness, with only a little illumination coming from the hall behind.

Bleak projected his image, formed of energy from the Hidden and twisted light, into the little swath of light falling on the opposite wall. He'd worked up the trick in Afghanistan and never used it till now.

The image was blurry, but Bleak was standing across the room from the door—while the Bleak that had been standing in the doorway seemed to vanish.

Reflexively, Zweig swung the gun toward the image.

"No, you fool!" Forsythe shouted, as Bleak spun left and grabbed Zweig's wrist with his right hand, used his left hand and foot to pull him off-balance.

The agent's gun hand flailed and Bleak forced the pistol toward Zweig—as the gun went off.

A blue muzzle flash showed Zweig taking the shot from his own gun under the chin—and out through the top of his head.

"Billy! Gulcher!" Forsythe shouted. "Prove you're of some damn use!"

Bleak snatched the gun from the dying man's limp fingers, the reek of blood and shattered brains strong in his nostrils as he aimed the pistol toward Forsythe—who had taken a step toward Bleak.

Stymied by the gun, Forsythe froze in place—mostly a silhouette in the dim room, the right half of his face lit from the open door.

"Swanson," Bleak said, "can you get General Erlich out of here?"

Even as he said it, as Swanson began helping the wheezing Erlich toward the door, Bleak knew he was under psychic assault.

Several things happened in a few seconds.

He was already feeling the strain of so much work with the Hidden, and he swayed, now, under the onslaught from Billy. It was like a hand made of icicles pushing against his chest, trying to stab its way inside. Bleak used the Hidden's energies to keep those gouging supernatural fingers back. But he was weakening—and he knew if that ethereal hand reached into him, it would take him over.

And that would be the end of him, in this world; the end of Loraine, and quite possibly the end of the world as anyone knew it. He had guessed what Sean was hinting at, in the pocket world.

And still the hand pushed, he felt it forcing its way through his defenses; he felt its subzero fingers clutching for his soul.

Bleak called out, inside himself, *Spirit of Light, guide me.*

No answer.

Hey—Mike!

He felt something then—something subtle, but clear enough. A kind of wordless suggestion: if he increased his inner receptivity to the Hidden, help would come. He had to open himself to it, without opening himself to Billy's diabolic influence. He concentrated, dividing his attention, one part to keep back the boy's influence—keeping back, really, the thing that was using Billy—and the other part opening to help from the higher forces that charged the Hidden.

And something flooded into him.

Suddenly he felt as if he were a lightbulb, switching on. A flash of piercing blue-white light—emanating from Bleak himself . . . from his whole body.

Billy screamed and clawed at himself; Forsythe bellowed in rage. Gulcher had covered his eyes—sensed something of the sort coming.

The pressure, the probing, was gone. Forsythe was standing there, in the dark corner, breathing hard—a very visible target. And Bleak had a gun in his hands.

I could kill him right now, he thought, feeling the gun heavy in his hand. He suspected that General Forsythe was the source of the worst rot in CCA. Was the locus of the threat.

But . . . Forsythe was unarmed. Bleak had never in his life shot an unarmed man.

And if he killed him—he'd be killing an innocent man. Because the threat wasn't *Forsythe*—it was what *controlled* him. Which was something that a bullet couldn't destroy.

There was no easy answer. Bleak shook his head and stepped back into the hallway, helping Erlich and Swanson through. Someone else came after them—Gulcher, hands raised as if surrendering. Bleak sensed no immediate threat from him, let him come out, then turned his attention to the door handle.

He slammed the door shut and pulsed energy from the Hidden, down through his arm, his hand, into the door handle—

welding the lock closed. Locking Forsythe in with Billy Blunt.

"Nice trick," Swanson muttered, turning to look warily at Gulcher. Erlich was leaning on Swanson, gasping raspily, his lips going blue, the scarlet mark of Swanson's fingers on his neck. Getting some air, but not enough.

Swanson turned to look at Bleak. "Now—who the hell *are* you?"

"Gabriel Bleak. Army Rangers, out of Kabul. No longer active duty." Bleak saluted, though he was no longer in the army—and way out of uniform. It felt natural to salute the general; it felt good. He handed Swanson the pistol, butt first. "In case you need this, sir."

"Bleak." Swanson pocketed the pistol. "I've heard." He looked at Bleak appraisingly. And nodded to himself.

Bleak decided he'd made the right move, giving Swanson the gun.

"What about him?" Swanson asked, nodding at Gulcher.

Gulcher slowly lowered his hands. "We could make a deal. Let me go and I'll tell you all kinds of . . ." He hesitated, looking past them.

Bleak turned to see three black berets coming around the corner of the hallway, submachine guns at ready.

Bleak hesitated—then he heard someone running behind him, turned to see Gulcher running down the hallway, the other direction. Taking advantage of Swanson, Erlich, and Bleak blocking the hall between him and the sentries.

Gulcher paused at the turning in the hallway—grinning at Bleak. "You keep 'em busy, pal—I'm for the open road!"

Then he dodged around the corner.

"'Pal,' he says," Bleak muttered, turning to face the three excited, uncertain soldiers.

Swanson stepped between Bleak and the black berets. "You there—stop pointing your guns at your commanding officer."

The three men stopped, glanced at one another in confusion, lowering their weapons—two of them were the Hispanic-American sentries Bleak had avoided outside, newly rearmed; the third was the man who'd taken a shot at Bleak in the hall. A sergeant with a gaunt face, ears that stuck out. "Sir," the sergeant said, "we're under the command of General Forsythe. I'm going to send one of my men after that guy who took off down the hall—he hasn't got freedom of the facility. We can't stand down without—"

"Sergeant!" Swanson barked. "Open your goddamned eyes. General Erlich is in a bad way—and that has priority. I outrank Forsythe and I've relieved him of command. You're all staying with me. We're going to get General Erlich to oxygen and a gurney. Now!"

"But that man there"—the sergeant nodded at Bleak—"he broke in here, sir—"

"That man just saved General Erlich's life," Swanson snapped. "Unless you keep wasting time. Now call for medics!"

Bleak was already stretching his senses out, looking for Loraine.

There—he sensed her down the hall, past the soldiers. "General—will you trust me a little more?"

Swanson nodded, as he lowered Erlich to the floor. "You men let him go . . . help me with this man. Did you call for that medic?"

The guards reluctantly stepped out of the way to let Bleak hurry past them.

He hurried off to find Loraine Sarikosca, thinking, *Now I've killed someone else. Zweig. Right then, he needed killing. But it really should bother me more than it does.*

A voice spoke, then—in his mind, but not from his mind: "*Gabriel Bleak. There's hope for you.*"

"Is that you, Michael?" Bleak asked, muttering the question aloud.

But the voice said nothing more, and Bleak was running, had to slide panting to a stop when he got to Room 32.

SWANSON WAS AFRAID THEY were losing Erlich. He could still feel his hands on Erlich's neck. His heart still thumped from the inward panic he'd felt, when he'd choked Erlich, aware of what he was doing and unable to stop.

The calls had been made, and in less than two minutes a medic rushed up, a woman in an army nurse's uniform pushing a gurney from the facility infirmary.

General Swanson and the soldiers lifted the wheezing Erlich on the gurney.

Then Swanson gave a set of terse orders to the three black berets. "You three bust into that room. You'll find a dead man—and you'll find General Forsythe . . . and you take General Forsythe prisoner. And that boy with him. You will ignore every single word Forsythe says to you *and that is an order*! You'll bring him to me in restraints, right outside the infirmary. He's under arrest. I believe the boy in there is out of commission now, but you'd better give him a sharp knock on the head before he can do anything to you."

"That Billy Blunt kid? Yes, sir, it'll be a pleasure."

"Zweig is in there, dead, by the way. Send a detail to clean that up." Swanson walked off with the medic, helping push the gurney. "Hold on, there, Larry, we'll get you to oxygen . . . just lay still."

It took the three sentries a full minute to get the door to the conference room open. A final kick sent it swinging smartly inward, and they stepped nervously into the dark room. One of them switched on a flashlight . . . to find Billy Blunt curled up on his side, next to the corpse of Drake Zweig. The boy was staring into Zweig's dead eyes. Billy was breathing . . . but seemed, otherwise, as lifeless as Zweig. No need to hit him.

"You okay, kid?" the sergeant asked.

Billy only said one thing, and it's all he would say, for a long time after. "The light. The light looked right at me."

"Jesus!" the youngest of the three sentries blurted, gawking at Zweig's body. "That's ol' Zweig with his head shot half off!"

"Yes, it's what remains of him," said someone sitting rigidly in a chair, in a dark corner of the room. He stood up, stretched, and stepped into the light. General Forsythe.

"The boy's useless, now, I'm afraid," Forsythe said, looking regretfully at Billy. "Damaged. Probably for good. Saw too much of himself, in that light." Forsythe looked back at the sentries. "You boys took your time getting in here."

"Sir," said the sergeant, swallowing, "you're under arrest. By order of General Swanson. Please come with us." He couldn't quite bring himself to point his weapon at Forsythe.

"All right, son—we'll get this straightened out." Forsythe smiled genially. "I won't hold anything against you. You're under orders."

Forsythe strode across the room as if he were still in charge, walked out the door. The sergeant stepped out behind him—and encountered the heel of the general's hand, flat on the black beret's forehead.

The sentry went rigid—the general jerked the submachine gun from his hand, reversed it, and shot him through the sternum, point-blank.

He squeezed off two more bursts, killing the other sentries before they could get their weapons in play.

Then General Forsythe walked away, humming tunelessly to himself.

EIGHTEEN

Bleak had to burst the lock on the door of Room 32.

He walked in, finding the air stale, and the room looking almost barren, with no furniture, no windows; yet complex with the geometry of magical symbols on every wall. And two people waiting in it. Loraine was sitting in a corner next to a dozing middle-aged man in glasses, suit and tie. The tie was painted with flowers.

She sat up, beaming when Bleak came in—then remembered to seem less glad to see him. "You finally made it," she said, standing.

"What made you so sure I was coming?"

"I . . ." She raised her eyebrows. She blinked. "Um—I'm not sure. But I knew."

"Who's he?"

She looked at the man slumped in the corner. "Dr. Helman. Head honcho here—under Forsythe. Seems to be in some kind of trance." She turned to Bleak. "Gabriel—we need to get away from here fast. I thought I heard shooting, but—"

"You're right about Helman, but wrong about leaving," Sean said, coming into the room and closing the door behind him.

Bleak spun toward his brother, Sean, thinking he should simply tackle him and try to knock him cold, before he could do any magic. Or he could set the floor on fire around him, with a couple of energy bullets, to hold him off—and maybe get Loraine out of here. Or . . .

Or nothing. He couldn't do anything. Not yet. Bleak just stared at him. *This is my brother. Sean Bleak. In person.* Not an astral projection. This was his brother in the flesh, after being gone all those years.

Embraces were out of the question. Everything about Sean, that sickly grimace of a smile, the hunched shoulders, the burning eyes . . .

Everything said that Sean would not permit himself to be touched by his brother. He stood, motionless, near the closed door, emanating raw hatred.

I should make a move, Bleak thought. But he felt paralyzed. Straitjacketed by emotion. *That's my brother.*

Slowly, Sean turned his head to take in Helman. "I planted a little something in his pocket, earlier. Used it to send him a trancing spell. Helman did surprisingly well at resisting. Babbling on and on for quite a while. I always despised him. But he's a rag doll now. Never was anything but a silly little pawn." Sean ducked his head to look balefully at Bleak. "It's no accident you're here, Gabriel—you know that, don't you? You were supposed to be here a little earlier . . . you got rerouted. Apparently we should have swept for ghosts when we got rid of that Scribbler of yours. But you're here now. . . . And you will help me. You *will* work with me. Our two opposing forces will open the doorway and Moloch will be here—and the Great Wrath will do as I command."

"That's not what Helman thought," Loraine put in. "He says your Outsider will do as it pleases, once it's fully here. It's just using you."

Sean chuckled. An unpleasant sound. "You'll see. The plan is great, and grand. Forsythe appreciates me. He's been there for me—not like our old man, Gabe. He's made me part of the big design."

"I can't help you, Sean," Bleak said, his voice hoarse. "Not that way. I can help you by taking you away from here. We can get you therapy. You've been traumatized by what happened to you."

"*Everyone's* been traumatized!" Sean snapped, taking a furious step toward them, arms rigid at his sides. "Everyone! They look around at the world and they go, 'Oh my God, it's full of cruelty and parasites and disappointment and abandonment and sickness . . . and then you die!' *Everyone* breaks, inside, when they realize that!"

"You know there's more to it than that," Bleak said.

He had to *do* something to stop this. But that was little Sean—grown big . . .

"What 'more to it'—our glorious life after death?" Sean jeered. "But first—you have to die! You choke to death from lack of oxygen . . . your heart stops! Cancer, emphysema, a stab with a knife! Dying hurts . . . and it seems to take an eternity, Gabe. And then! *Then* you get that glorious afterlife . . . to be a confused ghost, walking in circles! Or if you leave this world, most of you fades away, and what's left reincarnates! Back to the same dreary old grind! Life after death isn't much consolation, Gabriel. Best you can hope for is to be the slave of some angel somewhere!" Sean snorted with contempt.

Bleak shook his head. "There are other ways to see life. And death. You've been surrounded by some pretty twisted people, Sean. You don't get the chance to meet the other kind. Not everyone is damaged—not everyone has given up. A friend of mine survived the Nazi death camps—survived it in every way, Sean. It's possible to heal."

Sean snorted. "I don't want to heal! I like what I am! Now you think about this. Not only are you not in this room *by accident* . . . but neither is *she*." He pointed his left hand at Loraine. "Something's right there, in the room beside you, girl—invisible. Waiting for me to give it more life."

And from the tips of his fingers issued a stream of blue energy, infused with crackles of red. Bleak started to summon up energies to block it—but it had already infused the shape of the invisible being that had been waiting in the room all this time. The outline of something big, and sinuous—a *familiar*, one of Sean's "especialities." Its glossy brown-black insect head was the first part to visually materialize, spitting and hissing close to Loraine, making her gasp and flatten back against the wall.

In a heartbeat, four more yards of the familiar filled in, from the head down along its twisting, its interior parts first, then its armor-plated body—thick as a giant anaconda—with thousands of little sticklike, clawed arms threateningly waving. The familiar was a giant centipede—its faceted eyes, big as silver dollars, glittering with malevolent intelligence.

The supple creature was already whipping twice around Loraine, squeezing her like a python. The sharp hooks of its glossy brown-black mandibles snapped at her neck, its clawed legs clutched at her clothing, yanked at her hair. Its coiled body compressed her right arm crushingly to her ribs; her left arm was free, and she tried to tug the jointed coils from her, looking desperately at Bleak, eyes wide.

Bleak started instinctively toward her—and the giant, demonic centipede admonished him by tightening its grip on her, making her squeal with pain. It snapped at her hair—snipping away a piece of it, chewing it meditatively in its mandibles.

Bleak got the message. He stepped back. "I . . . Loraine . . . just . . ."

Sean chuckled. "Just *what*? Oh, don't look so anxious, Gabey! If you don't try that again, it won't hurt her! If you don't try to jump me and you do what I tell you—why, you'll get your Gothy little hottie back alive and only a little bruised! Just do the working, complete the summoning with me"—Sean's voice dropped a guttural octave as he finished the sentence—"*and she will not have her eyes chewed out.*" Sean glanced musingly at Loraine, squirming in the familiar's tightening grasp. "It'll go for the eyes first . . . then the brain. But—not as long as you behave yourself, Gabriel. Look—it's holding off!"

The centipede familiar snapped its mandibles near her eyes, making her draw her head back an inch, all the room she had. She bit her lip to keep from screaming. The creature had a strong grip on her—but didn't increase it. And it turned to look at Bleak, spitting and clicking, as if to await his decision.

Bleak felt waves of sick loathing and fury—loathing for what Sean had become, fury at himself for walking into this, for not getting Loraine out of here sooner.

He should never have taken that cup from Shoella. He should have been looking for this woman.

For U.S. Central Containment Authority agent . . . Loraine Sarikosca.

His senses keening now, he could sense her connection to him—feel in the deep core of his being that she was The Other. He'd been trusted with the jewel of all rarities. The possibility of perfect love. And he'd let this happen to her.

"The familiar responds to my thoughts, Gabriel," Sean said, taking up a place in the center of one of two interlocked silver pentagrams etched on the floor. "So if you try to interfere with it—or me—I'll make it kill her—bang!" Sean snapped his fingers. "Just like that! In a split second! You really have no choice in this.

This is your *soul mate*, Bro! Something ordained by the universe itself. And it says you are driven to take care of her, no matter what. *You can't let her die.* Emotionally"—he spread his hands and tilted his head, his squiggling smile almost comic—"you're incapable of it! We're counting on that. So—shall we start?"

"Gabriel . . ." Loraine's voice was almost inaudible. "I have to die sometime. It's something I can bear. Don't."

"What exactly do you want me to *do*, Sean?" Bleak asked. Desperately thinking that he could do the ritual—and somehow reverse it later. Send the thing they were to summon back.

But deep down, he doubted it. He'd need Sean's help, to send the thing back—and Sean would never give it.

Sean made a sniggering sound of triumph. "*Excellencio!* Now, Gabriel . . . move to the center of that pentagram opposite me."

Bleak moved to the point opposite—and heard a slithery thump. He looked at Loraine, saw she'd shifted, pitching on her right side, taking the twisting coils of the serpentine insect with her, so that it snapped at her in anger, cutting her cheek slightly with its mandible. She was lying close by the still-tranced Dr. Helman.

"Don't make it angry," Sean warned her. "I control the familiar—but it has a certain amount of autonomy. It might just choose to take a bite out of you."

The centipede's mandibles snapped at her face; she squeezed her eyes shut and turned her head. "Gabriel . . ."

"Hang on," he told her, inwardly calling for guidance. But he was a forest fire of emotion, inside—the roaring of the flames made any contact with the Spirit of Light impossible.

"It's easy," Sean said. "Just pay attention, Gabriel. We're going to reach out, into the field of the Hidden. It's so powerful around us now! It's bristling with energy because you and I are close by . . . and because your li'l love, there, is handy. It's all part of the equation! Now reach out, Gabe, form your field of control, I'll form mine, and we'll push the two against one another, so they contact, but don't try to push me back—just hold it there. I will call out certain names. You call them in *turn*, after me—make them ring out strong in your mind! You know the drill! And combined with our power, they'll open the doorway—and the Great Wrath will come through!"

"The artifact will stop it," Loraine rasped.

"You are so sadly uninformed, Little Miss Loraine," Sean jeered. "It's weak enough now to let Moloch in—if I have my brother here to help me. When Moloch is here to serve me and Forsythe, we'll empower the wall again—fully! But some of us will be protected from it . . . through Moloch! CCA agents will be protected from the artifact's suppression. . . . Something you don't know about, Gabe, Mr. Grand Wisdom! You don't know about that device! We will control it, so that some are able to project magic and no one else will! And Moloch will be our magical powerhouse. Our great ally! He is a being of a different order, and once he's here, its energies will not slow him down! Forsythe and I will control him . . . and through him, the country!"

"No!" Loraine said, her voice barely audible. The words choked out as she went on. "Forsythe *is* Moloch now. Forsythe is not your friend, he's a—"

"Shut up, you lying bitch!" Sean snarled, turning to her. And the centipede familiar tightened its grip so that she wheezed for air.

"Ease up on her, Sean—or she'll die!" Bleak warned him. "You won't have any hold on me if she dies!"

"Then tell her to shut up!"

But Sean eased the thing's grip and she breathed again.

"Sean—you're saying that CCA has a way to limit magic to American agents?"

"Through Moloch . . . it can limit the power to American agents—to us! ShadowComm will be done . . . all over the world the magic will belong to only a precious few of us!" Sean gestured grandiloquently. "To Breslin himself, in time! Moloch can give him the power too!"

So Moloch wanted to take control of the president.

"But, Sean . . . listen—"

"And then," Sean went on, eyes bright, "we take over the Pentagon—no more resistance there. They will have to do just as we say. . . . And it begins today! Moloch has promised that the real power will come when we open the way for him."

"It'll come through and it'll make you its slave!" Bleak told him despairingly. "Don't be stupid! You're the sucker here, Sean!"

"No—Forsythe told me! If I let it through, I command it!"

"That's a lie! Loraine's right—who do you think speaks through Forsythe? It's lying to you! The predators of the Wilderness have always lied, Sean!"

"They can't lie to me if I control them . . . and that is what I am going to do today. You are part of this ritual . . . but it is I who am the High Magician here. It is so ordained! Now . . . reach out . . . or we see what happens when we squeeze your destiny woman long and hard enough."

Sean caused the giant centipede to tighten its grip just enough to make Loraine cry out in pain.

"All right!" Bleak shouted. "Ease up on her!" He took a deep breath, the air shivering in and out of him. He had never felt this much fear before. Except . . . in childhood. "Just—let me concentrate!" He closed his eyes. Felt the shape of the field around him, the shape of his own participation in the energy of the Hidden. A man's personal energy field was shaped like a brain, big enough to contain his whole body. As if he were standing within a transparent brain. And Sean had created an identical but opposite field, facing him, pressing against his field, as if they were forebrain to forebrain, the fields sparkling, crackling at their points of contact.

Bleak caught flashes of Sean's thoughts. Bits of memory. The two of them as small children, chasing a chicken across a yard, laughing. Kicking through piles of dead leaves.

Men looming over Sean, as he lay in bed, pressing something to his face.

Rooms. Locked rooms within locked rooms. Tests . . . A gigantic ache of loneliness like a barren plain shrieking with a cold wind.

Then Sean was intoning names. Bleak made himself begin to intone the names along with Sean.

Oh, God. Help me. God forgive me. What am I doing?

But as Sean Bleak intoned each name of power, Gabriel Bleak repeated it . . .

"Asmodeus . . . *y* Moloch!"

"Asmodeus . . . *y* Moloch!"

"Tetragrammaton . . . *y* Moloch!"

"Tetragrammaton . . . *y* Moloch!"

On and on, name after name, till they came to the point where Sean began his sole invocation, his arms lifted, his hands shimmering with dark energy . . . and between his hands a window opened, into the Farther Hidden, the After the After, the place beyond beyonds, and something was approaching from that beyond-the-beyond: a vast creature that emanated hunger, a creature that looked like living wheels within living wheels, each wheel serrated with inward-turning teeth, and an eye on a stalk in the centermost of the wheels, the stalk stretching out toward them.

Moloch was coming. To change the world.

Sean opened his mouth to cry out the final invocation.

"I'm sorry, Gabriel!" Loraine yelled.

There was a gunshot . . . loud in the barren room. Gun smoke wisped.

The window into the Wilderness fizzed with a confusion of

energies—and seemed to swallow itself. It vanished. Moloch was gone—back to the spiritual wilderness.

Sean was standing there, staring at Bleak—then blood began trickling from his mouth.

Bleak suddenly remembered Sean just before they'd taken him . . . at the Dairy Queen, with chocolate syrup, from a dipped ice cream, streaming from his little mouth, just like that blood.

Sean went to his knees and lifted his hands palms upward—his empty hands.

He stared at his empty hands.

Then he slumped over. So that Bleak could see the small, round bullet hole in the side of Sean's head.

His brother, Sean, was dead. Really dead this time.

Bleak turned and looked at Loraine—and saw the centipede draining away . . . the energy draining out of its form as it had come. In two heartbeats, it was gone.

Loraine lay there on her side, weeping, Helman's .25 pistol held loosely in her limp, outflung hand. "I'm sorry, Gabriel . . . Had to do something." She lay close beside the moaning figure of Dr. Helman, who had clasped his knees against himself, was rocking in place. "Oh, no no no no . . . ," he moaned.

"Helman had a gun in his coat," Bleak said, thinking it through, out loud. Barely able to think at all. "You took Helman's gun . . . and you . . ."

"I killed your brother," she sobbed. "You can't love me. I killed your brother and you can't love me now."

STANDING BESIDE GENERAL SWANSON, in the facility's security center.

Bleak watched the surveillance footage showing General Forsythe hurrying out of the building, submachine gun in hand, calling out to Gulcher, who was staring at the electric fence, at the back gate, trying to figure out how to get over it.

"The sentries were running around inside, like chickens with their heads cut off," Swanson said, "looking for whoever shot their boys."

On the monitor, Forsythe walked to the gate, took something from his pocket, pressed a button, and the gate rolled back.

Gulcher stared at Forsythe. Didn't look glad to see him. But after a moment, his shoulders slumping with resignation, he walked off beside Forsythe.

"That was just, what, half hour ago," Swanson said wearily, rubbing his eyes. "I have some men out looking for them, but Forsythe kept a car at a lot down the road, and there's an airfield five minutes from here. And General Forsythe had a private jet out there. A CIA loaner—Gulfstream IX—kind of thing they used for rendition." He grimaced. "Lord, those three young men—I left them with that lunatic."

Bleak guessed Swanson was blaming himself for the deaths of the black berets. A feeling he understood.

"How is General Erlich, sir?" Bleak asked.

"They've got him breathing, his color's coming back. I still can't wrap my head around it—that it was me who . . ."

"It wasn't you, General. Not really."

"Big mess here. Men dead, and Helman—in some kind of coma. Stuck in it, seems like." Swanson chewed his lower lip, glancing at Bleak. "You been briefed on the artifact in the north?"

"Not exactly."

"I'm going to take a chance. I need somebody to help me contain this thing. I don't trust anyone in CCA and no one else has the background. Or the talents." Swanson shrugged. "It's not procedure. But you told me what you found out. And this is an emergency. I'm going to make a judgment call and tell you some things. . . . You were puzzling about the artifact . . ."

It only took five minutes to tell. About Isaac Newton, the Lodge of Ten. The wall of force.

Bleak felt shaken to the core, realizing how much of his life had been affected by the artifact.

He looked closely at General Swanson. "And you need someone from ShadowComm—someone with the right abilities—to fight a rogue from CCA. Sir, that's—"

"Yeah, I know. It's ironic. You going to work with us or not?"

"On *this* . . . I will. On one condition. There are people contained in this building—imprisoned. Maybe in other CCA facilities. I want them all released. You have the authority to do it. And I think you're a man of your word. Otherwise"—Bleak shook his head—"I can't trust CCA enough to work with it."

"You know if Forsythe destroys that thing out there . . . if he opens the doors completely . . . if he messes with the artifact . . ."

"Oh, it might make the world pretty damned different. Could be it'd help people like me, more than hurt us. But I'll work with you. *If* . . ."

Swanson grunted. "Guess I can't order you, you're not army anymore. All right. I was probably going to do it anyway. Any containees we have in any facility will be released, on my order, immediately. We'll transport them wherever they want to go. I've already ordered some women who were used in an experiment to be transported to their countries of origin. We'll pay them off, maybe they'll get over it. May as well go the whole route. Shut this thing down and—"

Swanson broke off. Bleak suspected the general was going to say, *And start from scratch.* He probably had a plan for a different kind of control agency. Something he didn't want to tell Bleak about.

They'd deal with that later. Right now . . .

"General?" They turned to see Loraine in the doorway, looking a bit rumpled but more in command of herself. "I just checked . . . Forsythe's already heading north in the Gulfstream."

"What's he plan?" Swanson asked.

She shook her head. "I don't know for sure."

Fourteen minutes later.

My brother is dead. I failed to help him . . . I should have saved him . . .

They were in a Humvee, Loraine and Bleak, riding to the airfield, with special papers from Swanson, driven by the same driver who'd brought Loraine to Facility 23, when Bleak realized that someone was sitting in the empty seat between him and Loraine. A ghost. He'd half expected Sean—but he felt immediately that it was someone quite different.

"Cronin?" he said, turning to look closely. The implications dawning on him.

The old man was sitting placidly beside him, slightly out of alignment with the seat. As if he were moving along on a different plane of relationship to the ground, not actually carried by the Humvee.

"Yes, Gabriel."

"You're . . . you've passed on?"

The driver was staring at Bleak in the rearview. "Uh—someone want to tell me who he's talking to?"

"Don't worry about it," Loraine said. "Just do your job."

"Yes," Cronin said. "I've moved on. A simple heart attack— *ach*, not so simple, I was in hospital, it took several hours. Two heart attacks really, to do it, *ja*? Did you ever read that Mr. C. S. Lewis? I read him in German but I think it's much the same. The author says that when you die, that's like having a tooth pulled, it seems to go on and on and it's awful but . . . at last the tooth is out, and you feel much better. That is not bad, such a description."

He sat in profile, staring ahead, as if looking up the road, not looking at Bleak. But Bleak felt Cronin looking at him, somehow, anyway.

"Cronin . . . you can see Isaac now."

Cronin sighed. "Not long ago, he moved on. I see he is well, in the high afterworld. Not so easy to see him yet. But . . . I see you—my other son."

Bleak's heart seemed to clench in his chest, like wringing hands. "I'm going to miss you."

"Maybe I stay in touch. And don't worry for your dog, after the first heart attack, I thought maybe I don't die today, but maybe I'm there for a while. I called your friend Donner, on that cell phone you gave me—he has Mr. Muddy now."

"Thanks."

"I heard you calling out, in such pain, a little while ago. So I look for you, I follow the traces, I come. You seem not so bad. But you are going to something . . . what it is, you don't know."

"That's right. Do you?"

"I have spoken to some who died here. A man, his name was Krasnoff. He says this thing that controls your running general, this Forsythe—it will destroy the thing in the north. I don't know what this thing is, but he says maybe you know. He says a deep darkness will come for the world then, when the Great Wrath comes through. This is not what it wanted, but it is another way. So it destroys this thing—and it comes. You understand this?"

"I think so. Cronin—"

"I cannot remain. This is a big effort, already. If I could get a headache, I would have one. But listen—you need anything else? Something more from me? Something to help?"

"There is one thing you could do . . ."

They spoke for another minute, then Cronin nodded . . .

And was gone.

GULCHER FELT AS IF he'd been swallowed by this Gulfstream jet, flying north, north, and more north. It was comfortable in here, he even had a drink in his hand; it was pretty quiet, what with the new engines, but he felt like he was that Jonah in the whale. No deal with God to get out. Just waiting to be digested.

General Forsythe sat across from him on the aisle, sitting up with his eyes closed. Twitching every so often, as he communed with . . . something. Gulcher could see a lot of movement under the general's eyelids, like the guy was in heavy REM sleep. A little saliva dribbled from the corner of Forsythe's mouth.

A pilot in civvies was in the cockpit, radio switched off—no radio contact was probably against Canadian aircraft regulations. And that was it, the pilot and Gulcher and Forsythe, no one else in the private jet. Unless you counted the thing that had taken Forsythe over. But then, it wasn't exactly *here*.

Gulcher finished his bourbon—cadged from the minibar in the back of the plane—and thought about trying to slip back and get another, while Forsythe was sitting there with his eyes shut. But he'd been told "only one" and—

"You are right as rain to hesitate, there, Gulcher," Forsythe said suddenly, his eyes still shut. "I told you one thing—you don't want to do another."

So the general—or the thing that controlled him—was monitoring Gulcher as well as everything else. No privacy left. Nothing.

Should have gotten away faster, Gulcher thought. *Had a chance . . . he caught me at the gate—*

"You had *no* chance to get away from me," Forsythe said, turning his head toward Gulcher.

But his eyes stayed shut. The eyeballs wheeling jerkily about under those lids. The face with the closed eyes was turned toward Gulcher as if Forsythe were blind.

"I am operating under limitations, until I can come fully into this world," Forsythe said.

There was a resonation with those words, in Gulcher's

mind . . . like Moloch's voice. The voice that had come to his mind that day he'd broken out of one prison and into this one—a prison he hadn't known he was in, until lately.

"But those limitations," Forsythe went on, "don't apply to you and me anymore. I have no need, here, of the one who whispered to you. I am more closely connected to you, now, Troy Gulcher—we've grown together, you and I, over the course of time!"

Gulcher noticed how "Forsythe's" whole way of talking was different, now, when they talked alone, most of the time. Dropping the General Forsythe pretense.

"You are still useful to me," Forsythe went on. "You're designed to control certain entities with great precision and reach. More reach than you realize."

Has to be a way to get free.

"There is no way free of me this side of death, Troy," said Forsythe, in a strangely companionable tone. "Now . . ." He paused, tilted his head. Eyes still shut, moving under the lids. Looking at what? "We're going to land at a strip not far from our ultimate goal. And we're going to shift over to a helicopter that will take us to the compound. On arrival at the base, soldiers will approach the helicopter with the intention of arresting or killing us. Calls have been made, you see. But you will deal with them. And then, another craft will arrive . . . and as for that . . ."

Forsythe's eyes abruptly snapped open.

His eyes had had become the color of phlegm and blood.

"And as for that," Forsythe went on, perhaps aloud and perhaps not, "consider that it is better to give than to receive, as someone once said."

A LONG TRIP, FAR to the north.

Loraine sitting next to Bleak, who was by the window in the rattling, echoey military transport plane, provided now by General

Swanson. Bleak could feel the atmospheric cold, seeping through the window glass.

Sometimes they talked, almost whispering. Mostly Loraine, telling him everything she knew about Forsythe, CCA . . . and Gulcher.

The rest of the time Bleak sat staring out the window, down at rugged brown land, flecked with green, studded with gray-black outcroppings, passing far below with illusory slowness. A few twisty roads, the goggle shape of a lake, the occasional snowy peak.

Pushing farther, farther to the north.

The wall in the north, Bleak thought. *At last.*

"Bleak," she said huskily, as they flew over the Hudson Strait, "I'm sorry I had to shoot him. I just—"

"You know, Agent Sarikosca—it wasn't *over* yet, with Sean . . . when you did it." He wasn't sure if it was true, but he had to say it. "I might've found some way to stop him. To stop what was going on. I *might* have saved him."

She nodded. Her eyes filling. "I know. But I *couldn't take a chance*. He had to be stopped right *then and there* . . . to be sure. It wasn't just about us."

"I see that, but . . ." Bleak shook his head. He knew she'd had a reason. A good reason. But there had been a chance he could have saved Sean—*and* stopped Moloch.

Or perhaps not. He'd never know, now.

The plane pressed on. A stop at a small base, so they could shift to a helicopter. There was no place for a plane to land at the compound.

Almost running, heads down against the wind, across an expanse of tarmac to the new Greenhawk copter. Another takeoff.

It all seemed to take forever. Her eyes were red, as she rode beside him, both of them with their backs to the vibrating inner hull of the helicopter. But she was calm now. Looking miserably resigned.

Bleak knew he should reassure her: *It's not your fault. It had to be done.*

But his usual inward command of himself seemed crippled, when he thought about Sean. He felt barely able to speak.

He had been in the same room with his brother, at last. Then . . .

She had shot him in the head. He saw it replayed, over and over in his mind.

But they flew on, all the time knowing that General Forsythe was ahead of them—had a jump on them, on a private jet—a CIA Gulfstream, then a DIA chopper. The general and Gulcher. How was Forsythe going to use Gulcher?

But Bleak knew. He'd use him as a weapon.

Attempts at calling ahead for Forsythe's arrest had come too late—despite Swanson's urgent request, the Canadian government refused to shoot down the general's jet.

It was a hard request to explain.

And by the time they could give the Canadians enough explanation to get more troops, more protection, to the artifact, it would be too late.

Could be just as well. Those troops might well simply die out there, anyway, if Bleak didn't intervene first.

The chopper ran full bore against a headwind, risking a crash on orders from Swanson. The engines roaring in their ears.

How many hours had passed, in just getting here? How far ahead were Forsythe and Gulcher?

IT SEEMED TWILIGHT WHEN Bleak and Loraine's helicopter arrived in the airspace near the compound around the artifact, but this time of year it might seem like twilight in the arctic circle for hours on end.

From the air, at about three hundred feet, they could see another, smaller helicopter, the one General Forsythe had used to get here from the airfield, standing near the Quonset huts.

And they saw the bodies of dead soldiers, scattered in front of the main building.

The air force pilot of their chopper, Purvis, was a short but broad-shouldered man in AF flight coveralls, lieutenant's bars. He was one of Swanson's aides—a volunteer and the only man who'd come with them. Bleak had turned down the offer of a marines escort. He didn't see any point in anyone else dying. Before it was necessary.

Purvis glanced back at them, made a sign that they were to land.

And then Purvis's eyes froze. That's what it looked like to Bleak—as if they turned to ice.

The pilot pulled off his headset, unhooked his seat belt, and stood up . . . giving up control of the helicopter.

The chopper began to bob, shimmying, turning wildly in place . . . in a moment it would start spinning.

"Something's got control of him!" Bleak yelled, over the engine noise. He could see the entity, like a face formed in steam, simmering around the pilot's face, there and gone . . . sinking deeper into him. Firming up control.

"Gulcher!" Loraine blurted.

The pilot was lurching toward them, his face settling into sheer malevolence.

"I can't fly a helicopter!" Bleak told her, getting up, forming an energy bullet in his right hand.

"I had some emergency training but—"

The helicopter cabin tilted, Bleak staggered—grabbed at the port bulkhead with his left hand as it righted, almost at random. Managed to steady himself, but then the pilot was lunging at him. Bleak aware that Loraine was stumbling toward the cockpit of the helicopter.

Bleak flung the energy bullet, but the wobbling of the chopper threw him off and it only hit Purvis glancingly, searing through the fabric of his jumpsuit, burning into his left shoulder, making a shallow crater of burned uniform material and red-black flesh. Purvis snarled with pain but it didn't slow him down. He lunged, his powerful hands clamping onto Bleak's face and head, thumbs gouging at his eyes.

Bleak wrenched himself back, feeling those steely thumbs prying at the edge of his eye sockets—but then the chopper went into a sickening spin and both men were flung by inertia to the right, onto the deck of the helicopter's cabin. Purvis immediately pitched himself at Bleak, knocking him back onto the deck—and vising his hands on Bleak's throat.

The chopper was steadying, under Loraine's control . . . but that seemed to work in Purvis's favor, as he used his brawny chest, his weight, and the leverage of his feet against the deck to press down on Bleak with his upper body. His hands twisting Bleak's head on his neck.

He was trying to snap Gabriel Bleak's spine.

Bleak resisted with all the strength of his neck and shoulders. But the pressure was incessant and increasing, making white and blue spots flash across his vision. Slowly his head turned creakingly to the left . . . and if he stopped resisting, even for a split second, Purvis would break his neck.

Bleak smashed his fists at Purvis but the angle was wrong, he couldn't get any real punch force from beneath. And Purvis was a powerful man—Bleak tried to pry at Purvis's arms but felt no give from muscles about double his own.

His neck muscles were screaming with pain; the pressure was building. He heard a creaking sound in his head. Purvis was going to rupture his spine at the neck. He had no choice. . . .

He slapped his hands onto the lower part of Purvis's head, either side of his jaws, pressed them there, drew energy from the

Hidden, forced it up his arms, into both hands, and into Purvis's skull.

Purvis's head began to glow, at first the multicolor shimmer of an energy bullet, as Bleak pumped the power into his skull.

The sparkling spots over Bleak's vision were almost filling his sight. But still he drew the energy from the Hidden, trying to make Purvis recoil from the heat he pumped into him . . . hesitating to go all the way with that energy.

Yet Purvis's grip never eased. He was under Gulcher's control—would fight to the death. So the only way to stop him . . .

But Bleak had never gone this far with this kind of power. And this man was an innocent—just a puppet.

He seemed to see that teenage boy in Afghanistan again.

This man will die today, Gabriel. Cronin's voice. *You cannot save him. Send him on, to us. We will care for him. It is not this man you fight against.*

Bleak sobbed—and forced full power into his hands.

Purvis's head pulsed with the Hidden's concentrated incandescence, now glowing cherry red. He screamed—

And the pilot's eyes boiled out of his skull. He convulsed, back arching in agony . . . and let go of Bleak. Tipped over to the left.

Bleak struggled to sit up, gasping, straightening his aching neck . . . and saw, through the cockpit hatch, the ground rushing toward the windshield of the helicopter. They were coming in at a steep angle . . . they were going to crash!

"Loraine!" he shouted, trying to get up.

But then the chopper suddenly angled sharply up, and he slid back along the deck, trying to find something to brace against—and felt a crashing thump, then another, loud enough to make his head ring. Heard a prolonged metallic grinding.

The helicopter spun once across the ground.

And stopped, in a cloud of dust and oily smoke.

Bleak lay there a moment, rubbing his strained neck . . . then sat up, wincing, coughing in the foul air. Loraine loomed through the dust and smoke. Helped him to his feet, telling him apologetically, "I can't really fly one of these things except in the most, you know, theoretical way."

"You got us down alive."

"Oh, God . . ." As she saw Purvis. His face charred, eye sockets empty. "Did you have to?"

"I had to. Come on."

They climbed out of the helicopter—an awkward climb. The chopper was tilted all wrong, the slowing rotors barely clearing the ground on its port side.

They stepped away from the chopper, coughing in the plume of smoky dust, looked around. Men were sprawled in drying pools of blood. Some of them, even in death, still clutching assault rifles.

But one of those bodies lifted up, started crawling toward them. An unarmed young soldier, moaning softly.

Forsythe had used Gulcher to take out the compound's defenses. Probably turned half the soldiers on the other half. But he hadn't quite killed them all.

Loraine and Bleak went to the injured man, about forty feet from the chopper. The man lay on his belly, whimpering. Sensing the soldier wasn't under Gulcher's control, Bleak gently turned him on his back. Loraine knelt beside him.

A young marine. He had a bullet hole in his chest, right side.

"Everybody . . ." A bubble of blood appeared at his mouth. He was young, blue-eyed, and pale with blood loss. "They just . . . went crazy."

"Take it easy, marine," she told him, taking off her coat, folding it under the soldier's head for a pillow. "We know what happened. Just rest—help is coming. They're getting clearance. Be here in about half an hour. Medical team and everything."

Bleak looked around for Forsythe—and didn't see him. But he

could feel the background signal of the artifact—something he'd felt, most of his life, never entirely sure what it was. It was coming from the dig, down the hillside.

A cool wind blew a scent of sea, from Baffin Bay, not far off; mosquitoes buzzed. Somewhere overhead, a gull shrieked.

Bleak said, "Wait here, Loraine."

"No," she said flatly.

"You have to help this man. There'll be medical supplies in their admin building, there. Could be others alive."

"Bleak . . . Gabriel . . ."

"*Just . . . wait . . . here,*" he said, with all the conviction he could project.

She looked at him. Then she pointed. "It's that way." She went to the admin building to search for bandages, medical supplies.

Feeling the breeze ruffle his hair, and reaching out to feel the environment on a much deeper level, Bleak strode toward the artifact—the quick stride becoming a jog, then flat-out running, as he reached the spiraling ramp and saw, at the bottom of the dig, two men close by the artifact.

One of them, Forsythe, was attaching something to a pagoda-shaped, green-gold metal artifact rising from the pit.

"Gulcher!" Bleak shouted. "He blows that thing up, you'll be up to your neck in competition!" He jumped from one ramp down to another, cutting through the curves of the spirals, heading directly toward the center, forcing his way through a labyrinth. Gulcher turned toward him, frowning. Forsythe was making an adjustment.

Bleak almost stumbled over the body of a white-coated middle-aged man. And immediately saw the man's ghost, appearing beside him, sitting on the rim of the ramp, looking confusedly at his body. Shot through with bullet holes.

"Come with me!" Bleak shouted at the ghost. "Join the others! The one who killed you is there!"

He ran past the ghost, calling out through the Hidden—and summoning its energies, to coalesce inside him, as he went. Until he was just a few strides from the two men and the artifact.

That's it, he thought. *The artifact.* That thing was a big part of the secret behind his life, behind who he was—dug up, exposed, but still cryptic, part of its origin still a mystery.

Then General Forsythe turned to face him—grinning. His hand on a switch, which was black-taped to a plastic explosive, wired to a side panel on the artifact.

"Close but no cigar," Forsythe said. "It's all ready to go."

Bleak was already concentrating the energy of the Hidden around the artifact—creating a cushion. Holding its few moving parts in place. Forsythe growled to himself as he attempted to press the button. Which wasn't working, as long as Bleak could keep the locking field in place.

But Bleak knew he couldn't stop him this way for long.

"Gulcher—," Bleak said, taking a step closer, forming energy bullets in the palms of his hands. "That thing blows up, they'll swarm over the planet and that means you too!"

"Oh, a few eggs will be broken, but it'll be a fine omelet," Forsythe said, reaching for something behind him. A gun he'd left lying on a segment of the artifact. "I had hoped to come in exclusively—through you and your brother—but this way will work, in a pinch. Once the artifact is down, I'll be able to come through completely, way ahead of . . . what did you call it? Our competition. I may have to divvy up the world, but there's so much life to be sucked up here, I won't mind so much. And so . . ."

He swung the submachine gun toward Bleak—who threw the two energy bullets, left and right, striking the submachine gun.

Forsythe shouted in pain and dropped the weapon—then he realized that Bleak couldn't still be controlling the bomb and throwing energy bullets too, and he turned, lurching toward it . . .

And Gulcher stepped in, smacked Forsythe hard in the jaw, with his right fist.

Forsythe went over backward, falling in the dirt. He glared up at Gulcher. The voice that came out of Forsythe wasn't Forsythe's. It phased in and out of audibility, almost warbling. *"You little . . . worm. That . . . will get you an . . . eternity in my jaws."*

"I'm sick of all you fucking big shots," Gulcher said. "I want to know if what he's saying is true. That assholes like you will be all over this planet."

"All over it, yes," Forsythe said, staring at Gulcher . . . getting control of him again. *"And scraping scum like you from our boots."*

Bleak focused, concentrated . . . and called, within himself, to his allies. The artifact's power was more concentrated here, but Bleak could still contact the Hidden.

Forsythe stepped over to Gulcher, put his hand on his head — and hissed, *"Down!"*

Gulcher went limp — and slumped to the ground, against the cowling of the artifact. He sprawled against it, making odd little sounds . . .

As Bleak concentrated, adjusting field strength, Forsythe went on, in his normal voice, reaching for the bomb, "Not only is it true, Gulcher, but this explosive is strong enough to take you right out of this life — and right into my jaws as I come into this world."

But his finger stopped a quarter inch from the detonator.

He seemed paralyzed . . . as Bleak focused the Hidden's energies around Forsythe . . . from all sides. Pressing . . .

Then Forsythe, slowly and painfully, turned to face Bleak — and the thing inside Forsythe started pushing back. The field, in the conflict, became visible. The violet-blue shape of giant hands around Forsythe, closing in on him, to squeeze the intruder out — and the red-energy outline of Moloch, flickering in and out of visibility, showing itself, exerting all the strength it could send through the crack it used to penetrate the human world. Bleak felt it writhing in his field of control.

And he felt himself faltering. The thing was sickening to be in contact with. It was so profoundly nonhuman, its appetites so vast, so alien, he felt an ineffable repugnance that made him recoil in sheer existential horror. He grimaced—and went to his knees, struggling to keep the energy field in place, to increase the pressure. Trying to get help from the refined energies the Spirit of Light had opened to him. But still the defiant pressure grew.

"Now!" Bleak shouted. "Cronin—tell them! Do it now!"

And then they were there, those Bleak had summoned: the ghosts of the scientist who'd died in the dig pit, and the marines who'd died in the compound, and Krasnoff, and Scribbler, and the three sentries who'd died at Facility 23, and Cronin himself. They all appeared around Forsythe, standing in a ring facing him, their hands lifted, touching the field . . . adding their psychic strength to it. A circle of ghosts acting as an astral magnetic coil to increase Bleak's power.

The field compressed around General Forsythe; staticky and flaring with internal conflict, becoming darker, more intense, as it closed in around him . . . pressing the possessed man from all sides. It wouldn't crush his body. Refined, it would pass through the physicality of his body, like a net through water. And it *was* a tightening net, dragging psychically through the general.

Forsythe screamed as the energy net closed inescapably around him—squeezing, pressing.

Then there was a flash of blue-white light. And it was done.

They'd forced out the spiritual alien, the intruder—*pushed it* out of the man, into the open.

Bleak saw it for a moment, just the portion of it that had entered the world, hovering there, a rearing bulk of glossy green-black, largely taken up by a leechlike, circular, serrated mouth, with more serrated mouths inside it. Poised over Forsythe like a giant Venus flytrap . . . staring furiously at Bleak with its single polyp eye the color of bloody phlegm. It squealed, ear-piercingly, just once . . .

Then it contracted, shrinking from yards across to a pinpoint in a second . . . and snapped out of the world with a crisp *crack!* that echoed through the dig site.

General Forsythe fell flat on his face, in the dirt.

He lay in the grit, squirming, babbling to himself. "What did I do what did I do what did I do what did I do I can still feel it I can still feel it I can still feel it what did I *do do do do do DOOOOOOOO* . . ."

Bleak stepped over to the plastic explosive, pulled out the wires, dismantled it, as the ghosts moaned softly to one another and faded as if blown away on the rising wind.

Cronin was the last to go. "Good-bye, *mein Jungen* . . . good-bye . . ."

"Thanks for coming back to this tired little world, Cronin," Bleak said. Feeling a sudden stab of loneliness. "See you someday. Thanks for always being there, and . . ."

But Cronin was gone.

Then Bleak stepped back and looked at the artifact. This thing limited his power. It had granted him, and ShadowComm, by accident or by someone's strange design, more power than their kind had in the past. It helped keep the predators of the Wilderness at bay—but even without that, would it be good to get rid of it? Or had Newton been right . . . that they weren't ready?

Gulcher lay there, against the artifact, muttering to himself.

Bleak figured he should kill Gulcher. But Troy Gulcher looked stricken; as shattered, as impotent, as Billy Blunt and Forsythe.

What about Sean? Where was he now?

Turning away from the artifact, the wind blowing dust in his eyes, heartsick, Bleak tried to tell himself that Sean might be wandering the world as a ghost . . . or reincarnated. But he knew different, deep down.

He knew that his brother was somewhere in the Wilderness. *Sean.* Keeping to the shadows of the Wilderness, trying to hide from its predators, and trying to remember why this had happened to him.

AN URBAN RIVERBANK, A warm, sticky night in New Jersey. Twenty-three hours later.

The decaying dock where Bleak had met with ShadowComm before.

They were all here now, more than Bleak had ever met. Every one of them watching Bleak closely as he walked up with Loraine Sarikosca at his side.

He and Loraine hadn't had much time to talk, since the events at the artifact. Since the artifact had been reburied and left to do its job as well as it might. They'd been too busy to talk. Supposedly. Coordinating with Swanson. But maybe they'd just avoided it.

Oliver was there, scowling beside Pigeon Lady—covered in blue-gray fluttering, some of the birds real, some familiars. And Giant was there, and the others—as well as some Bleak didn't know. A young, plump, cocoa-colored woman in a Gypsy dress, but no Gypsy; a tall albino with long white hair and a black suit; a small blond girl with a python that wasn't really a python twined around her waist . . . and many others.

"We've been trying to find Shoella," Oliver began.

"She's not in this world at all," Bleak said. "But she hasn't died. She's in a pocket world of her own creation—trapped there. It's pretty bad. I think she's probably found a hiding place there. I'm hoping to find some way to get her out."

"Oh, fucking hell," Oliver said. "She's trapped. And you had nothing to do with that?"

"No. That was her doing, man. Hers and . . . CCA."

"CCA?" Oliver said. "I heard some stuff. About a predator named Moloch chewing through those assholes. And CCA let some people go. But Scribbler . . ."

"Scribbler didn't make it," Bleak said. "But he's freer now than he's ever been."

"Yeah? And you want us to help Shoella?" Giant asked, looking at Bleak with rank suspicion.

"With that—and with other things. Troy Gulcher is still out there. He disappeared from the hospital—and the familiars that were released by Moloch, those are still floating around the world for Gulcher to use. And there are others—lots of other black souls that Moloch empowered. They're hostile to us. They're a whole different species of shadow. They'll find us and kill us if they can—because they don't want anyone to have the power but them."

"Maybe or maybe not," Oliver said. "How do we know any of that's true?"

"You saw the one that summoned the fire imps," Bleak pointed out. "You think he was alone? You think he'd stand with us?"

"Why should we trust you—and her?" Oliver nodded at Loraine. "She's an agent of CCA."

"CCA no longer exists," Loraine said. "But some of us were hoping to . . . to work with you. In some other way."

"With Breslin in charge?"

They all laughed at that.

Loraine smiled. "I know. But he's been taken down a few pegs. There is some . . . testimony. Behind closed doors, in Congress. Not for public consumption but—he's being reined in. He'll be gone next election."

"Believe that when I see it."

"About believing," Bleak said. "I want you to go ahead and look into my mind—Loraine's too, if she's willing. Send your familiars to look. See if you can trust me."

The ShadowComm drew off, in a group, to confer. Bleak and Loraine waited. A tugboat hooted on the river; a siren moaned in the distance.

"Gabriel," Loraine said, in an undertone. "We haven't had much time to talk."

"We'll talk later, Loraine," he said gently. "We have to think about what all of it means—if it's true about you and me. It's a big responsibility. It's so rare. But . . . maybe we can't do it this time around." Meaning, in this life. "Maybe it'll have to be . . ."

Then Giant walked importantly up to them, the others following him. "Pigeon Lady will look."

"Okay," Bleak said.

Loraine hesitated. "Will this be like . . . when Forsythe . . ."

Bleak shook his head. "No. That thing was predatory. It's different. It's intrusive but—not like that. Not violent."

"All right—then let's do it."

Pigeon Lady walked up to them—as the others backed away. Then the pigeons covering her seemed to explode, outward, toward Bleak and Loraine . . . the ones that weren't real pigeons, the familiars, flew right at their faces, blocking their vision, covering everything, a flurry of wings and glittering pink eyes and gray-blue feathers that filled the world.

Bleak closed his eyes and felt them flying *into* him, and through him, as if his body were a man-shaped building, and the birds were flying through its open windows, seeking.

He smelled them, acrid; felt them, sharp-clawed.

It was over in twenty seconds. Another burst of flurrying—and they were gone.

All that remained was a slight headache . . . and a faint nausea.

"Oh," Loraine said, swaying.

Bleak caught her in his arms to keep her from falling.

"I wonder if she's faking that," Giant said.

"Shut up, Giant," Oliver said.

"They're okay," Pigeon Lady said. "We can trust them. Bleak is telling the truth. And with Shoella gone . . . we need someone who can call the shots."

"I guess so," said the albino. "Let's vote. But I think it should be him. He's the one that took down the CCA."

"What the hell," Giant said boomingly. "I'll vote for that. Until Shoella returns . . . let it be Gabriel Bleak."

THE NEXT MORNING. SUNNY and bright, not yet hot. Bleak and Loraine were walking along a street in Harlem, with Bleak's dog, Muddy, running ahead of them. Loraine wore jeans, and a sleeveless, red T-shirt, red high-top sneakers.

Bleak wore a long, untucked white shirt, jeans, boots, with a vintage rock T-shirt under it: HAWKWIND. And over one shoulder he had slung a backpack.

It was a run-down street, its gutters cluttered with trash; buildings were boarded up on the left. But at brownstones farther down, people sat companionably on the steps. The closed-down school was still shuttered, across the street. Turfies milled on the sidewalk near the school fence, talking; people in hoodies, glancing suspiciously at Bleak and Loraine.

Pigeons fluttered suddenly, in front of them, and Loraine visibly shuddered. "Oh, God, I'm not quite over that. You made it sound like nothing. But . . ."

Bleak chuckled. He wanted to put a reassuring arm around her. He wasn't sure if it would be welcome. She seemed scared of their special status, together—and Sean's death hung between them, not quite resolved.

"Why'd you want to come back here?" Loraine asked. "Where you killed that speed dealer."

"Thought he might still be here. He doesn't seem to be. I wanted to have a shot at telling him to move on. I don't feel right when I . . ." Bleak shrugged. "Never felt good about killing people. I was pretty good at it once—but never learned to *like* it. Even knowing there's life after death. 'Cause you're ending something you don't have a real right to end. Zweig's death—that was his doing. But still . . . I had a nightmare about that one, early this morning."

She thought about it, then nodded. "What's in the backpack?"

"Ah. About that." He put his hand in his left pants pocket and closed his fingers around the talisman—this one altered a bit from the design that Shoella had used. "I spent yesterday doing some research. Refining Shoella's technique. Talking to the Talking Light . . . I can talk to it better now. Now we've made more contact. And it told me."

She looked at him. "Told you what?"

"That you'd better take my hand now."

She frowned—but she shrugged and took his right hand. They walked a few steps more. He called to the dog and it ran back to him, snuffling. "Stay real close, Muddy. Real close."

The dog seemed to understand, following along pressed against Bleak's left leg as they walked a few steps more . . .

And the street transformed around them.

Up ahead, the Harlem street glimmered and shifted, warped, and was gone—replaced by a country landscape. There were trees that hadn't been there before. A stand of pines. And just this side of the pines a curving line of green rushes marked out a stream running by a cottage, half broken-down, overgrown on one side with wild roses . . . a grassy field beyond it . . . a hawk circling in the immaculate blue sky . . .

Loraine gasped. "What . . . where's Harlem?"

"Look behind you."

They both turned—Harlem was back there, visible through a circle of watery light. A cab was pulling up, a skinny, pockmarked, overly made-up white woman getting out beside a broken fire hydrant. Gang tags decorated the streetlight posts. A skinny cat ran up the chipped steps of a brownstone. A plane traversed the thin, smoggy clouds just above the skyline.

"It's still there," Bleak said. "You have only to turn around, walk back. Get that cab before it leaves. You don't have to go with me."

She looked at him, squinting a little against the sun—the other sun. "And the backpack?"

"Stuff we might need. If we stay in that cottage. It's a pocket world—an idealized world outside of time, a paradise I created between the planes—a living world, all to itself. This one is based on some land near my parents' ranch in Oregon. I used to stay in that little cottage overnight. It needs fixing up. The fishing's good. I've got a sleeping bag."

"Just one?"

"Just one. If you want to come with me."

"We couldn't just stay there. We have things we have to do in . . . in this world."

"Yes. But time passes differently there. We could spend a long time alone together. Finding out what it means, when people are meant for one another."

"What! You've never even kissed me, you son of a bitch!" She laughed.

Bleak grinned, dropped the backpack, and kissed her. The dog barked, someone on the street hooted at them.

She broke the clinch and stepped back. "Let's not waste any more time here."

Bleak picked up his backpack. She took his hand.

And the three of them, Bleak, Loraine, and Muddy, turned . . . and vanished from the Harlem sidewalk.

About the Author

John Shirley is the author of many novels, including *Demons, Crawlers, In Darkness Waiting, City Come A-Walkin'*, and *Eclipse*, as well as collections of stories, which include *Really, Really, Really, Really, Weird Stories* and the Bram Stoker Award–winning collection *Black Butterflies*. His newest novels are *John Constantine: Hellblazer—War Lord; John Constantine: Hellblazer—Subterranean*; and, for Cemetery Dance books, *The Other End*. Also a television and movie scripter, Shirley was coscreenwriter of *The Crow*. Most recently he has adapted Edgar Allan Poe's "Ligeia" for the screen. His authorized fan-created Web site is www.darkecho.com/JohnShirley and his official blog is www.JohnShirley.net.